BLOOD RITE

STEPHEN PENNER

ISBN-13: 978-0-6-1558459-1

ISBN-10: 0-6-1558459-1

Cover image from joshuahorn.com. Used with permission.
Cover design by Stephen Penner.

BLOOD
RITE

1. Heir Apparent

He had no idea what was happening.

The year-old boy slept peacefully within a magnificent, solid mahogany crib, his opulent sheets enveloping him in illusory protection. While across the impeccably decorated nursery, through the elegantly dressed window, silver moonlight streamed in over the child's angelic face. Indeed, so sound was the baby's slumber that he didn't stir at all as the watery light spilling across his soft features was blocked by the cloaked figure who stepped silently to the edge of that magnificent, solid mahogany crib.

A woman's strong, fine hands reached down and gently lifted the infant from his cotton womb, trading him his cotton sheets for the equally luxurious warmth of a waiting silk blanket. The boy cooed contentedly as he nestled against his kidnapper's breast and returned to whatever happy images fill a yearling's dreams.

Several silent moments passed. Then the happy images were sliced violently away. A muffled yelp, followed by a smothered wail, rebounded dully off the walls of the nursery; and a woman's fine, strong hand hurried to paint the words in blood on the wall above the crib:

'I AM RETURNED TO FULFILL THE PROPHECY'

And then, with even more haste, the same hand scrawled

out another bloody phrase, this time on the polished wood
floorboards next to the bleeding child:

     ' *A THÁINMHNE NA DOHRGHATAS, SLÁINAICH AN
LÁINABH A'SIO'*

'Forces of Darkness, Heal this Child.'

2. The First Hours

Inspector Robert Cameron stood motionless, his hands shoved deep into the pockets of his crumpled blue suit, and stared down at the bloody pattern etched at his feet. Again.

He was a large man, six foot three with broad shoulders and thick muscles beneath his forty-something skin, and he towered incongruously within the infant's nursery. Closely cut, snowy-white hair retreated sharply from either side of his furrowed scalp to an increasingly large bald spot at the back of his head. His tired blue suit dated from the Thatcher administration; his frayed red tie, hanging limply between his unbuttoned coat sides, from the one before. Intelligent blue eyes shone out from their recessed sockets as he stood in the middle of both the nursery and the cacophony which had seized the residence.

Officer MacGregor was sliding the diminutive baby furniture away from the walls for Officer Richards to peer behind. Flashbulbs from Officer MacAllister's camera lit the room repeatedly while Officer Henderson began to dust both the crib and the windowsill for fingerprints. From down the hall Cameron could hear the soft, choked sobbing of the nanny, being both half-consoled and half-interrogated by Officer Wilkins; he'd have to make sure

Wilkins printed her before he let her leave. And Sergeant Willis was downstairs, undoubtedly failing utterly to prevent the lord of the house from leaving.

Cameron raised his gaze and stared several moments at the bloody phrase above the crib, drying brown, its drips extending almost to the floor. He was of the opinion that the gory script was just for show—to make the kidnappers appear to be more than just that, and to ensure the ransom would be paid quickly and without questions. After all, it was almost certainly not the boy's blood. Cameron doubted the body of a one year old even held enough blood to spell out the shocking graffiti on the wall above the crib. But he had to concede that the lad's blood could well have been the source of the enigmatic phrase drying sticky to the priceless wood floor next to his own dull, worn, black shoes.

Cameron rubbed a hand over his head and chewed his cheek contemplatively. Then he pulled his pipe from his coat pocket and lit the bowl, still packed with last night's tobacco.

He told himself it was just another kidnapping.

He told himself they'd get the ransom note within the hour.

He smacked disappointedly at his pipe and told himself to be sure to put some fresh tobacco in it once he was back at the station.

And then he told himself to wait until the end of the day for the ransom note not to come before calling her in on the case.

3. Maggie Devereaux

'*The University of Aberdeen Summer Research Institute of Irish and Scottish Studies,*' announced the banner draped from the registration desk.

"So which workshop do you want to go to first?" asked the friend as she lifted a brochure from the table.

"Hmm, let's see," answered Maggie Devereaux, perusing the list of events within her own pamphlet. "Anything but Old Gaelic."

Ellen Walker laughed at this reply. She was a young, gregarious woman, with a mop of dirty blond curls atop a ruddy face. When she smiled her cheeks pushed her blue eyes shut, leaving her strong, white teeth to dominate her visage. "Now that is a surprise," she chuckled. "And a relief. I thought for certain I'd spend the entire conference trapped in lecture after lecture on the latest theories of dialect variation in ninth century Old Gaelic narration."

Now it was Maggie's turn to laugh. Hers was a pretty round face beneath thick, straight auburn hair falling just to her shoulders. Unlike that of her Scottish friend, the petite American's smile did not render her eyes invisible, but rather added extra sparkle to the caramel-colored irises flashing behind her small and fashionable glasses. Her full lips held an understated smile as she crossed her arms faux-accusatorily. "You say that like it's a bad thing."

Another laugh from the blond Scot. "Well ..." she started.

"No, it's okay." Maggie waved away whatever her friend was about to say. "Believe me, I understand. After spending the last year studying Old Gaelic in one form or another," she paused and smirked enigmatically, "I think I've mastered what I can. I'm ready to move on."

Ellen nodded in reply. "Fair enough." She glanced down at her watch, then again at the brochure. "And speaking of moving on, we should probably decide which session we're going to. They start in five minutes." She glanced critically at the choices in her pamphlet. "What about the panel discussion on 'Scotland, Ireland and the Romantic Aesthetic?'"

"Sounds delightful," Maggie said with an affected air. "Let's away."

And with that, the brunette American and the blonde Scot stepped lively from the registration table to the free coffee across the lobby, before disappearing up the nearby stairs to their chosen workshop.

While the woman in the corner, her green eyes blazing, looked over her newspaper and watched their every move.

***

Maggie fiddled briefly with the lock then threw open the door to her new flat.

"Welcome," she announced with a flourish of her arms, "to Chez Devereaux!"

"Aye, well, thank you then." Ellen peered inside from her spot atop the *Ceud Mìle Fàilte* printed on Maggie's welcome mat— Gaelic for 'A hundred thousand welcomes'—then traversed the threshold and assessed the dwelling from its foyer. "And a bonny nice chez it seems at that."

"Why thank you, kind lass," Maggie mimicked the Scottish burr good-naturedly. She'd gotten rather good at it over the last ten months.

"I imagine you're glad to have moved out of your aunt and uncle's house, aye?"

"Oh, they're wonderful people," Maggie was sure to say of her Scottish relatives who'd hosted her during her first year in Aberdeen.

"Is that a 'yes?'" Ellen pressed, a sardonic grin exposing her teeth.

"That's a yes," Maggie admitted. "It's nice to have my own place. Would you like the tour, then?"

"Oh, aye. But of course."

"All right then," Maggie was happy to comply. "I'll give you the quick tour, then go fetch those DVDs on the American Revolution. I'd never really considered the connection between the Highland Clearances at the hands of the English and the American Revolution a generation later with all the patriots of Scottish descent. Sounds like an interesting angle."

"I'll keep you advised of my progress," Ellen assured as she stepped further into the flat. "And thanks again for letting me borrow them. Most British accounts of the American Revolution have a slightly different take on it than I expect I'll find in your videos."

"I can imagine," Maggie smiled. "So anyway: the tour." And with that Maggie escorted her guest fully into the small, but impeccably decorated flat. It boasted a single bedroom and a single bathroom, both of which Maggie pointed out from the foyer before stepping through a short hallway into the living area. The sitting room to the left held a miniature sofa between two comfortable looking armchairs, all in a classic ivory and smothered in vibrantly colored throw pillows. Two glass-topped end tables stood at either end of the sofa, supporting photographs and carefully arranged knick-knacks. Against the far wall loomed two huge bookshelves, packed full with books of every shape, color and size, and a smaller but similarly laden bookcase supported the small television in the corner. To the right was a small, sharp looking kitchen, with ash cupboards, handsome gray countertops, and a selection of shiny steel pots hanging importantly from a rack suspended elegantly from the tall ceiling.

Finally, every available inch of wall space was absolutely filled with framed prints: watercolors, landscapes, photographs, old maps of every part of the world, and so on. The most striking of these was a reproduction of a portrait, hanging importantly above the couch, its subject gazing across the living room and out the window toward the top of the King's College Tower visible only a few short blocks away.

"Who's that beauty?" Ellen asked, practically mesmerized by the portrait. The beauty in question was clearly a young noblewoman from some bygone era, with an aristocratic visage, a red velvet gown, long blond hair done up in strands of pearls, and clear blue eyes shining cat-like down through the centuries.

"That," Maggie was almost irrationally proud to say, "is my great, great, great, great, great, great, great, great, great," she paused for breath, "great grandmother. One Brìghde Innes, daughter of the Innes chieftain."

"Do tell," Ellen replied, duly impressed.

"She married one of the sons of the Gordon chieftain, thus becoming Brìghde Gordon, but she named her daughter Margaret NicInnes Gordon so the name wouldn't be lost."

"Are you named after her daughter then?"

"Not as such," Maggie answered. "That is, I don't think I was named 'Margaret' after her. But every daughter of every daughter after her had the middle name of NicInnes, all the way down to me, Margaret NicInnes Devereaux."

"NicInnes," Ellen repeated, then translated the Gaelic: "Daughter of Innes." She returned her attention to the portrait. "So when is this from?"

"It was painted in 1621. It's printed at the bottom there. See?"

Ellen leaned onto the sofa back and squinted at the words she found there. "*Bean-Slànaighear*. 1621." She considered the Gaelic for a moment. "*Bean-Slànaighear*. That means 'healer,' doesn't it?"

"Aye," Maggie resumed the brogue, then thought better of it. "Brìghde Innes, Healer. She was born in 1600, so she would have been twenty-one when this was painted."

"Well, I must say," Ellen stood up straight again and considered the portrait with a fist to her chin. "This is most definitely cool. Quite brilliant really. Where is the world did you get it, though? Did you have it shipped over from the States?"

"Not hardly," Maggie replied. "No, I didn't even know it existed until I got here last fall. I just ran across it in an old art book at the university library."

"You didn't steal it from the library, did you?" Ellen asked, aghast at the very notion.

"Of course not," Maggie defended. "It was a library book. I'd never steal a library book. But I was telling Iain about it—"

"Iain?" Ellen interrupted in a sing-song voice. "Your wee Iain?"

Maggie could feel the blush begin to sear her cheeks. "First off, he's hardly wee," she replied instinctively. Then, in an effort to maintain her dignity, she smoothed back her thick brown hair and went on, "In any event, Iain has a good number of connections in the Highland memorabilia industry. I just happened to mention the portrait to him once and without my even knowing it he made some calls, found an enlarged copy of the print at some out of the way shop in Inverness, and *voilà*, it's on my wall. It was a late birthday gift."

"It was a thank-you-for-not-leaving gift," Ellen opined cynically.

"Yeah, well maybe that too," Maggie conceded, the blush returning. "Anyway," time to change the subject, "how about those DVDs? I'll go fetch them. Wait here; I'll be right back."

Ellen assented with a laugh and a nod as Maggie turned and disappeared down the short hallway. It took Maggie only a minute or so to retrieve the disks. Like the rest of her flat, her bedroom was in a constant state of order. 'A place for everything and everything in its place.' And the DVDs were in their place: her closet shelf; informative or not, videos, she felt, really had no place on a bookcase. She pulled the three-disk set down from their perch and strolled triumphantly back into the living room.

"Here you go, Ellen."

Ellen spun around from her position by the far end table. "Oh, brilliant. Thanks again." She stepped over and accepted the DVDs from Maggie. Then she paused and tentatively motioned toward a silver-framed photograph on the nearer end table. "Speaking of family ties," she said with a grin, "is that wee lass you?"

The photograph was of three women: one an older woman, probably in her fifties; another a young woman in her twenties with long, dark hair cascading onto her shoulders in loose ringlets; and the third a young girl, five years old at the most, with thick dark hair, wide, intelligent-looking eyes, and a band-aid on her chin.

"Yeah," Maggie replied with a smile, "and grandma." Then

she sighed slightly and pointed to the young woman hugged between the girl and the grandmother. "And that's my mom. This was when I was about five," Maggie explained. "So my mom would have been 30 or 31." Maggie paused, then went ahead, "It would have been about three years before she died."

A tight frown cramped Ellen's mouth and she nodded sympathetically. "Aye. You told me that once. Sorry to have brought it up."

Maggie smiled and waved the suggestion away. "Oh, please. It's been, gosh, nearly seventeen years now. I can talk about it. In fact, I kinda like to talk about her." She picked up the photograph and inspected it. "I actually remember the day this was taken. I'd tripped and cut open my chin. It really hurt. But my mom cleaned it up and made it all better. She was really good with that kind of stuff."

"A healer herself, aye?" Ellen offered.

A broad smile blossomed across Maggie's face and her eyes sparkled at the suggestion. "Aye," she agreed happily. "A family tradition perhaps."

"Well, then," Ellen broke in, her empty stomach suddenly asserting itself. "Are you ready for dinner?"

"Oh, aye," Maggie set the picture back down and picked her faux-brogue back up. "I ken this lovely wee place Iain show't me. Fair bonny it is."

Ellen laughed and shook her head. "You know," she began as they walked toward the door, "we don't really sound like that."

"Yeah," Maggie replied matter-of-factly, in her flat American tone, "I know." She locked the door behind them and they headed off to dinner.

***

"Okay, granted," Maggie conceded, running a frustrated

hand through her auburn locks. "But you have to admit that palatal mutations only account for a portion of the dialectical variation of—"

Beep! Beep-Beep! Boop! Beep!

A cellular phone interrupted the debate. It was ringing somewhere inside the restaurant, although actual ringing having become somewhat passé, the phone was playing the techno-pop version of 'Rule Britannia.'

"Hello?" It was the woman at the next table. She was facing away from Maggie and Ellen, but her gentleman friend was offering an embarrassed grin in exchange for the several disapproving glances he was receiving.

"Now?" the woman asked, obviously perturbed. Maggie noticed that she had short, straw-colored hair above her black jacket. She looked familiar.

"Right, then," the woman barked into the phone. "Fifteen minutes." The voice was familiar too.

The woman beeped her phone off. "Sorry, Richard. I have to go. Duty calls."

Maggie was so intent on trying to recognize the woman's voice that she failed to realize she had begun staring, rather rudely, right at the woman's head. So when the woman turned around and their eyes met, Maggie was almost as surprised as the other woman looked.

It was Elizabeth Warwick. Sergeant Elizabeth Warwick. Of the Aberdeen Police Department. 'It's pronounced "Warrick,"' Maggie could hear the sergeant's voice echo from their first meeting months earlier. It was Sgt. Warwick who had come to Maggie's aunt and uncle's home to investigate the King's College murders last fall. It was Sgt. Warwick whom Maggie had gone to with an offer to help in the investigation, only to be politely rebuffed. Maggie had wondered whether she wouldn't be forced to reveal the source of her knowledge, but thankfully it hadn't come to that. Warwick didn't know her secret.

But as they locked gazes, Maggie was startled by the expression she found in the police officer's dark eyes. It wasn't just surprise at seeing each other again—there was something else there as well. Something probing. It combined appraisal with knowledge...and something more. Maggie felt like a book being read.

"Miss Devereaux," Sgt. Warwick said formally, even as she stood up and pulled her small, efficient-looking purse over her shoulder.

"Sergeant Warwick," Maggie replied almost sadly. She wondered where last fall's 'Maggie' had gone.

Then Sgt. Warwick strode quickly and officially to the exit as Richard signaled for the check.

"Do you know her?" Ellen asked her dining companion.

Maggie frowned. "I think so."

***

"Well, dinner was nice," Ellen said as Maggie opened the door to her flat. Time to call it an evening. "Same time tomorrow?"

"Absolutely." Maggie paused in the doorway. "Let's meet at the registration table again."

"It's a date," Ellen ratified. Then, with a sly smile, she added, "But don't tell Iain."

Maggie laughed despite herself and felt a pleasant flush sear to her cheeks. "Time to go, Ms. Walker," she announced with finality. "I'll see you tomorrow."

Still blushing slightly, Maggie locked the door behind her and then strolled lazily to the couch and plopped herself down.

And that's when she saw it.

'A place for everything and everything in its place.' A dogma for orderliness. But also one for protection. If everything is in its place, and you have something you want to keep hidden from prying eyes, then it's a simple matter of making sure that its place is somewhere out of sight. Any diary-writing teenage girl with a little brother can confirm that. But as even most of them eventually find out, it's almost impossible always to remember to return everything to its place—especially when you had no idea when you dashed out the door that morning that your friend was going to ask to borrow your videotapes on the American Revolution, and you, forgetting that you'd left your 'diary' out, led your friend right to it.

But although what Maggie saw sitting on the floor, clearly visible beneath the end table between the sofa and the farther chair, was a book, it was no diary.

It was an ancient book she'd found in the sub-basement of the University of Aberdeen's Historic Collections the previous fall.

It was written in a forgotten dialect of Old Gaelic, a dialect whose very existence had initially been hypothesized by a Professor Robert Hamilton of the University of Edinburgh, but which Maggie herself had first discovered, cracked and translated.

And it was a collection of pagan magic rites and spells, a grimoire scrawled down by hand in the half-legible script of some long dead Celt.

None of which was terribly interesting except for one additional fact.

She looked down at the ancient tome. "*Bhaitit inh chaoimraighanh anh'í chonric hrésia cho inh Talaom. Da'slaointi grád ó nádúhr ochus ail hrésia cho inh naim do'bhaichaidad.*"

The magic was real.

The book rose smoothly off the floor and into Maggie's waiting hands.

She had come to use the magic sparingly—for various reasons—but she always enjoyed the rush it gave her. However, as she accepted the book from the air, there was no smile on her face.

She had never shown the spellbook to anyone. Anyone. And its 'place' was most definitely out of sight in Maggie's bedroom. But she had left it out of its place that morning when she'd hurried out the door for the conference. So the question was: Had Ellen seen it?

Ellen hadn't mentioned it over dinner. It was possible Ellen hadn't even seen it lying there, or at least hadn't paid it a second thought. On the other hand, it was a rather striking volume, with an intricate, raised cover in black leather and a large metal clasp hanging broken and open across its closed pages. It would have been hard to miss.

Maggie frowned, her stomach in a knot.

Had Ellen noticed it? Picked it up? Perused it? Maybe even recognized it for what it was?

But then why not mention it when Maggie returned with the videos? Or over dinner? Why pretend she hadn't seen it?

Maggie closed her eyes and tried to calm her racing heart. Her skin burned at the thought of someone—even a friend—discovering her secret. She stood that way for a very long time, eyes squeezed shut and mouth clamped into a deep, creased frown. Finally she regained herself somewhat and opened her eyes. No point in panicking, she assured herself. She stepped back, sat down on the couch, and delicately opened the cover, the rigid spine crackling at the effort and the ancient clasp jingling lightly as it passed over the yellowed pages within.

Maggie nodded at the words she found there, as one might nod to an old friend across a crowded room, and a faint smile again played across her lips. She hadn't understood, or even recognized, the words when she'd first encountered them the previous autumn.

But she had nevertheless labored to understand them and had eventually recognized them to be a lost dialect of Old Gaelic, enabling her to translate and master them. So that now when she looked down at the ancient Celtic words, not only did she read, '*Inh Laibpohr Dohrgha Tiassain Ochus Damnasiadh,*' but she understood: 'The Dark Book of Rites and Damnation.'

Maggie tucked her thick, auburn hair behind her ears and turned the antique pages delicately, flipping cautiously through the priceless Gaelic spellbook. Handwritten words and freehand diagrams reflected off her lenses.

The levitation spell.

The divining spell.

The transmutation spell.

When Maggie reached the end of the tome, having briefly scanned every already-memorized spell secreted between its covers, she carefully closed the book again. Then she looked over at the photograph of her mother and up at the portrait of her ancestor.

Why, she wondered, *isn't there a healing spell?*

***

Dessert. Maybe dessert would take her mind of her ancestry, her spellbook, and the state of her secret. Milk and cookies. A bit juvenile, she knew, but pleasurable nonetheless. And television. If cookies and television couldn't distract her troubled mind, nothing could. Soon, a plate full of chocolate wafers in one hand and a tall glass of skim milk in the other, she crossed over to the living room, eschewing the day's still unread newspaper for the TV remote.

Plopping down on the sofa, she clicked on the 'tele' just as the local evening news was starting. She propped her feet on the coffee table and shoved the first wafer in her mouth. Ahh.

"—top story tonight is the kidnapping of one year old Douglas MacLeod, son of the MacLeod Chieftain David MacLeod, and heir apparent to the chieftaincy of MacLeod of Lewis. Initial reports lacked details, but the infant was secreted from his third-story bedroom sometime between ten o'clock last evening and eight o'clock this morning when his absence was first discovered by a nanny."

Interesting enough, Maggie supposed and she set the remote down on the table, picking up in its stead her glass of milk. Then, refocusing her attention on the television, she dropped the glass of milk onto the floor. She ignored the flowing liquid and stared in disbelief at the image on the screen.

"—police are said to be focusing on the dramatic warning written in blood on the wall above the crib. Early speculation connects this to the famous Fairy Flag of the Clan MacLeod and the legend of the MacLeod Banshee. This photograph, taken shortly after the police arrived—"

Maggie's ears shut off and her eyes drank in the words. Not 'I AM RETURNED TO FULFILL THE PROPHECY,' but: '*A THÁINMHNE NA DOHRGHATAS, SLÁINAICH AN LÁINABH A'SIO.*' Just in view on the floor beside the empty crib.

"Holy crap," she gasped in disbelief, but before she could grab a pen and copy down the phrase, the image flicked back to the anchorwoman who began introducing the next story.

Still ignoring the puddle of milk beneath her, Maggie scrambled off the couch and darted into the kitchen, snatching the newspaper off the kitchen table and sending envelopes flying. I have got to start reading this when I get home, she chided herself as she tore the paper open. The article started on page one, just below the fold, but the photograph was on page five.

The photo confirmed what her brain had first known when it had seen the bloody inscription on the flickering television monitor. The words were written in the same lost dialect of Old

Gaelic as her spellbook—a dialect which, until now, she had been certain no one else in the world but her knew.

As her eyes were filled with the age-old words, her mind juggled four equally disturbing questions:

What prophecy?

Why would the child need to be healed?

Who wrote this?

And perhaps most frightening to the young American who had just committed to spending her foreseeable future in Scotland:

Do they know about me?

4. MacLeod

"Why the bloody hell are you wasting time talking with me?"

David MacLeod's face was almost as red as the sunset blazing outside his 36th floor office windows, with their panoramic view of the Grampian Highlands to the west and Aberdeen harbor to the east. "You should be out finding my son!" Then, just to make sure he'd been understood, he added, "You bloody idiot!"

Aberdeen Police Inspector Robert Cameron sighed heavily, wearily. "Now, just calm down, Mr. MacLeod," he started. "I've plenty of lads out combing the streets for your son. But we need to talk to you a bit as well."

"Talk to me later, Cameron," MacLeod growled. He stormed out from behind his massive oak desk and right up to the inspector. Although MacLeod was a large man in his own right—six feet tall with broad shoulders supporting a chiseled jaw and thick, curly black hair—nevertheless he had to tilt his head back to look up at the equally solid six-foot-three Inspector Cameron. "Right now: you find my son."

Cameron truly enjoyed being a police inspector and so resisted his urge to head-butt one of Scotland's more powerful political and business leaders. Instead, he took a deep breath and, without stepping back, replied in as calm and forceful a tone as he could muster, "Mr. MacLeod, without information from you, my men will not be able to focus their investigation properly and you will hamper, perhaps even foreclose, our ability to find your son."

MacLeod's deep blue eyes flared and his face grew even more crimson. "How dare you speak to me that way?!" He stormed three steps away and then spun around again, his arms waving frenetically. "You're a bloody policeman! A policeman! Do you understand who I am? What I am? I'll have your badge, Cameron! You'll be sweeping rubbish by noon tomorrow!"

Cameron noted with some regret that MacLeod was now out of head-butt range. "Mr. MacLeod," he calmed his voice even further—it was an old police trick, but one that usually worked. "I need your help to—"

Bzzztt!! The intercom.

MacLeod threw his arms in the air again, then bounded to the desk in a single step and slammed on the flashing red button on his telephone—all in one angry motion.

"What?!" he demanded in the speaker.

"Um," a hesitant female voice replied, "there's a Mr. Genworth here in the lobby. Says he's from the Aberdeen Herald. Would you like to speak with him?"

MacLeod closed his eyes and drew in a long, painful breath before responding. "How," he asked in a tone whose controlled anger was perhaps even more frightening than his previous explosiveness, "in the bloody hell did he get up here?"

"Um," the voice started again. Cameron suspected she often started her sentences with that word. "I— I'm not sure. Someone must have let him up from downstairs."

"Then 'someone' is sacked!" MacLeod shouted into the

speaker, spit striking the slatted plastic. "And Miss Logan?"

"Um, yes?"

"If that bastard reporter is not out of my lobby in the next ten seconds," the frightening calmness had returned, "so are you. Do you understand?"

"Um. Yes."

MacLeod let go of the red button and then grabbed a hold of his desk with both hands, his head hanging from his strong neck and his shoulders shrugging in a deep sigh. Cameron shifted his weight uneasily. Best to give him a moment.

"Cameron?" The calm but scary voice. "Don't think I've forgotten about you."

MacLeod slowly turned around.

"I'll give you one last chance, policeman." He tipped his head back and looked wide-eyed at the inspector. "You leave right now. You find my son. And you keep your job. Understood?"

"MacLeod," the 'Mr.' was noticeably absent. "I've been threatened by far more important people than you." Cameron wasn't sure if that was true, but it was a good reply. "If you don't want me to do my job properly and find your son, that's your business. But this 'policeman' finds that a wee bit interesting—"

"Cameron!" MacLeod's face flamed crimson again. "I'll—"

"You'll do as he asks."

Both men's heads turned to the doorway where stood a woman of commanding stature and appearance. She was tall—at least 5'9"—with a slim athletic build and short, sandy blonde hair. She wore a two piece navy blue suit which made her look in uniform even while out of it. A shining silver badge hung prominently from her small leather purse. "Or you've no hope of ever seeing your son again."

"Who in the bloody hell are you, girl?!" MacLeod was beside

himself now.

"This is—" Cameron began but the policewoman waved him off.

"I'm Sergeant Elizabeth Warwick," she began, "and I stopped being a girl some time ago." She stepped fully into MacLeod's office. "And whether you're willing to accept it or not, Mr. MacLeod, I'm your best chance at seeing Douglas alive again."

"Cameron!" MacLeod's crimson face turned to the inspector even as he threw his open palms toward Warwick. "Do you let all your inferiors speak that way?"

Cameron smiled. "I may outrank her," he replied, "but she's not my inferior. And she's right. If anyone's going to crack this case, it's Warwick. She's my best officer. That's why I called her in."

"Your best man is a woman?" MacLeod asked incredulously.

"My best officer," Cameron repeated coldly, "is Sgt. Warwick."

MacLeod shook his head violently and began storming around the room. "No, no, no, no! That is it! You're both—"

"You still don't have a ransom demand," Warwick interrupted in her best English accent to emphasize her southern roots. She looked at her watch. "It's now nearly seven o'clock. As many as twenty-one hours have passed since your son disappeared. You won't be receiving a ransom note. Your son wasn't abducted for money." MacLeod looked at the sergeant; she had his attention. "That's bad."

"Whoever abducted your son," she continued, "did so without anyone in your townhouse noticing a thing. Douglas was spirited out of a third story bedroom by a perpetrator or perpetrators who did so without leaving any trace as to how they entered or exited. They knew exactly what they were doing. It was well planned." She paused. "That's bad."

MacLeod just stared at her.

She looked down casually at her perfectly painted fingernails. "Do you want me to discuss the blood?" she asked without looking up.

MacLeod eyes flared again and he squeezed his fists even tighter. "What I want you to do, girl, is get out of my fu—"

Bzzztt!!

MacLeod looked wildly at the phone.

Bzzztt!!

He slammed down on the red button again. "What?! What, God damn it?!!"

"Um," the same timid voice. "Your appointment is here."

MacLeod shook his head in disbelief. "My what?! My appoi—" Then his eyes lit up in recognition. "Oh. Right." Then politely as a vicar, "Thank you, Miss Logan."

He released the red button, then turned around slowly to face the two police officers. He straightened his fine white linen shirt, adjusted his expensive Italian silk tie, and took another deep breath. When he spoke, his voice held a force it had lacked even in his loudest bellows. "Leave," he instructed, pointing to the door. "Now."

"Mr. MacLeod—" Cameron started. He was tiring of this game.

"It was not a request," MacLeod interrupted. "I will talk to you, Cameron. But not now. Tomorrow. I'll send for you. But right now: leave."

Warwick looked to the inspector. It was his call.

For his part, Cameron had not failed to notice that MacLeod had finally agreed, at least in principle, to speak with him. That was progress anyway.

"Right then," Cameron nodded decisively. "But I'll expect to hear from you by noon tomorrow. Or else I'll be back tomorrow evening. And in far less patient a mood." He turned to the door. "Come on then, Sergeant."

MacLeod, who was still pointing at the door, did not reply, but watched with stony countenance as the police officers exited his office. Then he lowered his arm, shrugged mightily, and sat down on the front edge of his desk, head bowed and strength streaming down his back.

He didn't look up as a side door to his office opened and in walked his appointment. Gazing floorward, he quietly greeted his guest. "Taggert."

The man was shorter than his host by several inches, but a large man nonetheless—burly even. His broad shoulders and barrel chest were trapped inside a dark sweater and black leather jacket. Dark wool pants hung comfortably to the top of black leather shoes. Atop all this was a large head, its smooth, fine, black hair just beginning to recede, with thick dark eyebrows arching over eyes so light blue they were almost white. The chiseled jaw bore no facial hair, no scars, and, despite the gray beginning to fleck his hair, no wrinkles. He flashed strong, white teeth when he spoke. "David."

The clan patriarch looked up then. And for the first time that day, a smile struggled across his face.

Taggert crossed the room and shook MacLeod's hand. "You look tired, David," he observed.

"Aye, Taggert. That I am." MacLeod nodded. "And worried. What do you know?"

The visitor shook his head slowly. "Not much, I'm afraid."

"Not much?" MacLeod stood up sharply. "I don't pay you to know 'not much.'"

Taggert met MacLeod's gaze squarely. "Sure you do, David," he replied with a grin. "That's precisely what you pay me for. And then to find out."

MacLeod tried, but couldn't suppress his second smile of the day. A tired, defeated smile, but a smile nonetheless.

"You're right, Taggert," he admired with a slap to the man's shoulder. "Of course you are." Then MacLeod walked over to the various crystal decanters on the solid mahogany sideboard across the room. Picking up the Glenfiddich and two cut crystal glasses, he turned back toward the desk. "So then, what do you think?"

Taggert waited for a moment then took his freshly poured whisky from his benefactor. "I think," he sipped from the glass, "that I don't know what to think."

"Damn it, man!" MacLeod slammed his drink down onto the desk. "Don't play games! Not with Douglas."

Taggert nodded even as he took another sip. "I'm sorry, David. I didn't mean to sound flippant. I know this is important. The most important assignment you've ever given me, I'm sure. But that's why I'm being careful. I need more information before I start making any hypotheses. I don't want to trouble you with half-baked theories that might well prove wrong."

"Taggert," MacLeod's eyes flared desperately even as the third weak smile of the day presented itself, "I'm half-mad with worry already. I don't care if your theory is baked at all. I won't hold you to it. But damn it, man, tell me what you're thinking, whatever it is, so at least I'll have some idea of what to expect."

Taggert nodded again, then pursed his lips and thought for a moment. He set his drink down on the desk. "You're son's alive," he started. Then he raised a cautionary finger, "I think. If they'd wanted him dead, he'd be dead. They could've killed the lad where he slept."

MacLeod cringed and dropped his eyes.

"But you've no ransom note," Taggert continued. "That's

bad."

MacLeod looked up at this echo of the policewoman's words, but didn't say anything.

Taggert turned and looked out the window. "Not overly surprising, though. Those words on the wall: 'I am returned to fulfill the prophecy.' That might have just been for show—to make sure you paid the ransom quickly and without question. But I don't think so. The bastard—or bastards—who did this are obviously motivated by something other, something more, than money."

"So what's all this about a prophecy then?" MacLeod asked, perturbed by his next thoughts. "You don't think it's the banshee, do you?"

"The banshee?" Taggert asked incredulously. "Well, no," he chuckled, "I don't think the banshee's returned to steal your son."

"Well, of bloody course not," MacLeod railed. "But do you think that's what's meant by it? That that's what we're supposed to think?"

"Well, David," Taggert sipped from his glass, "I might. And the media certainly does. Very interesting angle. But there's one thing that gives me pause."

"What's that?"

"That other phrase. The one written in blood on the floor. I can't see any reason to add that if you're pretending to be the MacLeod Banshee returning from the Fairy Realm to steal the MacLeod heir. There's a disconnect there that isn't explained by any banshee."

"So why was it written?" MacLeod asked. "And what the bloody hell does it say anyway?"

"I don't know," Taggert admitted. "On both counts." He sipped again from his glass. "But I will, David. I will."

MacLeod frowned down at his own drink, considering the

bloody script. "It's not Gaelic, is it?" He knew the language, but only as much as his position required.

"No," Taggert replied with certainty, then hedged his bets, "At least I don't think so. I know Gaelic well enough and it's gibberish to me. Still..." He thought for a moment. "Have you many Gaelic-speaking enemies, David?"

MacLeod released a tired laugh. "I've enemies who speak every language, Taggert. English-speaking, French-speaking, German-speaking. Name the language and I've got enemies."

Taggert frowned in thought. "All right then." He crossed his arms and cocked his head at his benefactor. "I name Gaelic."

"You want me to list my Gaelic-speaking enemies?" MacLeod laughed to the confirming nod of his companion. "Well, I don't know for sure, of course. I've never catalogued them by language. I only meant—"

"I know what you meant, David," Taggert interrupted. "But I want you to consider who from the Gaelic-speaking community might be interested in taking your son away, for whatever reason. Those words may not have been Gaelic, but we may have been meant to think they were."

MacLeod frowned. "Well, I'm not truly sure just now, Taggert. Can I think about it a bit?"

"Aye, David," Taggert replied as he stepped back over to the desk, "but hurry. We don't have much time. Douglas is alive—I think—but there's no guarantee how long that will last." He picked up his glass and drained the last of the whisky. "So I'm back to work. I'll talk with you tomorrow."

Taggert turned to leave, but MacLeod grabbed his arm. The force of his grip surprised both men. "Taggert." MacLeod's eyes were red-rimmed and pleading. "Find my son."

Taggert paused, then laid a hand over the one seizing his

bicep. "I'll do everything humanly possible, my friend. You have my word."

With that MacLeod released his grip and Taggert walked silently out the same side door he'd entered through.

MacLeod looked down at his clenched fists and slowly shook his head. "I hope that's enough."

5. Legends

'MacTary's Woolens - Est. 1897'

The large, handsome sign hung perpendicular to the shop's forest green facade, and its white letters, outlined in gold, stood atop the painstakingly reproduced red, white, yellow and light blue tartan of the Clan Innes—the clan of the shop's owners, Alex and Lucy MacTary, and also the maternal clan of their American niece, Maggie Devereaux, who hesitated for only a moment before grabbing the brass door handle and pulling open the heavy door. As she did so her eyes were filled with the large brass door knocker of the Innes Clan crest: a boar's head inside a circular leather strap bearing the motto, 'Be Traist.' Middle Scots for 'Be True.' Maggie smiled at the familiar words as the door swung past her.

Inside, the shop was empty. No customers at nine o'clock on a Tuesday morning in late July. The floor-to-ceiling shelves, packed full with bolts of fabric, stared silently but companionably at her over the tables of sweaters, shawls and kilts. To the right was the counter, complete with computer, cash register and last minute purchases such as clan badge refrigerator magnets and clan tartan bookmarks. She nodded to herself; she'd definitely come to the right place. As if to confirm this thought, the Innes tartan curtain behind the counter parted and in walked the other reason—apart from her studies—that young Maggie Devereaux had decided to stay in Scotland.

"Well, good morning, Maggie!" called Iain Grant, the MacTary's twenty-five year old store manager, as he walked in from the storeroom carrying several bolts of fabric. He was dressed for work in a cobalt blue button-down shirt and khakis. His large black shoes matched the thick, sable hair falling loosely over his sparkling eyes, which always looked more blue than Maggie remembered. Through the cotton shirt, Maggie could see his biceps bulging from the weight of the fabric. "I didn't expect to see you this morn."

"And hello to you too, Iain," Maggie replied to the handsome Scot. She surveyed the empty store. "It doesn't look like you expected much of anyone this time of day."

"Och, I suppose not," he agreed with a boyish smile. "So let me just set these down and I can give you my undivided attention."

Maggie smiled at the thought. "Please do."

As Iain crossed the small shop and began quickly shoving the bolts of fabric onto an already full shelf, Maggie turned her attention to the refrigerator magnets affixed to the side of the metal cash register. She quickly found the MacLeod badge—or more correctly, both MacLeod badges. One had a bull's head between two flags and the motto, 'Hold Fast.' The other had a radiant sun and the motto, '*Luceo Non Uro.*' Maggie's four years of college Latin let her understand this second motto: 'I Shine, Not Burn.' But despite this fortuitous opportunity to use her rarely useful Latin, Maggie frowned at the unexpected development of encountering two separate badges for what she had presumed was only one clan. But she took solace in the fact that she'd come to the right man—a man who made his living selling Scottish memorabilia to tourists.

"So what can I do for you then, Maggie?"

"Well, Mr. Grant..." Maggie fluttered her eyelashes coquettishly at the tall Scotsman.

"Uh-oh," Iain laughed. "You want something."

"Just information," she assured sweetly. "I was at home, you see, and I was thinking to myself, 'Maggie,' I thought, 'if I needed to learn something about the history and legends of one of Scotland's greatest clans, who would I ask?' And then I thought, 'Why, Mr. Grant, of course!' That's what I thought."

Iain shook his head. "You've a way about you, you do, Maggie Devereaux. And you've that look in your eye, so I don't suppose there's much use in trying to resist your charms."

Maggie drew herself up and set her fists on her hips. "What look in my eye?" she demanded.

Iain laughed again. "The one that tells me you've set your mind on something," he explained. "And if I don't be careful I may end up driving you to the ends of the Earth—or at least the ends of Scotland—on some fool's errand that you won't fully explain to me. That look."

"Oh," Maggie nodded, a grin curling in the corner of her mouth, "that one." She thought for a moment. "Then I guess you'd better answer my questions well or I'll drag you to Argyll and back."

Iain considered this, then bowed deeply, an arm in full flourish, and offered, "At your service, Milady. What would you like to know?"

Maggie laughed. *That's more like it*, she thought.

"First question:" she pointed to the MacLeod magnets, "Why two crests and two mottos?"

"Och," Iain waved a disinterested hand toward the cash register, "that's easy. There's two Clans MacLeod."

"Two?"

"Aye. MacLeod of Harris and MacLeod of Lewis. Harris' badge is the bulls' head and Lewis' is the sun. The clan split into two branches, och, sometime in the 1300's, when the chieftain's two sons each claimed the chieftaincy. The two men were friendly enough to each other, but each established his own clan and became his own chieftain. One branch became the MacLeods of Harris and the other became MacLeod of Lewis. So two badges. They've different tartans as well. Harris' is a blue and green; Lewis' a fine yellow."

"Okay," Maggie made a mental note of the information.

"I should also point out that Clan MacKenzie has the same motto as MacLeod of Lewis. *'Luceo Non Uro.'* That's on account that they claimed dominion over the clan some time back, based on some questionable lineage. Or at least the MacLeods questioned it. There was a bit of fighting over it, but nothing too major."

"Uh, okay," Maggie accepted this additional factoid. "Thanks, I guess."

"Well, I had to add something, didn't I?" Iain crossed his arms and cocked his head half-critically. "To be completely honest, I'd expected better of you."

Maggie looked up at him in surprise.

"I'd expected," Iain continued, "something a bit more taxing of my abilities."

"More taxing," she confirmed with a raised eyebrow, "of your abilities?"

"Aye," Iain said proudly. "Two Clans MacLeod is common knowledge; even the MacKenzie motto being the same is fairly well known. Haven't you anything more interesting? Something I could regale the 'toorists' with? Maybe something about," he lowered his voice dramatically, "the Fairy Flag?"

Like flies to honey, she thought with a sugar sweet smile. *And he obviously hasn't read today's paper yet. Good.*

"The what?" she asked innocently.

"The Fairy Flag," Iain repeated, "of Clan MacLeod fame."

Maggie smiled at how well this was progressing. "All right then, how's this: 'Mr. Grant, sir,'" she exaggerated her American accent into a genuinely unpleasant twang, "'could you tell me about the Fairy Flag?'"

Iain pursed his lips. "Hm," was all he said.

Maggie looked sideways at the reaction. "Now what's wrong?" her normal voice had returned. "Don't you know anything about it after all?" That would be irritating.

"No, no. That's not it," Iain insisted. He squinted an appraising eye down at the diminutive brunette. "I'm just trying to decide which version to tell you."

"Which version?"

"Well, aye. There's at least two different stories surrounding the origin of the MacLeod's Fairy Flag." He pulled the MacLeod of Harris magnet from the cash register's side to fiddle with while he spoke. "There's the more historic version and then there's the more fantastic version. Although I'd wager one is about as true as the other. Still, I'd expect you to be more interested in the historic one. But then again, when I try to guess what you're thinking, I'm usually wrong. Hence," he concluded, "my dilemma."

Maggie blinked. "'Hence?'"

"Aye," Iain stood up straight. "I read books too, you know."

"Still. 'Hence?'"

"In any event," Iain pressed on, "which version would you like to hear?"

Maggie pushed her glasses back up her nose as she considered her options. "Let's start with the historic version."

"Are you sure?"

"Yeah, yeah. Historic." Maggie rolled her hand at him. "Let's just hear it, laughing boy."

Iain matched the description despite it. "You're in quite the mood," he said amicably. "All business."

"Yeah, yeah. Anyway..." She rolled her hand at him again.

"All right, then. Historic version." He paused to collect his thoughts. "Well," he began in a voice not quite his normal one, "as you know, Scotland was long plagued with Viking invaders, and indeed many clans are descended from the Norse. That includes the MacLeods by the way. 'Leod' comes from the Norse *'ljot,'* meaning 'ugly.'"

Maggie laughed at this useless but amusing piece of information, then encouraged him to continue with another roll of her wrist.

"Anyway," Iain complied, "in 1066, shortly before that other, slightly more famous battle against the Normans, the Anglo-Saxon King Harold fought a battle against Viking invaders on the coast of Yorkshire. The Vikings fought beneath a well-known and rightfully dreaded battle flag known as the 'Land Waster.' Despite the superior numbers of the Vikings, the Anglo-Saxons were victorious, and the Land Waster disappeared. It somehow later came into the possession of Godred Crovan, son of the King of Iceland, who had succeeded in establishing himself King of the Isle of Man. His descendants ruled Man until the mid-1200s. The flag then passed into the possession of the more-or-less nearby MacLeods, who by that time had set up residence in Dunvegan Castle on the Isle of Skye. And the Fairy Flag has been there ever since."

"Wow," Maggie opined as Iain nodded proudly and returned the Harris magnet to the cash register with a satisfying smack, "that was really unhelpful."

Iain's shoulders dropped noticeably. "Well, my apologies, Milady," he said sarcastically.

"No, no, the story's fine." Maggie waved her hands at him. "Very interesting. And very well told, I might add."

Iain bowed his head politely at the compliment.

"But," Maggie continued, "it doesn't really explain the 'fairy' part."

"Och, right," Iain finally understood. "That'd be the fantastic tourist version," he explained.

Maggie smiled. "By all means, then. Tell me the fantastic tourist version."

Another debonair smile lit the Scotsman's face, a dangerous glint in his eye. "Woold ye like th' toorist accent, as weel, then?"

Maggie crossed her arms. "Please, no."

"Ar' ye shoor then, me lassie? It'd be nae trooble at all."

"Aye, Ah'm quite shoor," she mimicked. "And don't call me 'lassie.'"

Iain laughed. "All right then. The Fairy Flag," he announced in his usual Scots lilt. He looked up at the ceiling as if about the deliver his report on 'What I Did this Summer.' "Back in the day—"

Maggie immediately interrupted. "Which day?" She wanted to get the details down.

"Ah," Iain flashed that 'you're-going-to-buy-a-kilt-from-me' smile, "no one kens for sure. It was long, long agoo." He stopped and smiled. "'Ago.' Sorry. It was long ago, in the legendary prehistory of the Clan MacLeod, when the Chieftain was a good and handsome man—and all the young ladies who had the good fortune to meet him quickly fell in love with him."

Maggie rolled her eyes. Or so he thought.

"One day," Iain continued, "the Chieftain was walking across a bridge when he encountered one of the Shining Folk—a *bean-sidhe*."

"You don't speak Gaelic," Maggie instinctively interjected.

"Just enough for the tourists," Iain flashed another smile. "Besides, *bean-sidhe* is practically English anyway: 'banshee.'"

"Thanks for the translation," the Ph.D. candidate in Celtic languages said sarcastically. "Good accent, by the way."

"Thank you. I think I even know what it means. 'Shining woman,' right?"

Maggie smiled. "No, actually." She liked correcting a Scotsman's Gaelic. "'*Bean*' does mean woman, but '*sidhe*' doesn't mean 'shining.' I think it's an old word for 'hill.'"

"Hill woman?" Iain questioned.

"Yeah," Maggie double-checked the translation in her head. "Didn't they used to think the Little People lived inside the hills?"

"'Shining Folk,'" Iain corrected, "not 'Little People.' And I think that may be right. It sounds familiar."

"It might also come from *bean-sìth*," Maggie hypothesized aloud. "It sounds the same—'she'—but it's spelled: s, i-accent, t, h. It's an older word for, well," she sought a concise definition but found none. "It kinda means the fairy realm, kinda means magic, things like that."

"Alright, then: *bean-sìth*." He tried the word on for size. "'Fairy woman.' 'Woman of magic.' Right. That'll work with the story."

"Oh, well, good." Maggie returned the smile. "Glad to have helped."

"Hm." Iain considered whether interruptions—even informative ones—were really all that helpful. He decided not to voice his thoughts. "Anyway, where was I? Ah yes, the Chieftain was crossing a bridge when he came upon the fairy woman—for as we all know, the Shining Folk are often encountered over bodies of water."

"Of course," Maggie agreed perfunctorily.

"Well, when she laid eyes on the dashing young chieftain she too was overwhelmed by his beauty and goodness, and she fell immediately and deeply in love with him. And this time, the Chieftain also fell deeply in love with her."

Iain paused and pulled another magnet from the cash register to play with absently while he continued his tale.

"But this *bean-sìth* wasn't just any *bean-sìth*—she was the daughter of the King of the Shining Folk. The Princess of the Fairy Realm. She went to her father and asked permission to marry the MacLeod Chieftain. But the King forbade it."

Maggie found herself frowning at this development.

"Shining Folk were forbidden from marrying humans," Iain explained. "Humans grow old and die, but Shining Folk are immortal. And the King didn't want to see his beloved daughter's heart break."

A wrinkle creased Maggie's brow even as she nodded at this logic.

"But the King could see that his daughter's heart would be broken in any event if he prevented the marriage, and so he relented and allowed her to marry the mortal. But the marriage could last only a year and a day. After that, his daughter would have to return to the fairy realm."

The crease deepened.

"So, the Chieftain and his fairy bride were married in a joyous festival and nine short months later the Clan could again celebrate—this time the birth of a son to the happy couple. But time couldn't be stopped, and soon enough the year and a day had passed, and the King of the Shining Folk appeared to take his daughter home. Only now the daughter's heartbreak had been doubled, for she had to say goodbye not only to her beloved husband, but to her infant son as well."

Dang, Maggie thought.

"Before she left, however, the Princess made her husband promise two things. First, that her son should never be left unattended, for she couldn't bear the thought of him being alone. And second, that her son should never be allowed to cry, for she would be able to hear his wailing even in the fairy realm and she knew she wouldn't be able to bear the sound of his cries. The Chieftain promised his bride these two things, they kissed one last time, and then...they parted."

I don't think I like this story, Maggie decided with a pout.

"Well," Iain sighed heavily, "the Chieftain was heartbroken. And his unhappiness was felt throughout the Clan. Nothing could rouse him from his depression and he withdrew inside the walls of his castle. Eventually, though, his son's first birthday approached, and the people of the Clan decided to throw a great festival in celebration—and in the hopes that it might pull the Chieftain from his melancholy.

"The festival was a success. Everyone danced and sang and rejoiced, and eventually even the Chieftain himself came out of the castle to thank his clansmen. So grateful was he for their love and support that he too began to dance and sing and celebrate the anniversary of his son's birth. Meanwhile, his yearling son was still inside the castle, sleeping peacefully and attended by a nurse. But the nurse could hear the joyous celebration and even though the Chieftain had given her strict orders to remain with the child, she nevertheless crept out onto the castle roof to watch the festival. And the young boy was alone."

Uh-oh, Maggie's eyes widened at this development.

"Sure enough," Iain continued, "the little boy woke up and began to cry. But with all the celebration, no one could hear his cries—no one save his mother in the fairy realm. Well, as soon as she heard the wails, she instantly returned to her son's side. She picked him up and wrapped him in a silk blanket, cooing in his ear and quieting his cries. Then, just as the nurse finally returned to her post, the Princess set her son in his crib, kissed his head, and disappeared in a flash of light.

"Years later, when the boy had grown, he told his father of what had happened, and how when his mother had cooed in his ear, she had told him to keep the silk blanket for protection, for it was enchanted. It would protect the Clan MacLeod—the clan of her child—but only that clan and only three times. Anyone not of the Clan who should touch the enchanted silk would disappear into a cloud of smoke. Thrice the Clan could use the magical fabric to summon the Shining Folk to their aid—but only thrice, after which the silk would disappear forever.

"It's said," Iain couldn't help but exaggerate his brogue as he approached the finale, "that the silk blanket was turned into a flag and has been used twice to summon the Shining Folk to the aid of the Clan. Once to stop the invading forces of the Clan MacDonald from eradicating the Clan, and again to reverse a cattle plague which threatened the entire Clan with starvation. And now the Clan MacLeod has only one use left—one more time they can wave the Fairy Flag thrice in the air and summon the Shining Folk to their aid, before the prophecy is fulfilled and the Fairy Flag disappears back to the Fairy Realm."

Maggie stood silently as Iain concluded his presentation, squeezing the magnet in his hand triumphantly.

"How was that?" he asked finally.

"That," Maggie nodded, "was perfect."

Iain smiled broadly. "E'en wi'oot the' accent?"

"Especially wi'oot the accent," Maggie replied deadpan. Then she snatched the magnet from Iain's hand and looked down at the radiant sun and its motto, '*Luceo Non Uro.*' After a long moment, she returned the magnet to the cash register and took a step toward the door. "Thank you, Iain. You've been a great help."

"Are you leaving then?" Iain was surprised by her sudden departure.

"Yeah. Sorry, but I've gotta go now. The conference starts up again soon."

She smiled, but her eyes held that far-off look—another look Iain knew only too well.

"Well good-bye for now," Iain offered. Then added, "You'll be sure to notify me before you run off on some fool's errand, right?"

"Hm?" It took a moment, but her eyes returned to focus on his and a sardonic smile cramped her mouth. "Oh, of course," she laughed. "I'll probably need a ride." Then she turned again and Iain Grant watched with his own smile as the pretty young American exited into the bright Aberdeen morn.

6. An Old Gaelic

"*Tapadh leibh*. Thank you." Prof. Robert Hamilton concluded his address to the twenty or so students, faculty and interested others who had come to his half hour of fame at the University of Aberdeen's Summer Institute of Irish and Scottish Studies. It had gone rather well, he thought. "I'll be happy to linger and answer any other questions you might have."

"C'mon, Ellen." Maggie stood up and grabbed the arm of her sandy-haired Scottish friend. "I want to talk to Professor Hamilton."

"Aye. I expected as much," Ellen smiled, displaying her large, white teeth. She dislodged her arm from Maggie's grip and pointed to the glossy brochure she held in her other hand. "But don't dally too long. I don't want to be late to the presentation on Scottish devolution."

"Right," Maggie quickly agreed as she stepped into the line which had formed to speak with the professor from the University of Edinburgh; Maggie was third in line. "This'll just take a minute. I want to go to that other one too. Sounds very interesting."

"Are you interested in home rule for Scotland, then?" Ellen asked, a bit surprised. Maggie's interests had always appeared more linguistic than political.

"Well, not exactly," Maggie frowned. "I mean, I'm not not interested in it. But I was thinking they might talk about some other stuff too. Like whether they'll ever make Gaelic an official language. I think it's ridiculous that Welsh is an official U.K. language, but Gaelic isn't."

"Plenty of people speak Welsh, you know," was her friend's reply.

"I'm not saying Welsh shouldn't be an official language," Maggie tried not to sound exasperated. There was just the one person ahead of her now. "But Gaelic ought to be too. It's offensive."

Ellen had to laugh. "And you're not even a Scot."

Maggie laughed too. "Maybe I'll get naturalized."

Before Ellen could reply again, Maggie stepped forward and grabbed the academic's hand. "Professor Hamilton!" She shook the old man's hand warmly, and a bit too enthusiastically. He was in his early 70s, with a neatly trimmed white beard descending from a wispy wreath of white hair around his otherwise bald and age-spotted cranium. Rather large, thickly framed glasses hid his intelligent eyes, and his slightly stooped figure was draped in a tweed jacket, brown sweater and brown pants. "My name's Maggie Devereaux. I'm so glad finally to meet you. Honored."

"'Honored,'" the old Scot repeated with a laugh. "I'd no idea my reputation extended across the Pond." He'd recognized her accent. "Are you American, then?"

"Yes," Maggie practically admitted, "but I'm studying here at Aberdeen. For real. Like a real student. Not study abroad."

Take a breath, Devereaux, she told herself.

"I'm pursuing," she gathered her wits, "my doctorate in Celtic Studies. Gaelic." She pronounced this last word 'Gah-lick,' like the Gaelic word for itself, *Gàidhlig*.

Hamilton's bushy white eyebrows raised in genuine

amusement. "An American who speaks Gaelic! How wonderful! Well then, what can I do for you?"

Ellen looked impatiently at her watch, but Maggie ignored her.

"Well, I've kinda started to focus my research on Old Gaelic and—"

"You have?" Ellen interrupted. "I thought you'd abandoned that direction."

"No, Ellen," Maggie's voice was almost as icy as her stare, "I haven't." She turned again to Prof. Hamilton. "Anyway, I wanted to ask you a question about your article from last year. The one about that long lost dialect of Old Gaelic?"

Hamilton's face was a blank.

"The dialect used primarily in religious ceremonies?" Maggie prompted.

Still no reaction; the same puzzled frown.

"There's no actual record of it? You just hypothesized its existence from a few references in surviving works from the same period?"

"Ah, yes." Finally the light bulb went on. "Yes, the so-called 'Hamilton dialect.'"

Hamilton-Devereaux dialect, Maggie smiled to herself. "Right. That one."

"Sorry," Hamilton removed his glasses and rubbed them on his jacket. "I'm afraid that was not one of my better papers."

Maggie was stunned by this characterization.

"I think I'd been a bit too hopeful on that one," Hamilton continued. "Too eager to see something that wasn't really there, I suppose."

"Oh, no!" Maggie protested rather too loudly. Hamilton quickly replaced his glasses and stared at the young American. "No, not at all," she continued more quietly. "In fact, I— I think you were exactly right. I— I want to— That is— I'm hoping to find proof of the dialect. Proof of its existence."

Ellen stared at her friend in disbelief.

"Well, then," Prof. Hamilton chuckled. "I wish you luck. The paper wasn't very well received, I'm afraid. It actually provoked a rather caustic reaction from one of the faculty here at Aberdeen. MacInnes, was it?"

"Macintyre," Maggie Caroline NicInnes Devereaux quickly corrected, lest her own ancestry be impugned.

"Right. Macintyre." Hamilton frowned at the name. "Rather overly hostile, I thought."

"Yeah, well, he had his own issues." Maggie decided not to relive the unpleasantries just then. "In any event, I think you were right. In fact, I know it. But— But do you have any more information about it?" Her voice almost betrayed her desperation.

Hamilton rubbed his bearded chin and frowned at his feet. After several moments—wherein Ellen let out only two rude sighs—Hamilton slowly shook his head. "No, Miss Devereaux. I'm afraid not. Everything I had I put in that paper."

Maggie frowned defeatedly. "Okay. Well, I guess—"

"But—" Hamilton interjected with an academic's grin. "If you're really interested in Old Gaelic religious texts, I may have a suggestion."

"Yes?" Maggie's eyes widened. C'mon, Hamilton. Give me something good.

"Old Gaelic," Hamilton observed slowly, "is the same as Old Irish. It's merely a difference in nomenclature."

"Right." Maggie blinked at this most elementary truism of Gaelic studies.

"And there's an exhibition," Hamilton continued, "of Old

Irish religious texts going on right now at Trinity."

Maggie blinked again. "Trinity," she repeated.

"Trinity College," Hamilton elaborated.

Maggie nodded slowly.

"It's in Ireland," Ellen broke in.

"I know that," Maggie shot back. "I was just thinking." She paused. "So there's an exhibition?"

"Yes," Hamilton answered. "As I said, of Old Irish religious texts. It's actually a rather extraordinary exhibit. Illuminated manuscripts, by their nature, are usually in Latin. They were produced by monks and as I'm sure you know, the Church rather looked down on the use of the vernacular until, well, 1968 or so. But these manuscripts are in Old Irish. Mostly translations of the Bible, although I believe one of them is known as the 'Spellbook of Ballincoomer.'"

Maggie's eyes lit up at this title.

"So, that exhibit might be worth your time," Hamilton continued. "But you'll want to hurry. I do believe it ends soon. Perhaps next week."

Maggie completely failed to respond. She appeared to have forgotten anyone else in the room. Ellen stepped forward instead and shook Hamilton's hand, "Thank you, Professor Hamilton. It was good of you to talk to us."

Hamilton smiled warmly. "You're welcome, miss. And good luck to you and your friend." Then he turned to speak with the man in line behind them.

"Are you ready finally?" Ellen asked Maggie as she pulled her away by the elbow.

Maggie's brow was creased in distant concentration, but she managed to shake her head and regain her wits. "Er, yeah," she stammered. "I'm finally ready."

And as Ellen fairly stormed out of the lecture room, Maggie trailed behind, a hopeful smile playing at her lips.

Ireland, huh?

7. A Single Step

'Argyll Ferry Dock'

The sign was large, blue with white letters, slightly rusted, and looming impatiently over Maggie's shoulder.

She looked at her watch. Eleven fifteen. "I guess I should get on board," she tried to sound happy.

"I guess so," Iain replied, his smile also fading just a bit.

"Yeah, I want to get a good seat." She thought of the motion sickness pills in her bag. No need to share that little personality quirk with him just yet. "Next to a window or something."

Iain nodded and looked around at the other passengers beginning to board the ferry to Belfast. "Aye, you'll be wanting to get on board then."

An awkward moment ensued as they both vainly resisted the impending parting.

"Well, all right, then," Iain tried.

"Right," Maggie echoed, trying not to be sad. She was a strong independent woman. No reason to be sad. "And you'll pick me up Saturday?"

Iain's smile returned to full force. "Two-thirty," he confirmed. "I'll be here."

Maggie smiled back at him. Then she remembered the time. "Damn," she said softly, almost to herself. "Okay. I've really got to go."

"All right then. Bye." Iain just stood there.

Maggie did too.

Finally she stepped forward, grabbed him by the back of his neck, and kissed him goodbye. Hard. "See you Saturday, *mo chridhe*."

Iain wiped the lipstick, but not the puzzled smile, off his lips. "'*Mo chridhe?*'"

"Look it up," she shot back as she pulled her bag over shoulder.

Iain shook his head amicably. "See you Friday."

"Thursday," Maggie confirmed before turning around and walking toward the boat, genuinely irritated with herself for the sad, empty feeling filling her stomach.

***

In the event, there were few passengers aboard the ferry and Maggie had had no difficulty in finding a forward-facing seat, a fact for which she was quite grateful once the ferry began its undulating journey. She had initially considered trying to spy Iain from a window, but had ultimately decided against it. It was only a few days after all. She needed to stop acting like a lovesick schoolgirl. Still... those blue eyes.

Maggie shook her head and laughed quietly at herself. Time to focus on more serious pursuits. She slid her small suitcase against the ship's hull and pulled her far too heavy backpack onto her lap. Inside the bag, she immediately spotted that morning's Aberdeen Herald—already half-crushed under her Dark Book. She'd brought along the ancient, and heavy, tome because she was fairly certain she'd want it with her while in Dublin. Not only for her impending studies, but also for peace of mind. She couldn't bear the thought of the book being damaged or destroyed while she was away. Better just to schlep it along. She pried the newspaper out from under the leather-bound text and unfolded it. Turning to page three, she quickly found the article she knew would be there:

KIDNAPPED MACLEOD HEIR STILL MISSING

Aberdeen—Police insist they are making progress in the kidnapping of one year old Douglas MacLeod, only son to David MacLeod, Chieftain of MacLeod of Lewis. While no suspect is yet in custody, police have begun contacting several persons of interest and assure that it is only a matter of time before the infant is reunited with his father...

Blah, blah, blah. Maggie skimmed down the page.

...The phrase 'I am returned to fulfill the prophecy' has naturally led to rumour that the MacLeod clan is being stalked by the ghost of the MacLeod Banshee, a mythical fairy woman who...

Yeah, yeah, yeah. So much garbage, Maggie opined. *And anyway, they won't tell the story as well as Iain.* She smiled at the thought of the handsome Scot, then shook her head and returned to her scan of the article. *Aha,* here we are. She pushed her glasses back up her nose and pulled the newspaper closer.

...Much speculation has also surrounded the apparently nonsensical words written in blood near the foot of the child's crib. Believing that the phrase might be Gaelic in origin...

Well, duh! Maggie rolled her eyes.

...Believing that the phrase might be Gaelic in origin, police contacted several local linguists from the University of Aberdeen. While they agreed that the words appeared similar to Gaelic, they ultimately concluded the phrase to be written in a language other than the endangered tongue.

Idiots, Maggie sneered.

...The words were also presented to Prof. Robert Hamilton, a visiting academic from the University of Edinburgh. Fortuitously in Aberdeen for a conference, Prof. Hamilton is widely recognized as one of the world's leading authorities on Celtic languages and Scottish Gaelic in particular.

All right! I told you it was a good article, Maggie thought with a smile. *Go on and tell 'em, Hammy. Tell 'em it's your dialect. Er, our— our dialect.* Maggie suddenly regretted never having published an article about her find. But she could hardly blame herself for having wanted to keep the Dark Book to herself. No, her academic fifteen minutes of fame would have to come from some other source.

...Prof. Hamilton also confirmed that the words were not Gaelic in origin.

"What?!"

Maggie looked around sheepishly at her fellow passengers, several of whom had glanced her way at the sound of her uncontrolled exclamation. Smiling weakly, she returned her attention to the newspaper article:

...Prof. Hamilton also confirmed that the words were not Gaelic in

origin. Hamilton explained that there are certain letter combinations one would expect to see in Celtic languages.

"If this were truly a Gaelic dialect," Hamilton said, "one would see these combinations. Even if this were some strange, forgotten dialect of the tongue, one could still expect to see consistent mutations from the standard. And although this is a rather short phrase, such combinations are simply not present here."

Hamilton concluded with the following foreboding opinion: "Whoever wrote this may have wanted us to believe it was Gaelic. For what reason remains to be seen."

Maggie set the newspaper down in disbelief.

"Now why would he say that?"

8. The Scientific Method

The white cinderblock wall was fairly covered by the enormous map of Aberdeen. It was the only thing even close to a decoration in Sgt. Warwick's spartan office. She had been meticulous in hanging the map, centering it exactly on the wall, equidistant not only from floor and ceiling but also from each of the adjoining walls. She'd measured three times to confirm exactly where the top corners should be affixed and she'd double-checked they were properly placed after hanging it. She was absolutely certain it was level and straight. Which is why it irritated the hell out of her that it looked crooked.

It had been a small task to deduce that the apparent slant was an optical illusion generated by the asymmetry of the image itself, particularly the large blue slash of Aberdeen Harbor and the North Sea which ran down the entire right side. But this deduction had done little to alleviate her irritation at the situation, or the temptation, like just then, during the time she found herself distracted from her work by the faux-crookedness, to just rehang it, slightly askew, in order, ironically enough, to make it look straight.

There was an undeniable logic to this solution if one accepted the premise that the entire purpose of hanging any picture straight is to make it look straight. In the case of her map, there was in fact no strictly utilitarian function in exact straightness: no robotic arm would be descending from the ceiling and relying on the exact positioning of the map to place a push-pin; and she had no intention of ever using the ceiling or floor or walls as reference points from which to locate a particular street or alley or quay. Therefore, given that the image itself created the illusion of slantedness, it should be possible to use the image to create a similar, but opposite, illusion of straightness. All she had to do was abandon the scientific method of measurement for the more holistic approach of artistry. Make it look straight, even if, in fact, it wasn't. And finally be done with it.

But then it would be crooked. And she'd know it. And it would drive her crazy.

No, better to be straight and appear crooked than vice versa.

And as far as being distracted by the map's positioning, that was simply a matter of will power. Warwick tore her eyes from the veins of the cities streets and once again glared down at the file on her desk. '*MacLeod Kidnapping*' said the file tab just above the obligatory law enforcement case number.

Back to work, she ordered herself.

She liked to review her files first thing in the morning, before the clamor and clatter of the shift change at eight o'clock. Refresh her memory, try to spot new angles, reconsider old ones she'd slept on. But that morning she was having trouble focusing and she let her gaze float to the green metal four-drawer file cabinet against the wall to her left, directly opposite the not crooked map.

When she'd first started out, some seven years ago, a rookie copper, still wet behind the ears and walking her first beat, there had been no shortage of sage advice from her older, more experienced colleagues. The words of wisdom ranged from the obvious ('Try to get to work on time') to the dubious ('The less detail you put in your report the more you can adjust your testimony at trial') to the downright strange ('You'll want to keep a salt shaker on your windowsill'). But one pearl of wisdom had stuck with her, perhaps because it had been wrapped in a compliment—and a challenge. It had come from a grizzled old lieutenant in the major crime unit—Lt. Robertson. It was after she'd been working a few months and had begun to develop a reputation as a hard-working and efficient officer who could not only stop the crimes she witnessed, but solve the ones she hadn't.

She'd stopped by Robertson's office to drop off a supplemental report for one of his cases; she'd logged some of the evidence into the property room or some such. A written report wasn't really necessary but she'd done one nonetheless. Robertson, seated at his desk, took it from her, glanced it over, then looked up at her with an inscrutable expression tucked away in the wrinkles around his eyes.

"Have a seat, Warwick," his gravelly voice invited as his hand gestured amicably toward the single guest chair opposite him. He was old, at least for a cop—well into his sixties, with white hair cropped close to his wrinkled, browning scalp. Thick wrinkles creased his pudgy, white-stubbled face, while light blue eyes shone out beneath bristly white eyebrows. "You've a moment, no?"

"Of course," Warwick knew to reply. She was still new, so even though she was confident in her abilities, and growing more confident each day, still, when a senior officer—a lieutenant no less—asks one to have a seat, one has a seat. She sat down. "Thank you."

"I've been hearing about you," Robertson began. "Good things," he quickly assured. "All of it. And I've seen your work. Top notch, that."

"Thank you, sir."

"Ah, well," Robertson twisted his bulky frame in his chair, "from what I hear, you've got the makings of a fine copper. Likely be a detective someday. Maybe even Detective Sergeant. Although, I'll tell you, back in my day, women—" He caught himself, and Warwick observed the slightest of blushes atop the lieutenant's ears. "Well, never mind that. Anyway, I'm nearing the end of my run here, so I figure it's only right if I share a few tricks of the trade with some of the younger lads. Er, and lasses," he was quick to add.

"Well, thank you, sir."

Robertson frowned slightly, then the frown gave way to a yellow-toothed grin. "And you can stop with the 'sir.' All it does it remind me I'm old."

"All right, then, er..." She wasn't sure what to call him, so instead just trailed off.

"See," Robertson continued, "the thing is, the good ones—like you—they start showing themselves quick. You can always tell the future detectives, even right from the beginning."

Warwick wasn't sure what to say, or whether a response was even invited. So she remained silent, satisfied to nod attentively.

"And it's no secret you're going to go far here. I wouldn't waste my breath with most of the lads hereabouts, but you—you've got what it takes. You'll be sitting here one day," he patted the arm of his chair. "So I suppose I ought to tell you a thing or two if I can manage it."

"Thank you, s— Thank you."

Robertson squeezed his eyes shut and tipped his large head back for several moments. Finally he leaned forward and opened his cobalt eyes again. "Organization," he proclaimed. "That's the key to this job. There's too damned much to do really. At least there's too much to do to have the time to do it as well as you and I would like to do. That's the challenge, aye? Finding the time to do the job to our level of satisfaction. And that's where organization comes in."

He levitated a hand across his desk. "No files," he observed. And sure enough, the desktop was bare, save the report Warwick had just brought and a small black notebook. "A desk is no place for files. I've tasks to do, but I keep those written down here," he patted the notebook. "When you need a file, get it. When you're done, put it back. That," he pointed to the tall metal object over Warwick's right shoulder, "is what file cabinets are for."

"Now, speaking of file cabinets," Robertson continued; he was on a roll, "Get yourself a good one. With four drawers. You'll want four drawers."

"Will I then?" It seemed a polite encouragement.

"Aye, you will. Put your open cases in the top drawer. Soon enough you'll have too many and you'll need the second drawer for them as well. The third drawer is for your solved cases what still need a bit of follow up, a last supplemental report or what have you."

"And the fourth drawer?" Warwick was curious now.

Robert grinned. "Use the fourth drawer for your unsolved cases."

Warwick glanced over, casually she thought, at the bottom drawer. I won't be needing that, she assured herself. When she turned back to Robertson he was grinning at her.

"I see that look on your face, lass," he half-laughed, "and that's why you'll be a detective someday." His grin broadened, but his eyes grew suddenly tired looking. "But you will be needing that bottom drawer. Like or not, we all do, eventually."

Warwick scowled at the sturdy green metal file cabinet across her office. It was the same one Robertson had had. She'd commandeered it when he'd retired. His little talk had succeeded in convincing her to get herself a four-drawer file cabinet and to assign its drawers as he'd suggested. But only so she could make sure that the bottom drawer remained empty—physical testament to her ability to leave no case unsolved.

And in the several years since making detective, she had indeed managed to keep the bottom drawer empty. Except for that one damned file.

In truth, it wasn't truly unsolved. Not in her mind. It was just that she valued her career too much to fill out the final report on how it had all turned out. If she did that, it would be her last report—before being forcibly removed to the Aberdeen Sanitarium.

Warwick tore her eyes from the file cabinet, then crushed them shut and rubbed them with the heels of her hands.

This wasn't working very well. Between the not quite crooked map and the not quite empty bottom drawer she'd managed to waste enough time that the shift change was beginning. Departing officers were booming out last good-byes while arriving policemen were greeting each other enthusiastically, catching up from yesterday afternoon, discussing what was on the tele last night and so on, all voices loud enough to penetrate easily past her mostly closed office door, and filling her office with the amicable, but distracting, cacophony.

With some effort she glared down again at the file before her. She knew it wasn't really the distractions; it was the case. Usually she had little difficulty ignoring whatever distractions tempted her. But usually she was also quick to find the chink in the case's armor; that point of weakness through which she could enter the enigma and unravel it from within. But that opening had avoided her as yet. And she found herself quite irritable—and easily distracted—when considering the MacLeod case.

It wasn't as if she'd never investigated a kidnapping before.

Even one without a ransom demand; indeed, a lot of them didn't come with ransom demands. It was pretty risky business to maintain communication, however guarded, with one's victim, who in all likelihood had brought law enforcement into the matter. No, most kidnappings seemed to involve angry relatives who'd lost custody battles; they had no intention of returning the child and thus no need for ransom notes. Of course, most of such kidnappings also didn't involve words in blood dripping down walls or smeared across floors.

She reached into the case file and pulled out the photograph of the bloody words. Not the ones on the wall; she found those surprisingly uninteresting, at least relatively speaking. What she really wanted to look at were the other words. The nonsensical ones written in blood at the side of the crib. And looking at the image, Warwick couldn't help but be reminded of the photographs of a similarly bloody pattern scrawled across the ground—the photographs in her 'unsolved' case file.

She let her eyes slide again to the bottom drawer of the file cabinet, and for not the first time she wondered whether she shouldn't contact a certain American student at the College. And the similarities between the MacLeod kidnapping and last fall's King's College murders were enough to give the detective sergeant pause.

Maybe she should abandon her usual scientific method of police investigation for a more holistic approach of solving the case with any and all resources—however arcane.

But Warwick just shook her head and for not the first time rejected the idea of contacting the American student.

Motive, means, and opportunity.

Deduced   through   observation,   hypothesis,   and experimentation.

The scientific method. It worked in the laboratory and it

worked in the field. Warwick was determined to solve the case the scientific way.

And Devil take Maggie Devereaux.

9. Observation

The blazing summer sun blistered the soaring summer sky. Only the thinnest wisps of clouds hovered between the radiant golden orb above and the soft emerald grass below. The lush field spread out over lazy, loping hills only to rebound off distant shrubbery and coalesce beneath the earth-stained feet of a five year old girl named Maggie Devereaux.

Maggie looked down at her childish body, past the yellow floral sundress, at her wiggling toes, thick blades of the greenest grass shooting up between them. She raised her face to the sun, sending her thick auburn hair cascading down her back. Too bright to look at, still the sun warmed her closed eyes and smiling young face. Birds sang from nearby trees.

She lowered her face again and when she opened her eyes she noticed for the first time the big red barn on the other side of the field, just past the ripples of gentle grassy hills ahead of her. Following her childish impulses, she began to run toward the candy-apple structure—the run of a five year old: awkward and flailing, but earnest.

Then she heard her mother's voice.

"Margaret! Stop!"

Maggie did as she was told, coming to a galloping halt still far from the barn. She turned around to see her mother standing in the tall grass behind her. She was wearing an identical yellow print dress, and a large hat shielding her face.

"Don't," was all her mother said.

Maggie's face screwed up into a frustrated scowl. She looked over her shoulder at the barn again, then back at her mother.

"Don't," her mother warned.

Maggie frowned. Her young brow creased with decision, and she turned around again. She was going to the barn; her mother could just try and stop her.

But the barn was gone.

Where it had stood was now just an empty knoll, sun drenched grass beyond the gently rolling hills she'd abandoned to look at her mother. Angry as a five year old can be, she turned again to face her mother.

But her mother was gone too.

Alone in the desolate field, her toes stained with earth, five year old Maggie Devereaux looked up to the distant sun and began to sob.

Then, like a bubble floating to the surface of the waves, twenty-seven year old Maggie Devereaux woke up. But the sobbing still echoed in her heart.

Wow, she thought as she rubbed her eyes with the heels of her hands. *I didn't like that dream very much.*

She squinted at the red digital numerals of the hotel room clock. 7:18. Way too early to get up. Way. She rolled over, pulling the covers snugly over her shoulders, and fell right back to sleep.

***

Taggert looked down at his wristwatch. 7:19. Late already. He'd stayed up too long the night before, but that was no excuse. He'd spend the rest of the day playing catch up.

With a disgusted frown he pulled his bag snugly over his shoulder and headed out the door.

***

There was someone at the door.

Knock! Knock! "Maid service!" called the Irish voice on the other side.

"Uhnngh-uh," Maggie tried to reply as she propped herself up in the far too soft and comfortable bed. She cursed herself for having forgotten to put out the '*Do Not Disturb*' sign. "No," she called out. "No, thank you. Not now."

"All right then, love," came the muffled reply, and Maggie could hear the cleaning cart being wheeled away.

She let herself plop back down onto the overly soft pillows and waited a long moment before rolling over and again squinting at the clock. 9:23.

Ugh, she thought. *Time to get up.*

She forced her feet out from under the thick covers and hung them off the edge of the bed. She also managed to lean herself up into a mostly upright position, but then she just sat there, toes brushing the carpet and eyes quite closed.

Then, remembering the in-room coffee machine, a smile crossed her sheet-creased face. She opened one eye and confirmed the apparatus' position on the small table across the chamber.

"Things are looking up," she said aloud as she finally stepped out of bed and crossed over to the coffee maker with its one bag of generically packaged 'COLUMBIAN COFFEE.' Soon, the machine was engaged and the sounds and smells of brewing coffee ushered Maggie off to the bathroom for her morning shower.

A short time later found Maggie cleaned, dressed and standing before the mirror, one hand holding a half-drunk cup of coffee and the other tucking thick strands of brown hair behind her small ears. She pulled on her glasses and checked her appearance. She'd opted for the light blue summer dress she'd brought; it was sunny out and this way she could avoid long pants without looking like a 'toorist' in shorts. Comfortable sandals hugged her immaculate feet and with her free hand she pulled the last of her accoutrements from her jewelry bag. It was a necklace, with the silver pendant her grandmother had left her in her will. The pendant of the Innes clan crest.

Maggie held the necklace up so the clan crest danced happily before her face, its polished silver reflecting brilliantly. The crest was the same as on the MacTary's door knocker: a boar's head surrounded by a representation of a leather strap. She admired the flawless silver finish, then set her coffee down just long enough to clasp the necklace around her throat and let the pendant topple onto her chest. Looking in the mirror, she couldn't help but smile at the reflection of the motto etched inside the silver strap: 'Be Traist.'

***

'*Do Not Cross*'

Taggert frowned at the familiar words printed on the plastic police tape. Then he shrugged and raised the barrier just high enough to duck under it, letting it slide off the back of his black leather jacket. It was the same police tape he'd once helped to wrap around older crime scenes: blue and white plastic, twisting and bouncing as Taggert walked efficiently toward the back of MacLeod's townhouse.

It had been easy enough to distract the two policeman assigned to guard the residence. A simple firecracker had been sufficient to convince the lad out front to call for the lad out back to 'come round front.' A few moments later found the back entrance unmonitored. Not that a quick phone call from MacLeod wouldn't have resulted in similar access to the townhouse, but it would also have brought with it considerably more attention than Taggert's now unnoticed activities.

And it wouldn't have been nearly as much fun.

The back door was locked, of course. But Taggert had a key, of course, and he quickly slipped inside his client's Aberdeen home. The ancestral seat of the MacLeods—both Lewis and Harris—rested some distance from Aberdeen, at Dunvegan Castle on the western Isle of Skye. But such residential occupation was a formality at best. In truth, both chieftains spent most of their days away from Skye. For his part, David MacLeod split his time between London, where he tried to keep a hand in any affairs of state which might affect him, Edinburgh, where he hoped to keep an eye on the upstart Scottish Parliament which threatened to affect him, and Aberdeen where he needed to stay abreast of his vast holdings in the North Sea oil industry which were certain to affect him. As a result, the patriarch of MacLeod of Lewis was possessed not only of an enormous residence and estate on Skye, but also a large home just outside London, a stately city residence in the shadow of Edinburgh Castle, and the smaller, but lavishly furnished, Aberdeen townhome through which Taggert silently crept.

MacLeod had not been back since the previous morning when his son's disappearance was first reported. Neither had the nanny he took with him wherever he traveled. Only the police had haunted the abandoned townhome since then, and now they too had fled its curtain-darkened confines.

Taggert walked through the back kitchen very slowly. Not out of fear of being seen, or out of concern of making too much noise, or even out of respect for the young boy whose disappearance had brought him there, but rather so he could thoroughly scan every visible nook and cranny for any clue the police might have overlooked—and therefore not corrupted.

The flour canister was approximately two inches forward from its brethren containers.

The lace curtains on the small window over the sink were mostly closed, hanging about a half-inch apart and a bit left of center.

The coffee maker was perfectly clean.

Taggert noted all this and more but didn't break his slow, measured, methodical stride as he crossed the black and white marble floor. He might well come back to inspect the room more closely, but there was another room which demanded his full attention and it would be folly to delay its inspection any more than these initial observations required. He stepped through the wooden doorframe into the hallway, then turned toward the staircase to his right. The nursery was on the third floor.

Visual inspection of the stairwell during the ascent confirmed only one thing: at least a half dozen different police officers had repeatedly traversed the steps, rendering further examination pointless. Taggert sighed, not surprised, and began the ascent.

Although no longer a young man, Taggert was fit and so he stepped onto the third floor breathing only slightly heavier than he had on the first. Fifteen feet later, his breathing still controlled, he stood at the threshold of Douglas MacLeod's nursery.

Where kitchen and stairwell had still appeared somewhat lived-in, the nursery was starkly ransacked. And although the police had undoubtedly gone over it with a fine-toothed comb, they had apparently started with a sledgehammer. The scene was thoroughly corrupted. Every last piece of fabric—from the curtains which had undoubtedly hung on the window to the sheets which must have covered the plastic coated mattress—was gone. Shipped off to forensics, no doubt. Similarly, each piece of furniture had been pulled away from the wall, leaving scuff marks crisscrossing the hardwood floor; the dresser's empty drawers still jutted out and the changing table's foam pad hung askew off the edge. The only piece of furniture which was still in the same place Taggert had seen the previous morning—before the police had first arrived—was the crib. The bloody words on the wall, now dried dark brown, still arched above it, and the half-legible stains on the floor still crouched evilly around the base of young Douglas' bed.

Taggert shrugged his bag off his back and set it on the floor. Time to get to work.

***

An approving smile unfurled across Maggie's face as she walked through the elegantly intricate archway of Regent House and into the grounds of Trinity College Dublin. As she crossed the white cobblestones of Parliament Square, with its scattering of summer tourists, cameras slung of their shoulders and multicolored jackets tied around their waists, Maggie considered Hamilton's description of the exhibition. 'Illuminated manuscripts ... in Old Irish ... one of them is known as the "Spellbook of Ballincoomer."'

She had her own spellbook of course, tucked safely away in the backpack she always kept with her, but she was excited at the prospect of an illuminated spellbook. For where her Dark Book had dealt with dark spells, such as human sacrifices, Maggie was hoping that an illuminated spellbook might deal with brighter spells. Spells such as healing. Hope brimming onto her smiling face, she bounded happily up the steps of Trinity College's Old Library.

"Good Morning, Miss," said the woman behind the reference desk. She was a bit shorter than Maggie, several dozen pounds heavier, even more years older, and sported a loose gray mop of hair and small glasses which hung quite officially onto the ball-like tip of her nose. "How can I help you?"

Maggie's light grin deepened into full smile. So far on her trip to Ireland she had yet to encounter anyone who did not appear genuinely delighted to be of even the slightest assistance. "I'm looking for the exhibition," she explained.

The woman smiled. "All right then. Which one?"

"Right." Maggie realized that Trinity College probably had dozens of permanent exhibitions in addition to the multitude of temporary ones like the one she'd come to view. "The one with the ancient manuscripts."

The woman's smile was joined by a warm glint in her eye. "Which one?" she repeated with a slight chuckle.

"Right. Sorry." Maggie laughed lightly herself. "The one with illuminated manuscripts from the 9th Century."

The woman's raised eyebrow repeated her question for her.

"In Old Gaelic," Maggie finally explained.

"Ah, yes." This had narrowed down the quest sufficiently. "An excellent exhibit. Runs through tomorrow."

"Tomorrow?" Maggie asked, her disappointment permeating the word. "That's it?"

"I'm afraid so."

"But tomorrow's Thursday," Maggie protested. "Shouldn't it run through Friday or something?"

"Well, sometimes the books need to be returned sooner than that," the woman explained. "Although," she defended, "that particular exhibit will have run a full three weeks."

Maggie nodded and frowned at herself. It was hardly this woman's fault that Maggie had only just learned of the exhibition. "So where is the exhibition housed?" she asked.

"That'd be in the 1937 Reading Room," came the reply.

Maggie paused. "The 1937 Reading Room?" she repeated.

"Right," the woman assured simply.

Maggie considered for a moment. "Should I ask?" she inquired.

The woman smiled. "You could. But in all honesty, it's probably not worth the answer."

"Okay, then." Maggie liked that response. "So where is the 1937 Reading Room?"

The woman pointed back at the door through which Maggie had entered. "Go back outside and turn left. It's the smaller building, tucked between the Old Library and the Theatre. You can't miss it."

Maggie thanked the woman for her help and headed back out into what she expected was probably rare Irish sunshine. The 1937 Reading Room was indeed easy enough to spot, its classical facade facing the Square immediately next door to the Old Library, just before the Public Theatre as the woman had assured. Maggie let her eyes dance lazily about the Square to her right as her feet motored toward her goal to her left. Among others, there was a group of four tourists—two married couples, Maggie guessed— standing at the edge of the grassy Library Square and pointing toward a map or some such in one of the women's hands. A short distance away were two older women, their white tennis shoes gleaming in the sun, who were crossing the cobblestones toward the small chapel opposite the theatre. A heavy set woman with dark hair and dressed all in black was standing at the side of the chapel looking right at Maggie. And a few students were scattered about the lawns next to Regent House.

Maggie stopped and looked again toward the chapel.

But the woman in black was gone.

Hmm, Maggie thought, an unexpected shiver climbing up her spine. She wasn't sure what to make of that.

Another look confirmed the woman was out of sight. Maggie wanted to think that the woman in black had been staring at her, but couldn't quite convince herself that she was really that important.

Not yet anyway, she joked to herself. Then she turned to her left and completed her journey to the 1937 Reading Room.

It was smaller than she had expected. Only one story and not much larger than an average home. Once inside, however, the smallness gave way to a certain academic grandeur and Maggie quickly found herself at the welcome counter. It was attended by a rather tall, rather thin man in his late 40s, with thick black eyebrows which almost, but not quite, made up for his deeply receding hairline and badly thinning red hair. "Can I help you, then, Miss?" he asked with usual Irish warmth.

"Yes," Maggie replied with equal pleasantness. "I'm looking for the exhibition."

"Which one?" His smile was, luckily for him, disarming.

Maggie took a calming breath. "Manuscripts. Illuminated. Ninth Century. Old Irish."

"Ah, right." The man smiled. "The one we've here."

"Right." Maggie was willing to entertain the notion that perhaps some people might start out at the 1937 Reading Room only to be directed elsewhere on campus. After all with a name like 'the 1937 Reading Room,' one could only suppose it housed manuscript exhibitions. "The one you have here."

"Well, then," the man laughed, "you have, of course, come to the right place." He pointed to the door past his desk. "It's right through there."

"Great," Maggie enthused. "Thank you very much."

She started toward the door, only to be stopped by the polite, but serious, cough of the tall, balding man. "Er, miss?"

Maggie turned around again. The man was tapping on the sign affixed to the front of the welcome desk. The sign Maggie had overlooked when she'd first approached. The sign with the admission prices.

"Oh. Right. Sorry." She tried not to feel stupid and quickly fetched the student admission price from her bag. "Here you are."

The man eyed it critically. Obviously his Irish pleasantness was being tested. "I think you're a bit short here," he said as gently as he could, then reached down and tapped the sign again.

Maggie double checked the sign, then explained, "I'm a student."

"You are?" He eyed her critically. She was twenty-seven, after all.

"A doctoral student. At the University of Aberdeen."

The critical gaze intensified.

"In Scotland."

The man laughed. "I know it's in Scotland, Miss. It's simply that you are obviously not Scottish. Are you Canadian, then?"

Again her accent had betrayed her. Damn. "American, actually."

"Ah, I expected as much," he replied with a satisfied nod.

"But I'm a student at the University of Aberdeen," Maggie insisted. "Directly enrolled."

The man pursed his lips, but then shrugged. "Well, then," he dropped the money into a previously unnoticed cash drawer, "please go ahead. It's the third room on the left. Enjoy the exhibition."

Grateful not to have had to extract her student ID from her bag, Maggie thanked the man and pushed open the door to the exhibition halls.

Walking into the third room on her left, she was greeted with absolute silence and only one other patron, a young woman with short red hair who was hovering near a window, whispering into a cellular phone and temporarily ignoring the exhibit behind her. Maggie grabbed a pamphlet from the introductory display standing near the entrance. '*Old Irish Illuminated: The Vernacular Works of Ireland's Ancient Monasteries*'

Oh goody, Maggie thought to herself, and she bounded forward into the exhibit.

There were seven manuscripts displayed, each atop a large wooden pedestal and each quite thoroughly sealed under glass. The exhibitors had obviously elected which pages to display and visitors would simply have to content themselves with viewing whichever pages had been so chosen. Arranged in a loose scattering, with no recognizable geometric pattern, the podiums suggested a zig-zag stroll as the most appropriate method of viewing their treasures. Maggie walked up to the first manuscript.

Sure enough, it was in Old Irish. Or Old Gaelic, she thought. Whatever. But reading it was more difficult than she'd expected. It wasn't just that Modern Gaelic, rather than Old Gaelic, was her specialty, but also the fact that the letters had been drawn more than written. Their resultant illegibility was compounded by the fact that the 9th Century equivalents of 'r' and 's' looked nearly identical, and that of 'g' almost entirely unlike the letter known today. But careful, patient study of the first sentence unlocked its prose: '*Ocus conaca Día an leus, co fail é maith; ocus cuit Día an leus á an dub*': 'And God saw the light, that it was good; and God divided the light from the darkness.'

Genesis 1:1, Maggie remembered from Sunday School.

Maggie scanned the pages. In addition to the fact that each

letter had been rendered in flawless brushstrokes, the first letter of this first page of the Bible—the 'O'—took up fully one quarter of the page. The intricate Celtic knotwork inside and behind the letter was even more stunning for the gold leafing affixed to it. Down the entire left hand side of the page was a border filled with even more knotwork, inked red beneath the evenly spaced embellishments of gold leaf. It was as beautiful as any illuminated manuscript Maggie had ever seen, and for her, the fact that the blue painted letters were in Old Gaelic rather than Latin only added to its beauty.

Maggie then made her way through the remainder of the exhibition, only vaguely aware of the young woman with whom she shared the room. The next several texts were also translations of the Bible, and Maggie began to wonder whether any of the volumes were spellbooks as Hamilton had promised. In the event, the seventh and final text proved the professor right.

The brass nameplate on the podium read: '*The Spellbook of Ballincoomer.*' Apart from this title, the only indication that this equally breathtaking manuscript was not another translation of the Bible was the meaning of the ancient words themselves. Still acclimating her eyes to the ornate letters, Maggie contented herself simply to peruse the intricate green script, reading what she could and skipping for just then any words whose meaning did not immediately jump to mind. But then, as she neared the end of the page—the second page, the right hand page—her eyes darted ahead slightly and caught glimpse of a word she couldn't help but recognize. A word she'd seen only just recently in the Modern Gaelic, but whose Old Gaelic ancestor was little different. And while it was the second word of the sentence, it was the last word on the page, and seeing it, Maggie ached to shatter the glass and turn the centuries-old page to read what lay just overleaf.

The word: *ben-slániger.* 'Healer.'

***

Taggert retracted his measuring tape and jotted a final note in his notepad. Then putting both the tape and the notepad back into his bag, he slung the sack over his shoulder and turned to face the room one last time.

He crossed his arms and surveyed the room. He was satisfied. For now.

But just as he turned to the door, the last glimpse of the room was processed by his brain and he realized he'd just seen something he'd overlooked until that exact moment. He turned back around and confirmed what his eye had told his brain.

Taggert frowned at the gory stains on the hardwood floor. The letters which had been scrawled in blood had eventually dried up, their liquid returning to the atmosphere and their solids sinking into the porous surface of the wooden planks. In so doing the sharp lines of the letters had become blurred, some areas being absorbed more fully than others. The result was that although one could still make out most of the original inscription, significant parts of it had disappeared into the darker areas of the wood. As a result, one word in particular stood out to Taggert from its dried up brethren. Not because of its physical appearance, but because of its new spelling. Having lost several letters to the porous wooden floorboards, the remaining letters—'SLÁN'—stood out more or less legibly from their lighter wood to the left. And as a result, Taggert realized he would have to reassess his assumptions and form a new hypothesis.

He'd told MacLeod that the inscription wasn't Gaelic.

He'd been wrong.

Taggert spoke Gaelic, and his curious mind had wandered enough along that path during his lifetime to know at least a few of the Old Gaelic roots of the language. He knew '*slán*' meant 'heal' in

Old Gaelic.

And now he knew that whoever had kidnapped Douglas MacLeod knew that as well.

10. The Father

"The police officer is here, Mr. MacLeod." The intercom squeaked just slightly at the 's' sounds.

Silvery smoke wafted heavily from the cigar pinched between the fingers of MacLeod's left hand even as his right finished the note it was scrawling in the file. He took a long drag off the cigar, held it for a moment, then exhaled slowly before finally reaching over and pressing the intercom button on his telephone. "Send him in."

Three seconds later the door from the lobby opened and in walked a her.

"Aw, Christ," MacLeod spat as he leaned back in irritation. "It's you. Where the hell is Cameron?"

"He's busy," Sgt. Elizabeth Warwick replied from the doorway.

"Too busy for my son, is he?" Another drag on the cigar. "So he sends a lass?"

"It's my case." Warwick stepped into the office and over to MacLeod's desk. "Deal with it."

"Listen, eh—Wilcox, was it?" MacLeod started.

"Warwick. Like the castle." Warwick sat down opposite her

subject. "And you can do the listening. You don't have to like me. And I'll refrain from sharing my current opinion of you. But it's my case, so we're doing this. And that's that."

MacLeod stared at the blond policewoman for several moments. Then he looked at the clock on his desk. Half past four. He sucked again on his cigar and exhaled the smoke slowly out of his nostrils. Warwick supposed he thought it made him look like a dragon. She thought it drew attention to the fact that he needed to clip his nose-hairs.

"You've five minutes," he said finally.

"It'll take seven," Warwick replied as she retrieved her notepad from her inside jacket pocket. "And you'll give them to me."

MacLeod smacked his lips, then lowered his gaze to the paperwork strewn across his desk. He took up his pen again. "You'll no mind if I work while you interrogate me." It was a statement, and he began scribbling more half legible entries into the file.

"No ransom note yet," Warwick began. This itself was barely a question.

MacLeod paused, his writing hand momentarily stilled. Without looking up, he replied quietly, "No."

"All right then. Since the kidnappers have declined to divulge their identity, we can start with the more obvious suspects. Do you have any enemies?"

MacLeod couldn't help but smile at the question. "Aye, lass. I've a lot of enemies." He looked up at her. "I'd have expected you to know that. You'll no earn my respect with questions like that."

"I'm not after your respect," Warwick retorted, although she fought an angry flush from her face. "I'm after information. Let's start with family."

"Family?" MacLeod set the pen down.

"Right. Your son is family and he's who's missing. So we'll start there."

MacLeod drew another intake from the cigar. "All right."

"Let's talk about Janet."

"She goes by 'Jessie,'" MacLeod replied through a cloud of smoke. "And I'd rather not."

"Too bad." Warwick didn't wave the cigar smoke away; that would have given him satisfaction. "Janet 'Jessie' Sterling. Douglas' mother, correct?"

"Aye, and soon to be my ex-wife." MacLeod raised the tobacco to his lips again. "And not soon enough."

"When was the last time you spoke with her?"

"Several months ago," was the immediate response.

"Months?" Warwick tried to control the surprise in her voice. "Douglas is only—"

"A year old," MacLeod finished her sentence for her. "Aye, and it's been months since I've spoke with Jessie."

Warwick considered for a moment, then followed up. "Haven't you spoken with her about this?"

MacLeod shook his head slowly. "Nae. All contact is through our attorneys."

"All right then." She jotted a note in her notepad. "Any other family?"

"I've a brother in Australia," MacLeod offered casually. "I'm fairly sure he didn't do it."

Warwick had to ask. "Why Australia?"

"Simple enough, I suppose." MacLeod temporarily abandoned the work before him. "Business took him there. The weather kept him there. Going on twenty years now."

"Anyone else?"

MacLeod rubbed his chin. "Nae. That's the family. My

parents are dead. My brother's in Australia, I can't stand to see my soon-to-be ex-wife, and my son has been kidnapped." He inhaled again from the cigar. "And, I might add, you seem to be doing precious little to change that last state of affairs."

"Business." Warwick ignored the barb. "What about business rivals?"

"You think a business rival kidnapped my son?" MacLeod was incredulous. "Are you daft, lass? Why would anyone do that?"

"It's not always clear," Warwick replied coolly. "Perhaps to distract you."

MacLeod picked up his pen again and returned to his work. "Nothing distracts me."

"Do you have any upcoming deals? Anything that would demand your complete attention?"

"Everything demands my complete attention," MacLeod snapped. Then he took a deep, smoke-free breath, and added, "If it's my business dealings you want to know about, you'll want to talk with Barry Nelson, my C.O.O. He handles the day-to-day."

Another note in the pad, then, "What about politics?"

"What about it?" came MacLeod half-laughed reply.

"You've political enemies, as well?"

"Most likely."

"You oppose Scottish devolution."

"Absolutely," MacLeod scowled and took another drag from the nearly spent cigar butt. "Ridiculous notion that Scotland would be better off independent within a united Europe. The U.K. was united under a Scottish king, and the Scottish parliament voted to unite with the English one. Why the bloody hell do we need our own bloody parliament when we've already got M.P.s in London? It makes no sense. It's just another layer of politicians and bureaucrats who'll nationalize every last oil field in the name of Bonny Ol'

Scotland."

Warwick looked at MacLeod for a moment before offering her observation. "Including yours."

"Well, bloody hell yes, mine!" MacLeod slapped the desk. "Christ, woman, I don't bleeding care if they nationalize your oil fields—you don't have any!—but they damn well better keep their greedy hands off mine!"

"And do you find the notion distracting?" Warwick asked.

Another smile. "Not in the least."

The two stared at each other for a few seconds, then MacLeod broke off the gaze to glance at his watch. "Well, lass, your seven minutes is up, it seems."

"Not quite." Warwick didn't look at hers. "It's been six and half. I've one more question."

MacLeod crossed his arms and pushed himself back in his leather desk chair, waiting.

"Why," Warwick asked in a perfectly even voice, "did you lie to the police about when you discovered your son was missing?"

MacLeod paused for a very long time before responding, "How do you mean?"

"Don't screw with me, MacLeod." Warwick leaned toward the desk. "Just because I asked questions I already know the answers to doesn't mean I don't do my homework. Sometimes I just want to see if you'll tell the truth. But don't screw around on this one. We're both above that."

MacLeod raised his head slightly and looked at Warwick anew.

"You didn't find him missing at eight o'clock that morning."

"No," MacLeod admitted.

"More like six."

"Seven actually. Ten before."

"And it wasn't the nanny who'd found him missing, was it?"

"No. It wasn't the nanny."

Warwick narrowed her eyes. "And why hadn't the nanny checked on him before seven in the morning?"

MacLeod leaned forward and crossed his hands on his large desk. "I don't believe for a moment that you don't know the answer to that question."

Warwick allowed herself a smile. "You're right."

"And you're finished." MacLeod stood up and gestured toward the door, even as he returned his gaze importantly to the work on his desktop. "You'll let yourself out."

At this dismissal, Warwick nodded curtly and stepped to the door, satisfied with her eight minutes of work.

11. The Chief Operating Officer

"And who should I say is calling?" The handsome blond receptionist was pleasant enough, but she clearly understood and meant to perform her duty as gatekeeper—especially just before the end of the work day. Her serious brown eyes belied the warm smile on her burgundy lips.

"Aberdeen Police Sergeant Elizabeth Warwick," came the pleasant enough but also serious reply. "Please tell Mr. Nelson I need to speak with him regarding the MacLeod kidnapping."

The receptionist's mouth screwed up into a tight little knot as her face displayed the internal balancing of her obligations to her employer against her obligations as a good citizen. "One moment please," she finally replied. She glanced at what must have appeared to be the inadequate intercom, then stood up, straightened off her skirt and crossed the lobby to a pair of dark wooden doors through which she deftly slipped.

A few moments later the wooden doors clicked open again and the secretary stepped back into the plush lobby.

"Mr. Nelson will see you now."

Barry Nelson was standing just inside his palatial office and extended a friendly hand in greeting. "Good morning, Sergeant."

He was the definition of professional. Warwick guessed his age at about 45. He stood six feet tall, with short brown hair, just beginning to gray at the temples. A crisp white linen shirt framed a delightfully patterned red and gold tie, while his tan suit pants hung pleasantly to obviously expensive burgundy leather shoes. The matching suit coat hung neatly from a hanger on the coat rack a few feet behind him.

The office itself matched the man. It was a corner office, of course, and extended at least 30 feet from the entryway to the floor-to-ceiling windows which commanded a breathtaking view of the Aberdeen harbor—a similar view to that of his employer one floor above. But unlike the traditional cherry furnishings of David MacLeod, Barry Nelson had filled his office in the most modern-looking black steel and blue-tinted glass furniture, giving the distinct impression of a man both professional and modern.

He stepped aside. "Please come in."

Warwick shook Nelson's hand, they sat on opposite sides of Nelson's futuristic desk.

"Thank you for agreeing to see me," Warwick began, "particularly in light of the time of day." Neither bothered to look at the clock; they both knew it was quarter of five.

"Of course, Sergeant," Nelson replied with an engaging smile. "Anything to help David. Although I should warn you," he raised a cautious but friendly hand, "if we go much past five, you may have to take the matter up with my wife. We have rare plans for dinner tonight and she's meeting me here at the office."

"Then by all means, I'll try to be brief," Warwick assured. "I am, of course, trying to be as thorough as possible in identifying potential suspects in the kidnapping of Mr. MacLeod's son. Given the size and diversity of Mr. MacLeod's business holdings I felt it prudent to pursue this area as well. And Mr. MacLeod indicated that you handle his business affairs."

Nelson laughed politely. "Hardly. I am the C.O.O.—Chief Operating Officer—for MacLeod Enterprises, an umbrella organization which handles most of David's investment and business pursuits. But as you can imagine— You've met David, have you?"

Warwick smiled. "Yes."

"Right. Then as you can imagine, David keeps a careful eye on all of his holdings." Although," he allowed himself a satisfied nod, "he does trust my judgment."

"Well, then. Let's get started. Could you briefly describe Mr. MacLeod's holdings, generally speaking?"

"Of course." Nelson leaned back and set his hands on his chest, fingertip to fingertip, as he gazed toward the ceiling. "David is clearly a very high worth individual. There is a sizeable sum which he insists be kept aside as instantly liquid. It is earning negligible interest but is available at his whim. The remainder of his assets is invested quite broadly in a variety of British, European and international vehicles. However, from a traditional standpoint, the primary industries would be oil, communications and agriculture."

"Agriculture?" This surprised Warwick somehow.

"Oh yes." Nelson was unphased. "Dairy farming primarily. And some agricultural research. Genetically enhanced foods and the like. There can be a rather high profit potential in certain areas of agriculture."

"All right."

"Although, to be clear, David doesn't hold a majority stake in any agricultural enterprises." Nelson spun slightly in his chair to get a better look out his window. "Similarly, David holds a significant, but minority, interest in several British media outlets."

"Such as?"

"Yes, well. I'd rather not list them specifically, unless it's absolutely vital. Given his status as Chieftain, he's rather expected to shy away from the media. But again, the profits can be sizeable, and he shows an interest in it."

"So those are all minority interests?" Warwick confirmed.

"Yes. Well, actually, no." Nelson corrected himself with a finger in the air and a turn back toward his guest. "We did just purchase a majority interest in a Gaelic language news site on the internet. I believe it's called 'an-diugh.co.uk.'"

"Anjou?" Warwick asked. "Isn't that French?"

"No, no: *An-Diugh*," Nelson corrected, but he essentially repeated the sounds the police officer had made. "It Scottish Gaelic for 'today.' We actually just purchased the site the other week and—" He frowned. "Well, actually, this may not be the best example after all. David has asked me to do a complete study as to the site's profitability. I'm not sure how that will turn out. It can be hard to get advertising on a site which can only be read by some seventy-thousand people, most of whom don't have any sort of high-speed internet access—if any at all, actually. So we'll see."

"And if it's not profitable?" Warwick asked.

"Then I imagine David will liquidate it."

Warwick thought for a moment then asked, "Are there any other Gaelic news sources on the internet?"

"Most likely," was the reply. "But *An-Diugh* was the—er, I mean, is the primary one." He smiled again.

"And from whom did Mr. MacLeod purchase *An-Diugh*?"

Nelson frowned in thought. "I really can't say just off the top of my head. Does it really matter? I'd have to have Laura look it up."

Warwick smiled politely. "Then please do."

Nelson paused, making no movement toward the intercom. Finally he sighed, then offered, "Marsaili NicRath. She was paid quite well for it, I can assure you."

Warwick thought for a moment herself, then tried, "An I.P.O.?"

Nelson's left eyebrow raised and he couldn't suppress an admiring smile. "Yes, actually. We succeeded in purchasing over seventy percent of the stock."

Warwick nodded, expressionless.

"But as I said," Nelson continued, "at quite a large profit for Ms. NicRath. David paid twice the initial offering price."

"Which drove away," Warwick surmised, "most of the competition."

"Yes."

"Except Ms. NicRath."

"Yes."

"Who bought the other thirty percent."

"Twenty-six actually." Nelson's smile seemed significantly less warm. "With a few shares spread around among some others."

Warwick considered all of this silently, then asked, quite earnestly, "Do you think you'll survive Ms. NicRath's minority shareholder legal challenge to the liquidation of her former company?"

The smile turned downright cold. "Hence the profitability study."

Warwick nodded slightly to herself. "All right then. What about oil?" *Time to push the interview along.*

"Ah yes. David's interests in the oil industry are quite broad."

"Does he control a majority share in any of the oil companies?"

"If he did," another engaging smile, "I wouldn't be in a position to say so. Not outright, anyway." A wink.

"Of course not," Warwick replied quickly. "Thank you. And is there anyone in the oil industry who dislikes Mr. MacLeod?"

Nelson pursed his lips and looked up at the ceiling again. "No, I really don't think so. David is very well liked among his colleagues in the industry."

"What about nationalization?"

A puzzled expression blossomed on Nelson's face. "Well, London already receives a healthy percentage of all oil profits..." he started.

"No, not London," Warwick clarified. "Edinburgh."

"Oh, you mean Scottish nationalization." Nelson nodded. "Yes. Right. David would be opposed to that. But it's not a real possibility in my opinion."

Warwick recalled her conversation of earlier that afternoon. "Mr. MacLeod seems to think it is."

"I know." Somehow the warmth returned to the curling lips. "But David's a bit of a worrier. I simply don't believe there is any way London is going to allow those revenues to be diverted from the Royal treasury."

"Unless Scotland becomes independent."

Nelson guffawed. "Even then, I'd suspect. And I should assert that an independent Scotland is a proposition of only the smallest possibility. I hardly think London will allow that to happen either."

"That presumes," Warwick observed, "that London's opinion will be relevant—let alone solicited."

Nelson considered this in silence until there came a sharp knock at the door. Warwick confirmed with a quick glance at her watch that it was exactly five o'clock.

"Mrs. Nelson," her subject observed unnecessarily, before calling out, "Come in."

Then Warwick turned to glimpse what she had to admit was one of the most beautiful women she had ever seen in her life.

Mrs. Nelson was tall, probably equal to her husband's six feet, even without the heels, and boasted long red hair which cascaded around her face and shoulders in waves of tightly wound ringlets. Large green eyes shone from a face of the purest porcelain complexion. Her body appeared to be of perfect proportions, the classical rounded curves at her bosom and hips combining seamlessly with the modern muscular tautness apparent at her stomach and legs. Her beige suit was of the highest quality and the skirt was actually a little longer than she could have gotten away with. Gold jewelry flashed from her ears, throat, wrists, fingers and her left ankle.

"Sergeant Warwick," Nelson waved toward the red-maned goddess as he stepped around his desk, "my wife, Caroline."

"Good day, Sergeant," Caroline chimed with perfect diction, her soft Scottish accent shining gently off each vowel. A smile lit the already incandescent face. "I've come for my husband."

"Of course." Warwick stood up and stepped over to the door. "We'd just finished anyway. I won't detain him any longer."

Caroline's eyes narrowed at the word 'detain.' "Barry," she purred, "you haven't you got yourself into trouble?"

Barry Nelson laughed but it was Warwick who replied. "No, Mrs. Nelson. I'm here regarding the kidnapping of David MacLeod's son. Just trying to get some background information to tease out who might have done this."

"Not the MacLeod Banshee, I suppose?" Caroline inquired. "Like all the papers are saying?"

"I expect not," Warwick replied humorlessly.

"Well, I apologize for the interruption, then." Caroline smiled. "But I must insist. Barry and I don't always get the opportunity to dine together and I'm afraid I can be quite possessive."

"Long hours, Mr. Nelson?" Warwick inquired of the businessman who was fetching his suit coat from its hanger.

"Sometimes," he replied as he slipped the coat on. "Although more often it's hers."

"Oh?" Warwick turned back to the scarlet beauty.

"I'm a physician," Caroline explained. Warwick found this surprising, and then was disappointed in herself for so finding. "Emergency at Aberdeen General Hospital," Caroline continued. "My hours are often less than standard."

"I can imagine," Warwick replied. "Which reminds me: I have one more question for you, Mr. Nelson."

Nelson almost succeeded in suppressing the concern from his face. "Oh? Well, then, by all means ask away."

"Yes, well," Warwick hesitated. A practiced hesitation. "It's difficult to ask the question without seeming accusatory, but I do need to ask it of everyone I speak with regarding the case. You understand?"

"I believe so," Nelson glanced sidelong at his wife. She was taller than him in the heels.

"Fine. Well, then. It appears that young Douglas was abducted sometime between eleven o'clock Sunday evening and eight the next morning. So if you could just tell me where you were during those hours."

"Home alone, of course." Caroline's voice startled both her husband and Warwick. "Where he should have been. I was working myself. A late swing shift turned into a graveyard shift. I arrived home around seven-thirty to find Barry sound asleep in the bedroom."

Nelson looked from his wife to the sergeant, his eyebrows

lowering again on the trip over. "So says she," he grinned.

Warwick smiled too, in departure. "Well, thank you then, Mr. Nelson. And nice to meet you, Mrs. Nelson. I'll let myself out."

12. Hypothesis

"Hello, miss. How may I hel—"

"The exhibition," Maggie interrupted. "The illuminated-manuscripts-ninth-century-Old Gaelic-Old Irish-whatever-exhibition. Do you have copies of the manuscripts?"

The middle-aged saleslady at the Trinity College souvenir store paused long enough for Maggie's rapid fire words to sink in. Finally, she managed to ask, "Copies?"

"Yes." Maggie had suddenly become very impatient. She needed to read that next page—and what lay beyond. But the library hadn't had any plain-text versions of the books. 'Try the gift shop,' the librarian had said. 'They might have reproductions for sale.' "Reproductions," Maggie explained. "Of the pages. Do you have any?"

"Well, now," the woman stepped out from behind the counter as she slowly surveyed the small shop tucked into the lobby of the Old Library, "let me see. We usually do have. Let's give a look, shall we?"

Maggie followed the plump woman around the narrowly aisled shop for what seemed an eternity. Finally the woman announced, rather proudly, "We have coloring books."

Maggie hadn't expected that. "Coloring books?"

"Yes." The saleslady pulled one from a swiveling metal rack. "They've beautiful illustrations. The children love to color in the knot work."

I'll give you knot work, Maggie thought as she tried to control her irritation at this particular turn of events. "Anything else?" she demanded through her teeth.

"Well, there's the booklet about the exhibition." The woman removed a thin, glossy book from the same wire rack. "It has some photographs of particular pages, I suppose."

"Great." Maggie snatched both books from the woman's hands. "I'll take them. Here." She thrust far too large a banknote toward the saleslady. "Keep the change."

The woman accepted the note and before she could protest its size, Maggie was out the shop doorway and through the Old Library's doors to the sunny courtyard beyond.

The woman slowly returned to her post behind her counter.

"Hmph," she observed to herself. "Americans."

***

The crofter's shack was nestled into a rolling fold of the lush green carpet draped over the rocky crags of the seaside cliff. The cliff was one of many forming the edges of the Isle of Skye. The North Atlantic waves beat rhythmically against the granite shore, their crash joined by the occasional cry of a seabird and the intermittent creak of the old man's rocking chair. Milky, cataract-covered eyes stared out toward the enormous orange ball of the setting sun, while his remaining senses reveled in the sound, spray and scent of the sea.

"<Hello, Michael,>" he said in gravelly-voiced Gaelic, even as his uninvited, but never quite unexpected visitor approached his home.

Taggert stepped onto the cleft stone front patio. <Hello, Niall,>" he replied. There was no second chair, so he sat down on the stones at the old man's feet. "<How are you, my friend?>"

Niall smiled a weathered, tooth-poor smile. "<Well enough, Michael. Well enough.>" He rocked a bit more, then asked in all sincerity, "<And how are you yourself?>"

"<Quite fine as well,>" Taggert replied as he too stared toward the sun's descent behind the black waves.

The two men sat for some time then, content to let the waves and birds carry the conversation. Eventually, Old Niall asked, "<So what can I do for you, Michael? You've come a long way from home>."

"<I suppose so,>" Taggert reluctantly agreed. He picked up a pebble, considered tossing it toward the waves, but thought better of it and let it fall again to the ground. "<But you're right. I do have a favor to ask of you.>"

The old man continued his creaky rocking. "<I'll do what I can to help, of course. But I don't know what this blind, brittle-boned old man can do for you.>" He laughed at this last part, but not much.

"<I don't need your eyes, Niall. Or your bones. I need your mind. And your experience.>" He picked up the pebble again. "<I've come across a phrase,>" he explained. "<It's in Gaelic—I think—but I can't read it all. I think it must be dialect, but I couldn't find it in any of the etymologies you've written.>"

"<Well, I couldn't write it all down,>" Nial joked nostalgically, and a bit regretfully. He tapped his temple. "<Some of it's still up here.>"

"<Aye, Niall. I know. That's why I've come.>"

Niall was glad for it. "<What's your phrase then, young Michael?>"

So Taggert gave him the phrase. And the old man told him what he could.

***

Maggie tipped back in her wooden chair, her pub dinner long finished, the plates laying discarded across her small table. Her afternoon of pouring over small photographs and black-outlined coloring book pages had proved to be only minimally useful. The 'Spellbook of Ballincoomer' had garnered less space in the booklets than its compatriots in the 1937 Reading Room. But what few images there were confirmed its title: It was a shopping list of various spells, incantations, and rites. And none of them seemed to call on the 'evil forces' mentioned so frequently in her own Dark Book of spells. Indeed, these new spells were of an undeniably positive nature—perhaps the reason a literate Christian monk might feel at liberty to record their words. Words which called on natural forces like the sun and the water to use their gifts for the benefit, not of the spellcaster, but of whomever or whatever the spellcaster's subject was. The few complete spells she could make out claimed to reveal, enlighten, strengthen and protect. But she couldn't find any that healed.

Apparently the page she'd seen that morning in the Reading Room had not been pretty enough to warrant a space in either the coloring book or the exhibition's promotional pamphlet. In the event, Maggie could find no reference in the reproduced Gaelic she'd purchased of any 'ben-slániger'—or of any healing spells such a woman might have used.

Still. Magic spells.

Spells that called on good forces for altruistic results. Not evil forces for self-serving results.

Spells that sought to amplify the natural order and harmony of the universe. Not to twist and violate that order to its own ends.

In short, Good Magic. Not Dark Magic.

And even though the spell she'd really wanted to see wasn't in that stupid coloring book, she'd still seen the word 'healer' that morning. She had no doubt. The Spellbook of Ballincoomer hid within its covers a healing spell.

She needed them simply to turn one more page. And luckily, the exhibition had one day left.

The descendant of Brìghde Innes looked at her watch and calculated how long it had taken her last time. Then she raised her hand just slightly, waving politely in the direction of a nearby waitress.

"Check, please!"

13. Experimentation

Maggie closed the door to her hotel room, locking it. She flipped the deadbolt. Then she latched the chain.

She surveyed the small room. There was just the one window. The curtains were open, letting the summer sun stream in even after eight o'clock at night. She considered leaving the curtains open—sunlight seemed appropriate somehow—but she knew better and crossed to the window to pull tight both the thin white external curtains and the heavy internal green ones. She surveyed the room. Unless the mirror over the desk was two-way, she was alone.

She set the booklets on the desk. She still couldn't believe she'd bought a coloring book. But in fact it had proved the more helpful of the two books she'd purchased. One of the pages from the Spellbook of Ballincoomer which had been worthy of transmogrification into black outlines on rough coloring book paper had actually contained a complete spell. A spell Maggie had been absolutely elated to see.

It was a levitation spell.

A levitation spell had been the first spell she'd mastered from the Dark Book. And now here she was with the same type of incantation only from a different source. Time to get busy.

She propped the coloring book open to the proper page, Old Gaelic letters large and outlined on the colorless paper. She set a small pen from the desk drawer directly in front of the book, centered on the desktop before her.

Then, closing her eyes, she spoke the spell. Not the newly-encountered words from the coloring book, but rather the well-learned levitation spell she'd mastered from the Dark Book. Just to be sure.

"<Tear asunder the bonds which chain this object to the Earth. Deny Nature its order and raise this thing to the hated sky.>"

The pen rose quickly into the air, to exactly the level Maggie intended.

Simple enough, she thought almost smugly.

But in truth, it wasn't as simple at it used to be. She'd avoided the dark magic lately. Not just because of the nightmares which inevitably followed its use—she'd gotten used to those—but also out of a general unease surrounding the magic. Since learning the true origins of the dark magic, she'd become increasingly reluctant to use it just for fun. It seemed... inappropriate somehow. And just a little dangerous. She let the pen descend back onto the desktop.

Okay, she thought to herself, *let's unleash a little light magic.*

She considered the colorless outline of the spell opened before her. She noted how very different the carefully illustrated letters were from the scrawled, black-ink words which filled her Dark Book. She was looking forward to accessing the light magic. She wondered whether she'd have good dreams that night.

She noted that the phrasing of this new spell was quite different from its dark counterpart. This new spell translated as: 'Amplify the natural separation of these objects. Tap into the order of the world and raise this object onto a bed of air.'

She wondered whether the pen would rise as quickly and as securely.

Then, just before she spoke this new levitation spell, she wondered why the light magic had ever been lost if this Spellbook of Ballincoomer—unlike her lost Dark Book of Rites and Damnation—had been available and understandable since the Ninth Century. She shrugged and let the question fall away, for now.

"<Amplify the natural separation of these objects. Tap into the order of the world and raise this object onto a bed of air.>"

Nothing. The pen didn't budge.

Maggie was genuinely surprised. And disappointed. Had she spoken it wrong? She reviewed the spell.

"<Amplify the natural separation of these objects. Tap into the order of the world and raise this object onto a bed of air.>"

Nothing.

Wow. This was unexpected. Maggie thought for a second, then raised her hand, "<Tear asunder the bonds which chain this object to the Earth. Deny Nature its order and raise this thing to the hated sky.>"

The pen shot up into the air. She frowned, and lowered the pen.

Okay, then. She steeled herself. She reread the coloring-book spell. Then she spoke it as forcefully as she knew how. "<Amplify the natural separation of these objects. Tap into the order of the world and raise this object onto a bed of air.>"

And nothing again.

Maggie stared at the pen for a long, long time.

"Damn."

She walked over to the bed behind her and plopped down. She laid on the bed, her legs still hanging over the edge, and thought. And thought. And thought.

Why isn't this working?

This should work.

She considered the differences between the two spells. Different sources. Different phraseology. Different words.

Different words, eh?

She leaned up and walked over to the desk. She picked up the coloring-book, studying the words carefully. Definitely standard Old Gaelic. Maybe the problem was in the language. Maybe she needed to use the Hamilton-Devereaux dialect. Maybe the spells had originally been in that dialect, but the monks had translated them into the more standard form. She'd been able to translate the Dark Book after identifying repeating mutations from the Old Gaelic. But there was no reason that couldn't work in reverse: translate the standard into the dark dialect by following the mutations backwards.

She pulled a small scratch pad with the hotel logo from the desk drawer and plopped back down on the bed, coloring-book accompanying her. After almost fifteen minutes of diligent work, she was satisfied with her attempt to translate the spell into her dialect. Tearing off the first page of the pad, she rewrote a clean version of the light magic spell. Then she stood up and returned to the guinea-pen. Looking down she spoke the new version of the spell, same meaning but different words:

"<Amplify the natural separation of these objects. Tap into

the order of the world and raise this object onto a bed of air.>"

Still nothing.

The light magic didn't work.
Maggie sat back onto the bed and hung her head.
But why not?

14. Alison Chisholm

"Mornin', Sergeant," said Officer MacNeily.

"Sergeant." Officer Preston.

"Morning, Warwick." Sgt. Thompson.

Warwick greeted her colleagues as she walked into the Aberdeen police station on Queen Street. Yesterday had been a good day of police work—followed by an average night's sleep—and she was eager to push forward with the investigation. Possibilities were already beginning to coalesce in her mind. Best to get some additional information before a bad hunch solidified into a poor course of action.

Her office was as orderly as she'd left it, the 'MacLeod Kidnapping' file still centered on her desk directly in front of her chair. She sat down, opened the file and set to her work

"Elizabeth."

Warwick looked up sharply to see Inspector Cameron's large figure in her door frame. Someone was standing behind him.

"Inspector." Warwick craned her neck slightly to catch a glimpse of the other visitor. Cameron entered the room fully, finally leaving enough space for the other person to step into the room herself.

"Elizabeth, I'd like you to meet Alison Chisholm." Cameron

waved an open palm toward the woman who had walked in behind him. She was just a inch or two shorter than Warwick's 5'9", with a similarly thin build, long wavy raven-colored tresses and eyes a brilliant green.

"Pleased to meet you, Sergeant," Alison Chisholm said as she extended a hand in greeting.

Warwick stepped around her desk and took the hand. "Likewise, er," she hesitated at her guest's title.

"Oh, right," Cameron interjected. "Sergeant. Detective Sergeant Alison Chisholm. From Glasgow. Glasgow Police."

"Good to meet you, Sergeant Chisholm," Warwick answered, wondering whether her work had been interrupted just to introduce a visiting police officer, "And what brings you to Aberdeen?"

"Ah, well, that's just it," Cameron started, a hint of pride ringing in his voice, "we're participating in a sort of exchange program. Sergeant Chisholm will be assigned to our department through August."

Chisholm smiled self consciously. No doubt she was looking forward to all the initial introductions being over.

"Exchange program?" Warwick asked, a bit taken aback. "Like at school?"

"No, not exactly," Cameron frowned at this simple comparison. "It's a new program to improve law enforcement here in Scotland. Get to know one another's methods and such. We send an officer there; they send one here."

"It does sound a bit silly," Chisholm conceded, "but they say it's already had some very positive results."

"Hmm. An exchange, eh?" Warwick raised a hand to her chin in contemplation. "And so we sent — ?"

Cameron cleared his throat. "Sergeant Willis," he explained. Then looking at Chisholm, expounded, "Very nice fellow, that Willis."

Just incompetent, Warwick thought with a smile. *And irritating in large doses. Well done, Inspector.*

"Well, nice to meet you, Sgt. Chisholm." Warwick took a step back toward her desk—and her case. "I'm sure we'll run into each other again."

Cameron cleared his throat again. "Ah, yes. Well, that's just it, Elizabeth."

Damn. She should have known something was up when he'd first called her 'Elizabeth.' He was usually better with formality.

"Sgt. Chisholm will be assisting you on the MacLeod case."

"Now wait a minute." Warwick raised her hands in immediate protest. "That's my case."

"Exactly." This one word response silenced Warwick for a moment as she considered it.

Cameron turned to his guest and gestured to his subordinate. "Elizabeth—Detective Sergeant Warwick, that is—is our best officer," he explained. "Indeed," he glanced quickly toward his favorite sergeant, "no doubt she'll have my job someday." A smile tried to push onto Warwick's lips but she stopped it. "And if you're going to learn our methods," Cameron continued, "I want you to learn from the best. Sgt. Warwick is our best."

"Thank you, Inspector, but—" Warwick started to protest, but then stopped herself. Cameron had obviously made up his mind. Might as well just make the best of it.

"I don't bite," Chisholm offered. She flashed a smile. "Truly. Well, only if I get really angry, but even then I usually don't break the skin."

The smile finally made it out onto Warwick's lips.

"It's settled then," Cameron patted Chisholm lightly on the back. "Show her everything, Elizabeth. And listen too. I'd wager we might learn a thing or two from our colleagues to the south."

With that, Cameron swirled out of the room and left the two women to get better acquainted.

After a moment of awkward silence, Chisholm spoke up. "I'm no Willis," she assured with a sly grin.

Warwick was so shocked by the comment that she couldn't help but laugh. She was able to stifle it again after a moment. "How—?"

"Oh, I've spoken with my colleagues back in Glasgow," Chisholm explained. "He's already made quite the impression. But I assure you, I was selected because I'm good. Not because my supervisor couldn't think of any other way to get me out of his hair."

Warwick smiled. "I think I'm going to like you, Alison Chisholm." She walked over and picked up the file. "C'mon."

"Where are we going?" Chisholm asked as she followed Warwick out into the hall.

Warwick smiled at her new partner. "We're looking into child care," she explained. "Come along."

15. The Nanny

Knock! Knock! Knock!

A few moments passed. Then a few more. Then just a few too many more before the doorknob finally turned and the door to the flat opened a crack.

"Hello?" said the large green eye on the other side of the door.

"Hello," replied Sgt. Warwick. "Are you Nellie MacQuarrie?"

The eye narrowed. The door didn't open any further. "Yes?"

"I'm Sergeant Elizabeth Warwick. Of the Aberdeen Police." She displayed her badge and ID to the door crack. "And this is Sergeant Alison Chisholm. May we come in? We need to speak with you."

The eye hesitated, then started to well up. The door swung aside and the beautiful young woman inside hung her head. "I know."

***

"It's all my fault," sobbed Nellie MacQuarrie. Her curly brown hair hung delicately to her shoulders, and her thin frame was squeezed into a red blouse and dark blue jeans. Black sandals wrapped around bare feet with toenails painted a surprisingly interesting shade of mauve. Warwick guessed she was 20. Maybe 19. "I should've been with little Douglas."

"Well, now," Warwick began. "It's hardly all your fault."

Nellie looked up, her eyes and lips swollen and pink.

"I should think," Warwick explained, "that Mr. MacLeod shares some of the blame."

Nellie smiled weakly. "I don't know..." she started. "I was supposed to stay with him. All the time, really."

"That's why your bed was in the nursery."

Nellie looked first to Warwick, then to Chisholm, unsure what to say.

"From what I understand," Chisholm interjected in as friendly a tone as she could, "Mr. MacLeod was well aware that you were not with Douglas that night."

Nellie's brow creased even as her green eyes widened.

"How long?" Warwick asked matter-of-factly.

"I— I beg your pardon?" Nellie wiped her nose on her arm.

"How long," Warwick repeated, "had you been sleeping with Mr. MacLeod?"

Nellie's brow furrowed and she looked from Warwick to Chisholm to Warwick again, her eyes mixing fear with uncertainty with shame. She hung her head again. "Not long. A few weeks, maybe."

Warwick and Chisholm glanced at each other and exchanged infinitesimal nods.

"Is that why he hired you as his nanny?" Chisholm followed up.

"No," Nellie was quick to assert. "No, not at all. Well, that is— Well, maybe, I suppose." She sighed and looked down at her tight, young body. "I guess it depends what you mean. But I was hired as the nanny first, then... Well, then the other things started later."

"All right," Warwick announced. Time to move on. She looked around the flat. "And are you from Aberdeen then?"

"No." Nellie wiped her eyes, and smiled. She seemed glad to move on to another subject. "I'm from the Isle of Skye. A small town called Struan on the western coast. It's not very far," she explained, "from Dunvegan. David—Mr. MacLeod—hired me back there. I wanted to get away from Skye. He wanted someone who was willing to travel and take care of Douglas." She paused and looked self-consciously at her body again. "And more, I suppose."

"So you traveled, got away from home," Warwick digested the information, "and then the affair started."

"Aye," Nellie sighed. "But it wasn't really an 'affair.' I mean, they're divorced."

Warwick frowned. "Actually," she corrected, "they're separated. The divorce isn't final yet."

Nellie's face screwed up at this news; her eyes began to tear over again. "Oh." She looked at the police officers again, her eyes searching for better news, but finding none. "But he said—"

"I'm sure he did," Chisholm interrupted. "Have you ever met Mrs. MacLeod?"

"No," Nellie assured. "But I understand she's a simply horrible woman."

"And yet," Chisholm observed, "they've a child in common."

Nellie paused, then cast her eyes down sadly. "Yes."

"Is that a possibility for you?" Warwick asked indelicately.

Another pause. "No. Not really. David's very careful about that."

Warwick nodded. "I'm sure." Then she pressed on. "Nellie, do you have any idea who would have wanted to do this? Any idea at all?"

Nellie frowned in thought, then turned away. She squirmed uncomfortably in her seat.

"Nellie?" Warwick prodded.

"No," Nellie shook her head as she looked away. "It's silly."

"Of course it's not," Warwick soothed. "What is it?"

The nanny glanced back to the officers, a crooked smile hanging self-consciously from her lips. "It really is silly," she assured.

"Fine," Warwick shrugged. "Maybe it is silly. But tell us anyway. It might help."

Nellie's face evinced her doubt about this last prospect.

"You never know," Warwick encouraged. "Let us decide. We'll take it with a grain of salt."

Nellie shifted again in her seat, her lips squished into a conflicted button. Then her eyes gleamed in decision and leaned forward, as if ready to tell the latest and juiciest gossip about the preacher's wife. "You'll have heard of the Fairy Flag?" she asked with wide eyes.

Warwick succeeded in not rolling her own. This was a road she did not want to go down.

But Chisholm didn't seem to mind. "'The Fairy Flag?'" she asked.

"Aye," Nellie lowered her voice and cast a careful glance over her shoulder. "No one knows this, but the Flag went missing almost two weeks ago."

Even Warwick couldn't keep her eyebrows from shooting up at this. It was hardly world stopping news, but the MacLeod's Fairy Flag did hold a certain notoriety in Scottish culture. She was surprised she hadn't heard of its disappearance. Alleged disappearance, she reminded herself.

"David—Mr. MacLeod, he'll deny it," Nellie cautioned. "But

it's true just the same. And now the MacLeod heir has gone missing." She lowered her voice. "I'm no saying the banshee came back and stole wee Douglas thinking him her son... but, well, I'm no not saying it either."

Warwick suddenly found herself quite tired of Nellie MacQuarrie. She turned to Chisholm. "Anything else, Sergeant?"

Chisholm thought for a moment, then replied, "No. Not now, anyway."

"Right then." Warwick stood up. "We'll be in touch. Thank you for your time, Ms. MacQuarrie."

Nellie stood up as well and sniffled deeply, the tears beginning to dry. "You're welcome. Thank you."

The three walked back to the door and Nellie opened it for her guests. "Good bye then."

"Good bye for now, Nellie," Warwick replied with a nod.

"Good bye." Chisholm joined in.

Then, just as Nellie MacQuarrie of Struan, Isle of Skye, had almost closed the door, Warwick put her hand out and stopped it. She looked Nellie right in her big green eyes. "*A bheil Gàidhlig agad, a Nellie?*" she asked.

"H— How's that?"

Warwick shook her head. "Nothing. Never mind." She smiled softly. "Thanks again, Nellie." And the two police officers turned and walked deliberately down the hallway.

Nellie MacQuarrie closed the door after them and locked it. She stood there for a very long time, unsettled and unhappy.

She wondered whether they'd noticed.

***

"So what was that gambit you just pulled?"

Warwick glanced over at Chisholm as they drove down King's Street. "Which?"

"That 'uh-vayle-gah-lick-whatever you said.' What was that? Gaelic?"

"It was supposed to be," Warwick laughed. "I don't really speak it," she assured. "But I thought I'd try to pick some up. Might be necessary for the case."

"Really?" Chisholm frowned contemplatively. "I thought you said those words in blood weren't really Gaelic."

"What I said," Warwick corrected with a raised finger and a friendly smile, "is that the experts say it's not Gaelic."

"Hm," Chisholm observed. Then, "So what did you say to her?"

"I believe I asked her if she spoke Gaelic."

"But she didn't," Chisholm recalled.

"Ah," the finger and smile returned. "She said she didn't. Or rather she indicated it by appearing not to understand what I'd said."

Chisholm shook her head. "You're a very exact thinker, Elizabeth Warwick."

"Thank you." She accepted the observation as a compliment. After a moment's reflection she asked. "Do you know any Gaelic?"

"Not really, no," Chisholm answered. "They say ten percent of the Gaelic speakers left live in Glasgow; but that's only about seven thousand people, and there are over seven hundred fifty thousand in Glasgow. That's less than one percent who speak Gaelic. I've heard it, but I don't speak it."

Then Chisholm considered the gambit Warwick had tried. "So what should Nellie have said, if she speaks it, I mean?"

"*Tha*," Warwick replied, pronouncing it like the English 'ha.' "There's no word for 'yes' or 'no,'" she explained, "so one simply repeats the verb back. It's like saying 'I do.'"

"Hmm." Chisholm considered this.

"Well, then," Warwick interrupted her consideration as they pulled to a stop in front of police headquarters. "I think we can call it a day. You should head home. But I'd like to start bright and early tomorrow. Can you be at the precinct at eight?"

"Yes," was the professional, unambiguous response. "In fact I'll be there at ten 'til, how's that?"

"Fine. We can run over the case in full again before we move on. If you're going to be my partner on this case, then you should know everything I know."

Chisholm smiled. "That's the plan."

16. Bad Dream

Falling.

Falling.

Falling.

The ground rushed up at her with the speed of an oncoming train. And just as she was about to impact, she found herself standing in the same grassy field. The same rolling green hills disappeared into the same distant bushes. And the same red barn stood invitingly just past the same grassy ridge to her left—only now it was a school house. Five year old Maggie Devereaux looked at the school house and took a sure step, ready to break into full sprint toward the structure.

"Don't."

Maggie cringed, then looked over her shoulder. It was her mother. In the same yellow dress. With the same hat shading her face.

But this time Maggie didn't wait for anything more. Her face set in a determined scowl, she took off running toward the schoolhouse, just as fast as her small legs could carry her. She ran and ran and ran. The schoolhouse was getting closer, but not fast enough. She'd expected her mom to yell after her by now. But the only sound was the wind rushing past her ears as she sprinted toward the crimson sanctuary before her.

Why wasn't her mom yelling at her to stop?

Maggie looked over her shoulder even as she ran, trying to see what her mother was doing behind her. But rather than her eyes catching a glimpse of her mother, Maggie's clumsy young legs caught on each other and she fell stumbling to the ground. The hands she put out to break her fall did little to soften the crash, and she succeeded only in scraping her palms on the hard ground hidden beneath the tall grass. Holding back the tears, she leaned up onto her bloodied hands to look at the schoolhouse so temptingly close.

But her mother grabbed a hold of her neck and shoved her face roughly back to the ground. "Don't!"

Maggie jerked awake.

Damn, she thought as she panted against the images still echoing in her mind, *that was... unpleasant.*

She looked at the clock. 8:15.

After a moment she sighed and sat up in bed, the sheets cascading onto her lap.

Might as well get up, Devereaux, she told herself. *You're sure as hell not going back to sleep after that.*

17. Turning Over a New Leaf

Come on, come on. Maggie stood impatiently outside the 1937 Reading Room in the cool Irish morning. Open already.

Her watch said 9:02.

Finally, the tall, thin, balding man from the day before stepped up to the doors from inside and unlocked them.

"Good mor—" he started.

"Morning." Maggie shoved a bank note in his hand as she pushed past. She ran ahead just as fast as her legs would carry her.

"Hmph," said the man. "Americans."

Maggie burst through the doors to the exhibition and rushed to the last of the seven podiums. She expected the page to have been turned from the day before, from the page that ended mid-sentence with the word ben-slániger—'healer.' She expected to gaze down on the next page, the page which would reveal the complete thought which had been so rudely interrupted by the mere fact that there was no more space left on the page.

But she found herself quite thoroughly disappointed.

The Spellbook of Ballincoomer was still there, the glass cover still protecting it from the hands of visitors. But it was most definitely not open to the next page.

"Damn it!" Maggie's voice echoed through the room.

She skimmed the display before her, trying to recognize enough words to get a feel for where the book had been opened to. But it was a simple glance at the relative thicknesses of each side of the open volume that revealed that the work had been turned ahead by several dozen pages.

Maggie scratched her head. "But why?"

"Well, miss," the thin man replied from behind his information desk, "the volumes are only here for a short period of time. There simply aren't enough days to display every page. Not like the Book of Kells which is here at Trinity permanently. So for each visiting text, we select the pages we feel were most attractive, the most interesting, the most historically significant."

"The least helpful," Maggie retorted as she stood in the lobby, arms crossed and quite irritated by this turn of events.

"Yes, well." He was trying not to get upset; but he hardly felt like helping the American at this point. "I suppose it depends on what one finds helpful."

"I'm sorry." Maggie ran her hands through her thick auburn hair. "I'm just... disappointed. I'd— I'd expected to get to read the next page."

"Ah, well. As I said, I'm sorry about that." He wasn't actually, but it was the polite thing to say.

Maggie tapped her toe in thought. "You don't suppose," she ventured, glancing sidelong at him as a smile played across her lips, "that you could turn it to the page I'm interested in, could you?"

The man's face showed genuine shock.

"Just for a minute or two," she assured. "I won't touch it. I promise."

"No," he replied sharply. "Absolutely not." He appeared offended at the very idea. "I mean, Good Lord, what if we did that for everyone who made a similar request? Why, it would destroy the manuscripts."

Maggie thought for a moment, a skeptical frown draped across her visage. "And exactly how many requests have you had like mine?"

The man straightened up a bit before answering, quietly, "Well, none actually. But that's hardly the point."

"Look, it would just take a moment," Maggie pleaded. "And it's very important. Really."

The man sighed. "I'm sure it is, miss, but it's simply not possible." He frowned. "Even if I wanted to—which, in all honesty, I must say I don't—but even if I did, I don't have the authority. The manuscripts are on loan to the Celtic Department. I just work for the library. And I have strict instructions."

Maggie's eyes continued her pleading, but to no avail.

"I'm sorry, miss," the man concluded. "It is simply not possible." He saw Maggie's lips part in protest. "Please don't ask again."

Maggie nodded in defeat and looked down at the floor. Now what?

But nothing presented itself and she walked dejectedly from the Reading Room into the mocking sunshine.

"Hello there!" The woman's shout completely startled Maggie as she stepped out onto Parliament Square. She looked wildly to her left where sat, on the grass next to the cobblestones, the young woman with whom she'd shared the exhibition hall the day before. "Back again, eh?" the woman asked.

"Er, yes." Maggie was quite surprised to see the woman again, let alone to be speaking with her. "Back again."

"Looking at the Spellbook of Ballincoomer again, I'd wager?" The young woman stood up and brushed off her seat before hoisting her bag over her shoulder. She was tall, a few inches above Maggie's 5'4", with reddish-brown hair cut short and spiky and bright green eyes. She wore a loose-fitting black linen top over a lavender skirt and brown sandals. She stepped over to Maggie and offered a smile that would charm the birds from the sky. "Before the exhibition ends?"

"Um, right." Maggie shifted her weight uneasily. "It's really quite beautiful, that one. The, um, what did you call it? The 'Spellbook of Ballincoomer'? Yes, quite beautiful. And of course, I came to see all of them. Not just that one. The Ballincoomer one."

"Well good thing you did," the woman observed with a casual glance toward the structure which housed the texts in question. "After today, they'll all be packed up and shipped back to their respective homes."

"Hm," Maggie said noncommittally.

"Have you ever been to Ballincoomer?" the young woman asked.

"Er, no," Maggie replied. "In fact, this is my first time to Ireland."

"Ah, well then," the young woman opened her arms wide. "*Cead Míle Fáilte!* 'A hundred thousand welcomes.'"

Cead Míle Fáilte, Maggie repeated in her head. Almost identical to the Scottish Gaelic, *Ceud Mìle Fàilte*.

"Thanks," Maggie replied, unsure what to say next.

"Well, look." The woman took a step toward Maggie, just an inch too close. "My name's Kitty. Kitty McCusker. And it just so happens I'm from Ballincoomer, way over in County Galway. The Spellbook is kept at the cathedral there, ironically enough."

Maggie nodded at the information, trying to figure out where all this was headed. Kitty pulled out her planner from her bag.

"I'm actually a student here at Trinity," she continued as she started to write something on a blank page in the back of her planner, "but I'm heading home for the summer this weekend." She tore off the planner page and handed it to Maggie. "Here. That's my number and address in Ballincoomer. If you'd like to see the Spellbook, and more of the Emerald Isle, you're welcome to stay with me for a few days."

"Wow." Maggie looked down at the paper. The Irish really are friendly. "Thanks. Thanks a lot. I don't know, though—"

"Oh don't trouble yourself. And don't feel obligated. Like I said, if you decide you'd like to come visit Ballincoomer, then ring me up. I'll be happy to show you around. And the cathedral would let you look at any pages you wanted."

"Uh, great." She glanced over to the Old Library. "Okay, uh, well, I should probably be going. Lots to do and all that." She held up the paper she'd been given. "Thanks again. It was nice to have met you, Kitty."

"Likewise, Maggie. And maybe I'll see you in Ballincoomer next week."

"Er, yeah. Right. Maybe so. 'Bye."

Maggie turned and headed toward the Old Library.

And as she watched Maggie Devereaux walked away, Kitty McCusker's friendly smile melted completely away.

18. The Rival

"Hm. I don't know, Elizabeth." Chisholm fiddled absently with the passenger side door lock as the patrol car sped down Aberdeen's M-7 motorway. "I suppose I see your argument, but it seems a bit of a stretch."

Warwick kept her eyes on the road, but frowned. But at least Chisholm was being honest. "I guess I'm just saying it's motive."

"Well, it's motive to be angry," Chisholm agreed, "but kidnapping?"

"Why not?" Warwick tried not to be irritated by this Socratic attack. "MacLeod buys her internet start-up only to shut it down. I'd wager that an all Gaelic website had printed more than one editorial piece advocating Scottish independence—and most advocates of an independent Scotland agree that the North Sea oil revenues would be essential to any such endeavor."

"Agreed, but—"

"And then when MacLeod's son is found missing," Warwick went on, "there's that cryptic phrase in blood. It sure wasn't English."

"Well, do we know it was Gaelic? I thought you said it was gibberish."

Warwick frowned again. "The linguists at the college said it wasn't Gaelic," she admitted with another frown. "They said it looked like Gaelic, but was probably only meant to do. Still, it wasn't English. We know that much."

"Well, we can hardly go around arresting everyone who speaks another language, now can we?"

Warwick sighed deeply. "That's not what I meant." She turned the car off the motorway. "But I'm not passing up a chance to interview someone who lost their entire enterprise to MacLeod and speaks Gaelic on top of it. I'm not ignoring that path."

Chisholm crossed her arms and sighed lightly herself. She looked out the window. "So what path are we on anyway? Where are we headed exactly?"

Warwick pointed ahead to the blue sign on their left. "Right up there." They reached the sign just as Warwick turned into the driveway and read the words aloud. "Aberdeen Recreational Facility."

Chisholm glanced over at the driver, a raised eyebrow inquiring of their purpose there.

"We're going to watch some shinty," Warwick explained with a smile as she pulled the car into a parking stall.

The Recreational Facility was in fact a large park, with three soccer fields, a clubhouse building and access to the Dee river. On that particular afternoon, one of the soccer fields had been converted into a shinty field, and two dozen or so participants were presently chasing a ball up and down the grassy rectangle waving long wooden sticks over their heads. Similar to field hockey, shinty laid claim to being a sort of national sport for Gaels, with leagues across Scotland and Ireland. Warwick herself had never been interested in the sport however, perhaps in part due to the violence and injuries which resulted from handing wooden clubs to twenty-odd people and telling them to swing at a small wooden ball as hard as they can.

"NicRath's secretary said she'd be at the shinty match today," Warwick explained. "I didn't want to wait, so I thought we'd come out here directly."

"Great," Chisholm squinted at the players they were approaching, and the fifty-odd spectators who were scattered about the edges of the playing field. "She's a shinty fan, then? How entirely Gaelic."

Warwick smiled and raised her hand. "Exactly," she exhorted.

They'd arrived at the edge of the field, the players hacking at the ball safely away at the other end. A group of five spectators had made camp at this particular end and sat atop a picnic blanket together with a cooler of beer and bag of some sort of unhealthy snack.

"Excuse me," Warwick began, showing her badge as casually as the gesture allowed. "We're looking for Marsaili NicRath."

A tall black-haired woman stood up and dusted some of the unhealthy snack off her shorts. "You've found her," she announced.

"Ms. NicRath?" Warwick asked in confirmation.

The woman smiled. "Not me, love." She turned toward the playing field and pointed. Warwick looked out onto field just as a short but strong looking woman with a long blond ponytail came running toward their end of the field, stick low to the ground, and teeth bared in determination. She planted one leg and let fly with a full swing onto the wooden ball racing away from her. The ball flew off the ground with a thunderous 'crack' and over the head of the opposing goalie, sending approximately half of the spectators into hysterics. "Her."

A goal having been scored, it was time to set up again, and

Marsaili NicRath circled back slowly toward the center of the field.

"Ms. NicRath!" Warwick called out. "Ms. NicRath!"

NicRath slowed her trot and looked around, finally catching sight of the officer, her badge displayed. Chisholm was just standing next to her motionless.

"May we speak with you for a moment?" Warwick yelled.

A teammate of NicRath's had run up to congratulate her and joined NicRath's puzzled expression at this interruption to their match. "Go on ahead, Mike," NicRath told her teammate. "I'll catch up in a bit. Think you can handle 'em without me for a few?"

"I don't know, Marsaili." He slapped her hard on the back. "But we'll try. Hurry up though, aye?"

NicRath diverted her path and trotted up to the police officers. "May I help you?" she asked, wiping her forehead dry with her jersey sleeve. "Now's not exactly a convenient time."

"Sorry, Ms. NicRath," Warwick apologized. "This should only take a few minutes. We just wanted to ask you some questions about David MacLeod."

"Ah, David MacLeod," NicRath began. "The bastard who's going to shut down my Gaelic-language internet site." Before Warwick could confirm this, NicRath continued, "And the poor father who's son was recently kidnapped, only to have cryptic, apparently Gaelic words scrawled at the cribside. That David MacLeod?"

Warwick smiled. "That's him."

"Right then," NicRath undid her ponytail, then pulled the sun-streaked strands back again. "I haven't the time right now, officers, so I'll be direct. I didn't kidnap his son and I don't know who did. Perhaps it was the MacLeod Banshee like all the papers are saying."

She finished wrapping the rubber-band around her

refurbished ponytail, then continued, "And before you ask: no, I'm no happy the bastard's going to be shutting down *An-Diugh*, but according to my lawyer I can't stop him either. But I can't imagine how that would be grounds for kidnapping his son. Besides, if I had kidnapped the lad, I certainly wouldn't have written out Gaelic on the floor like some bloody calling card—if you'll pardon the pun. And if I had done, I certainly would have spelt it correctly. Perhaps," she jabbed a finger toward the detectives, "you should consider the possibility that whoever did this wants to make it look like a Gael is the culprit, but didn't want to take the time to actually learn Gaelic."

Chisholm had to nod at this. She looked at Warwick, but Warwick was just staring at NicRath.

"I'd be happy to give you my fingerprints," NicRath went on, "but I haven't an ink pad with me just now, being as I am occupied. However, if you'd like a DNA sample to match the bloody fake-Gaelic," she bent down and smeared some blood from a still oozing wound to her shin, "I can offer this."

Warwick looked down at NicRath's outstretched hand. "Thank you, Ms. NicRath. But no. Not now anyway." She forced a smile. "Thank you for your time. We'll be in touch."

With that NicRath let out a grunt and galloped back onto the playing field.

Warwick matched the grunt and stomped back toward the car. Chisholm knew enough to follow close behind.

19. Testing Results

Taggert lifted his eye from the microscope and noted his final observation on the grid. Twenty for twenty. Uncanny.

Seven donors at each allele, each time.

Beyond uncanny.

Now he just had to figure out what it meant.

20. *Baile nan Cuimri*

Ballincoomer Abbey was monstrous. Not that it wasn't beautiful—quite to the contrary. All arches and spires and flying buttresses, stretching hopefully toward the heavens, its stones shimmering gray-green in the filtered late morning sun. Still, it sat perched ominously on the hill overlooking the small village of Ballincoomer, like a silent dragon glowering down on its next meal.

Although, Maggie supposed with a shrug, the locals probably didn't see it that way.

The hill itself appeared to have originally been man-made, the rest of the surrounding terrain being relatively flat, and the slow rising grade up to the abbey being typical of the mounds built under the earliest forts and keeps to dot the Irish landscape. This suggested to Maggie that the abbey had likely been built upon the ruins of some ancient fortress which had once towered similarly over the beginnings of the town below. This deduction was bolstered by the maze-like collection of stone ruins leading off from the rear of the cathedral, skeletal remains of half or mostly demolished walls, some still clinging to remnants of long shattered windows, and all crisscrossing and intersecting across the top of the ancient mound like the bony back of a sea serpent just breaking the water. The dragon had a tail.

Maggie hiked up the lazy road which wound its way up from the small downtown below to the large abbey above. Her full backpack made the going slow and the hill pulled at the muscles on the back of her legs, but it felt good to stretch her limbs after a long morning of traveling. She had caught the first train from Dublin to Galway, and had made good time, arriving in the western seaport in just under three hours. Ireland, she had noted, is not a large country. But from Galway she'd had to take a bus—a 'motor coach' as they called it, perhaps in an effort to increase its appeal. In the event, the 'coach' had proved to be very nice, with large comfortable seats and sides made almost entirely of windows through which to view the ride still further west.

Her only concern had been the alarming fact that the winding, twisting, undulating road appeared to be approximately the same width as the average driveway—and only slightly narrower than the coach. Eventually, though, she was able to release her terrified certainty that the coach would, at any moment, plunge off the road and down some cliff, and she relaxed as the bus traveled deep into the heart of Connemara, the western most part of County Galway, and of the Emerald Isle.

Once safely to her destination, Maggie was sure not to call on Kitty McCusker. For one thing, Kitty had said she wasn't coming home until the weekend, and it was only Friday morning. For another, something about Kitty gave Maggie an ill-defined, but undeniably uneasy feeling. She didn't like how Kitty had used her name so comfortably; she didn't know why, but that had sent off alarm bells.

So instead Maggie had quickly found a room at one of Ballincoomer's three bed & breakfasts. Her room had been decorated primarily in Connemara's best known export: its unique and beautiful marble, highly prized in all corners of the world. And while the top quality marble would be far too expensive to use to build an abbey, still Maggie could see, as she approached the massive wooden front doors of Ballincoomer Abbey, that the green-gray bricks from which the cathedral had been constructed were of an unusual quality and sheen, lower grade near-marble, she supposed, each stone catching and reflecting the sun in a shiny, slippery pattern. The dragon even had scales.

Inside, however, the dragon gave way to the sumptuous splendor of a richly decorated Catholic church. The cathedral was enormous, stretching back at least two hundred feet. Stained glass filled the uppermost walls, while dark wooden pews lined the floor. In between, statues and paintings filled alcoves and pedestals from the entryway to the altar, resplendent in carved wood, purple silk, and golden artifacts.

Maggie glanced around for some indication of where the famous 'Spellbook of Ballincoomer' might be kept. The smothering Christianity of the main chapel made her suspect the Spellbook might be housed in some side chamber, or perhaps even downstairs—if there was a downstairs. Maggie began a slow circuit of the outer perimeter, a mall walker in slow motion, in search of a plaque or sign. There were exactly three other people in the abbey, a young couple and an older man with thick gray hair; they were all up near the altar and all appeared to be tourists, judging by both their awestruck appraisals of the abbey and the cameras slung about their necks.

Twelve minutes into her search, and two-fifths the way around the church, Maggie met with success—of a sort. She'd found a sign. A small metal sign, white with a thin black border and carefully painted letters, announced: 'The Spellbook of Ballincoomer - An Leabhar Druidh a' Bhaile Nan Cuimri'.

Beneath these bilingual letters was a rather fancy and very well drawn arrow pointing left toward the arched entryway to a small alcove. Unfortunately, it also pointed to the iron gate which securely blocked entry to the darkened side chamber. Squinting between the bars into the dim room, Maggie could see a large, apparently informative display, in front of which stood a large, glass-topped pedestal. But she couldn't read the display, and the pedestal was empty.

"Damn," she whispered in the church, then was embarrassed she had.

Plan B, she thought to herself. *I wonder what Plan B is.*

She made a quick path back toward the main entrance. She thought she'd noticed an office or store room or some such in the foyer of the cathedral, off to one side near a rack of paper brochures. When she arrived there she noted that the door to the side room was ajar, the light inside was on, and the handwritten sign on the door read simply, '*Please Keep Door Closed During Mass*,' again followed by a translation into Irish Gaelic. She pushed the door open and peered inside.

It was a gift shop. Small and tasteful, it might have also doubled as an information desk, but its main function was clear. Of the four small walls in the cramped room, three held displays of books and postcards while the fourth housed the counter and cash register. The woman behind the counter looked up from her paperback novel and greeted her visitor.

"Good Morning," she boomed in the otherwise silent building. She was probably around forty, well-fed but not really fat, with thick, frizzy black hair cut mid-length and hanging simply from her face, brushing the intricately flowered blouse which extended down below the countertop at which she sat. The woman's next words startled Maggie, despite her being in the far west of Ireland and despite the signs she'd encountered so far. "*Dia dhuit.*"

Maggie blinked at the unexpected phrase, her mind searching frantically for meaning in the syllables. 'Jee-uh dwitt,' her language recognition center muttered to itself as it thumbed through the available papers and files until finally, after several seconds—in which Maggie was sure she looked a complete idiot— the proper reference was found. 'Jee-uh dwitt.' '*Dia dhuit.*' Irish Gaelic for 'God be with you.' The standard greeting in Ireland's Gaelic-speaking areas and a turn of phrase sufficiently uncommon in Scottish Gaelic as to initially evade Maggie's comprehension.

"Er, *Dia dhuit*," Maggie repeated back tentatively. Her specialty was Scottish Gaelic, not Irish Gaelic. Still, the tongues were very similar. Gaelic had been brought to Scotland in the Eighth Century by Irish missionaries and it wasn't until the Eighteenth Century that the Scottish and Irish versions of Gaelic had diverged enough to be classified as separate languages. As a graduate student in Celtic, Maggie had been expected to gain at least some knowledge of Celtic languages other than her concentration. There were six Celtic languages, grouped into two large families: North and South. The Northern family—also known as the 'Gadelic' family—consisted of Scottish Gaelic, Irish Gaelic and the recently extinct Manx; while the Southern family—'Brittonic'—consisted of Welsh, Breton and the long dead Cornish. Maggie had taken a course on Welsh, and had aced several Irish Gaelic courses—mainly because, already fluent in Scottish Gaelic, all she really had to do was remember the differences between Ireland's *Gaeilge* and Scotland's *Gàidhlig*. But she'd never had the opportunity to speak Irish outside the classroom—so she decided to seize this one. She thought for a moment, then tried, "*Conas atá tú?*" Irish, she hoped, for 'How are you?'

The woman's mouth curled into a cautious smile and she narrowed her eyes a bit to scrutinize her guest. "*Tá mé go maith,*" she replied. "*Agus tú féin?*"

Maggie concentrated on the woman's lips so she could see the sounds she was hearing. After a moment, the meaning revealed itself: 'Fine thanks. And you?'

"*Tá mé go maith,*" Maggie parroted back the phrase for 'I'm fine.' She wasn't sure what to say next—let alone how.

"*An feidir liom cabhru leat?*" the woman asked.

Or at least Maggie assumed it was a question. She hadn't understood a thing.

Don't panic, Devereaux, she told herself. Just ask her to repeat the question. "<Pardon? What did you say?>"

The woman's appraising gaze narrowed still further, but her grin broadened. "*An feidir liom cabhru leat?*" she repeated.

This time Maggie thought she heard the word for 'help.' Then she figured out the question: 'May I help you?' *Oh, okay. Right. Er...*

"*Tha. Tha mi a' rannsachadh an Leabhar Druidh na Ballincoomer.*"

Oops, Maggie immediately thought. *That wasn't Irish.* The sentence had rolled a bit too easily off her tongue; she'd dropped into Scottish Gaelic. The shop woman was thoroughly puzzled.

"Er, uh... <Yes>," Maggie tried again, translating the Scottish into Irish. "<I'm looking for the Spellbook of Ballincoomer."

The woman didn't reply right away. She had set her book down on the counter and was rubbing her chin contemplatively. Finally she lowered her hand and asked a one word question which Maggie immediately understood—and was humiliated by.

"*Beurla?*" she asked. The Gaelic word—both Irish and Scottish—for 'English.'

Damn, Maggie thought, thoroughly disappointed in herself. "Er, yes. I— I'm sorry. It's just that, well, that is—"

"Oh!" the shop woman interrupted Maggie's sputtering. "Oh, I didn't realize. Are you Canadian, then?"

The accent again. "Uh, no," Maggie smiled and ran an awkward hand through her hair. "American."

"Right." The woman nodded quickly. "I thought so. I am sorry, love. Your Irish had a strange ring to it, so I couldn't quite understand you. Especially that last bit."

Maggie grimaced. "That's because it was Scottish Gaelic," she explained, slightly red-faced. "I accidentally slipped into it. Actually," she felt the need to say, "I'm fluent in Scottish Gaelic, more or less. But I'm afraid my Irish needs some work."

The woman's head began nodding again. "All right then. That explains it. I thought perhaps you were from the southern *Gaeltacht.* Their Irish down there can be quite different sometimes."

"Well, thanks, I guess," Maggie replied, then asked, "Are they really that different?" She was genuinely curious. She'd learned that the differences in Irish dialects were exacerbated by the that the Irish *Gaeltacht*—the areas where Irish Gaelic was the predominant language—consisted of actually three separate and distinct areas: north, west and south. Small isolated islands of Irish separated by swift channels of English.

"Well, they can be," the shop woman started, "although I was surprised we were having so much difficulty communicating. But an American speaking Scottish Gaelic—well, that explains it. So," she slapped the counter gently, "what can I do for you?"

"I was hoping to look at the Spellbook," Maggie explained. No point in beating around the bush. She pointed vaguely toward the door and the chapel beyond. "But it doesn't seem to be on display just now."

"Oh, I'm afraid it's not here at all right now," the woman explained to Maggie's surprise and dismay. "It's away at an exhibition." She laughed lightly, transforming her eyes into arching slits. "It seems always to be away at an exhibition."

Maggie's dismay lessened slightly. "Well, actually, I think the exhibition just finished. Dublin, right? Trinity College? I saw it there, but then the exhibition ended and they said they sent the Spellbook back here."

"Dublin, you say?" The shop woman looked up at the ceiling. "Now, see, Dr. McCusker said as it was Kilkenny..."

"Doctor," Maggie interrupted, "McCusker?"

"Yes. He's the Deacon here. In charge of historical artifacts and such. Like the Spellbook."

Maggie cocked her head slightly. "Deacon?" She'd heard the term of course, but wasn't sure of its exact meaning in its present Irish Catholic context.

"It's like a priest," the woman explained, "only they can get married. And have children."

"Children," Maggie echoed back, not exactly a question.

"Yes. In fact, now that you mention it, Dr. McCusker's daughter, Kathleen, is a student at Trinity."

"Kathleen McCusker," Maggie tried the name. Then, at exactly the same time, they both said, "Kitty."

"Why, yes," the woman burst out. "She does go by 'Kitty.' Rather a common nickname for Kathleen. 'Kathy' is more the norm in the States, isn't it?"

"Er, yes," Maggie managed to reply, even as her brain replayed what she could recall of her two brief conversations with Kitty McCusker. She was fairly certain Kitty hadn't mentioned being the daughter of the man who kept the Spellbook. "So anyway," she decided to find out more, "you say the Spellbook is in

Kilkenny?"

"Yes. It was in Dublin, as you said, and was due back yesterday afternoon. But then Dr. McCusker diverted it to Kilkenny. Or was it Killarney? Kildare? No, it wasn't Kildare. Hmm..."

Great, Maggie thought dimly.

"Well, anyway," the woman continued, "Dr. McCusker said there was another exhibition the Spellbook needed to go to. I've no idea which. Usually I know these sorts of things—I'm the church secretary, you see, but I'd never heard of any exhibition in Kilkenny. Or Killarney. Whichever. Usually Dr. McCusker goes on and on about any loan of any artifact—very proud of the Abbey's collections, he is—but he was very short about this, now that I think about it. He just came in this morning, poked his head in the door, and said as the Spellbook had been sent to Kilkenny, should anyone ask."

Maggie frowned at this news. "Did he say how long it would be gone?" She supposed she could stay a few days in the little town, if need be. She didn't really want to, but she could.

"You know, he did say something about how long it would be gone. I remember because it seemed quite strange. He said, 'If anyone asks after the Spellbook, just tell them it's been sent to Kilkenny—indefinitely.' He said it just like that. 'Tell them it's been sent to Kilkenny,'" she paused dramatically, "'Indefinitely.'"

Maggie crossed her arms and tapped a finger lightly against her lips. "Is Dr. McCusker around today?" She was pretty sure she knew the answer.

"No," the woman replied as expected. "He's gone to Kilkenny as well, I'm afraid. To meet the Spellbook. That's how I know, you see. Not that he wouldn't have told me, but he made sure to let me know where he was going and such." She sighed and glanced affectionately at her surroundings. "Dr. McCusker does love this old Abbey. It's been his passion ever since he first arrived here, his and his wife's, God rest her soul."

"She died?" Maggie asked without thinking.

"Yes. A few years ago now. Car accident. Absolute tragedy. One of those fool tour busses came speeding around a curve and crossed the center line. Doctors said she died instantly. Poor Dr. McCusker. And poor Kitty. But I dare say she'd doing all right now. She loves this old Abbey too. And ever since her mother passed away, she's been hell bent on taking on her mother's role here."

Maggie just nodded, unsure how to reply. She felt bad for Kitty. Still, the whole thing was a bit strange.

"So anyway, you say the Spellbook won't be back for, well, for a few days anyway?"

"That seems safe to day," the shop woman agreed.

Maggie looked around the shop. Plan C. "You seem to have a lot of books for sale here. Are any of them about the Spellbook?"

"Well, yes, of course." The woman slid off her stool and stepped around the counter. "We've several books about the Spellbook. Picture books with photos of the pages, historical works, even a coloring book."

Maggie had to roll her eyes at that last one.

"So just what— Er. That is..." The woman stopped her walk along the shelves, leaving one outstretched hand resting on an empty space on the shelf. Her eyes scanned the remainder of the shelves beneath knitted brows. "Hmph," she said finally. "Well, I'll be."

"What is it?"

"Well, they're gone, aren't they?" The woman was dumbfounded. "Every last book we have about our Spellbook. We must have sold out."

Maggie doubted it.

The woman offered to check the back room, and Maggie accepted, although she was certain of the result.

"No, I'm sorry, miss," the shop woman apologized as she reemerged through a door behind the counter. "We've none in the back either. I am sorry."

"Don't be," Maggie managed to say. She'd had time to steel herself for the disappointment. "So there's no other information about the Spellbook? It is why I came to Ballincoomer after all."

"Yes, yes. Of course." The woman began wringing her hands. "Of course it is. But I'm afraid there's nothing available just now."

Maggie's brow creased, but then an idea came to her. "Is there a bookstore in town? One that might carry books about the Spellbook?"

"I'm afraid not," was the unhappy reply. "There's only the one bookshop in town, and Dr. McCusker owns it. But he keeps all the books about the Spellbook up here at the Abbey. Says as how it gives the tourists a reason to climb the hill."

"Lovely," Maggie said coldly, her irritation finally starting to show through her amicable facade.

"Hm. Well yes." The shop woman straightened herself up. "As I said, I am sorry about all this. But the Abbey has a great deal to offer aside from the Spellbook. I encourage you to look around the cathedral and the grounds. The altar is from the 15th Century. There's a statue of Madonna and Child carved from Connemara marble. And the organ is one of the largest outside of Dublin."

Blah, blah, blah, thought Maggie, only half listening. *How to find the Spellbook...*

"The grounds are also quite interesting," the woman went on. "This hill has been a place of great religious importance since before even the first Christian missionaries arrived from Britain. Several structures have been built here on the hill, each upon the ruins of the last. We've kept what's left of the walls and foundations of those temples and fortresses and you're free to stroll through them at your leisure."

Maggie managed a genuine smile for the very nice, very helpful woman. It wasn't her fault, after all, that the McCuskers had emptied the Abbey of any trace of the Spellbook. "Thank you very much for your help."

Maggie exited the shop into the cathedral, hiked her backpack up on her shoulders, and walked outside into the ruinous dragon's tail, a forced smile on her face and rising anger in her heart.

***

What the hell is going on? Maggie was beside herself.

I finally come across a spellbook of light magic—one with a healing spell, no less—one that might shed some light, so to speak, on both my Dark Book and my 'Healer' ancestor. But no sooner do I find it and glimpse a sum total of two unimportant pages then it's packed up and removed early from the exhibition. The curator in Dublin says it's gone back to Ballincoomer, and young little Kitty McCusker seems to confirm that, but when I reach the quaint little village in the western *Gaeltacht,* I discovers that Kitty's daddy, the Great and Terrible Dr. McCusker, has diverted it to Kilkenny, or Killarney, or Kill-a-Freaking-Mockingbird. Indefinitely. Oh, and the good doctor has gone with it, taking with him every last other damned book about the Spellbook.

She exhaled through gritted teeth.

Nice.

But despite herself, the history of her surroundings was starting to soothe her, and as she stomped through the grass and stones she could feel her heartbeat begin to slow.

There were seven ruined chambers in all, the most recent

abutting the present Abbey with the older ones receding away in reverse chronological order, so that walking through them toward the end was like a trip back in time. The march through the centuries was marked with brass milestones—small plaques embedded in the ground, not unlike grave markers, explaining a bit of the history and significance of each dearly departed building.

The first plaque was right next to the Abbey wall. It explained, in English and Irish, that the Abbey in its current form dated from 1853. The two ruined chambers closest to the Abbey had once been a dormitory of sorts, but had been destroyed in the Rebellion of 1848. Apparently some Nationalists had taken refuge in the dormitory wing of the Abbey, and the Loyalist commander, not thinking much of this, had sent a hail of cannon fire into the wing, to the predictable horror of the residents of Ballincoomer. What wasn't knocked down with cannonballs was burned by the fire started from the Abbey's own shattered lanterns. When all was said and done the dormitory wing was, well, in ruins, and a large gaping hole filled the wall adjoined to the cathedral.

In truth, however, these first two rooms were the best preserved. The walls were still original height in some places, with glassless windows peering down on the town below. The plaque went on the explain that while the practice up until 1848 had been to build or rebuild by cannibalizing whatever stones were left from the previous structures, the residents of Ballincoomer—at least the Nationalists who both attended the Catholic Abbey and had supported the Rebellion—wanted to keep the ruins as a memorial. The money to buy stones to repair the damaged cathedral wall had come from a favorite son who had made a good go of it over in Boston. He had been able to send back enough money to pay for the repair, thereby allowing the dormitory walls to stand as a monument to the Irish struggle for independence.

The next ruined room dated from 1713. It had been part of a larger chapel which had burned to the ground in an accidental fire. Although the fire had done little damage to the stone walls, what remained of them was still considerably shorter than the dormitory ruins, their stones having been removed to help build the new abbey. A quick scan of the ruined dormitory walls confirmed a great number of stones whose hue matched that of what remained of the chapel walls.

And so it went. Each room's walls were shorter than the last as the Ballincoomerians had built new church after new church next to and from the ruins of the last. This left the last skeletonized chamber to be barely a ruin at all. Of what had presumably been four walls, only two remained, rising no more than two feet off the ground at their tallest point. The final brass plaque stood guard next to this meek ending to the dragon's tail. Maggie stood over the plaque, her shadow falling diagonally across its face, and read.

'On this spot stood the original church building, erected c. 600-650 A.D. by the Welsh missionaries who founded Ballincoomer. Constructed entirely of stone and devoid of any mortar to hold the bricks together, the church followed the architectural style of other Christian outposts in Ireland. Of notable deviation at this site were the nearly ubiquitous carvings on the interior of the stone walls. The pictographs and their accompanying text, in both Old Welsh and Old Irish, are believed to have been the missionaries' first attempt to preserve and pass on their beliefs and teachings. The church was destroyed in 1210, during English King John's ill-fated attempt to subjugate Ireland.'

Welsh, huh? Maggie jutted out a thoughtful lip as she recalled the sign in the cathedral. "Ballincoomer," she said aloud, followed by the similar sounding, "*Baile nan Cuimri.*" Old Irish for 'City of the Welsh.' "That makes sense."

She thought she recalled learning that St. Patrick had been Welsh—or Briton, at least—and supposed that if she had been a Welsh missionary in the Seventh Century, she'd likely have headed to Ireland too; with the notable—and dangerous—exception of the Vikings, most of the rest of Europe was already Christian by then, thanks to the Romans.

Intrigued by this Celt-Celt connection, Maggie crouched down to inspect what was left of the engraved stones. Sure enough, every last one of them bore crudely carved diagrams, symbols and words. She could read the Old Irish well enough, but not the Old Welsh. At least she supposed it was Old Welsh. Apart from the information from the plaque, Old Welsh was also suggested by both an amazing frequency of 'ff,' 'dd' and 'll' combinations and a noticeable dearth of vowels other than 'y' and 'w.' Her single course in Modern Welsh was going to be of no use to her. She squatted down next to remains of the wall and searched for snippets of Old Irish to read.

Who knows, she thought, *maybe I'll find something interesting.*

By the time she'd finished the thought, she'd accomplished its hope. A few feet to the left of the plaque and half obscured by tall grass was a diagram surrounded by words in both Old Irish and Old Welsh. What caught her eye was the word '*fáitsine,*' Old Irish for 'prophecy.' Just like the word, albeit in English, in the newspaper photograph, scrawled above the MacLeod boy's empty crib. Maggie knelt forward onto the moist ground, slipped her backpack off, and, pushing the grass aside, examined the carving.

Only the bottom half of the diagram remained, its top half long since destroyed, or removed to build new walls. Still, what was there was more than intriguing. The bottom of a circle sat carved in the stone, its insides filled with busy, interlacing Celtic knotwork. The pattern of the knotwork suggested three equidistant points of some importance on the circumference of the circle, one each to the lower left, lower right, and, although no longer present, the top center. At each of the two lower points, 120 degrees apart, the knotwork came to a flourish, with words carved there. The words were in Old Irish, with what was presumably an Old Welsh translation beneath.

To the left was the phrase, 'The banshee shall return to claim her legacy.' To the right stood, 'The magic of the Celts shall be reignited.' But Maggie couldn't read the third and final inscription—because the brick was gone.

Moved by something more than mere curiosity, Maggie ran back toward the ruined walls behind her. She knew the chances of finding the missing brick were slim. Even assuming it had been commandeered to build a new wall, it was entirely likely that it had been shattered by a flying cannonball or otherwise destroyed. Still, she had to try.

The search of the first set of ruins back proved fruitless. She hurried to the next. And the next. It wasn't until the chapel from 1713 that she finally found it. Upside down and badly worn, half-blackened by soot, still, there it was about a third of the way down a four foot section of wall, its dull gray quite obvious among the darker reddish bricks of the ruin.

Although the position of the circle clearly indicated the brick was upside down, the letters appeared to be right side up, the tops of their letters hugging the outer circumference of the ring. Even so, they were greatly worn, their centuries old lines no longer discernible to the naked eye. Seized by an idea, Maggie ran back to her bag and extracted both a sheet of notebook paper and a pencil. She quickly made a rubbing of the first stone she'd found, with its two verses. Then she sprinted back to the lost stone, carefully positioned the paper over its pattern, and rubbed the pencil over the paper for all she was worth. When she'd finished she raised the sheet. What she found there, the completion of the unbroken circle of the ancient Welsh prophecy, chilled her soul:

'The ban-shee shall return to claim her legacy.'

'The magic of the Celts shall be reignited.'

And: 'Infantsblood shall be spilt onto ancestral earth.'

21. welshbookofsouls.co.uk

The shop woman had been right. Ballincoomer had only the one bookstore. However, the little town of one thousand residents boasted six drinking establishments, all but one of which specialized in beverages of the alcoholic kind. The exception was named 'Kafka's' and was a dimly lit, hole-in-the-wall café devoted to, according to its sign, 'Good Coffee and Better Connections.' This somewhat cryptic catch phrase was elucidated by two other signs, both in tasteful neon: 'We Serve Starbucks' and 'High Speed Internet Access.' Kafka's was an internet café. Maggie pulled open the unexpectedly lightweight door and stepped inside.

She fetched herself a short mocha from the bar to the left, then perched herself on a stool at one of a dozen state-of-the-art-deco computers lining the wall to the right. A few mouse clicks later she was staring at the 'Search.com' homepage. She paused, formulating her query.

She knew Scotland's national library was in Edinburgh. She knew England's was in London, and Ireland's in Dublin. She supposed then that Wales' national library was likely in Cardiff. But she thought better of surfing through every page devoted to Wales' capital city and instead got right to the heart of the matter, typing 'Wales library national' and clicking the 'SEARCH' button. Her surgical accuracy was rewarded and one click later she was downloading 'www.nlw.co.uk,' home site for the National Library of Wales in, not Cardiff, but rather the beautiful seaside university town of Aberystwyth.

In short order she had navigated to the search engine for the library's holdings. She was presented with several options. While *'Title'* would have been quickest, she was lacking that information. So too with *'Author'* and *'Call Number.'* This left *'Subject'* and *'Keyword.'* She cracked her knuckles and set to work.

It was nearly forty minutes later before she finally found it. Or at least she hoped she'd found it. 'The Welsh Book of Souls.' A handwritten manuscript from circa 500 A.D. The all too brief online entry described it as 'a cataloging of beliefs, myths and prophesies from the time just prior to Wales' conversion to Christianity.' Further remarks explained that some of the ceremonies described involved child sacrifice. Maggie knew it wasn't guaranteed to shed light on the cryptic carving atop Dragon Hill, but she also knew it was about as good a lead as she was likely to get.

She pointed the mouse onto the button marked 'holdings' and clicked. They had several copies of this 'Book of Souls.' The original Old Welsh manuscript was housed safely away in the Historic Collections. But there were also plain-text versions available in the general collections, and even two translations of the work into English. This last part was important. She knew she would be hard pressed to read the original.

Still... She tipped back on the tall stool, her feet swinging several inches above the floor. Wales, huh?

***

Taggert's face was a sickly, pale blue from the glow of the computer monitor in his otherwise shade-darkened study. His right hand rested on the mouse, guiding the device across its pad as its arrow-shaped alter ego glided across the flickering screen. Click after click led Taggert deeper and deeper into those rare, and seldom visited websites devoted to such esoteric subjects as dead languages and ancient manuscripts.

His left hand was taking notes.

***

The mocha was long gone, but Maggie still sat there, staring at the screen displaying the call number for the Welsh Book of Souls. She glanced down at the chocolatey remains in her paper cup and regretted not having ordered a tall.

Words and phrases danced in her head. 'Spellbook' and '*bean-slànaighear*.' 'Prophecy' and 'infantsblood.' 'Ballincoomer' and 'Aberystwyth.'

Ultimately she knew she had three choices.

First, she could wait around Ballincoomer — 'indefinitely' — and see whether Dr. McCusker ever returned and if so whether he'd bring with him the Spellbook of Ballincoomer. Despite her unexplainable misgivings about Kitty, the Spellbook held within its covers a healing spell, and therefore a possible connection to her 'healer' past.

Second, she could walk to the bus terminal and buy a ticket first to Dublin, then a ferry ticket to Aberystwyth, home to the Welsh Book of Souls. This book might hold within its covers more information about the prophecy etched on the abbey ruins, and therefore a possible connection to the present mystery.

Or third, she could just walk back to her hotel, forget all this nonsense, and get ready to head home to Aberdeen. For Aberdeen held within its city limits her new home, her new school and her new life, and therefore an undeniable connection to her future happiness.

She sighed a heavy sigh, then stood up, pushed her stool in, and swung her bag over her shoulder. Then she walked out onto the street and turned determinedly toward her hotel.

After all, she'd have to make arrangements to check out early if she was going to go to Wales first thing in the morning.

22. The Estranged Wife

Warwick looked at her watch and nodded. "Come on then, Alison. Our three-thirty should be here by now."

"Our three-thirty?" Chisholm looked up from the reports she was rereading.

But before Warwick could expound, Officer Kerr knocked on the inside of her door frame. The young patrolman, his short but thick black hair combed away from his strong face, flashed a smile at the visiting sergeant, then looked over to Warwick. "Your three-thirty appointment has arrived," he announced.

"See?" Warwick waved toward the blue clad herald. "Thank you very much, Kerr." Then pointing toward Chisholm, she executed the introductions. "Fraser Kerr, this is Sergeant Alison Chisholm of the Glasgow Police Department. Sergeant, this is Officer Fraser Kerr."

"Nice to meet you, Officer Kerr," Chisholm nodded in greeting.

"Please," another smile, one that made his blue eyes sparkle, "call me Fraser."

Chisholm smiled too at this display. "I'll consider it." Then taking a full look at the strapping young policeman, "I'll definitely consider it."

"Excuse me, Fraser," Warwick interrupted impatiently. "But you wouldn't know whether the interrogation room is free, would you?"

"I would," Fraser Kerr responded with a gracious nod, "and it is not." He jerked a thumb toward the hallway. "Russell's working over some bloke in there right now."

"Mm." Warwick pursed her lips. "What about the conference room?"

Kerr thought for a moment, then answered, "Aye, that should be free. The Inspector's got a meeting, but not until ten, I believe. So that should work."

"Wonderful," Warwick said. "Could you show our guest into the conference room? Sergeant Chisholm and I will be there in a moment. Then twenty minutes."

"Twenty minutes?" Kerr cocked his head.

"Right," Warwick confirmed.

"Will that be enough time?"

Warwick just raised an impatient eyebrow.

"That is," Kerr ran a finger inside his collar, "Russell usually takes longer than that."

"I'm not Russell," Warwick replied levelly. "Twenty minutes."

"Your wish, milady," he replied with a large smile and an exaggerated bow and slipped away.

"Well, he was cute," Chisholm observed with a devious smile.

"Yes and no," Warwick replied. "But he's helpful. And a good officer."

Chisholm rolled her eyes at Warwick's prudery, but only a bit and she was fairly certain Warwick hadn't seen. "So who's our three-thirty appointment?"

"Who else?" Warwick asked rhetorically as she stepped into the hallway. "The Lady MacLeod."

***

Whatever Warwick might have been expecting—and she wasn't really sure what that was—it was definitely not what she encountered when she and Chisholm walked into the conference room.

Seated at the far end of the table was a surprisingly young woman, slight of build, with cropped blond hair, heavy dark eye make-up, an extremely tight baby-doll T-shirt with the word 'diva' arcing beneath the pink collar, and a pair of very dark, almost black, blue jeans, which hugged her form almost as tightly as her shirt. Warwick couldn't see the girl's feet inside the black leather boots that disappeared up the jean legs, but she guessed several of the toes sported toe-rings to match the nose-stud which sparkled pink above the woman's left nostril.

The young woman looked up at the entering police officers. "Hey," she said in subdued greeting.

"Lady MacLeod?" Warwick tried to make it sound like a greeting, not a question.

"Please," the young woman cringed at the words. "Don't call me that. 'Jessie' is fine."

"Okay, Jessie. I'm Sergeant Warwick. This is Sergeant Chisholm." Warwick sat down at the conference table; Chisholm followed suit. "We're investigating the disappearance of your son. Thank you for agreeing to meet with us."

"Of course." Jessie wrung her hands. "I'm— I'm glad to do whatever I can, you know, to help or whatever."

"Great."

"Um, but—" Jessie clutched her small black leather purse

from the floor. "Do you mind if I smoke? I—"

"Not at all," Chisholm said before Warwick could answer, and slid an ashtray over from the far end of the conference table. "Here you are."

Warwick tried not to flash a disapproving glare at Chisholm. She'd talk to her about it later. Not only did Warwick not like cigarette smoke, but she would have preferred her subject to be a little edgy, eager to finish the interview as quickly as possible. It would have helped Warwick control the conversation that much more easily. Oh well.

Jessie took a long drag and exhaled rather a lot of smoke. "Thanks. Aye, that's better."

"So then," Warwick started, but she didn't get any farther.

"I didn't do it," Jessie MacLeod announced.

Warwick shook her head sharply. "What?"

"I didn't do it," Jessie repeated. "I didn't kidnap Douglas."

"Okay," Chisholm replied slowly. Warwick just eyed the young woman.

"That's why you wanted to talk to me, right?" She blew more cigarette smoke toward the floor.

"Well, we did want to talk to you about Douglas' abduction, yes." Warwick replied carefully. "But—"

"Well, I didn't take him. I mean, I wish I had. I should have. But I didn't. Maybe if I had— maybe then he wouldn't have been kidnapped, but, well, I didn't." She took a breath. "So I guess that's it."

Warwick pursed her lips. It was time to take control of the interview. "Okay. Let's start at the beginning then."

Jessie MacLeod rubbed her nose with her cigarette-less hand. "All right."

"You are Janet MacLeod. We've established that."

The young woman laughed slightly and looked at Chisholm. "Uh, yeah, right. I'm Janet MacLeod. Jessie."

"And you're David MacLeod's wife."

"Barely," was the reply. "The divorce'll be final next week."

"And how old are you, Jessie?"

She smiled, understanding the question behind the question. "Twenty-two. He's thirty-seven."

Warwick nodded. "All right. And where are you from? Not Aberdeen?"

"No, I'm from Fort William. Although, I've moved to Aberdeen now. I would travel with David sometimes for business and I liked it here. It's bigger than Fort William but still Highland. I like being in the Highlands."

"All right then," Warwick continued. Chisholm wondered whether she shouldn't be taking notes. "And how," Warwick asked, "did you meet David?"

Jessie shook her head and sucked on the cigarette again. "Aye, that's a story." She cleared her throat, just to note the drama of the impending information. "I was a waitress in a pub in Fort William. David came there one night for dinner. And after closing, David took me back to his hotel room and shagged me."

Nice, Warwick thought to herself, careful not to let the thought appear on her face.

"That's nice," Chisholm observed aloud, her sarcasm obvious.

"Isn't it, though?" Jessie laughed sardonically. "Real fairy tale stuff. But it gets better."

"Oh?" Chisholm seemed genuinely entertained.

"Oh yes." Another inhale of smoke. "I became his girl in Fort William. Whenever he was there for business, well, you know. A girl in every port, as they say. And it was fine, you know, because he was David MacLeod, Chieftain of the Clan MacLeod of Harris, and I was just Jessie Sterling, waitress. It was convenient for him. It was well enough for me. But you see, I'm one of seven kids. And my mum was one of eight."

Chisholm looked askance.

"We're quite fertile, we Sterling women," Jessie explained. "It didn't take long 'til I got pregnant."

"Ah," Chisholm replied.

"I figured I'd be a single mother. Or maybe— Well, I knew there were other options."

"But MacLeod wouldn't have it, would he?" Warwick asked.

"No," Jessie confirmed. "Surprised me actually. He took me for my word that it was his. And so there I was, twenty-one and pregnant with—"

"With the heir to the MacLeod Clan," Warwick observed.

Jessie took a last drag off her cigarette and crushed the butt in the glass ashtray. "Aye. The heir to the Clan MacLeod. So those 'other options' were out of the question. He wasn't about to see his heir aborted. Or adopted; one doesn't put an heir up for adoption."

"And you don't have an heir out of wedlock," Warwick observed.

"I do recall the word 'bastard' being thrown about a bit," Jessie confirmed with a grin. "Apparently it had the potential to wreak rather a lot of havoc on the eventual succession to the chieftaincy. Not to mention the general discredit it would bring to the clan. Particularly his half of it. I discovered that David has quite the inferiority complex about MacLeod of Harris versus MacLeod of Lewis."

"So he proposed," Warwick deduced.

"Yes. And quite a show it was too. On bended knee and all that." She flashed the large diamond ring she still wore on her left hand. "He didn't skimp on the rock either. And then," she paused and fluttered heavily mascaraed eyelashes, "we got married."

"Quite the courtship," Chisholm observed with a shake of her head.

Jessie laughed lightly. "Aye, but it wasn't so bad. He was actually very caring during the pregnancy—doting even. I was very well taken care of. All the best doctors and such. And then I gave birth to the most wonderful, beautiful baby boy."

Chisholm's face softened at the story. Warwick waited for it.

"A week later," Jessie continued, "he took Douglas from my very arms and served me with the divorce papers." She displayed an angry, clenched smile. "And I haven't seen my son since."

Warwick set her chin on her hands and frowned as she processed what she'd heard. It was time to ask the million pound question.

"All right. And where were you Sunday night? When Douglas was kidnapped?" Her voice was still friendly, almost casual, but the import of the question was clear.

"How do you mean?" Jessie blinked heavily and reached for another cigarette. After lighting it and exhaling the first dark smoke, she assured, "I told you: I didn't do it."

"Of course." Warwick didn't blink back even as the smoke wafted past her face. "So if you can just let us know where you were, we can confirm it and then officially eliminate you as a suspect."

"A suspect," Jessie almost spat as she took another long drag off her cigarette. Then, exhaling the resultant billow of smoke through her nostrils, admitted, "Well, that makes sense, I suppose."

Warwick smiled encouragingly. Chisholm had already leaned back in her chair and crossed her arms.

"Well, let's see..." Jessie began. "That was Sunday, you said?"

"Sunday night into Monday morning," Warwick clarified.

"Right." Another lung-full of cigarette smoke. "Sunday night I ate dinner out. With a friend."

"A friend?" Warwick echoed.

"Yes, a friend." She paused. "A gentleman friend. It was a late dinner. We finished around nine o'clock, so I don't suppose you'll need his name, will you? It could complicate ... other matters."

Warwick hesitated. Chisholm didn't. "That's up to you, Mrs. MacLeod. As Sergeant Warwick explained, the more you tell us, the easier it will be to confirm your alibi."

"Yes, well..." Jessie's eyes widened a bit at the word 'alibi.' "I had a late dinner with a gentleman friend and we finished up a bit after nine. We ate at *Le Bistro Écosse*, if that helps. Then we went out for a few drinks. That is, I did. My friend decided to go home."

"And where did you go for drinks?" Warwick this time.

Jessie paused again and flicked her cigarette in the ashtray. "I forget the name of the place. A small nightclub down on Dunfinnich Quay."

Warwick thought for a moment. "Club Frankenwald?"

"Yes." A guarded smile lit Jessie's face. "I believe that may have been it. Adorable place. I hadn't been there before. We stayed there until, oh, probably one o'clock."

"We?" Chisholm leaned forward

"Pardon?" Jessie inhaled again from her cigarette.

"You said 'we.' 'We stayed there until one o'clock.'"

"Did I?" Another flick of ash into the waiting glass receptacle. "I meant 'I.' I stayed there until one o'clock. I must have said 'we' because I was thinking about the people I met there. Jolly nice folks. Good fun. I had a wonderful time."

"And you wouldn't happen to remember any of those folks' names?" Chisholm inquired.

Jessie exhaled a large billow of smoke toward the visiting sergeant. "Afraid not."

"What then?" Warwick pushed her along.

"Then? Then I went home."

"Alone?" Chisholm prodded.

"Alone," Jessie confirmed. She shrugged. "Sorry."

Warwick clicked her tongue lightly. "So," she summed up, "you were alone from around one o'clock until you woke up the next morning?"

"Right," Jessie extinguished her second cigarette in the ashtray. "I woke up around nine." She smiled. "Maybe ten."

"And you've no one," Chisholm interjected, "who can vouch for your whereabouts starting at about nine o'clock Sunday, is that correct?"

Jessie pursed her lips to one side. "I suppose that's correct."

Warwick nodded her head. Chisholm shook hers. "That's not very helpful, Mrs. MacLeod."

"I suppose not," Jessie replied with a shrug. "But it's the best I can do."

An awkward silence fell upon the room. Chisholm decided to fill it. "Do you still have a key to the townhouse here in Aberdeen?"

Jessie grinned. "No. I had one before, of course, but I've returned it to him. Through my lawyer."

"Your lawyer?" Warwick felt obliged to ask.

"Aye. Glynis Campbell, in the Hastings Building."

Before Warwick could follow up a sharp knock resounded off the door. Warwick looked at her watch. *Right on time*, she thought. "Come in," she said.

Fraser Kerr pushed open the conference room door, an ink pad and paper towels in one hand, a rigid letter-sized card in the other—and a boyish smile still plastered on his face.

"We'll just need," Warwick explained with a gesture to Officer Kerr, "to get your fingerprints before you leave."

A puzzled expression traversed the young woman's face, but she shrugged yet again. "All right."

Kerr swooped in and deftly pressed Jessie's fingers to the ink pad, before rolling each fingerpad onto the card to obtain ten square smudges. He then handed her the paper towels, snapped close the ink pad and handed the fingerprint card to Warwick.

"Pretty bird," he whispered admiringly out of the corner of his mouth, but he escaped into the corridor before Warwick could administer any verbal or physical reprisal.

Jessie's voice pulled Warwick back to the task at hand. "Can I go now?" she asked wiping the ink from her fingers.

"Yes," Warwick replied "We've got your address. You're not planning on going anywhere any time soon, are you?"

"Just my lawyer's office later today. But she's here in town. Otherwise I'm not going anywhere."

"All right then." Warwick stood up, followed by Chisholm and Jessie MacLeod. "Thank you for coming in, Lady MacLeod."

The young woman laughed again. "Right. 'Lady MacLeod.' It sounds quite romantic." She shook her head as they walked into the hallway. "The exit's that way, right?"

"Right." Warwick pointed down the hallway, away from the direction of her office. "Straight ahead, then left at the corridor. Thank you again."

Then Lady Janet 'Jessie' Sterling MacLeod walked down the hallway and out to the lobby.

"Well?" Chisholm inquired.

Warwick sighed. "She's lying. I'm not sure about what yet, but she's lying."

23. Hard Evidence

It was nice to have Chisholm around, Warwick conceded to herself. But as she sat alone in her dark office—its confines lit only by the inadequate glow of her desk lamp, the MacLeod file spread out before her, and her fingertips brushing against the mug full of tepid coffee—she was also glad for the time to herself.

Chisholm appeared to be intelligent and insightful. And she played the role of sounding board expertly. Ideas, hunches and suspicions were developing at a more rapid pace than even Warwick was used to. That was good, given the imperative nature of the case, not the least of which arose from the exceptional vulnerability of the victim. But the partnership wasn't entirely benign. At this pace it had become difficult to impossible for Warwick to allow her unconscious mind to mull over the information they were obtaining, particularly amid the din of discussion with Chisholm.

Therefore, despite the clock hands having almost completed their race to the twelve, Warwick had no regrets for abusing her body with strong coffee and long hours.

She glanced down at the file—or rather at its guts splayed out in front of her. Somehow, this reminded her of her last case involving bloody patterns etched at a crime scene, and she frowned as, even against her will, her thoughts wandered again to the young American student she'd met during that earlier investigation. And again against her will, an idea—a decidedly un-Warwick-like idea flashed through her mind. But summoning her will, she dismissed it, and shook her head sharply against its return.

The late hour, she decided.

The station was rather quiet now, the hush of night exerting its influence even on a profession which could ill afford to sleep. Nevertheless, officers on swing shift were coming in for the night, while those on graveyard were heading out into the dark Aberdeen streets. Warwick raised her mug and drained the cool, bitter remains. Then she stood up and walked into the hallway. Richards should be in by now.

The gray linoleum corridor was calm. Echoes of voices and tired laughter trailed after her from the main lobby, but she was headed the opposite direction. She reached the back stairway and descended the rubber tipped steps surely, fatigue dampening any desire to hurry the descent into the basement. Then she walked back down a longer, gray our linoleum hallway to the small black sign with white letters, '*Forensics.*'

"Elizabeth!" Officer Jenny Richards shot up from her short desk behind the tall counter of the Forensics office. She was rather tall and extremely thin, with straight blond hair that fell limply to her shoulders. "What are you doing this time of night? Aren't you still working days?"

"Still on days," Warwick admitted cheerily, "but still working nights as well."

"Aw, I should have known." Richards leaned onto the counter from her side of it. "What can I do for you?"

"It's the MacLeod case. The kidnapping. Are the forensics

done yet on the townhouse?"

"MacLeod, eh?" Richards turned and crossed to the file cabinet at the back of the office. "Let me see what we've got. Come on back."

Warwick walked through the swinging wooden door at the far end of the counter and stepped up next to Richards, who was busy thumbing through a collection of six-by-eight-inch index cards in the second drawer down, her hair falling around her face.

"Here we are," she announced as she pulled out a light green card. Then turning again to her guest, "Yes. They're done. Finished them up this morning."

"And what are the results?" Warwick asked as Richards took the card over to a wall of file cabinets and began searching for the proper drawer. "Any prints?"

"Oh yes," Richards replied. "The room was filled with good impressions. All over the crib, the window sills, the furniture. Even the floor."

"Great." Warwick watched as Richards extracted a manila folder from the right-most file cabinet. "And were you able to match any of the prints?"

"Oh yes," Richards assured with a sly grin. "All of them actually. All of the good ones anyway."

"And?" Warwick widened her eyes.

"And," Richards couldn't help the mischievous gleam in her eye, "they mostly belonged to Mr. MacLeod. We matched them from his military records," she added in explanation.

"Well, that figures," Warwick replied, a bit disappointed. "What about the rest of the prints?"

"Well, a fair number matched up with the ones we got from the nanny. Er, Nellie something or other?"

"MacQuarrie." Warwick shrugged. "That's probably also to

be expected. Were any of hers near the window?"

"No, none from the window. Most were from the changing table and a couple from the crib railings."

"All right," Warwick was still hopeful, but she was having to work at it. "Anyone else?"

"Well, there were some that we couldn't actually match up," Richards started, "but given their relatively small size, and their locations exclusively inside the crib and on the changing table, I'm fairly certain they belong to the infant. We don't have anything to match them against, of course—most one-year olds have never had their fingerprints taken—but the only other possibility would seem to be that he was kidnapped by another infant. An unlikely proposition," Richards opined unnecessarily.

Okay, now Warwick was disappointed. "So, in summary," she raised an upturned palm in emphasis, "no useful fingerprints."

"No," Richards admitted, "no useful fingerprints. But it is noteworthy that the room didn't appear to have been wiped down in any way. Whoever did this simply succeeded in not leaving any fingerprints. And there are no marks indicating gloves. It appears they simply didn't touch anything."

Warwick frowned a tight little frown. "Well, that's something, I suppose. What else do you have? Any hair or fabric samples?"

"Nothing useful," Richards conceded. "The hair samples track the fingerprints: old man MacLeod's, the nanny's, or short and fine like an infant's. The ones we think are the lad's are blond and the photos we have confirm young Douglas was fair-haired. On the fabric, we found several threads of various types of fabric—cotton, wool, even silk—but nothing out of the ordinary, and nothing that really leads us anywhere. The problem is that the home was rather lived in. MacLeod had been in Aberdeen for two weeks already when the child was abducted, and he's owned the place for years. So there's bound to be fingerprints, hair and fabric all over the bloody place."

"Right," Warwick frowned again, and then leaned into a half-sitting position on the desk behind her. "Well what about the blood? That's not commonplace."

Richards laughed. "No, sure enough it's not." She took the file from Warwick and pulled out a few photographs of the bloody inscription. "I'm no linguist, so I can't tell you what it's supposed to say—"

"I'm working on that," Warwick interjected.

"—But I can tell you a bit about the substance itself."

"And? I guess the first question is: Is it human?"

"Yes, it's human," Richards face held no hint of additional information. Warwick would have to ask.

"Was it the boy's? Can we know?"

"We can know," Richards replied with a faint smile. "The blood on the floor matches the boy's. Or rather it matches his parents well enough that I'm as certain as I can be that it's the lad's."

"Okay. And what about the blood on the walls?"

"Well, I'm having a bit of trouble with that one yet," Richard's brow creased.

"Have you DNA-typed it yet?" Warwick pressed. "Will we be able to match it?"

"As to your first question," Richards replied pointing to a single raised finger, "no, I haven't DNA-typed it yet. As I said, I'm having a bit of trouble with that for some reason. Fairy dust, perhaps, from the MacLeod Banshee."

Warwick didn't laugh at all at this attempt at a joke; instead she offered an icy, impatient glare. Richards moved on.

"It should be done by early next week," she assured. Then

raising a second finger, she added, "And as to your second question, I don't know if we'll be able to match it. We'll need a known sample to complete a match. But we'll run it through the databases once it's typed."

"And if there's no match in the database," Warwick considered the suspects so far, "we'll get you a subject sample to compare."

Richards nodded, aware of the determination that lurked beneath the fatigue in Warwick's voice.

"All right then," Warwick wrapped up as she stifled a yawn. "Anything else?"

"Probably," Richards laughed. "But I don't know it yet. I'll call you once the DNA typing is done."

"Good. Great," Warwick allowed the next yawn to come to fruition, but hid it behind a fist. "I should get going then. Thanks for your help, Richards."

"Anytime, Sergeant," Richards smiled and waved her guest goodbye. "Talk to you soon."

And an exhausted Elizabeth Warwick walked slowly back down the long gray linoleum corridor.

24. *Croeso i Gymru* / Welcome to Wales

The Irish Sea can be surprisingly turbulent in midsummer and the passage from Dublin to Hogshead, Wales, had proved rather a bit too choppy for Maggie's tastes. But she had taken her motion sickness pills. And she'd tried not to think of the Lusitania. The subsequent train ride south along the Welsh coast was quite smooth by comparison and she arrived in the Welsh college town of Aberystwyth, relaxed and refreshed, at a little after three in the afternoon. Her hotel was conveniently located only a few blocks from the train station and within easy walking distance of the University of Aberystwyth, with its affiliated National Library of Wales. But first she had to check in.

"Good afternoon, ma'am." The young man behind the reception desk flashed a pleasant, toothy smile, apparently unaware or indifferent of the entirely untamed state of his thick brown hair. Faint stubble colored his chin and Maggie could see the pierced holes in his earlobes, although he'd apparently been instructed not to wear earrings while on duty. He appeared twenty, twenty-one tops. Still, he didn't need to call her, 'ma'am.'

"Good afternoon," she replied. "I have a reservation. Under 'Devereaux.'"

"Devereaux," the young man repeated, looking down at the computer screen hidden below the tall reception counter. "Let's see..." His eyes scanned the names: Hewlin, Stiles, McCusker... "Ah, here we are. Devereaux. Margaret, right?"

"Right."

"Two nights?" the clerk confirmed.

"Yes."

He tapped a few keystrokes. "Smoking or non?"

"Non, please."

"Right. Non-smoking." A few more keystrokes, then he pulled a plastic key-card from a drawer and inserted it into an apparatus that looked half-toaster, half paperweight. "Would you like a view room? We've one left."

"A view of what?" A fair question, she thought.

"A bit of the bay, but mostly of the college up the hill. It's quite picturesque actually. Wonderful gothic architecture."

"That does sound nice," Maggie started.

"It's ten quid more," the clerk finished.

Maggie paused. Ten quid would more than cover her dinner—for a few nights. But then again, a view of the college sounded nice. "What's my other choice?"

"Ah well." The clerk grinned. "That's the thing. The other view is the back of the shops across the alley. Loading docks. And it's ground floor. Otherwise, all the other rooms are smoking."

"The view room it is," Maggie quickly agreed and accepted her computer-coded key-card from the clerk.

"Room 407, ma'am." Maggie cringed at this second 'ma'am,' but declined comment. "Enjoy your stay."

"Thank you, sir." Maggie turned toward the lift as the clerk shook off his surprised grin and typed the '407' next to Mr. Hewlin's 201, Mr. Stiles' 316, and Ms. McCusker's '405.'

***

It's like music, Maggie decided as she walked up the street toward the university.

The sidewalks were filled with people finishing the business of their days, leaving work early, returning from shopping, heading out for tea, and to Maggie's genuine surprise and utter delight, almost all of them were chatting away quite unintelligibly in Welsh.

She found herself ridiculously pleased, as she crossed Thespian Street and began her ascent up the steep hill toward the university, that the language seemed so alive. Majoring in Celtic languages, let alone seeking a Ph.D. in the subject, could sometimes be a disheartening experience. The leading linguistic literature in the field tended to be analyses of how the latest dialect of Gaelic had succumbed to the hegemony of English. But rather than having to travel to the farthest reaches of the Scottish coast or the rocky, windswept fields of the west of Ireland to find Gaelic the everyday language, Maggie found herself strolling in the heart of Wales' premier university town surrounded by the lyrical cadence of an obviously still quite vibrant Celtic tongue.

Maybe I'll take another Welsh course after all, she thought as she continued up the hill.

This fancy was reinforced by the majestic spectacle which filled her eyes as she turned round to take in a view of the town from halfway up Penglais Road. The hill, and the city with it, sloped down and away from her, banking to the right to spill into the harbor and the Irish Sea beyond. At the bottom of the grade, nestled right against the crashing waves of the sea, stood the clearly recognizable bastion of the Old College, mammoth and gray, its gothic turrets rising into the sky as it sat guard along the seaside ring road.

Maybe I'll take that class here.

With the smile that lingers after gazing upon a beautiful landscape, Maggie turned and continued her ascent toward the hilltop section of the University of Aberystwyth where stood the National Library of Wales. Somewhat short of breath, she finally reached the unnamed drive which led to the Library and turned right, passing a long, gray, stone building that looked suspiciously like the Welsh equivalent of a student dormitory. Ahead of her stood her destination and she found herself quite pleased with its initial appearance. Identified by a tasteful sign reading, '*Llyfrgell Genedlaethol Cymru / National Library of Wales,*' the library was housed in a large, three-story building of white stone. Its neo-classical architecture was, while perhaps not regal, at least still impressive—it reminded Maggie of a very, very large bank. And somehow that worked for her.

A bank of knowledge, she considered as she pushed open the massive wooden doors and stepped inside.

The entry hall was the definition of grand, a red carpet extended across the dark hardwood floors and the walls rose in white columns to the vaulted, sky-lighted ceiling three stories above her.

God, I love libraries, she thought as she strolled through the lobby, her head tipped back so she could survey the full grandeur of the hall. And a national library at that! Who knew what treasures the collections held? Who knew what historical manuscripts peered down weightily from their bookshelf perches? Who knew what secret volumes hid in forgotten recesses? Who? Well, the librarian of course.

Maggie stepped up to the information desk.

"Hello!" she announced a bit too cheerily.

"Well, hello," responded the 40-something brunette librarian in her quaint Welsh accent. "May I help you?"

"Yes," Maggie beamed. "Yes. I was wondering if you could tell me where to find a particular book."

"Most likely." The librarian offered a bemused smile. "Do you have the call number?" A fair question.

"Oh." Maggie frowned. "Uh, no." An honest answer.

"All right then..." The librarian bent down and pulled out a lavender sheet of paper from under her counter. She slid it across to Maggie. "Here's a map of the library." Then she pointed to a row of computer terminals across the lobby. "You can search by title, author or keyword. Once you have the call number, you should be able to locate it on the map."

"Uh, okay." Maggie accepted the map with an embarrassed grin. "Right. Thanks. Thank you very much."

She tried not to notice the three separate wall-mounted dispensers of the lavender call number maps between the information desk and the computer terminals, nor the two more taped to the wall behind them. She hoped no one had overheard her exchange with the librarian. She simply sat down on the stool at the terminal to the far left and pressed 't' for a title search.

'welsh book of souls,' she typed.

The screen went white for a moment as the search page surveyed the library's holdings. Then, in amber print against the black screen, she was presented with five choices for 'welsh book of souls.' The last two indicated English translations.

She typed '4' and pressed 'Enter.'

The screen flashed again and she was given the record for the first entry:

Title: Welsh Book of Souls, The—English Translation

Call #: 204.7 w.481.1

Location: Printed Materials

Status: *Checked Out*

Darn, Maggie frowned. But then she shrugged, pressed the 'B' for 'Back,' then typed '5' and 'Enter.'

Title: Welsh Book of Souls, The—English Translation

Call #: 204.7 w.481.2

Location: Printed Materials

Status: *Checked Out*

And darn again. Maybe I'll be taking that Welsh course sooner than I'd thought. Another shrug, another 'B,' then '1' and 'Enter.'

Title: Llyfr Cymraeg Gwyffyn, Y (Welsh Book of Souls, The)

Call #: 204.1 w.480.1

Location: Printed Materials

Status: *Checked Out*

Hm. Her mouth squinched into a knot. 'B,' '2,' 'Enter.'

Title: Llyfr Cymraeg Gwyffyn, Y (Welsh Book of Souls, The)

Call #: 204.1 w.480.2

Location: Printed Materials

Status: *Checked Out*

Well, she sighed, *this is going about as badly as it can. One more chance.* 'B,' sigh, '3,' sigh, 'Enter.'

Title: Llyfr Cymraeg Gwyffyn, Y (Welsh Book of Souls, The)

Call #: 105.78 w.480.1

Location: Manuscripts

Status: *Manuscripts*

Maggie stared at the entry. *What do you suppose 'Status: Manuscripts' means?* she asked herself. *Maybe this is the original? Well, in any event it's better than 'Checked Out.'*

She stood up and crossed back over to the librarian, muttering only slightly over the bad luck that both English translations were checked out.

"Ah, yes," the librarian replied to Maggie's question, "that means that the entry is for the original manuscript. It may not be checked out, so its status cannot change."

"Okay," Maggie said slowly, her mind trying to catalogue her options. "Are the manuscripts accessible to the public? Could I go look at it?"

"Do you have the call number?"

Maggie grimaced; she hadn't written it down. "No. I forgot to write it down. Should I go get it?"

The librarian nodded with an apologetic, but still irritating, smile. Maggie crossed the room again, obtained the call number, then crossed back and provided the librarian with the slip of paper upon which she had scrawled it.

"Ah," the librarian began. "That is unfortunate."

Maggie waited, but apparently she was going to have to ask. "What is?"

"Well, some of the manuscripts are available to the general public. This isn't one of those."

"Swell." Now what? "What about graduate students?" she tried. It had worked the previous fall in Aberdeen.

"Yes, that will work," the librarian smiled. "As long as you have faculty approval."

Maggie grimaced again. "Oh. I'm not actually a student here."

The librarian simply nodded.

"Does it have to be faculty here, or faculty anywhere?"

"Well," the librarian began as delicately as she could, "certainly not North American faculty. Are you Canadian then?"

Again the accent. "No, American," she replied shortly. Then, "What about other U.K. faculty? I'm a student at the University of Aberdeen. In Scotland."

"I know it's in Scotland," the librarian sniffed. "And I think that will do. We have reciprocal agreements with most U.K.

colleges, and Aberdeen is certainly among those."

"Wonderful!" Maggie beamed. Then she shrugged, realizing that she was quite far from Aberdeen at that particular moment. "Uh, what kind of approval do you need? Written? A fax or something?"

"That would be preferable," was the somewhat equivocal reply. "A fax on letterhead from a professor at Aberdeen should be sufficient."

"Okay, great. Great." Maggie scanned the lobby; no telephones in sight. But she'd find one. "Should they fax it to you then?"

"They could do." The librarian fetched a scrap of paper from beneath her counter and scrawled out a number. "They can fax it here. 'Attention: Circulation' We should receive it."

"And what time does the library close?" The clock behind the counter read 5:07.

"At six." Then appreciating Maggie's resultant frown, she added helpfully, "The telephones are downstairs, near the café."

"Okay, great. Thank you. Thank you very much." Maggie hurried away and toward the stairs, slinging her backpack again over her shoulders. She just needed to find those phones. And figure out who in the world she was going to call.

***

"Hamilton," Maggie repeated into the receiver, a hand over her ear to block out what little noise there was around her in a vain attempt to comprehend the distant voice whispering into the other end of the phone line.

"Robert Hamilton.

"Okay, well, can I leave him a message?

"A message.

"Yes, my name is 'Maggie Devereaux.' 'Ma—' 'Maggie.'

'Devereaux.' Yes, 'Devereaux.' D-E-V— Okay. All right. D-E— Okay. Ready? Okay. D-E-V-E-R-E-A-U-X. Yes, 'X.' Right. 'Maggie.'

"No. Uh, no, I'm not actually a student of his. No. Well, I spoke with him at a conference last week. Last week. Right. In Aberdeen. I'm a student at Aberdeen. Yes, I'm sure. Yes, I'm American, but I'm a student at Aberdeen. Yes, really.

"Okay, well, the message is this: Would he be willing to fax a letter to the— fax a letter to the National Library of Wales— Yes, Wales. Right. The National Library of Wales. Authorizing me to view their manuscript collection. Manuscript collection.

"Uh, well, no. Like I said, I'm a student at Aberdeen. Yes, the University of Aberdeen.

"Well, I don't actually have a faculty advisor just now. Well, I just finished my first year, and well, it's a long story. I said, it's a long story. Anyway, do you think he might be willing to do that? Fax a letter to the library here? Right.

"Yes, I've got the fax number right here. Ready? Okay, here it is."

And Maggie provided the facsimile number for the National Library of Wales circulation desk, then hung up the receiver. Before the call, she had been concerned how, even if she obtained access to the manuscript, she would possibly be able to read its Welsh text. Now she was less worried about that. She was certain the telephone call would produce absolutely no results.

She looked at her watch. 5:15.

Time for a drink. And dinner. In that order.

25. The Dragon Rampant

Maggie had always been a sucker for symbols, especially nationalist symbols on flags and coats-of-arms—thistles, harps, lions, fleur-de-lis, and the like—so when she set out in search of a pub for dinner she knew she'd found her place in 'The Dragon Rampant,' a congenial looking establishment within view of the university's Old College and boasting a large wooden sign featuring the red dragon of Wales, only rather than in its traditional on-all-fours position as on the Welsh flag, the dragon stood menacingly on its hind legs, front claws extended forward, and red leathery wings flourishing behind. A quick peek at the front facade of windowpanes confirmed it was well frequented by students, some of whom had already arrived for an evening of dining, drinking, talking or all of the above.

"Just one?" asked the tall, lanky hostess from the bar near where Maggie walked in. The pub was essentially a single large room outfitted perfectly for social interaction. A well stocked bar stood against one wall and an alcove filled with pool tables and dart boards jutted out from another, with light wooden tables wrapped around the dark wooden walls and scattered across the even darker wooden floor.

"Yes, one." Maggie replied with a smile which almost hid her self-consciousness at dining alone.

"Right, then." The hostess stepped around the bar, grabbing a menu and stepping toward the tables. "This way please."

There were probably ten other customers in the pub just then, scattered about the bar and tables. None of them seemed to pay much attention to her as she was led to a four-person table near, but not quite at, a window facing the street. Obviously saving the better tables for larger parties. Maggie guessed it wouldn't be long before the pub was quite filled; there was already a certain buzz in the air as the day drew to a close and the evening set firmly in.

"Whatcha drinking then, miss?"

Maggie considered for a moment as she accepted the menu and sat down. Uncertain what the offerings might be, she elected to leave her inebriation to the good graces of her hostess and host country. "Beer, please. Whatever the local brewery is."

The hostess smiled. "All right, then. A pint of Flannery's." She took a step toward the bar, then shifted her weight back and turned round again. "Canadian?"

"American," Maggie corrected.

"Right," replied the woman. "I figured as much. Well, then: Welcome to Wales."

"Thank you," Maggie replied. She was already starting to feel better.

Two pints and half a dinner later and Maggie was downright happy. As expected, the pub had turned out to be quite the hotspot for Aberystwyth's collegiate residents. Within a half an hour every table had been occupied and the hostess had begun directing arriving patrons to tables with already-dining ones. It was one of those European customs which, while perfectly sensible from both a business and a social perspective, was still so entirely foreign to Americans as to keep Maggie slightly on edge as she waited for the inevitable question from a pair of strangers:

"Are these seats free?"

Maggie looked up at the two young women who were readying themselves to pull up seats at her table. "Of course," Maggie replied, actually relieved she was no longer dining alone. "Please sit down. And, er, hello."

"Hullo," echoed one of the women. She was thin, with fine, shoulder length blonde hair, and wearing a sleeveless yellow blouse and floral print skirt. "I'm Gwen," she announced. "Gwen Palmer. And this is Susan."

Susan had thick black hair cropped just below the ears and sported a red shirt and white trousers. She smiled a large friendly smile. "Hullo."

"Er, I'm Maggie." A distinctly non-British accent. "Nice to meet you."

"And you," Gwen replied. "Are you Canadian then, Maggie?"

"No." Now it was starting to get irritating. "American."

"Right." Gwen smiled. "And what brings you to Wales? Tourist?"

"No, actually," Maggie was glad to say. "I'm a student."

"Oh really?" Gwen looked to Susan then back again. "Here at the college?"

"Er, no. Up at the University of Aberdeen actually." Then she decided she should at least attempt to explain her presence so far south. "I'm here in Aberystwyth," she only had a small problem with the pronunciation, "doing some research for my studies."

"Brilliant!" Susan enthused. "And what are you studying then?"

"I'm studying—"

"You ladies know what you'd like?" The waitress had arrived, thoroughly oblivious to the quiet conversation she'd interrupted amid the growing din of the pub.

Gwen frowned at her menu, then asked, quite to Maggie's surprise and delight, "*Cymraeg?*"

Maggie recognized it as the Welsh word for 'Welsh.' She remembered that much from her single Welsh course—in part because it was similar enough to the Gaelic word for Welsh, namely '*Cumruis.*'

"<Of course,> replied the waitress with a casual smile. "<What would you like?>"

"<I'll have the fish and chips,>" ordered Gwen.

"<I'd like the fish and chips too,>" agreed Susan.

Maggie didn't understand a word of it. Not even anything that sounded like a cognate with Gaelic. She considered her plans for the next day. Uh-oh.

"Sorry, Maggie." Gwen returned to English. "What were you saying?

"Uh, right. I was saying that I'm studying Gaelic." She took a palpable satisfaction in this following Gwen and Susan's *Cymraeg* display.

"Are you then?" A large smile bloomed across Gwen's already pleasant visage. "How wonderful. Isn't that wonderful, Susan?"

"Oh yes," the brunette agreed. "Quite brilliant."

"But I'm afraid," Maggie continued, "that I don't know much Welsh. That was Welsh, wasn't it?"

"Ah, yes." Gwen seemed suddenly self-conscious. "That was Welsh. Sorry about that, but it's nice to use it when possible. Keep it alive and such."

Maggie nodded in understanding. Although Gaelic wasn't

her native tongue, it had been that of her Scottish ancestors. Perhaps that's why she'd excelled at the northern Gaelic languages, but had showed only minimal interest in their southern cousins, Welsh, Breton and Cornish.

"I did take a Welsh class a few years ago," Maggie offered. "Did pretty well in it, too. But I don't remember much anymore. I recognized '*Cymraeg*,'" she offered with a sheepish smile.

"Well, that's a start anyway," Gwen laughed. "And I bet your Welsh is still better than my Gaelic."

"Not likely," Maggie laughed.

"Ah well, I don't know a word of it," Gwen asserted.

"Me neither," Susan chipped in.

"Well, I suppose there's probably not much call for it around here," Maggie observed amicably. "Heck, there's not that much call for it Scotland anymore either, I'm sad to say. Except on the islands and the northwest coast."

"That is too bad," Gwen displayed a sympathetic frown. "All the more reason to keep speaking Welsh, eh, Susan?"

"Quite right," her friend replied.

"Are you both Welsh, then?" Maggie inquired.

"Gwen is," Susan replied. "But I'm actually from Man—the Isle of Man. I came here to study Celtic music and ended up learning Welsh as well."

This point was punctuated by the return of the waitress. "<Here you go,>" she announced in Welsh, transferring two plates and two pints from her tray to the table. Then, spotting Maggie's half-finished glass, she asked, in English, "Another pint, love?"

Maggie considered it—the beer was quite good—but decided to let the others catch up. "No thanks. I'm still working on this one."

The waitress smiled, then returned to the ever thickening

crowd.

Looking out into the crowd after the waitress, Gwen appraised first the game alcove, then her fish and chips. She turned to the American. "Do you play darts, Maggie?"

"Darts?" She hadn't expected that. "Er. I don't know. I suppose I've played them before, but—"

"Are you up for a game?" Gwen stood and lifted both her plate and her glass. Susan followed suit and both looked askance to Maggie. "There's a board open," Gwen explained, "and we can set our food on the counter there. What do you say?"

"Eh..." Maggie started.

"Winner buys the next round," Gwen offered.

"The winner, eh?" Maggie confirmed. She stood up and grabbed her glass. "In that case I'll be happy to play. There's no chance I'll win, and I can hardly turn down a free drink."

The three walked over to the one open dart board and Susan fetched the darts for them.

"So now, the point of this game," Maggie quipped over her beer, "is to throw the darts into the dartboard, right?"

Both Brits chuckled at this. "That is it, roughly," Gwen confirmed. Then she took a dart from Susan and sent it sailing not a centimeter from the bull's eye. "But there are some finer points."

"I see," Maggie replied, duly impressed. "And I just want to confirm: winner buys the drinks?"

"Well," Gwen started, "perhaps it should be loser buys the round, eh, Susan?"

"Oh, no," Maggie protested. "No bait-and-switches. You got me out of my chair on the promise of a free beer."

"And friendly competition as well?" Gwen raised an eyebrow and a dart.

"And friendly competition," Maggie acquiesced. She took a

proffered dart and weighed it in her hand and she squinted at the unfamiliar dartboard too far away. "Although I'm not sure how competitive I'll be. Let's keep the emphasis on 'friendly.'"

Gwen bounced her dart in her hand and leveled an intense glare at the dartboard. A dark smile hardened onto her face. "We'll see."

"Uh-oh," Susan laughed. "Gwen's into it. We may be here all night, Maggie."

Maggie smiled and thought of the other plans she hadn't made that night. "All right with me."

And it had been all right after all. Although normally a hopeless perfectionist at heart, Maggie knew she had no chance in this particular event and so was able to let go and just enjoy herself. Which turned out to be for the best. Gwen had won every game but one, and that one had been won narrowly by Susan. Maggie, for her part, had finished third—and last—in every game. But she was improving with each round. She was now hitting the dartboard with most of her tosses, a marked improvement from the first game when she had eschewed the colored corkboard for the large white wall behind it. Still, even after a few rounds, the darts which did strike the dartboard had an annoying habit of rooting into areas worth only five or ten points, while Gwen, and to a lesser extent Susan, had trained their projectiles to seek out the twenty-point row, and in particular those sections of the row worth double and triple points.

Oh well, Maggie thought as her last dart of the sixth game struck just outside the circle—next to the five-point row. She'd given it a good try. But it was getting late and she'd already had too much to drink. Time to head back to the hotel.

"Oh, come on, Mags," Gwen protested, appearing a bit tipsy herself from the rounds she'd been purchasing. "One more game. I'll even teach you a trick."

Maggie found herself intrigued. "A trick, eh?"

"Yes, a trick." Gwen looked sideways shiftily, then draped a secretive arm over Maggie's shoulder. She handed the American a dart. "It's not the dart," she explained. "It's the dart player."

Zen and the art of pub darts, Maggie thought as she tried not to laugh. "Okay..."

"You see, Maggie Devereaux," the confiding half-whisper continued. Susan leaned against her stool and waited patiently. "Most people think you have to learn how to throw a dart."

"But you don't?" Maggie deduced, fully amused.

"No." Gwen shook her head slowly. "You already know how to throw a dart."

"I do?" Maggie looked at the freshly perforated wall behind the dartboard. "I'm not so sure..."

"What you have to do," Gwen explained further, "is access the skills you already have and harness them for darts."

Now that seemed almost coherent. "How's that again?" Maggie asked, suddenly truly interested.

"Well, you see." Gwen released Maggie's shoulder and rolled a dart in her hand. "There's not much point in learning how to throw a dart. Not much practical in it. It's not what they call a 'transferable skill.'"

Maggie laughed and imagined the want-ad: 'High Tech worker sought. Dart players encouraged to apply.'

"It's better, therefore," Gwen continued, "to find something you already know how to do and transfer that to darts." Gwen looked at her expectantly.

Maggie thought for a moment. "I know how to speak Gaelic," she offered. *Not helpful*, she thought, *but true.*

"Hmm," Gwen frowned. "That is a good thing, but it likely

won't transfer easily to darts. No, think of something you've used to move an object through the air."

Maggie's eyes widened involuntarily as she remembered the ancient Gaelic words. '*Bhaitit inh chaoimraighanh...*' She could see the Dark Book floating up to her hands. Maybe the Gaelic could help after all...

"And use that," Gwen smiled, almost knowingly, "to guide the dart home."

Maggie took the dart and Gwen stepped back, leaving Maggie to stare at the dartboard some three meters away. She turned the dart slowly in her hand. It made sense. If she could levitate a book, or a ballpoint pen, surely she could guide a thrown dart into the bull's eye. And she could probably do it without actually uttering the spell aloud. Her control of the magic had been getting stronger. If she just adjusted the spell slightly...

She looked over to Gwen. Then to Susan. Then to the dartboard, and to Gwen again. Gwen nodded, then her soft smile melted and an urgent seriousness seized her visage. "Go on, Maggie," she whispered.

Maggie stared again at the dartboard, spinning the dart deftly in her hand. She narrowed her eyes and nodded her head in decision. Then she hurled the dart toward the bull's eye.

"Five!" shouted Susan with a laugh. "Too bad, Maggie."

"Oh, darn." Maggie shrugged good-naturedly and turned back to her companions. There was no way in hell she was going to use the magic in a crowded bar, no matter how many pints she'd had. "I guess I'll have to keep working on it."

Gwen laughed too, lightly, and stepped over to slap Maggie gently on the back. "Oh, well. Don't worry though, Maggie. I know you have it in you."

Maggie thanked her new found friends and then finally

excused herself for the evening, leaving a few pounds for her dinner, and parting with Gwen and Susan amid earnest promises to maybe run into each other some time. As the door to the outside closed and Maggie Devereaux passed the row of windows on her way back to her hotel, Susan MacGowell turned to her companion and asked solemnly, "So, what do you think?"

Gwen Palmer paused for only a moment before answering. "Definitely."

26. Too Damned Late

The pen flew several inches wide of the poorly sketched bull's-eye taped to the wall, flying up and over the desk and striking the hotel room wall in a clatter of plastic and failure.

"Definitely," Maggie observed to herself, "a good thing I didn't try that at the pub."

The levitation spell had successfully attached to the thrown writing instrument, but rather than guiding it home to its target, the spell had quite noticeably altered the projectile's trajectory upwards, as if jerked on a string. That might have been difficult to explain to Gwen and Susan.

Maggie stepped over and picked the pen up off the floor.

"<Break the bonds...>," she whispered in her Old Gaelic dialect, and the pen floated effortlessly from her hands. With some concentration she guided it slowly over to the desktop and brought it to rest next to the bull's eye pad. Then she yawned. Time for bed.

She'd been tired when she'd gotten back to the hotel, but she'd had to try the dart trick at least once, just to see if it would work. That having been ascertained—no, it wouldn't—she was now ready to put the day behind her and get some shuteye. The morning's traveling and the afternoon's walking had settled on her like a heavy overcoat. She felt lucky to have the energy to brush her teeth before climbing between the covers.

The bed was even more comfortable than she could have hoped for. She let her thoughts drift over the happenings of her day. She was beginning to lose control of the images as her mind succumbed to sleep. Somewhere in the Aberystwyth night a car alarm went off. Not too near and not for too long before its owner disengaged it, but it was just enough to pull Maggie momentarily back from the transom of dreams. She rolled over, pulling the sheets to her chin, and murmured in her sleep, "No, I don't speak Welsh."

***

'A is for Alba.'

'B is for Breizh.'

'C is for Cymru.'

The alphabet border wrapped itself importantly around the top of the deserted classroom, over the green slate chalkboard, down the side wall, across the rear wall behind her, and back again, repeating its liturgy every 26 characters. The institutional clock over the door set the time at 3:46 and Maggie found herself alone in the small schoolhouse.

The combination chair/desk she was seated at was also small, too small really for a highschooler, and her knees pressed uncomfortably against the underside of the writing board. Atop it rested a thick, edgeworn, ugly textbook, laying open and staring up at Maggie as she hunched over uneasily in the miniature chair. Her foot bounced nervously, driving her knee into the desktop and sending the entire desk-chair into creaking convulsions. This caused the finely printed words in the desk book to blur, further slowing her reading, which succeeded in making her that much more anxious, in turn driving the foot and leg to bounce even more intensely. The school day had already ended. And she still had so much to learn.

"You'll never finish in time."

Maggie looked up to cast an angry eye at her mother. She stood just a few feet away, just in front of the large, boxy teacher's desk. Her flowered dress was now accompanied by a simple white cardigan sweater and she held her hands casually folded in front of her. "Why bother?"

Maggie glanced at the clock again. 3:59. "There's still time," she insisted.

"No, Maggie." Her mother took a step forward. "It's too late."

Maggie's brow furrowed, sending a deep crease up her young forehead. She gazed down again at the textbook. Its words seemed even smaller, each page a collection of four columns of illegible fine print. She was ready to turn the page, but she couldn't move her arms; they were pinned beneath the small desk, jammed between her legs and the underside of the wooden writing surface. Fully trapped, she looked up again at her mother.

"There's still time," she repeated, but her voice belied even her own doubts. "I just need a little more time."

Her mother stepped forward and lifted Maggie's chin with her hand. "No," she whispered. "It's too late."

Maggie's face crimped again as her eyes looked first to the textbook then again to her mother. "There's so much to learn," she lamented. "I just need a little more time."

Maggie's mother smiled and nodded, then opened her mouth to reply. But rather than words, thick red-black blood oozed from her parted lips. She dropped her hand from Maggie's chin and her eyes rolled up into her skull even as her body stiffened with an upward jerk and a faint, gurgled squeak. Maggie could hear the skin split and the flesh tear as her mother's face and neck were ripped down the middle, spilling blood and bile onto her desk and textbook. The fissure tore down the length of her mother's body, staining the sweater crimson and blotting out the flowers with pitch. Blood sprayed from the resultant cavity and Maggie, trapped in the school desk, could only watch in helpless horror as the dress followed its owner in shredded bifurcation—and from within the gory husk emerged a scarlet skinned demon, long ragged horns curling evilly from its forehead, uneven yellow fangs pushing from its mouth, and rippling steel-cable muscles exploding from its gore-soaked chest and arms.

"NO!" it shouted into Maggie's face and soul, its breath caustic with her mother's blood. "IT'S TOO LATE!!"

Maggie wanted to scream but she could find no wind to do so. Instead she fought for breath as she sat upright, sweat-soaked, in her hotel bed.

"Ho— Holy hell," she finally managed to say, one hand clawing at her chest for air, the other covering her mouth in horror.

She knew it had only been a dream, but the vividness of the nightmare lingered despite the onset of consciousness. She could still smell the blood. Her mother's blood.

She threw back the covers and stumbled weakly to the window, quickly parting the shades and opening the pane. The fresh air cooled her sweaty body as she looked out over Cardigan Bay. The morning sun was shining off the water and she could hear birds in the distance. The air was sweet with the scent of saltwater and breakfast.

"I think I'm gonna be sick," she managed to say and ran to the bathroom.

27. Xqrjl h'Gyuxvwwlyi Qxq

Climbing the hill from her hotel to the library, the summer sun caressing her back and neck, Maggie questioned the wisdom of having skipped breakfast. Normally a 'breakfast-is-the-most-important-meal-of-the-day' sort of person, Maggie had nevertheless passed on any food that morning, the stench of the nightmare still fresh in her nostrils. But now that her body was being asked to actually do something, the dull, easily enough ignored void which had filled her stomach had been replaced with a sharp nausea which both punished her for having not eaten and dared her to try now without vomiting. She halted her ascent to catch her breath— and to let the nausea subside.

Looking around she noticed that she was standing across the street from Bronglais Hospital. She also noticed that the clinic appeared to be roughly halfway up the steep hill from the Old College by the harbor to the Penglais campus, where stood the residence halls. She wondered how many of the hospitals patients were exhausted students who had stupidly skipped breakfast that morning.

She then turned back whence she'd come and caught a glimpse of the sun's glimmer off the waves of the harbor. A grin escaped onto her face and she inhaled deeply. Aberystwyth was undeniably beautiful from this vantage point. And the nausea had finally passed, leaving behind a decidedly more polite request for food. Or at least coffee. Maggie looked up the hill and considered the near certainty that Prof. Hamilton had in fact not faxed any permission letter to the library. That should only take a minute or so to confirm. Then she could grab a bite to eat, maybe at the library's café, while she considered what her next step would be.

And speaking of next steps, she thought with a pained smirk, then lifted her foot and renewed her assault on Mount Aberystwyth.

The confines of the library were a cool and welcome relief after the sunny climb. Maggie eyed the computer terminals suspiciously as she crossed the lobby to the circulation desk. Just a minute to confirm no letter from Edinburgh, then off to breakfast. She wondered whether the Dragon Rampant served eggs.

"Good morning, miss." It was the same woman as yesterday.

"Good morning." Maggie smiled, still somewhat hopeful, but undeniably realistic about her chances. "I was here yesterday afternoon and I wanted to look at the historical manuscripts. You said, that is, um, I'm a student at the University of Aberdeen and you said if I could get a letter from a professor...?" Not terribly coherent, but adequate.

"Right, right." The librarian remembered their conversation. "You were going to call someone, I believe?"

"Er, yeah." An embarrassed frown cramped Maggie's lips. "I ended up having to leave a message. So I don't know if anything got sent. But I asked them to fax it here."

The librarian nodded understandingly. "Well, then, let's take a look, shall we?"

She crossed over to a fax machine half-hidden behind a file

cabinet and cubicle partition and began sifting through the pages which had recently been spat out by the apparatus.

"University of Aberdeen, you said?"

"Yes, but—" She didn't get the chance to explain about Hamilton and Edinburgh.

"Here we are," the woman announced and returned with a single sheet. Maggie was stunned. "From a Professor MacKenzie?"

Maggie was stunned. *MacKenzie?* she thought, thoroughly puzzled. "But I don't know any—" But she stopped herself just in time to avoid endangering her access to the manuscripts. She didn't know who Prof. MacKenzie was, but he had just given her the key to the manuscript room. "That is, I don't know how to thank you." *Pretty good save,* she thought.

"Not at all," the woman replied, but Maggie was already examining the page in her hand. It was on University of Aberdeen letterhead and addressed, as she had asked, to the 'National Library of Wales, Circulation Desk.'

Dear Sir or Madam:

This letter is meant to confirm that Margaret C. Devereaux is a doctoral student in good standing at the University of Aberdeen, Scotland. Accordingly, we would respectfully request that she be given full access to any and all materials which such status entitles her.

Sincerely,

Prof. S. MacKenzie, Ph.D.

Department of Celtic

Well, I'll be damned. A bemused smile lit Maggie's face. But who the hell is S. MacKenzie?

"Miss?" The librarian's voice pulled Maggie back to her surroundings. "Is everything in order?"

"Er, yes," Maggie replied. "Yes. Quite in order."

"Well, then," the woman opened a drawer in the counter and extracted a key. "Here is the key to the manuscript collection. It's on the fourth floor, up the lift then around the bend and at the end of the hallway."

"Thank you." Maggie took the key gladly. Then she glanced down at the fax from the mysterious Prof. MacKenzie. "Can I get a copy of this? You know, just for my records?"

"I don't see why not," replied the librarian, and within a few moments, Maggie was strolling down the hall, key in one hand and eyes perusing the surprising letter. She had forgotten entirely about breakfast.

At the far end of the hallway stood a rather nicely painted burgundy door with a rather nice black and white sign that read, simply enough, '*Manuscripts.*' Maggie inserted the key into the doorknob and popped the door open.

Inside was a pristine and very comfortable modern chamber, some twenty feet wide and twice as deep. An institutionally patterned beige carpet blanketed the floor beneath a score of extremely solid looking black metal bookcases, all spaced well apart from one another. Several tables and chairs, all in a lightly stained pine, spread out ahead of her in front of the windows and across a sort of lobby formed between the nearest end of the bookshelves and the door. To her right was a row of half a dozen microfiche machines and an equal number of computer terminals. To her left were study carrels next to a wall of windows, all sporting a microfiber shade which filtered the potentially damaging sunlight without blocking it out altogether. Additional lighting was provided by attractively modern chandeliers, gold and wood half-spheres spaced evenly across the whitewashed ceiling. A central air system hummed quietly overhead and kept the room at a comfortable coolness. Almost too cool for Maggie who had worn another light summer dress and sandals for another sunny late July day. But her joy at her unexpected access to the manuscript collection more than warmed her inquisitive little self. She swung off her backpack, heavy with the Dark Book, and set it on the table nearest the door, then she pulled from a zippered pocket the slip of paper from yesterday—the one with the manuscript's call number— and dove between the shelves.

Her first order of business was not locating the manuscript. Rather it was to ascertain whether anyone else was in the room. She followed the hum of the central air down the length of the middle of three long corridors formed by the rows of bookcases. Then she doubled back around, circling and crisscrossing where possible to confirm she was alone. Having worked her way back to her backpack, she was satisfied she had the room to herself. The coast was clear.

Now to fetch the manuscript. According to the neat plastic signs at the end of each row of bookshelves, her quarry awaited her down the far right aisle. Call number temporarily memorized, and eyes scanning the texts on the shelves, she walked slowly, but purposefully toward the Welsh Book of Souls. When she reached the location where the manuscript should have been, she looked up on the shelf and shook her head in disbelief. It was actually there.

She pulled the manuscript from the shelf, or more correctly stated, she pulled form the shelf the protective box which housed the manuscript. A sturdy cardboard, it had affixed to it blue plastic tape with white letters spelling out 'Y Llyfr Cymraeg Gwyffyn / The Welsh Book of Souls.' Maggie pulled open the box and peered inside, both seeing and smelling the ancient text. *Jackpot*, she thought.

She hurried back to her table. She wasn't thrilled about sitting so close to the door where anyone, or almost anyone, could just walk in while she was doing what she was about to do. But it was the best place to sit, and she too would be able to see if someone came in. And stop.

She carefully extracted the bound manuscript from its protective shell and set the box neatly at the far corner of the large table. Then she set the true goal of her search before her and smiled—a happy, relieved, nervous smile.

The book itself was beautiful. Its cover was red and simple; no raised latticework to speak of. The leather had peeled away slightly from the lower right corner, exposing the thin wood beneath. Not surprising for a book nearly a thousand years old. Upon the cover stood the title, ornately worked into the leather, almost all of its gold-leafing lost over the centuries: *Y Llyfr Cymraeg Gwyffyn.*

Maggie was delighted because she simply adored the smell and feel and wonder of old books. She was relieved because she'd actually gained access to the book that morning despite her certainty that she would not. And she was nervous because she knew it would come to this. She turned the cover and stared down at the first, ornately scripted page, filled with the ancient Welsh words.

And Maggie had absolutely no idea what they meant.

If she couldn't understand Modern Welsh—and she couldn't—then there was no way in hell she was going to understand Old Welsh.

Well, almost no way in hell.

The modified levitation spell on the ballpoint pen hadn't been the only new spell she'd crafted from the building blocks of the already memorized catalogue of black magic hidden within her Dark Book. It was simply the only one she'd actually tried. But there was more than enough raw material in the black ink scrawlings of the spellbook to cobble together a second spell. A spell of understanding. Of translation.

She had been struck, when she'd first completed her translation of the Dark Book, by how similar its spells were to feats accomplished routinely by modern science. Levitation, like floating magnetic monorails above the crowded streets of Tokyo. Divination, not unlike the work of DNA experts in murder investigations, identifying who was where by clues left behind. And transmutation, the dream of the alchemists, realized the conversion of hydrogen to helium, and a whole lot of energy, in the yet to be perfected nuclear fusion fuel-cells. Indeed it was this last example that had seized her imagination.

Cold fusion was probably still several decades off, but it was today's dream, and if the last fifty years or so had proved anything, it was that the gulf between science fiction and household appliances was simply one of time. Talking computers, orbiting space stations, and of course, that most vital of interstellar necessities—from Captain Kirk to Ford Prefect—the universal translator.

Not really a huge science fiction fan, still Maggie had seen and read her share. And it had always irritated her to a nearly irrational degree, how easily people from different nations, planets and galaxies were always able to communicate, as if English, not even the most spoken language on Earth, were somehow the accepted lingua franca of the entire universe, save the planet Klingon. She knew that it would be nearly impossible to craft a compelling story if none of the characters could communicate, but as someone who had spent literally years of her life in libraries and classrooms memorizing vocabulary lists, verb conjugations, noun declensions and adjectival inflections, it had always angered her that no spaceship ever seemed to have a 'Languages Officer' who could beam down to the planet with the away team, standing proudly next to her captain, ready to perform the most essential function of any sentient species: communication. But apparently that wouldn't be interesting enough. Instead the solution of cheap gadgetry had been adopted, with some cheezy-looking device or other, dutifully labeled 'universal translator,' forever replacing the scintillating adventures of Star Linguist Commander Margaret Devereaux.

But what really bothered her was that, despite the easy out such a device would provide those wishing to avoid the issue of language differences, it was nevertheless based at least somewhat on reality—a hallmark of good science fiction—and might therefore, someday, actually work. So she had had to admit, with begrudging irritation, that this dream of speculative fiction, this 'universal translator,' might actually prove to be the solution to the very real language barrier which she knew would lay, concrete like, between her and her comprehension of the Welsh Book of Souls.

Languages are not word-for-word translations of each other. 'It's a language,' her high school German teacher had always said, 'not a code system.' Indeed, the United States military had successfully used the Navajo language as an uncrackable 'code' during World War II precisely because it was not a code. Concepts and ideas and thoughts and wants and emotions can be expressed in any number of ways, so a simple word-for-word translation system could never work. But all languages, spoken or written or signed, function on the same basic principle: some external stimuli—a series of spoken sounds, letters or characters on a page, a flurry of gestures—being received by one or more of the sensory organs and passed onto the language recognition center of the brain, where the stimuli is converted from what it is to what is meant by it. From sounds to ideas, from letters to concepts, from gestures to emotions. From the communicative convention to the idea that convention symbolizes.

'Smoonyakh' is nonsense to an English speaker because her brain has never learned—through immersion or study—that that particular combination of sounds holds any meaning beyond the mere sound of it. But the brain of a Gaelic speaker from Scotland's Western Isles would immediately recognize it as the concept the English speaker labels as 'think.' And when the Gaelic speaker hears the question, '*Dè a tha thu a' smaoineachadh?*' the same synapses fire in his brain as those in the German speaker's when he hears, '*Was meinst Du?*' or the English speaker hears, 'What do you think?'

Learning a language—really learning it—is the effort, sometimes Herculean, to get one's brain to fire its synapses in response to the sounds and sights of the target language in the same way it already does to the sounds and sights of the native one. The tools include study, repetition, grammar, memorization, and immersion, to name just a few.

Not 'universal translators.'

But what if a device really could be constructed which artificially stimulated the appropriate synapses in the appropriate order? Not unlike the stereo speaker that mimics the sounds of the actual orchestra?

And what if Maggie could cast a spell that did the same?

She was about to find out.

Of course she knew there was no small danger in this. She hadn't yet directed the dark magic against herself. And the thought of allowing the magic direct access to her brain filled her with a healthy dose of concern. On the other hand, the dark magic already had gained at least some access to her mind, as evidenced by the nightmares she endured after each use of it. But more importantly, there was the child.

She'd not forgotten the purpose of her detour to Wales. The

trip to Ireland had enjoyed dual goals. When she'd heard from Hamilton about the Old Gaelic exhibition she had of course wondered how it might relate to her dark dialect and the kidnapped child next to whose crib words of that dialect had been scrawled in blood. But it had been the promise of the white magic—of healing spells and the connection to her great-times-ten-grandmother, the Healer—that had converted a questionable whim into a ferry ticket and hotel reservation.

But the trip to Wales held a single purpose. The stone carving from Ballincoomer Abbey had listed three events: 'the banshee shall return to claim her legacy,' 'the magic of the Celts shall be reignited,' and 'infantsblood shall be spilt onto ancestral earth.' It was this last event which she had found particularly distressing. Hence the trip to Aberystwyth, in search of more details surrounding this prophecy, to confirm whether it was the prophecy mentioned, in English, on the wall behind the empty MacLeod crib—and if it was, whether she could do anything to stop it. Because even adrift in an ocean of uncertainties, Maggie was sure of one thing: the police had no idea about the Welsh Book of Souls. She suspected that once Prof. Hamilton had provided his expert opinion that the bloody words on the floor were nothing more than gibberish, Sgt. Warwick and the rest of the Aberdeen P.D. had likely given no more thought to the scrawlings, other than perhaps D.N.A. analysis of the blood to confirm it was the boy's.

All of which left Maggie as the only one pursuing the linguistic clue left behind by the kidnapper.

Space Commander Devereaux reporting for duty.

So Maggie had two choices: find someone who could translate the Welsh Book of Souls for her, or learn Old Welsh herself in the span of a single day. But the former option was fraught with danger; anyone who spoke the tongue might be in league with the kidnapper, and she was uncertain how her own interest might be easily explained. She still wondered whether the kidnapper, who had used her dark dialect on the floorboards of the MacLeod nursery, didn't already know about her. And if she hadn't already been certain when she arrived at the library that morning that she couldn't know whom she could trust, the unexpected letter from a hitherto unheard of 'Professor S. MacKenzie' of the University of Aberdeen had sealed it. Maggie hadn't even contacted Aberdeen; her call had been to Hamilton at Edinburgh.

Which left the latter option: learning Old Welsh in a day. And there was only one way to do that. So, as nervous as she was to try crafting an original spell to inflict on her own synapses, she needed only to remind herself of one thing: the life of a helpless child hung in the balance.

She really had no choice. The magic might be dark in origin, she told herself, but she was sure she could harness it for good. She had to. That would have to be enough.

She looked down at the manuscript. She readied herself. Then she closed her eyes and spoke the translation spell.

Her scream rebounded off the bookcases. Ten dozen ice-covered steel spikes impaled her frontal lobe, only to dissolve into liquid fire and explode along every synapse of her brain, reducing the pathways to ash. She couldn't see because her eyes had rolled up into her head. She couldn't hear because her ears were bleeding. And the only reason she didn't scream again was because she'd forgotten how.

She lay there for an indeterminate time, eyes closed and chest heaving, aware less of her surroundings than of her detachment therefrom, as the jelly of her mind slowly rebuilt itself, a jolt of electric agony accompanying every reconnected synapse.

Finally it subsided. One of her eyelids fluttered open and the eyeball rolled down to obtain an up-close view of the formica table top upon which her face was resting. Gingerly, she lifted her head and with some trepidation opened her other eye.

She was still alive. That was good.

The room was still there. That was also good.

As was the manuscript. Thrice good.

She must have shoved it to one side as she collapsed onto the table. A fortunate event, in turned out, judging by the blood which her nose and ears had deposited onto the table top. She wiped the blood from her nose with the back of her hand and fumbled in her bag for tissues to mop up the rest. Once this task was completed and she confirmed the bleeding had stopped, she shoved the wet rags into her pocket and turned her attention back to the manuscript.

She opened her parched mouth to say something—something witty to calm her nerves and dispel the last aching from her sinuses—but nothing came to mind. So instead she closed her mouth again and reached for the ancient Welsh text.

The first thing she noticed was that she couldn't see the text. She could read it, but she couldn't see it. Not in the traditional sense anyway. She couldn't see any letters on the page, but it wasn't blank either. More like a blind spot in her vision. A colorless blur where the words should have been. But when she looked there, the expected image of words was replaced with a less expected direct understanding of their meaning, ringing clearly inside her mind. Her brain was refusing to acknowledge the letters transmitted by her optic nerve, electing instead to simply skip that step and move directly to the translation of those symbols into the proper linguistic concepts. She couldn't see the letters, but she understood the words.

'Welcome, dear reader,' she understood, 'to the Welsh Book of Souls. Contained within these pages is the sum total of the knowledge of Our People.'

She could hear the English words in her mind. She supposed she heard English because even directly translated words needed some medium to manifest their meaning, and English was her mother tongue. But her Gaelic was pretty good too. Focusing on Gaelic, she reread the sentence. This time she heard the same introduction, but in Gaelic.

Hot damn. She slapped the table. It worked!

Not without side effects, however, she was compelled to notice. Being blind to the words she was reading proved to be a bit more irritating than she might have imagined. She had to put her finger on the page and follow it with her eyes, lest they inadvertently drop to the next line and begin instantly translating the words found there. It was like guiding a magnifying glass over otherwise illegible fine print. Her brain could immediately understand anything displayed to it, but it had to be presented in the right order.

Still, it worked, and once Maggie had gotten a hang of 'reading blind' she found herself sailing through the pages as easily as if she'd written them herself. The prophecy she was seeking turned out to be toward the end, but she was having so much fun 'reading' that she was in no hurry to finish. Even once she encountered her linguistic quarry she was tempted to continue reading to the very end, just because she could—but she resisted the temptation. She hadn't forgotten the purpose of the mission which had compelled her to cast the potentially dangerous spell. Slowing herself with a deep cleansing breath, she repositioned her finger and let her mind translate the invisible Old Welsh words:

'The Teutons have arrived on our Celtic Isles. Despite the assurances of our military leaders, it is foretold that they will not be defeated. Indeed the wars which shall follow shall last a thousand years,

and will end in the near destruction of the Celts. Our enlightened ways shall be supplanted by the barbarous rituals of the invaders. Magic and Nature shall fall to Sword and Axe. What was ours shall become theirs and we will risk losing what we were, the links to our past all but severed by time and defeat.

'But all hope is not lost.

'A millennia hence in tragedy shall we find victory. The blood of our descendants shall reestablish their connections to the power and magic of their Celtic forebears. The cost shall be great, but the reward greater. So is it written — so shall it come to pass.'

This preamble was then followed by the same image Maggie had seen etched in the stones of Ballincoomer Abbey: a knotwork circle. It was essentially identical to its stone cousin save that it was far more beautiful in illuminated red ink and gold foil. The circle held three points which, as near as Maggie's magic-addled mind could tell, anchored roughly the same information she had previously translated the old fashioned way — save that where the Irish stones held phrases, the Welsh pages boasted near-paragraphs:

'A woman of magic, the ban-shee, shall return from the West, alive with power and determined to reclaim her legacy.'

'Two infants, a boy and a girl, one from each of the two great clans, shall suffer their throats to be slit, their blood spilt into the earth of their earliest ancestors.'

'The magic of the Celts shall be extracted from the dust of the ancient past, its glory and power reignited in the ban-shee.'

Then beneath this, text again, exhorting simply: *'She shall return to fulfill the prophecy.'* Just like on the wall above Douglas MacLeod's empty crib, save in the third person rather than the first and the simple future rather than the present perfect.

Maggie closed her eyes — in part to rest her enchanted brain from the stimuli of the ancient words, in part to consider their meaning. After several moments she opened her eyes again, but her gaze was distant.

Two? she asked herself in no particular language.

***

Part of the problem with crafting the translation spell turned out to be, ironically enough, the very fact that she didn't know Old Welsh before casting it. Because of this gap in knowledge, she had been unable to pursue a more focused approach to understanding the manuscript. Hence the direct assault on the language recognition centers of her frontal lobe, rendering them capable of understanding anything it encountered.

An interesting side-effect—one she hadn't expected—was that Old Welsh was not the only language she could now understand instantaneously. A glance at the interior of her Dark Book resulted in the identical sensation she had had with the Old Welsh manuscript. Her eyes couldn't make out the individual words, but her mind understood them anyway, and in a purer way than even her arduously gained fluency in the Old Gaelic dialect had allowed. The same proved true for the call number signs on the bookcase ends as well as each and every title she passed on her way to returning the Welsh Book of Souls to its spot on the shelf. Blind to the words themselves, she could not possibly have identified what language they were written in—Welsh, Old Welsh, English, French, Zulu—but she understood each and every title perfectly.

The effect seemed also to spill over past visual stimuli. The simple experiment of speaking aloud confirmed that her hearing, and her aural comprehension, had been similarly affected.

She whispered, "Well done, Devereaux."

She heard nothing.

But she understood, 'Accomplished/Completed + Good/Well + Me/Self/Name.'

And so she became quite relieved that she'd decided to make the spell temporary. A lifetime of linguistic deafness seemed certain to prove annoying. She only hoped she'd succeeded as well in the temporal aspect of the enchantment as she had in the substantive.

She repeated her test phrase, this time in a normal voice, focusing on the rounded lips of the 'W' and the dental pressure of the 'D's, and working hard to form the right sounds even if she couldn't hear them. She supposed it was similar to what deaf people must do, unable to hear the sounds they produce and therefore focused on the mechanics of creating them.

Again she understood what she'd said. But again she couldn't hear her words, although the hum of the central air was fully audible.

Oh well, she thought. *Hopefully the spell will wear off soon.*

She tried not to be too worried. There wasn't anything to be done about it just yet, save waiting for the spell to wear off. And if it didn't, she could always try to craft a second spell to undo the effect—an antidote of sorts. In the meantime she could read Tolstoy in the original.

Maggie closed the door to the Old Collections behind her and confirmed it was locked. Then she sought out the stairs. Any curiosity she might have had as to what the elevator buttons might look like while the spell was active were far outweighed by her desire to minimize any human interaction until after it wasn't. She descended the four flights down to the ground floor, and headed straight for the circulation desk around the corner. As she reached the corner she considered whether she needed to vibrate her throat to make the 'TH' in 'thank you' sound like the one in 'thatch' and not the one in 'that.' She had no time to consider the 'G' in 'Gwen.'

Gwen Palmer stepped right in front of Maggie and said

something the American couldn't hear. 'Hello, Maggie,' rang inside Maggie's head.

"Eh, hello," Maggie replied as best she could.

'Do you have a cold?' Gwen asked in silent inquiry.

I must not be doing a great job of annunciating, Maggie deduced. "Yes, actually," her mouth replied precisely. "I must have stayed out too late last night." Maggie laughed lightly, relieved not to have to mimic that sound, and was even more relieved when Gwen returned the laugh.

'Are you doing some research then?' Maggie understood Gwen to ask.

"Er yes. The Old Collections." No point in denying it. "I found some interesting texts for my research."

'That's good,' Gwen nodded companionably. Maggie tried to concentrate on the woman's lips as she spoke, but Gwen kept moving her head. 'Well, look,' came next into Maggie's brain as Gwen looked away to the wall clock, 'I can't really chat. But I saw you and I wanted to say hello.'

"Okay. Great." That was a relief. "Well, good to see you, Gwen."

'Good to see you too, Maggie.' The words instantly translated in Maggie's mind as Gwen flashed a friendly smile.

Maggie nodded in reply and stepped lively toward the circulation desk. She elected just to nod and smile as she returned the key to the Old Collections. Then she made a bee-line for the door.

Gwen hadn't moved from her spot. Rather she stood glaring after Maggie as the American hurried out into the Aberystwyth late morning. And Gwen didn't break off her cold stare even as an elderly tourist woman came over to speak to her.

"What a remarkable conversation," the old woman enthused,

looking first to Gwen then to where Maggie had exited. "I've never heard anything like that before. Tell me, young lady, was that Welsh you were speaking?"

Gwen Palmer's eyes narrowed to harsh slits as they clung to the still swinging exit doors. "Yes," she hissed.

28. Marketplace of Ideas

Oh, man. Oh, man. Oh, man. Maggie hurried down the hill toward the harbor and business district. *That was close.*

She should have stayed in the Old collections room until the spell had worn off. But who knew when—or even if—that would ever happen. The shop signs she was passing were still the illegible, fully understandable blanks she'd encountered in the Welsh Book of Souls. And the lilt of the passersby mirrored that of Gwen Palmer, entirely inaudible and perfectly comprehensible. But the truth—the pathetic and pedestrian truth—was that simple hunger had forced her out of the room sooner than might have been wise. It was nearing noon and she still hadn't had a bite to eat that day. She hadn't even had any coffee to suppress the appetite which had finally asserted itself once the brilliance of her successfully cast spell had diminished the horror of the previous evening's nightmare.

Oh, well, she smiled at her deftly executed one-way conversation in the library lobby. No harm, no foul.

The next order of business, then, was breakfast. Or lunch, she supposed. Food, in any event. Perhaps a little stand or café where she could just point at a croissant and smile. Then the half-smile which clung to her lips blossomed into full grin as she glanced up at a sign approaching on her right.

'*Archfarchnad,*' it read.

And she had no idea what that meant.

She never thought she'd be glad not to be able to read a foreign language, but given the circumstances, she was ecstatic. Not only would she be able to hear her own voice again, but more importantly her home-brewed spell had turned out to be a complete success, right down to its temporary effect.

"You're a regular Samantha Stevens," she told herself. But her self congratulatory smile faded as the last syllables faded again into comprehensible silence. Glancing again at the sign, she watched with begrudging interest as the words morphed slowly from a collection of identifiable but incomprehensible Latin letters to invisible, fully understandable concepts in her mind. 'Grocery.' Then the sign morphed back to its unintelligible Welsh, the translation lingering behind in Maggie's memory. As she waited and allowed her perception of the sign to change yet again, she realized that while the spell was indeed wearing off, it was not entirely finished with her yet.

Oh, well. Maybe by the time I get to the market... She shrugged and continued on her way.

***

The market was a beehive of bilingual activity. Fruit stands jostled against craft carts against bakery wagons. Merchants hawked flower bouquets on one corner and cheeses on another. All the signs, hand-written and professionally printed alike, were in both Welsh and English, and the shouts and laughs and calls of merchant and customer were similarly a mix of the two tongues. For the most part, much to her delight, Maggie was able to appreciate all this; the translation spell had all but worn off, only the last remnants hanging on stubbornly, not unlike the sensation after a long airplane flight when one's ears haven't quite popped yet, despite several minutes already on the ground. She could tell she was only a short time from once again being completely ignorant of Welsh, and she could hardly wait.

As she milled through the crowd, she consciously focused in on the conversations swirling about her, listening to the words to see whether she could understand their meanings.

An overweight vendor in a dirty apron held a bag of potatoes aloft. "Two quid per kilo!"

A tall blond man inspected a clay pot. "*Oes coffi gyda chi?*" he asked.

A scarf-headed woman walked past, cooing to the baby in her arms. 'Hush, baby girl, hush.'

An elderly woman in a woven shawl squinted up at the sky. "Looks like rain."

The various word and phrases flowed into Maggie's ears. She couldn't see all the speakers, and amid the cacophony of ideas she couldn't distinguish between traditionally spoken English and magically translated Welsh. But eventually her eardrums popped and Maggie knew the spell had finally passed. A relieved smile on her face, she stepped up to a bakery cart with a sign reading '*Bara/Breads*' and asked, quite happy to have to do so, "Do you speak English?"

"Why of course, love," came the reply from the stout woman behind the bilingual sign. "What would you like?"

"I would like a croissant," Maggie replied, relishing in the sound of her own voice. She pointed to the largest, most buttery-looking crescent roll in the pile before her. Then she had a thought. "Actually, make it two."

A few steps away was a beautiful slate fountain, its central column rising a good ten feet into the air with clear, cool water spilling out into a large circular pool boasting a tile bottom, submerged coins, and a rim more than wide enough to be used as a bench. Although most of the stone circle was already occupied by a varied collection of market-goers and/or tourists, a few spaces still remained and Maggie quickly parked herself in the nearest opening, a cool, wet breeze on her sun-heated back, and half of the first croissant already in her mouth.

Her hunger being thus addressed, Maggie could return her attention to her morning's work—and the unexpected problem it had presented. She had been cautiously confident that the prophecy of the Welsh Book of Souls would speak to the kidnapping of a young boy, and in that, she supposed with another bite of croissant, she had been right—sort of. But the prophecy had actually spoken of two children: a boy and a girl. And to the best of her knowledge, there was no related kidnapping of a little Scottish girl. She supposed it a safe bet that a second kidnapping complete with bloody inscriptions was likely to have made the papers and the evening news. So she was left to wonder whether her trip to Wales hadn't turned out to be just a wild goose chase after all, its only benefit having been the resounding success of her translation spell.

She swallowed the last of the first croissant and bit off the first of the second.

She deduced silently, as she people-watched the market crowd, that there were two possibilities. First, the prophecy in the Welsh Book of Souls was not the prophecy referred to in the bloody inscription above Douglas MacLeod's crib, in which case she'd just wasted two days in beautiful, sunny Aberystwyth, Wales. Or second, it was the same prophecy but she just hadn't heard about the second kidnapping yet.

Another bite of croissant.

She couldn't quite believe she had the wrong prophecy. In

part, she hated to admit she might have been wrong. But moreover, it was that last sentence after the diagram in the Welsh Book of Souls. 'She will return to fulfill the prophecy,' it had said, just like on the wall above Douglas' crib. Maggie had thought at first that the bloody words might have referred to the prophecy of the return of the MacLeod Banshee. But it seemed more likely that it referred to this prophecy of kidnapping and infanticide. Which left the second alternative.

Another mouthful of roll.

'One each from the two great clans,' the prophecy had said. But which clans? Maggie wondered. The MacLeod boy was heir to the MacLeod clan, one of Scotland's ancestral aristocracy—certainly a 'great' clan in the broader sense of the word. But what of the girl from the other great clan? Which clan would that be? Again, it seemed likely that the kidnapping of the child, a daughter, of a second Scottish chieftain would have made a splash on both the front page and the evening news. But there had been no such reports.

And another bite. The last of the second croissant waited nervously in her hand.

So maybe the kidnapping just hadn't happened yet. And maybe, with proper thought, it could be avoided—if the second 'great clan' could be deduced. Assuming MacLeod was the first great clan, what made them so great? Maggie tried to remember her Scottish history. There had been a time, she recalled vaguely, when Western Scotland, primarily the Hebrides and surrounding islands, had been a sort of quasi-independent kingdom—under the romantic name 'The Lordship of the Isles'—while the remainder of Scotland was ruled from Edinburgh. Had the MacLeods been the royal family of that western duchy? And had that left the Stuarts, Scotland's ancient monarchy, in charge of the eastern half of fair

Alba?

MacLeods and Stuarts. Maybe that was it. It made a certain sense. Although Maggie couldn't help but wonder why a Welsh book of prophecies would care overmuch about the royalty of the northern Celts. Still, if that was what the prophecy meant, then the girl to be kidnapped would be a Stuart. But Maggie had most definitely not heard anything about any Stuart child being kidnapped. There was no way that wouldn't have made the news. But then she wondered something else: were there even any Stuarts left?

Hadn't the Stuart line died out after Bonnie Prince Charlie, having failed in his 1746 attempt to regain the British throne, died childless? His only sibling, Henry, was a priest and had therefore also, one could assume, died without issue. That would mean there could be no Stuarts to kidnap. So no MacLeod-Stuart pair. Hmm.

Maggie swallowed her last bite of croissant.

But then again, there must be someone now who's head of the Stuart Clan. The clan couldn't just exist without a chieftain, could it? There must be someone to raise the clan standard at the Highland Games in Braemar each year. There must be someone, somewhere, who—whether they know it or not—can trace their lineage back to some great monarchy of the second great clan.

These thoughts and more swirled in Maggie's head as she continued to people watch. Then the crowd parted somewhat and her eye caught the figure of a young woman stepping out of the butcher shop across the cobblestone square. What grabbed Maggie's attention was the abnormal—almost urgent—cock of the woman's head as she stepped up to the baby carriage she'd left outside the shop, her one hand holding aloft two small, brown paper wrapped packages, and her other reaching in no doubt to pull back the blankets beneath the pram's awning.

The woman's hand followed this innocuous motion with an agitated flurry of searching, the blankets and other coddling being pulled up and over the sides of the carriage. Then the hand retracted, cold and limp looking, as the woman began to bounce lightly on the balls of her feet. Her head jerked frantically from the pram to the butcher shop to the crowded market and finally back to the pram which Maggie knew was empty.

The nervous bouncing increased to near jumping in place and the wrapped meat fell disregarded to the cobblestones at her feet. She ran shaking hands through her long black curls and even from that distance, Maggie could see the mascara beginning to smear at the corner's of the young mother's eyes.

The woman looked again into the butcher shop, then again to the empty pram. And as the gray-black tears began to stream down her cheeks, she pulled at her sable curls, looked to the sky and screamed the pain of a mother whose baby has just been kidnapped.

For ritual sacrifice, Maggie knew. And she was off like a shot.

She darted through the crowd, scattering 'Excuse me's and 'Pardon's at the marketgoers past whom she desperately clawed. The young mother's sobs trailed after Maggie as she headed back the way she'd come. She wanted to help the heartbroken woman, but knew any aid she could offer would come not from consoling the woman beside her empty pram, but rather from retracing her own steps from when she had entered the market. For she knew two other things as well. First, she'd found the right prophecy. And second, she had seen the kidnapper with the child.

'Two infants ... one from each of the two great clans...'

Stupid translation spell, Maggie cursed to herself as she craned her neck to try to catch some glimpse of the scarf-headed kidnapper. The spell had succeeded in translating the unknown words into understandable concepts, but then her brain had insisted on relabelling these concepts in a language she knew. But concepts are ambiguous, whereas words are not—or at least are less so. So when confronted with an Old Welsh word consistent with the concept for 'family,' her brain had looked perhaps first to the English 'family,' then perhaps to the Gaelic equivalent '*clann*,' and opted finally for the compromise word, 'clan,' an English word borrowed from the Gaelic. Cognates and circular labeling had led to a mistranslation.

Not 'two great clans,' Maggie realized as she reached the edge of the marketplace, 'two great families.'

North and South. Gadelic and Brittonic. Scottish and Welsh. MacLeod and whatever Welsh surname the little girl who'd just been kidnapped bore.

Maggie scanned the horizon in vain for any sight of the woman who'd brushed past her on her way out of the marketplace. No sign of her. Maggie felt sick to her stomach, aware that the translation spell had been doubly flawed.

In the staticky flicker of the fading spell, Maggie had failed to notice that she hadn't actually heard the words uttered by the scarf headed kidnapper—she had simply understood them. They could have been in English; they could have been in Welsh. They could have been in her lost dialect of Old Gaelic. Maggie would never know.

A final scan of the area confirmed that the kidnapper was gone. She'd vanished. And the infant girl with her.

'She shall return to fulfill the prophecy.'

Maggie's soft faced hardened into a determined scowl. The prophecy shall not be fulfilled, she swore to herself, and headed back into the crowd.

Marching back to the butcher shop proved considerably easier than running out of it, in part because she'd shed the urgency to push past people, and in part because the mass of people had begun to thin. While misery loves company, the feeling is rarely mutual, especially when the misery is a stranger's and offering comfort might mean getting involved. But while Maggie might not be able to offer much comfort, she could offer something perhaps more valuable: information. Information which might prove to be the only lead to catching whomever stole the poor mother's baby. The woman could take it or leave it, but Maggie couldn't keep what she knew—however incredible—to herself. If the woman thought Maggie was crazy, then fine—Maggie could just leave, no harm done. It wasn't like she would be relaying her fantastic story to the police or anyone like that.

The crowd was even thinner back by the butcher shop. A crusty half-ring of gawkers had solidified some fifteen to twenty feet away from the still weeping woman. She sat alone on the stone steps of the shop, her head in her hands and her back rising and falling sharply in hyperventilating sobs. Her black hair hung over bony knees which were pulled up and bent in to meet each other above pigeon-toed feet. The packaged meat lay discarded in its original landing spot near the pram, tragically empty among its numerous blankets. Eyeing the uncaring crowd disapprovingly, Maggie pushed through their number and walked up to the crying woman.

"Miss?" Maggie bent over and set a gentle hand on the woman's back. "Miss?"

The young woman looked up with a start but with less surprise than Maggie would have expected. Her red-rimmed eyes and gray streaked cheeks displayed a visage apparently numb with grief.

Maggie sat down next to her on the step. "I think," she began simply enough, "I may have some information about who took your baby."

Just then a strong hand from above gripped Maggie's shoulder. She looked up and around, the surprise on her own face not at all hidden.

"Have you then?" asked the large policeman towering over her. "And who the hell are you?"

29. Just the Facts, Mag

"Good Morning, Miss Devereaux."

Sgt. Jeremy Llewellyn's voice was taut and angry as he paced restlessly before the table Maggie was seated at. His inhospitable demeanor matched perfectly with the intimidating stone walls of the Aberystwyth Police Department's interrogation room.

"Good morning," Maggie replied, rather coolly, she thought, considering the circumstances.

The room was small, with four cinderblock walls painted a sickening shade of green. A large metal door, painted an equally unpleasant blue loomed to Maggie's right, while opposite the door was a long, horizontal mirror that reflected Maggie, the police officer looming across the table from her, and the second officer seated in a pink plastic chair in the far corner.

"Thank you for agreeing to meet with us." Officer Jessica Kernough said from her seat in the corner. She was an attractive woman in her late twenties, with shoulder length, strawberry blond hair and feminine curves suppressed beneath her bullet-proof vest and black police uniform.

Llewellyn was considerably less attractive. He was tall and

thin, with needle-like features, small teeth and an unpleasant squiggle of brown hair atop his long head. His chest was incongruously thick, shrinking quickly to a narrow waist and long, spindly legs.

"Well then, Miss Devereaux." Llewellyn stopped in front of her and leaned onto the table. "Let's get to it, shall we?"

Maggie nodded cautiously. "All right."

"You told Officer Bradley," he peered down at her over his long, pointy nose, "that you had information regarding the kidnapping of the Owen girl."

"Actually," Maggie disagreed, "I never told the officer that."

Llewellyn straightened up at this. "You didn't?"

"No." Maggie knew this was splitting hairs, was a bit silly, and was probably just going to antagonize them. "I told Ms. Owen that." But she had to buy herself some time to think.

Llewellyn pursed his lips with a clicking, puckering noise. He looked to Kernough, but she just smiled and nodded him back to work. Turning again to his subject, he flared his nostrils, then proceeded. "Miss Owen, then," he corrected. "A single mother by the way. Which is unfortunate."

Depends on who the father was, Maggie opined to herself.

"In any event," Llewellyn pressed on, "would you agree then that you told Miss Owen—in the presence of Officer Bradley—that you had information regarding the kidnapping of her daughter?"

Maggie shifted uneasily in her chair. It was one thing to try to console a heartbroken mother with a little information—however sketchy, unbelievable, or carefully edited—to give her some hope that her child might be found. It was quite another to tell the police that the child had been kidnapped to be sacrificed to a dark Celtic god in the hopes it might rekindle an ancient magic—a magic which works, by the way—to aid in driving the English from the British

Isles.

"Something like that," she admitted. Reluctantly.

"'Something like that?!'" Llewellyn kicked the table sending it spinning at once toward and away from Maggie, careening to her left and leaving her quite exposed to the angry policeman. "What the bloody hell does that mean?! Either you have information or you don't! If you don't, then why did you approach the Owen woman? And if you do, why won't you tell us?"

He stepped right up to her and lowered his voice to a growl. "What are you hiding?"

Maggie looked up at the police man with knitted brows. She didn't need this. And she was pretty sure she didn't deserve it either. Llewellyn was staring down at her, his chest beginning to heave and red blotches crawling up over his jaw. A short fuse apparently. Uncertain how to reply, Maggie looked over to Officer Kernough for help. Somewhat to her surprise, she got it.

"Calm down, Jeremy," Kernough counseled with a graceful wave of her hand. She stood up slowly and crossed over to Maggie's table as she offered, "Don't mind him too much, Maggie. He takes his job quite seriously." Kernough smiled—a warm generous smile, with burgundy lips and perfectly even, white teeth. "But we all do, don't we?"

Maggie nodded. "Sure."

"And our job," Kernough pointed to herself and her partner, "is to find whoever took Ms. Owen's baby and bring them to justice." She half-sat on the edge of the askew table to Maggie's left, even as Llewellyn slunk away into an impatient pacing. "But do you know what else our job is, Maggie? Even more important than that?"

Maggie's knitted brow creased in contemplation. "What?"

"To find Ms. Owen's baby," Kernough tilted her head softly,

sending her thick hair gently swinging, "and bring her home safe."

Maggie nodded and smiled weakly. She was starting to relax a bit. "Right," she offered. "Of course."

"You can help, can't you, Maggie?" The head tilted back, pulling the strawberry tresses with it. "You want to help, don't you?"

Maggie's face betrayed her unique dilemma. "Yes," she said. *But you won't believe me*, she thought.

"So help us, Maggie. Help us bring little Holly Owen home to her mother safe and sound." The reassuring smile faded just the right amount to communicate the seriousness of the request. "Whatever it is you know, Maggie, tell us. Please."

Maggie thought for a moment, brow still creased and mouth pulled tightly shut. Llewellyn had stopped his pacing and stood scowling expectantly at her. Kernough leaned in just slightly, still smiling. Maggie liked her perfume.

"Well, I—" Maggie began with a glance to both Llewellyn and Kernough. Then she decided to just speak to Kernough. The Good Cop, Maggie was well aware. But better than talking to the bad one. And clichéd police tactics or no, Kernough had a point—to a point. "I think I may have seen the person who did it."

Kernough gave an exaggerated, but satisfied nod. Llewellyn provided an impatient "Hmmph" and resumed his pacing.

"And what did this person look like?" Kernough inquired casually yet professionally.

A frown pulled at one side of Maggie's face. "Well, I didn't get that great a look at her really. She was walking past me." The frown spread to the other side of her visage. "She had a scarf on her head and was wearing sunglasses."

"Oh, bloody helpful, that," Llewellyn grumbled under his breath without breaking stride.

Ignoring him, Maggie pressed on. "She was carrying a baby girl and walking away from where the baby carriage was."

"Okay," Kernough nodded as she pouted in contemplation. "What color was the scarf, if you remember?"

"Er..." Maggie replayed the vignette in her head. "Red, maybe? Or pink. I think." Another frown. "I guess I'm not totally sure."

Another "Hmmph" from across the interrogation room.

"All right." Kernough gave another patient nod, her hair bouncing pleasantly. "Did you notice anything else about her appearance? Her clothing? Any marks on her face?"

Maggie concentrated for several seconds. It had happened so quickly. "No, not really. I wasn't really paying that much attention. I mean, I didn't realize I'd be here talking with you."

"Of course, of course," Kernough started with another reassuring, hair-bouncing nod. But Llewellyn interrupted.

"I've a question for you, lass," he fairly shouted as he stepped back up to Maggie's chair. "How'd you know the baby was a girl?"

Maggie blinked up at the imposing police man, her brown eyes wide behind her glasses. *Wow,* she thought. *Now that is a good question.*

And one that struck at the heart of her dilemma. Kernough was right: she did want to help. But the problem lay in the inescapable fact that if she told them the entire truth, they'd think she was an absolute loon. Not only would she run the risk, however small, of being locked up in a mental institution, but any truly helpful information she did have would likely be completely discounted as the ravings of a madwoman.

"Well, er..." she used to buy herself a moment.

On the other hand—the devil to the nut-house's deep blue

sea—if she strayed too far from the truth, she ran the risk of unintentionally misleading the investigation, sending the officers down a primrose path of unjustified and inaccurate deductions. A good example was now staring her right in the face—along with Llewellyn's reddening expression and Kernough's encouraging visage. All she had to do to confirm that the baby she'd seen was in fact a girl was to tell them that she heard the woman say, "Hush, baby girl." But she would also simultaneously mislead—perhaps— the police into concluding that the kidnapper was speaking English, when in fact, not only might she not have been, but properly identifying which language the woman was speaking could prove crucial to the investigation. If it had been Welsh rather than English, then that fact alone would narrow the list of potential suspects from the approximately one billion English speakers worldwide to the somewhat smaller number of 500,000 Welsh speakers—only 250,000 of whom, Maggie supposed, were women.

So she could claim that the baby was dressed all in pink with a chiffon bow in her hair. But the truth was that she didn't really recall what the child was wearing; and if she got it wrong—a distinct possibility given her lack of recollection on that particular point—the only thing she'd convince the officers of was that the child she'd seen was absolutely, positively not Holly Owen—when Maggie was absolutely, positively certain that it was.

So how could she both convince them that the child was a girl, and simultaneously avoid misleading them about what language the kidnapper had been speaking—all without signing her admission papers to the nearest sanitarium?

"I think it was something she said." Maggie finally replied.

Well, it's true, she supposed with an inward frown.

"Something," Llewellyn repeated with unmistakable derision, "she said? Who? The baby? She's only one year old!"

Maggie tried to keep a pleasant expression. At least she was getting a little extra time. "No, no. The woman."

"And what did she say, Maggie?" Kernough stood up again and looked down at her encouragingly.

"I can't recall exactly," Maggie replied carefully. "It wasn't really what she said. It was more the way she said it."

"The way," the same derisive tone from Llewellyn, "she said it?" His face was losing its redness, leaving behind purple blotches on his jowls and throat.

"Um, yeah." Maggie shifted uncomfortably in her chair. "It was, you know, the way you'd talk to a girl?"

Llewellyn's incredulous mouth somehow combined a pucker with a frown. He looked sidelong to Kernough who only shrugged in reply.

"Could you tell what language it was?" Kernough asked.

Maggie cocked her head innocently. "What language?"

"Was it English? Or Welsh? Could you tell?"

"Hmm," Maggie nodded sincerely as she pondered the question. "You know, come to think of it, I guess I can't really say what language she was speaking." She grinned from Kernough to Llewellyn and back. "Sorry."

Llewellyn's expression didn't budge, but Maggie could hear a tongue click behind it. "Anything else?" she asked eager to be on her way. She'd told them what she could. The rest would have to be up to them. "If not, I'll just be goi—"

"No," Kernough interrupted. "Sit down." Then she crossed to the exit and cast a cold glance back to Llewellyn. "She's all yours."

The brief echo of the metal door closing behind the exiting Kernough left Maggie feeling quite puzzled—and more than a little vulnerable. She turned her gaze from the door to look up at Llewellyn, whose yellowed teeth were exposed in a cold grin.

"You're a smart one, eh, lass?" he asked with a sneer.

Maggie was smart enough not to respond.

"Well, you'd better wise up!" Llewellyn shouted into her face. "You're a bleeding suspect in a bleeding kidnapping! You've been evasive and deceitful in your answering of questions! And you're damn well lucky I don't arrest you here and now on the spot!"

Maggie's eyes widened in horror. "Arrest me?"

"Yes, arrest you!" Llewellyn's face had returned to its unpleasant crimson. "Good Lord, girl, for all we know you were about to deliver the ransom demand when Officer Bradley stopped you!"

"B—But..." This was unreal. Arrest me?

"You won't even admit what language that woman you claim you saw was speaking!"

"I don't know what language she was speaking!" Maggie yelled back, her voice bolstered by the truth of her statement. "Why would I even tell you about her if I was conspiring with her?"

"Maybe," Llewellyn leaned in close to Maggie, his breath stinking of coffee and cigarettes, "because there was no woman with a baby."

"No woman with—?" Maggie started, leaning away from the officer.

"No woman!" Llewellyn shouted over her. "No baby! No scarf! No sunglasses! Just you! And you made the whole story up just to throw us off the scent."

"Made it all up?" she asked quietly, utterly flabbergasted by the accusation.

"Tell me, did you have it all made up in advance, just in case you got nabbed? Or did you just make it up on the spot when Bradley caught you?"

"Caught me doing what?" Maggie demanded, crossing her arms as her initial shock at the bevy of accusations began to give way to offended irritation.

"Delivering the ransom demand!" Llewellyn's entire face was red now, even his ears. It made his hair seem even more unkempt.

"I wasn't delivering any r—"

"No use, lass!" Llewellyn shot up and threw his arms wide. "Time to fess up!"

"Fess—?" Maggie shook her head in disbelief. "What are you talking about?"

The red-rimmed eyes flared. "I'm talking about you. I'm talking about kidnapping." Then the eyes narrowed menacingly. "And I'm talking about prison."

"Prison?!" Maggie screeched, her own eyes flying wide behind their tortoiseshell rims. "What—?"

"Right. Prison." Llewellyn took several steps away, then turned around slowly. "You're looking at twelve years, you know."

"Twelve years?" She hated that she was repeating back everything Llewellyn was saying, but she was having trouble believing how the conversation was careening out of control.

"Maybe ten with good time." Llewellyn squeezed his fists tight. "Or—if you help us—maybe we can work something out with the prosecution."

"Prosecu—" She stopped herself. She closed her eyes and shook her head slowly. "Okay, now wait." She raised a tired palm and opened her eyes again. "Just wait. What are you saying?"

Llewellyn pushed his scarlet face into something a bit more humorless than a stone wall. "What I'm saying is that unless you start cooperating, you're looking at twelve years in a British prison. And don't think your American citizenship will help you any; we've plenty of Americans in our prisons. The United States government doesn't go out of their way to help convicted felons. Particularly kidnappers. You just better hope that baby's still alive. If she turns up dead, you'll be arraigned tomorrow on murder, not just kidnapping."

"Mur—" She couldn't finish the word.

"But if you're willing to help, well then maybe—no promises, mind you—but maybe—"

"Llewellyn!" Kernough was standing in the doorway.

Maggie hadn't heard the door open over the din of surreality spewing out of Llewellyn's mouth; but she was glad for it. "Inspector wants to see you."

Llewellyn sighed audibly through stained teeth. "Now?" His eyes were wide and his face still crimson. "Can't it wait?"

"Inspector says it's about the Hughes case." Kernough shrugged. "They found the murder weapon."

Llewellyn exhaled loudly through his nose. He glanced over at Maggie, who lowered her eyes in response, then back to Kernough. "Damn it." He pumped a fist in the air, then turned to point at Maggie. "I'm not through with you."

Maggie mixed a grimace with a sneer and managed not to reply, 'Delightful.'

The door clanked loudly behind Llewellyn, and Kernough stepped quietly over toward Maggie. Silently, she pulled the table back into position and Maggie was glad to have something to hide behind. Kernough fetched her own chair from across the room and sat down opposite Maggie.

Maggie didn't say anything. Her head was still spinning. Murder?

"He's right, you know," Kernough said softly, a slight nod toward where Llewellyn had exited.

Maggie stared at Kernough blankly.

"The mirror," Kernough explained with another nod of her head. "It's two-way. There's an observation room on the other side. We always have another officer observe.

Maggie nodded. It made sense. Another witness to the confession, she supposed.

"Llewellyn's got quite a temper," Kernough finished her explanation, "so we make sure he doesn't go too far."

"Oh." Maggie preferred her own explanation to Kernough's. She thought for a moment, then asked, almost conversationally, "So who's watching now?"

Kernough glanced comfortably toward the mirror, a soft smile unfurling across her lips. "No one."

Maggie nodded again. She looked down at the table top, unsure what was coming next.

"But he is right, you know," Kernough repeated.

Maggie looked up at the officer, her brow creased in confusion and amazement. "About what?"

"You're looking at a lot of time. Probably ten years."

"But—"

"I know." Kernough raised a hand. "But you have to know it sounds incredible. Unbelievable really. You saw a woman you can't describe, speaking a language you can't identify, and carrying a baby who just seemed like a girl." She shook her head. "I don't think a jury will believe it."

Maggie let out a short burst of nervous laughter. "A jury?" This was getting crazy.

"Well, of course you'll get a jury. It's a felony." She bit her lip and nodded thoughtfully. "But you never know, they might buy it. Hard to say. But the judge sure won't. And he's the one who'll set your bail."

Apparently it was repeat day. She stopped fighting it: "Bail?"

"Yes. At the arraignment. Even without any criminal history, you're probably looking at 500,000 pounds on a kidnapping charge. The judge'll be worried you might flee back to the States." Kernough shook her head slowly. "And if it's murder, well then it's no bail of course. You'll be held in custody until the trial."

"Well, of course," Maggie quipped humorlessly. How is this happening?

Kernough nodded again, her soft green eyes fixed on the floor. "But if you helped us. Especially right now—when we might still be able to save the girl—well then, the prosecution would be very grateful."

Maggie just stared at Kernough, entirely dumbfounded.

"Truth is, Maggie," Kernough reached out and touched Maggie's forearm, "no one's going to believe your story. Even if it's true. And I know you were holding back on us there, Maggie. You weren't telling us everything." Maggie looked away. "The jury will know it too," Kernough pressed on, "and you'll spend twelve years in prison. Whether you did it or not."

Maggie didn't look up.

"On the other hand," Kernough retracted her arm and sat up a bit. "If you tell you were involved—even minimally—and you made up the story about the scarved woman because you got scared, well, people will understand that. People will believe that."

Maggie looked up but didn't get a chance to say anything before Kernough went on.

"Tell us you were approached by some woman, someone you didn't know but can actually describe. Maybe she offered to pay you something if you delivered the ransom demand. Maybe a small percentage. Tell us you needed the money for school. People will believe that. And maybe you'll get lucky and we'll find the person who's really responsible. And then you'd get the credit."

"You want me to lie?" Maggie was incredulous.

"I want you to do what's best for you," Kernough sighed, that same beautiful smile hanging onto her lips. "If you cop a plea to a simple count of rendering criminal assistance you'd get off with just a year of probation."

Maggie blinked. "But I didn't do anything."

"It doesn't matter, Maggie," Kernough tilted her head in sympathy. "No one's going to believe you. And you'll go to prison."

Maggie ran her hands through her thick auburn hair and let out a long, low sigh. She pulled off her glasses and rubbed the red marks on the bridge of her nose. "Okay. You want me to say what, then?"

Kernough smiled. "Say you were just walking along when some woman approached you and asked you to deliver a ransom demand to the Owen woman. She offered you a hundred quid. You thought it was just some sort of joke. And you needed the money."

Maggie looked across the table to the police officer, her caramel eyes wide.

"I will personally see to it," Kernough assured, "that you get off with just probation."

Maggie rubbed her eyes again, then replaced her glasses. She ran both hands through her hair again and tucked the thick locks behind her ears. She took a very deep breath. She exhaled it very slowly. She looked down at the table. Then she opened her mouth and spoke, very quietly.

"I saw a woman," she began, "at the market. She was walking toward me." Maggie looked up and met the police officer's gaze. "She was wearing a scarf on her head and sunglasses covering her eyes. She was carrying a baby. As she walked past me, I heard her say something to the baby. I don't know what she said. I can't even tell you what language it was. But something she said made me think the baby was a girl. I kept walking and saw a crowd around a young woman who was sitting next to a baby carriage and crying. For a reason I can't explain I thought the baby I'd seen was hers. So I went to tell her what I'd seen and that's when the policeman stopped me."

Kernough held Maggie's gaze throughout the recitation. The smile was gone. She started another slow nod, and Maggie looked away, having nothing more to say.

The metal door clanked open again. Kernough didn't wait to be addressed before standing up and pushing past Llewellyn on her way out.

"All right, lass," Llewellyn hissed as the door thunked close behind him. "One more thing. Then," he practically choked on the words, "you're free to go."

Thank freaking God, Maggie thought, and her exaggerated sigh of relief shed the tension from her neck and shoulders.

"You can leave," Llewellyn explained, "after we take your prints."

Maggie looked up sharply. The tension was back—and then some. "My prints?" She was doing it again. "My fingerprints?"

"No, your bleeding pressed flower prints," Llewellyn spat. "Yes, your fingerprints."

He placed a single sheet of heavy duty paper and a small inkpad on the table in front of her. "Your left hand first," he instructed.

"No!" Maggie heard herself shout. "You're not taking my fingerprints. I didn't do anything wrong."

Llewellyn glowered at her. "That's as may be. But we still need your prints. And you're not leaving until we get them."

Maggie cast her gaze about the room helplessly. Finally she crossed her arms with authority. "No," she decreed. "You can't take my fingerprints."

Llewellyn frowned at her in puzzlement. Then he shrugged, stepped over to the mirror and tapped on it. "It's not a request," he explained.

The door flew open and in stormed Kernough and two very young, very large, very strong-looking patrol officers. Kernough's soft smile was nowhere to be seen. "Don't make this more difficult than it has to be." It was a warning, her voice like ice. "It will be much easier if you cooperate."

"But—But I have rights," Maggie insisted. "You can't just take my fingerprints when I haven't done anything wrong. It's— It's— It's un-American."

Llewellyn snorted at this. Kernough just replied coldly, "This is Britain, not America. We do things differently here."

"I'll say." Maggie looked past Kernough at the hired muscle behind her. "No wonder we left."

"That's it!" Llewellyn slammed his fist down in the table. "Just give us the damned prints! Left hand first."

Maggie glared through narrowed eyes at Llewellyn, at the fingerprinting paraphernalia, then at Kernough and her goons. This was too much. "Nope." She shook her head defiantly. "You're gonna have to take them."

"Fine." Llewellyn seemed almost happy at this. He nodded to the two gorillas in police uniforms and in a few moments they were rolling Maggie's ink-wetted fingers across the page. Left hand first. Then right hand. Maggie didn't resist, but she didn't help either. When they'd finished, she wiped her fingers off on the flimsy paper towel Llewellyn provided.

"You can go now," Llewellyn barked.

Maggie bent down, picked her backpack up off the floor and swung it over her shoulder. The enforcers had already left.

Kernough held the door open and Llewellyn turned to watch Maggie exit, his back to both the table and the fingerprint card atop it. He noticed neither the subtle flick of Maggie's wrist, nor the tiny black spot which appeared at the center of the fingerprint card.

"*Liosc*," Maggie hissed angrily under her breath as she passed through the doorway. Her Old Gaelic dialect for 'Burn.'

Llewellyn stared after the American and waited for Kernough to close the door. When he finally turned around he had just enough time to run over to the table, push the flaming fingerprint card onto the floor and stamp it into crumbling, illegible black ash.

30. The Lawyer

"I hate lawyers."

Sgt. Warwick pulled open the door to the Hastings Building, directly across the street from the Aberbeenshire Courthouse and home to over a dozen barristers and precisely three solicitors.

"Even prosecutors?" Chisholm asked as she followed her colleague into the lobby. "They're lawyers as well, you know."

Warwick pressed the button for the lift and thought for a few moments. "No," she said finally as the lift doors opened, "I don't trust them either."

***

It hadn't surprised Warwick that Glynis Campbell's office was in the Hastings Building. It also hadn't surprised her that Campbell's office was on the top floor. And considering the circumstances it hadn't really surprised her that Campbell had agreed to see them on such short notice. What did surprise her was the person she saw exiting Campbell's office and ducking toward the stairs just as she and Chisholm stepped off the lift exactly seven minutes early for their appointment.

"Ms. NicRath!" Warwick called out. "Is that you?"

Marsaili NicRath turned and let her hand fall from the

stairway door handle. "Hullo." Her smile was forced. "Officer Warwick, was it?"

"Detective Sergeant, actually," Warwick corrected. "And it's pronounced 'Warrick'—like the castle. You'll remember Detective Sergeant Chisholm?"

"Of course." NicRath nodded politely. She was attired quite differently from the last time they'd spoken with her. Rather than a dusty, sweaty shinty uniform, she sported a sharply tailored lavender business suit, the straight skirt stopping just above her knee. Her fine blond hair was pulled back from her face again, but rather than stuffed into a simple ponytail, it cascaded down the back of her neck from several golden hair clips. Pearls adorned her ears, throat and wrists and she was wearing just the right amount of make-up for the successful business woman. "Good afternoon, Sergeant."

Warwick wasted no time in posing the obvious question. "So what brings you to Ms. Campbell's office?"

NicRath took a moment before answering, obviously weighing her options. She elected for the simplest. "She's my lawyer."

Warwick nodded thoughtfully. "For your fight against David MacLeod?"

NicRath cocked her head slightly and considered her response. "You mean the matter regarding *An-Diugh*?"

"Are there others?" Warwick's raised eyebrow feigned only casual interest.

NicRath smiled. "No."

All three women stared at one another for a moment, then Warwick signaled the end of the impromptu interview; they had other business to attend to. "Well, it was good to see you again, Ms. NicRath. I'm sure we'll be speaking with you again sometime."

NicRath had to laugh as she pressed down on the door handle. "I'm sure you're right. Good day, Sergeants."

Chisholm waited for moment after the doorway to the stairwell clicked shut. "That was interesting, eh?"

"Oh, very," Warwick agreed. "I'll be interested to see what Ms. Campbell has to say about it. But don't mention that we saw her until I do, all right?"

Chisholm raised her eyebrows, but then nodded. "All right."

Warwick didn't bother saying 'Good' before walking over and entering Glynis Campbell's law office.

***

"Ms. Campbell will be with you in a moment," the young male receptionist assured the police officers after brief introductions. "She's just putting some files away."

Warwick and Chisholm thanked the young man, with his stylish sideburns and gel-spiked hair, then sat down patiently in two of the leather wingback chairs which decorated the smallish, plant-filled waiting room. After less than a minute, the door to the office at the end of the hall opened and Glynis Campbell, Barrister, stepped out into the lobby.

"Sergeant Warwick? Sergeant Chisholm?" She was probably in her early 50s, with thick and wiry brown hair tamed into a knot at the base of her skull. She wore small half-lens reading glasses, their gold chain draped around her neck, and a conservative business suit in either black or a very, very dark blue. The tasteful ruffle of a cream-colored silk blouse was visible at her throat, while her skirt fell almost to mid-calf, revealing the bottom of strong-looking, stockinged legs which ended at very expensive-looking black leather heels. She motioned her visitors into her office. "Please come in."

Warwick and Chisholm both stood and walked the short

distance into Campbell's office. "Thank you for agreeing to see us," Warwick began. "We appreciate the courtesy."

"Yes. Thank you for your time, Ms. Campbell," Chisholm agreed. "I'm sure you're a busy woman."

Campbell laughed—a short but warm laugh, just the right length and appropriate enough that Warwick almost thought it was genuine. "Quite busy, to be sure," Campbell replied in a thick brogue as she closed the office door. She sat down at her desk and motioned to the officers to sit as well. "But I cut my last appointment short a bit and I don't have to be in court until two-thirty."

"Funny you should mention that—" Chisholm started.

"I hadn't realized you had court today," Warwick interjected, her irritation fairly well masked; Chisholm sat back in her chair. "I hope we won't make you late."

Campbell waved away the suggestion. "Don't worry yourself, Sergeant Warwick." She nodded toward her office lobby. "Charles will come fetch me when it's time to go. He'll not let me be late, and it's only just across the quay." She leaned back in her chair and grabbed a hold of the arms rests. "So, then. What can I do for you?"

"Well, as you know," Warwick began, "we're investigating the kidnapping of Douglas MacLeod. And Mrs. Janet MacLeod mentioned that you are her attorney."

"Jessie." Campbell smiled just the right amount as she spoke the name. "Yes, I did represent Jessie in the divorce action. A very nice woman. Unfortunate situation."

"I'm sure," Warwick replied. "Could you tell us a little about Jessie?"

"I'd be happy to," Campbell replied with a full, friendly smile. Then the smile made an endearing transformation into a cautious grin. "Within the limits of attorney-client privilege, of course."

"Of course," Warwick sighed. Then she set to work. "When did Jessie become a client?"

"The divorce papers were served on her in early May. I filed my formal Notice of Appearance on the matter the first week of June."

"How much does she stand to gain from the divorce?"

"In truth, she'll lose several hundred thousand pound as she goes from holding a joint tenancy in all of the MacLeod properties to receiving a monthly alimony stipend."

"Who will have custody of Douglas?"

"We've a petition before the court to award primary custody to Jessie."

"Will the fact that Douglas was kidnapped while staying with his father help Jessie win custody of her son?"

"The court will consider all relevant factors when rendering a decision on custody."

Warwick nodded thoughtfully as she considered the information provided. She looked over to Chisholm, who appeared quite satisfied with the exchange. So Warwick turned back to Campbell. "You didn't really answer any of my questions," she observed pleasantly.

Campbell laughed again, this time genuinely. "I'd hoped you hadn't noticed."

"There's no use to repeating the questions, is there?" Warwick inquired casually enough.

"No, not really," Campbell admitted.

Chisholm looked first to Campbell, then to Warwick, both of whom ignored her. She leaned back into her chair and crossed her arms.

"All right then." Warwick sniffed slightly and sat forward in her chair. "Let me try some more general questions."

"An excellent idea," Campbell agreed and she too leaned forward.

"When a couple divorces, are all of the assets automatically divided fifty-fifty?"

"No," Campbell replied. "Not automatically. It depends on the nature and extent of the holdings and the manner and time in which each was obtained as it relates to the dates of the marriage."

"So, if a wife received an inheritance before the marriage, she could keep that as separate property?"

"If she kept it entirely separate during the marriage, yes." Campbell seemed to be enjoying the hypothetical legal analyses.

"What about an inheritance received during the marriage?" Warwick inquired further. "Or wages for that matter? What about wages earned during the marriage?"

"The inheritance could still remain separate," Campbell pontificated, "if it were kept separate throughout the marriage. But wages are a different story. The law is fairly well settled that wages earned during a marriage, and any assets purchased with such wages, are the property of the marital community. The law recognizes that one spouse may be able to earn more money because the other has elected to stay home and take care of the house."

"Interesting," Warwick nodded along. "And what would happen if, say, one spouse went bankrupt between the filing of the divorce papers and the finalization several weeks later?"

Campbell considered the question with a frown. "How do you mean exactly?"

"Would the court," Warwick clarified, "award alimony based on the assets at the time of the filing of the divorce, or based on the assets at the time of finalization?"

Campbell squinted slightly as she contemplated the query, and her answer thereto. "Usually the numbers are worked out some time before finalization."

"But if there's a change in finances before finalization?" Warwick pressed. "Would it be too late to change the numbers?"

Campbell paused again. "No, I suppose not," she admitted. Then her practiced smile returned. "Although the judge would likely be irritated."

"I should imagine so," Warwick replied warmly. "Although in my experience, most judges can be rather irritating themselves sometimes."

Campbell laughed at this and Chisholm too chuckled. "That," Campbell pointed an amicable finger toward Warwick, "is certainly true."

The three women let their light laughter subside, then Warwick, a pleasant smile pasted across her face, attacked. "So what will happen when the Bar Society finds out about the blatantly unethical conflict of interest you have in representing both Jessie MacLeod and Marsaili NicRath?"

Campbell's lingering smile fell from her face like so much lead. Her eyes narrowed and for the first time the wrinkles that flanked her eyes and mouth became noticeable. She raised an offended eyebrow. "Excuse me?"

Chisholm's eyebrows were also raised; she was staring at Warwick, awaiting her partner's reply.

"It seems to me," Warwick began coldly, "that your representation of Marsaili NicRath's claim against David MacLeod is in direct conflict with your representation of Jessie MacLeod."

Campbell's other eyebrow raised, but then she regained her visage into one of amused interest. "Does it?" she asked smugly.

"Pray, do enlighten me."

"Right." Warwick took up the task effortlessly. "As Jessie MacLeod's attorney, it's your job to obtain as large and as favorable a settlement as possible for her in her divorce from David MacLeod. And you've just confirmed two things for me: first, that any assets obtained entirely during the marriage are subject to division by the court; and second, that the relevant date for dividing those assets is the date of finalization. Therefore, it is in Jessie's best interests that David MacLeod's assets be as large as possible at the time of divorce."

She took a breath, then continued. "Now, one such asset is *An-Diugh*, Marsaili NicRath's former company, which Ms. NicRath has hired you to regain. But if you succeed in wresting control of *An-Diugh* from MacLeod, then you will have also lessened the marital assets to be divided by the courts in the divorce action, thereby reducing Jessie's settlement." Warwick smiled coolly. "I'd call that a conflict of interest. What would you call it?"

Chisholm turned back to Campbell, who had remained quite calm during this assault on her professional integrity.

"I would call that," Campbell replied calmly, "a potential conflict of interest." She folded her hands atop her desk and proceeded. "If Mr. MacLeod is possessed of and awarded the entirety of *An-Diugh* at the time of finalization of the divorce settlement—which is how the settlement is currently arranged— then Mrs. MacLeod will receive other assets of equal value to ensure equal division of the marital assets. If Ms. NicRath then succeeds— after the MacLeod divorce is final—in regaining ownership of *An-Diugh*, then that will affect Mr. MacLeod's assets only. And when that happens, not only will I have obtained my goal in representing Ms. NicRath, but I will also have insulated Mrs. MacLeod from any detrimental impact such divestment might have had, had it occurred prior to the finalization of the divorce." Campbell hadn't smiled throughout her explanation, but now allowed a satisfied grin to emerge. "And, as a bonus to both my clients, David MacLeod will get doubly screwed."

"And of course," Warwick replied evenly, as if she'd expected this reply, "you've advised both Ms. MacLeod and Ms. NicRath of this potential conflict of interest."

"Of course," Campbell replied quickly, then added, "Not that it's any of your business. But they were each in agreement as to my continued representation."

Warwick smiled her own evil little smile. "And screwing David MacLeod?"

Campbell produced her laugh again. "Especially screwing David MacLeod." She looked down at her watch. "Now, if you'll excuse me, Sergeants, I need to be getting to court. Charles has been derelict in his duty. No doubt intimidated by the imposing presence of law enforcement. But really, I must be going."

Chisholm stood up readily, followed slowly by Warwick.

"Oh, just one more thing," Warwick said almost casually as she stood up. "When we first spoke to Mrs. MacLeod—Jessie—we didn't realize you represented her. She didn't mention your name until we'd nearly concluded the interview. But we'll likely need to speak with her again, of course. I assume you'll want to be present, so should I contact Charles if we need to schedule a time?"

Campbell's fine face displayed patient amusement. She dismissed the suggestion with a wave of her hand and toss of her head. "Oh, no need, Sergeant. I trust you. And I trust Jessie. She's no more the kidnapper than is the MacLeod Banshee. You may speak with her as much as you'd like. I'm sure I don't need to be there."

"Thank you." Warwick offered a polite nod. "We'll let ourselves out."

Glynis Campbell returned the officers' thanks and then Warwick and Chisholm exited the comfortable office and rode the lift back down to street level.

"Well, you were right," Chisholm could barely wait to point out. "Jessie lied to us. She said she'd been served with divorce papers a year ago."

"Right." Warwick nodded distractedly. "And we know Glynis Campbell isn't everything she appears to be."

Chisholm cocked her head. "How so? She seemed very nice. Even agreeing to let us talk to Jessie without her."

Warwick shook her head. "No," she replied. "She wasn't being nice. No attorney worth their salt would let a client speak with the police without being present themselves. It was either stupid or inexperienced."

Chisholm frowned. "Well, she didn't seem stupid or inexperienced," she opined.

"No," Warwick agreed, "she sure didn't."

31. Search and Rescue

The problem with police records wasn't gaining access to them. Hacking into government databases was child's play. The real problem was the delay in entering the information into the databases in the first place. An officer investigating, say, a kidnapping wasn't likely to pause his investigation long enough to make sure some pencil-necked number-cruncher could keep his beans counted. And especially not until the case was solved, lest there be a tally somewhere of the officer's currently unsolved cases.

So Taggert turned to the most reliable source for stories of tragedy and heartache: the media. 'Police Beat' sections from newspapers throughout Britain.

Aberdeen... Edinburgh... York... Manchester... London...

It was, he hoped, simply a matter of time.

Cardiff... Aberystwyth...

32. Blood

"So, what've you got for me, Richards?" Warwick leaned onto the front counter of the Forensics Department office. "Anything good?"

"Afraid not." Officer Richards frowned as she pulled the file out from under two others on her cluttered desk. "We can't I.D. anything from the blood."

"No matches, you mean?" Warwick considered the thousands upon thousands of known D.N.A. profiles on file throughout the U.K. and abroad. They couldn't have exhausted all the databases yet.

"No," Richards shook her head. "I mean we can't even type the D.N.A. from the blood. It's thoroughly corrupted."

Now Warwick frowned. "Corrupted? It can't have degraded. D.N.A. doesn't degrade."

"Not degraded," Richards corrected. "Corrupted." She pulled several sheets from the file folder and turned them for Warwick to see. Warwick recognized them as D.N.A. fingerprints: the graph-like profiles obtained through the D.N.A. typing process. The graphs on the sheets were noticeably dissimilar. "Every time we type a sample, we get multiple results at each allele."

Warwick examined the proffered pages. "What does that mean?"

"It means," Richard grinned, "the sample is corrupted. Mixed. This isn't one person's blood. It's a mixture of blood from more than one person."

Warwick was at a loss for words. She hadn't expected this. "Are you sure?"

"Aye," Richards shrugged. "So D.N.A.'s not going to help you any. The only thing I can say for sure is that the lad's blood is probably in there. Every now and again one of the cells will have an XY male chromosome. But most of the time it's all XXs. The kidnapper likely mixed the boy's blood with her own or someone else's."

"Well, thanks anyway, Richards," Warwick tried to laugh it off. "I guess I'll just have to do it the old fashioned way. Thanks for the good work anyway, Richards."

"Not at all," Richards replied. "Have a good night, Sergeant."

Warwick returned the well wish then exited into the corridor. Things were going nowhere fast.

33. More Blood

The first order of business was to get the hell out of Dodge.

Maggie knew the police would discover the burnt remains of the fingerprint sheet quickly enough. She supposed it wouldn't take them too long to figure out what hotel she was staying at and track her down. So she hightailed it back to the Dragon's Arms and checked out, impatiently agreeing to pay for that coming night's lodgings as well, given the late check out. Then she snatched up her bags and walked as quickly as she could to the train station, wondering the whole way whether she was being followed—or worse, pursued.

She took a certain dramatic pleasure in asking the ticketing agent for "a ticket on the next train out of here," even though that ended up being a rather uninteresting inter-city run to Llanwnog. But the key had been to get out of Aberystwyth before Llewellyn hunted her down and dragged her back in for more fingerprints, more questioning, or, God forbid, her arraignment. And Maggie knew the odds of that happening were far greater if she was sitting in the train station waiting lounge in Aberystwyth, rather than Llanwnog.

From Llanwnog, she made her way to London North, where

she was offered two choices: a high speed train to Edinburgh, arriving at 1:12 a.m., with the connecting train to Aberdeen not for some three hours; or a slower direct train, complete with private sleeper compartments, and arriving in Aberdeen at 8:04. With a tired smile and a flash of plastic, Maggie purchased both her ticket to Aberdeen and her pass to the sleeper compartment. The train would be boarding soon. She was glad.

***

It had been a long, long day. The train started rolling out of the station shortly after she settled into her compartment. A small, cramped little thing, still it offered sanctuary and rest. She locked the door behind her, pulled the shade, stripped to her underwear, then turned off the light and slipped into the narrow bed jutting out from the wall just as quickly as she could.

She had feared the lurching of the moving train might induce sleep-depriving motion sickness, but to the contrary, the gentle rocking of the compartment began immediately lulling her off to her dreams.

She replayed the day in her head. The police interrogation and subsequent flight from Aberystwyth lingered foremost in her tired mind. But the day had begun with the Book of Souls and the magic spell she had used to read it. She had, over the last months, come to accept that use of the black magic invariably led to unpleasant dreams; and there had certainly been nights when she'd laid awake in bed, her trepidation against the coming visions preventing her from slipping easily into slumber. But after such an exhausting day, the morning's magickry seemed vastly distant. So, as she rolled over one last time and pulled the blankets up to her chin, ready to succumb at last to sweet, rejuvenating sleep, she forgot entirely to be afraid of the coming nightmares.

She would not forget again.

***

The earth was scorched. Not flat and hard like a stone cliff. Not dried and cracked like an empty riverbed. But scorched. Burnt and melted and ruined. Burnt like human flesh is burnt, with no hope of ever healing. The blackened earth stretched out, jagged and cropped, as far as she could see, to the far off horizon, where it met with the purple-gray sky, a sun-blocking blanket of cold, low clouds. The only feature visible for miles was a circular crevasse filled with fire, protecting a granite castle within. The castle she had to enter.

For inside was an innocent young girl named Maggie Devereaux.

So outside, the guilty young woman named Maggie Devereaux threw back her leather cloak, squeezed the silver clan crest hanging from her throat, and confirmed the presence of her razor-sharp *sgian dhu* dagger in her belt. Then she took her first deliberate step toward the fire-belted castle.

Damn them all. She would not fail.

The first demon appeared at the edge of the infernal moat. It shot up from the earth in a geyser of fire and stench, blocking her path to the single stone bridge across the flaming cavern. The beast was tall, probably seven feet, and thin—the way an unbreakable steel cable is thin. Powerful, red-skinned legs supported a hair-covered torso and four grotesquely long arms each ending in a spiked claw. Its head was small with jagged, twisting horns and a large, pig-like snout. It opened its fang-filled mouth and let out a roar that shook the very air.

"You shall not pass!" the demon declared.

Maggie squinted against the sound and reek of the bellow, then she adroitly dropped to one knee and unleashed a spell form her outstretched hands.

"<Cancel the forces which bind this matter! Disperse this form across the winds!>"

A blinding blue light shot from within the demon and the beast exploded in a ball of flame and fury.

Well done, Maggie thought to herself, and she started across the bridge.

Flames rose past her, shooting upward to further scorch the already blackened stone beneath her feet. She didn't she the next demon—it waited to appear until she'd been momentarily blinded by a flare from below. When she regained her sight, the demon was there in front of her. Before she could react, a razorlike claw lashed out and slashed her face, catching her just under her left eye and slicing so deeply across her nose that all the cartilage was severed, leaving the cute button tip fully separated from the bridge, blood pouring down her face and shocked, labored breathing bubbling from the wound.

"You shall not pass!" screeched the second demon.

Lashing out instinctively, and squeezing her eyes shut against the pain, Maggie repeated the spell, sending the second demon to disintegrate into oblivion after the first. Then she fell to her knees in shock. She grabbed at her face with her left hand and squeezed her clan pendant with the other.

"<Reunite and replenish this flesh. Amplify its natural healing a hundred-fold.>"

She could feel and hear the severed flesh of her face grow back together and she sighed with relief as the pain vanished. Regaining herself, she wiped the blood from her face, stood up and walked to the end of the bridge.

The fire pit now safely behind her, she stared ahead at the keeps' entrance, not ten feet away. But she waited. She knew she would not traverse the gate unopposed. She stood ready.

Another geyser of flame shot from the scarred ground and before her stood her next opponent. He looked just like Iain, save the glowing red eyes in place of Iain's gorgeous baby blues.

"You shall not pass," it declared softly in Iain's familiar voice.

Unfortunately, the trick worked; Maggie hesitated, just for a moment, but long enough to allow the beast to pounce, transforming mid-leap into a scarlet-skinned, cable-sinewed monster.

Its gnarled, gray-yellow teeth sunk deeply into Maggie's shoulder. Knocked onto her back by the impact, she could feel the hot blood begin to spurt from her torn arteries. Pain clouded her thoughts as the demon began to thrash its jaws back and forth, tearing deeper and deeper until it reached bone. She found herself unable to find the ancient Celtic words necessary to free herself. Instead, she grasped desperately for the Highland dagger, clumsily unsheathing it before plunging its silver blade into the beast's back, pushing upward toward what she hoped were some sort of vital organs. With a cry of pain and horror, the demon released its bite and fell writhing off her, reaching in vain for the blade in its back.

Maggie considered her shoulder, but knew to take care of business first. She rolled on top of the demon and extracted the *sgian dhu* from the wounded demon. The she drew the knife slowly and deeply across the monster's throat, all but severing the crimson head, whatever life was left in the beast running out into a pool of fetid black bile atop the scorched earth.

She slid off the demon's vanquished form and fell onto her back. Raising a hand to her shredded shoulder, she repeated the healing spell. "<Reunite and replenish this flesh. Amplify its natural healing a hundred-fold.>"

The flesh of her shoulder immediately began to mend itself,

squeezing out the vile yellow pus left in her bloodstream by the demon's foul mouth. After a few moments, the shoulder was whole again. She stood up, set her jaw and walked into the castle.

The inner courtyard was deserted. The ground beneath her feet was a coarse black sand that crunched like shattered glass with each step. She paused. Across the courtyard, some fifty feet away, was the heavy wooden door to the dungeon. Where the little girl was. She readied herself, then took the next step.

The demons waited—until she'd gotten exactly half-way across, until she was in the center of the courtyard. Then they rose up around her, three of them, emerging from the black glass-sand like maggots from a corpse. Each was armed with a yard-long, blood-stained scythe. Two stood between her and the way she'd come; the third blocked the door to the dungeon.

"You shall not pass," they cried in ominous unison.

Maggie immediately destroyed the one before the dungeon door. A quick spell and wave of her hand and the demon dissolved into so much red goo. The door was clear. She ran for it. But she didn't know if she'd make it.

She didn't.

The first blow struck her ankle, slicing her Achilles tendon clean through and sending the ridiculously stretched tendon recoiling painfully up into the back of her knee. She fell awkwardly forward, hands outstretched, and skidded into the black glass-sand—shredding her palms and forearms, and slicing up her chin and cheek.

She managed to roll over just before the second blow struck, a slash into the top of her left leg. The scythe jerked her roughly across the glass-sand as the blade caught on the femur. Blood began to spurt from her leg with each beat of her racing heart.

She shrieked in agony, then grabbed at the scythe and

lashed out. Earlier the pain had interfered with her ability to remember the Old Gaelic; now her instinct to survive wrenched the words from their hiding spots. The demon disappeared in a ball of blue flame, its scythe melting in Maggie's blood spattered hand.

Then came the next blow, from the next demon. This one severed her right arm completely; the scythe blade buried itself a half-inch deep into her ribs. Blood poured from the stump.

A red blaze filled Maggie's vision for a moment, then her head rolled weakly to the side and she looked down. Her arm lay severed on the ground, blood oozing into the black earth.

With great effort, Maggie looked up at the monster above her. She couldn't make out any features in her rising shock, but she could see the hideous smile on the demon's wicked face. It yanked the scythe from her ribs and pulled back for a final swing. Her neck tingled in morbid anticipation.

She struggled to focus on the form retreating down her darkening tunnel vision. She only had time for one word.

"<Burn>."

The demon exploded in a titanic ball of fire, filling the courtyard with black flame. Maggie's hadn't the energy to cover her face against the blast; she could feel her hair burning off and her nose and ears melting. The pain was unbearable. As the flames dissipated, she lay bleeding and burnt and broken on the broken glass of the courtyard. Now she only had strength for one word: "<Heal.>"

She closed her scorched eyelids. "<Heal.>"

She reached for her severed ankle. "<Heal.>"

She laid a hand on her carved up leg. "<Heal.>"

She dragged her severed arm up to its shoulder. "<Heal.>"

It took several moments, but the pain began to subside. "<Heal,>" she whispered one more time, then she waited until the agony had fully passed. She opened her eyes without pain. Her legs were whole. Her arm was whole. And a hand to her head confirmed the skin there was also healed, unmelted and scar-free.

She sat up and took a deep breath. Then she stood up fully. Regaining herself, she brushed off her cloak and walked to the door. It was unlocked.

There were no demonic guards within the fortress walls, only a single stone staircase leading down. Maggie descended the rutted steps deliberately. At the bottom of the stairs, a granite landing opened onto a long, narrow hallway leading to a darkened chamber at its end. There was no door on the room, just a faint red flicker from some out of view light source. She tensed her hands in anticipation, then began the march down the length of the corridor, her boots clacking loudly on the age-old stones.

"I shall pass."

The room was small. A small fire burned in a small pit in the floor. In the back was a small curtain behind which, Maggie knew, was the small girl she'd come for. And between the fire and the curtain was a small, ancient-looking demon, sitting cross-legged and staring into the fire.

"You shall not pass," he said simply without looking up, and so quietly Maggie almost didn't hear it.

She sneered and stepped up to tower over the seemingly inconsequential demon-let. "And why not?" she demanded.

"Because," the demon looked up at her with an expression almost of boredom; then it sprang from its seat and grabbed onto Maggie's collar, its clawed hooves digging into her stomach, its breath rank with blood and death, "THERE IS NO HEALING SPELL!!"

Maggie crumpled to the floor. Her face was sliced and burnt. Her shoulder was torn and fetid; her legs carved and useless. Her arm lay severed at her side. A pool of blood poured out from under her, burning into black smoke as it reached the demon's fire.

She tried to speak, but couldn't. Shock was overwhelming her.

The small demon calmly removed Maggie's own *sgian dhu* from her belt.

"You shall not pass," he repeated, just as quietly as before.

Then he buried the silver blade into her heart.

Maggie awoke screaming. She sobbed uncontrollably as she reached first for her face, then her legs, then her arms, then her face again. She curled up into a ball, squeezing herself against the dream and rocking back and forth atop the covers as the train sped on through the cold, black night.

34. Home

The train jerked rudely to a stop, sending Maggie off balance and stumbling into the wall of her sleeping compartment. Regaining herself, and still numb from the nightmare and the sleepless dark that followed, she hitched her backpack up higher and stepped into the corridor to file out onto the platform of the Aberdeen rail station.

***

She walked up to the bus shelter, the light morning rain spitting on her face. The next bus to campus wasn't until 9:40. She craned her neck to look at the watch she kept looped to the outside of her backpack. 9:06. She turned back toward the rail station, the row of taxis there firmly in her sights.

***

She slammed the taxi door and shoved the driver far too large a bill. Then she lowered her head and trudged to her flat. It took a minute but she found her keys in an outside backpack pocket. She unlocked the door, stepped inside and dropped the pack in the foyer. Then she locked the door behind her and walked straight to her bedroom.

She thanked God she was tired enough to sleep.

And she asked Him to stop the dreams.

***

Apparently He didn't listen. She found herself again in the black glass courtyard. But as soon as the first demon sprouted from the earth Maggie screamed herself awake.

Hugging her heavy arms against herself, she rolled over onto her stomach and closed her eyes again.

***

Knock! Knock! Knock!

Maggie forced an eyelid open and rolled her eyes back down from inside her skull. She had finally been getting some almost halfway decent sleep.

Who the hell is that?

She'd stripped to her underwear before climbing into bed, so she grabbed her robe off the hook by the door and slipped it over her arms, tying the belt as she walked over to peer through the peephole.

Great, she frowned. What does he want?

She unlocked the door and opened it just enough to see Iain Grant standing, clearly agitated, on her 'Ceud Mìle Fàilte' welcome mat.

"What?" she demanded, her voice thick with sleep.

"What?!" Iain parroted incredulously. "What do you mean, 'what?' What are you doing here?"

Maggie paused long enough to confirm the question in her still sluggish mind. She blinked puffy, baggy eyes, then replied, "Sleeping."

Then she closed the door and stepped toward her bedroom.

Knock! Knock! Knock!

Maggie turned back and opened the door again.

"What?"

"Where have you been the last two days?" Iain demanded, shaking his hands at her.

Again Maggie paused before answering. "Wales," she replied and closed the door once again.

Knock! Knock! Knock! Knock!

Maggie opened the door and glared at Iain, but didn't say anything.

"Wales?" Iain was livid. "Wales?! What the bloody hell have you been doing in Wales?!"

Maggie took a deep breath. "Witnessing a kidnapping, being interrogated by the police—rather rudely, I might add—and then screaming myself awake from nightmares of my body being hacked to pieces."

Iain just stared at this enigmatic reply.

"Now," Maggie concluded, "go away." She shut the door a final time, latching the bolt and ignoring Iain's knocking until it finally stopped and she was able once again to slip into viscous, restless dreams.

***

All in all Maggie had stolen about three hours of poor quality sleep by the time she pushed herself again from the sweat soaked bed. The nightmares had softened slightly—the demons only hiding at the edges of her dreams, content to stalk her with red, glowing eyes—and she'd managed to get some rest.

She crossed the foyer to the bathroom and stepped into a scalding shower. Soon, fully dressed and partially groomed, she was locking her flat door behind her and pulling on her backpack, empty save the Dark Book.

Time to find out who the hell 'S. MacKenzie' is.

35. The Professor

The University of Aberdeen, in typical British fashion, was a stunningly beautiful affair. The Old Campus boasted a variety of breathtaking buildings, the masterpiece of which was the King's College, a gothic cathedral of a structure with an enormous stone crown atop intersecting skyward arches. Taylor, on the other hand, was anything but beautiful.

The Taylor Building, home to all of the university's language departments, was a series of utilitarian longhouses strewn end to end in a zig-zag fashion to trail haphazardly away from High Street, the main bisecting artery of the Old Campus. When Maggie had first arrived in Aberdeen she had been duly disappointed in Taylor's less than weighty appearance. Almost a year later, she still wasn't impressed, but she was getting used to it. She pulled open the door and walked to the reader-board in the lobby.

'MACKENZ E SARAH 124'

Several thoughts came to her. First, she was surprised that 'S. MacKenzie' turned out to be a woman. Second, she was disappointed in herself for being surprised. And third, she wondered where all the damned 'I's had gone.

Maggie quickly ascended the nearest stairs to the first floor and walked unhesitatingly to room 124. The door was open.

Inside, cramped behind the small desk which had been squeezed into the cell-like confines of the office, sat a very pleasant-looking woman in her mid-to-late forties, thoroughly engrossed in the novel she was reading. She wore a cream-colored blouse and had long, thick, brown hair which cascaded onto her shoulders in a foam of loose, natural ringlets. Sensing Maggie's presence, she looked up from her book and met her visitor's gaze. Her soft face, with attractive wrinkles radiating from the corners of her eyes, was a perfect companion to the soft brown tresses. And she had the most brilliant green eyes, which absolutely sparkled as she said, "Maggie?"

What really angered Maggie was the effect this had on her, namely to throw her completely off her game, and hand the advantage to the academic.

"Wha— Well... Yes," Maggie stammered. She struggled to regain her composure. "Professor MacKenzie?" she retorted. Considerably less impressive given the reader board downstairs.

The professor stood up and extended a hand almost to the doorway. "Sarah," she corrected warmly. "Come in, Maggie."

Maggie accepted the hand, warm and strong, and sat in the one guest chair that fit in the glorified closet.

"So," Sarah MacKenzie began before Maggie could, "the Welsh Book of Souls, eh?"

Again Maggie was temporarily stunned. "Er, um, uh... Yes. But how—?" Then she thought for a quick moment. "Oh, of course. The library would have told you the title."

Sarah just smiled and nodded pleasantly as she folded her hands together.

"Well, I," Maggie pressed on, "I just wanted to thank you. And to meet you." She crossed her arms. "You're new here, aren't you?"

Quite the question, Maggie knew, for a visiting student to pose to a professor whose soft brogue clearly identified her as a Highland native. The irony wasn't lost on Sarah and she laughed lightly.

"No, actually," she replied, almost pronouncing it 'noo.' "But I was on sabbatical last year, so you'd not have seen me about campus. You came to Aberdeen last fall, did you not?"

Maggie narrowed her eyes. It shouldn't have been surprising that this woman, after having somehow been forwarded Maggie's request for access to an ancient Welsh manuscript, would have been curious enough to take whatever simple steps were required to access Maggie's school file and discover, among other relevant facts, when she had arrived in Aberdeen. And Maggie was even willing to concede that the guess of her identity might not have been too surprising either, given the proximity in time since the request. But nevertheless it was—all of it—really quite irritating to her.

"Yeah," Maggie replied flatly. "And where were you?" Not pleasant, but direct. She was still tired—and still in a bad mood.

Sarah laughed again, but not too much. "Edinburgh, actually. Doing some research. That's where I met Robert— Professor Hamilton. When he received your request, he called me. You're a student here, not at Edinburgh, so he thought it best if an Aberdeen faculty replied. Professional courtesy."

Maggie pursed her lips. "I suppose that makes sense," she had to concede. She wanted to say something more but was unsure what.

Instead, Sarah asked, "So how did you like it?"

"How did I like what?" Maggie replied, still a bit slow on the uptake.

"The manuscript," Sarah explained patiently. "The Welsh Book of Souls. Did you enjoy looking at it?"

Maggie just stared at the professor. She'd had a bad day yesterday. She'd had a horrible night's sleep. Her Iain-interrupted nap hadn't been very helpful either. Her intent had been to come to campus to grill the smarmy little academic about how she'd come to be involved in the whole sordid affair. Instead, Maggie was the one off guard, fielding unexpected questions and comments, reacting instead of acting, and despite it all, and despite herself, she thought she might actually be starting to like Sarah MacKenzie, the professor's openness engaging and her soft face reassuring.

"Well, yes, actually."

"You know Old Welsh, then?"

Maggie was fairly certain she'd managed, except perhaps for a slight widening of the eyes, to keep a pretty good poker face. She realized for the first time that she hadn't really thought out this encounter very well. She probably should have anticipated this line of inquiry, but on the way over, when she'd imagined the impending conversation it had been she who had posed the difficult questions and it had been the professor who had been left squirming for answers. So now Maggie had about three seconds to come up with some plausible response, without the pause itself becoming suspiciously long. Mentally flailing about for some possible response, she recalled a book she'd read once wherein the heroine, a spy of sorts, had explained that the best lies are mostly truth, with only the minimum of fabrication necessary. It would sound more sincere, and be easier to remember.

"No, actually," Maggie started. "My focus is more on Old Gaelic." True. "I have taken a Modern Welsh course or two along the way." One, actually. "And I've been thinking maybe I need to learn Old Welsh too." I certainly thought that the night before last. "So I wanted to see an example." A very particular example. "I'd seen a reference to the manuscript somewhere." The ruins of Ballincoomer Abbey. "And thought it would be a good one to look at." To perhaps save a baby's life.

"Really?" Sarah seemed quite taken by the explanation. She pursed her lips and drummed her fingers gently against one another, obviously considering something. "Now, you don't have a faculty advisor, do you?"

"Um," she stuttered. The question seemed to come out of nowhere. "Well, no. I had one, Prof. Macintyre, but—"

"I understand he's on leave for the time being," Sarah finished the sentence diplomatically.

"Er, right."

"Well, then." Sarah's warm smile sent her green eyes shimmering again. "I've a thought. You said you're considering adding Old Welsh to your Old Gaelic. And those two happen to be my primary areas of focus. Plus I worked closely with Prof. Hamilton last year, and when I reviewed your university file, I noted that your initial research proposal involved following up on some of his work."

Maggie just nodded dumbly.

"So then, would you let be your faculty advisor?"

And Maggie's train of thought derailed. She struggled for a response.

"Uh." Not a great one, so she tried again. "That is, I— I hadn't expected to need one until the Fall. But, well, I mean, I suppose— I suppose I'll need one eventually just the same. And I did say I wanted to learn Old Welsh." I did say that, didn't I? "So I suppose it would make a certain sense..."

Maggie tried to calm herself and consider the offer. Despite Maggie's malicious intentions, Sarah MacKenzie seemed to be a genuinely nice person. She was obviously intelligent, a good listener, and shared at least some of Maggie's academic interests. In addition, she had also—in the form of a fax to Aberystwyth—already done Maggie a significant favor, without question or delay. And although Maggie had just met the woman, she had to admit she liked her. She reminded Maggie of someone, although she wasn't sure who just then—but she knew it was someone she liked.

"All right," Maggie said at last. She extended a hand across the desk. "Let's do it. Thank you very much, Prof. MacKenzie."

"Sarah," the pretty academic corrected again as she shook the hand of her newest student.

"Sarah," Maggie acquiesced.

36. Where the Light is Best

"Next stop: Llandrindod. Connections to Cardiff, Caernarfon and Aberystwyth."

Taggert noted the announcement but didn't look up from his newspaper as the Welsh countryside sped past his train compartment window. But he wasn't reading the paper either. He was thinking.

He couldn't help but remember the joke about the man who was looking for a lost coin on Fifth Street.

A friend comes upon the man, who by now is down on all fours next to the curb, searching for the coin. After discovering the man's plight, and wishing to offer his assistance, the friend asks, 'So where did you lose it?'

'Over on Fourth Street,' the man answers without looking up.

The friend is puzzled; they are on Fifth Street. 'Then why are you looking for it over here?' he asks.

'Because,' the man replies matter-of-factly, 'the light's better here.'

As the train rolled to a stop at platform 6 of the Llandrindod rail station, and he stood up to exit the train, Taggert wondered whether he was looking where the coin was, or just looking where the light was best.

***

"Jessie MacLeod!" Chisholm's shout from the office doorway sliced through Warwick's ruminations.

"How's that?" Warwick looked up from the file on her desk.

"Jessie MacLeod," Chisholm repeated as she stepped into the room. "I've been thinking about her."

"All right," Warwick encouraged. She leaned back in her chair. "And what have you been thinking about the Lady MacLeod?"

Chisholm stepped around one of Warwick's guest chairs and plopped down. She slouched down, obviously quite comfortable, and ticked off a finger. "First, clear motive. She's about to lose her only son. And to a jerk, at that."

"True," Warwick replied cautiously. She knew the next point. "And what about opportunity?"

"Ah, see," Chisholm touched her next finger. "Now that's where I've been thinking. Opportunity can really be divided into 'general opportunity' and 'specific opportunity.'"

"Do tell." Warwick found herself curious.

"Right. General opportunity," Chisholm continued, "is things like: Would she know where the child was? Is she familiar with the residence? Would she know old man MacLeod's schedule? The nanny's? Things like that. And see, Jessie's got all that."

"And specific opportunity?"

"Well, that's things like: Where was she that night? Could she have used her general knowledge of the place to take advantage of the situation on that specific night?"

Warwick nodded. She liked the analysis. "And what do you think? Could she have done?"

Chisholm smiled. "That depends."

"On what?"

"On whether her alibi holds up." Chisholm ticked off another finger. "And we know she's lied to us once already."

Warwick nodded again. "What time does *Le Bistro Écosse* open?"

"Eleven thirty." Chisholm offered a lop-sided grin. "Early lunch?"

37. Alibis

"Can I help you, miss?"

'Miss.' Warwick had to smile at that. She couldn't remember the last time someone had called her 'miss.' And the fact that the current speaker was a spritely, red-headed waitress probably fifteen years her junior only added to Warwick satisfaction.

"Can we speak with the manager, please?" She flashed her badge and I.D. "It's important," she added unnecessarily.

The young sprite swallowed hard, offered a more appropriate, "Yes, mum," and scurried away to find her boss.

It had taken Warwick and Chisholm some time to make their way to 'Le Bistro Écosse.' Kerr had called in for a sergeant just after eleven, just as the two detective sergeants were about to go check out Jessie MacLeod's alibi, Warwick answered the call and she and Chisholm met Kerr at Aberdeen General Hospital. Apparently the teenaged son of one of the patrol officers had decided to see what would happen if he swallowed a few dozen of his old man's pain pills. Luckily, Dad got off shift early and found him. Still, it was a delicate issue and Kerr had been right to call in a sergeant to review the situation. Once the boy was stabilized, Warwick had to spend a couple of hours interviewing dad, mom and doctor before finally returning to her other duties. And so it was shortly after five thirty when the manager of *Le Bistro Écosse* stepped into the waiting area of his establishment, his hand extended anxiously in greeting.

"Good evening, officers. How can I help you?" His voice betrayed his nervousness, cracking slightly on the words 'officers.' Police rarely brought good news. His palm was sweaty in its limp grip and after shaking both officers' hands, he retracted the extremity to squirm restlessly in its companion. Forty-something and noticeably overweight, he had thick, unkempt black curls atop a fatty, shaven face. His white, tie-less shirt was clean, but old, and his paunchy stomach pressed unpleasantly against his shirt as it curled under and into his black polyester pants. "Is something wrong?"

"No, no," Warwick assured. "Everything's quite all right, Mr.—?"

"Eh? Oh!" The squirmy hands flung wide. "Quentin. Michael Quentin."

"Everything's fine, Mr. Quentin," Warwick continued. "We were just hoping to have a minute of your time."

Michael Quentin relaxed appreciably; he exhaled audibly. "Well, of course. Of course, officers."

The three of them—Warwick, Chisholm and Quentin—took a booth near the entrance and soon Quentin was reviewing Jessie MacLeod's driver's license photo as he answered the detectives' preliminary questions.

He hadn't been on shift that night—he rarely worked past six—but soon the three of them were joined by a fourth, a miss Mary MacLachlan, one of the waitresses who'd been working the evening of Douglas MacLeod's kidnapping. Mary was even younger than the first waitress, with bright blond hair, cropped short and spiked with mousse or gel or whatever it was the kids were using these days.

"'Ello!" She immediately pointed to Jessie MacLeod's photograph. "That's Jessie, in' it?"

"You know her?" Warwick invited.

"Oh, right I do," Mary replied quickly. "A regular, she is. A right nice lady. An' a good tipper, too. Aye, I know Jessie. She's all right, she is."

Warwick nodded slowly, her bottom lip protruding slightly as she considered this verbal avalanche.

"You say she's a regular, Mary?" Chisholm inquired with a soft smile. She tucked her black curls behind her ear—a very disarming gesture.

"Right," Mary answered. "She comes in all the time. A right nice lady." Then she paused, threw a look around their immediate vicinity, then lowered her voice and raised a pierced eyebrow. "She's rich, you know."

Even Warwick had to smile at that.

"So," Chisholm pressed on, "do you think you'd remember whether she was here on a given night?"

"Oh, aye. Aye." Mary grinned slyly. "See I usually try to get her seated in my section, I do. Like I said, she's rich. And a good tipper." She tried to ignore Michael Quentin's disapproving glare.

"Was she here last Sunday night?" This time Warwick posed the question. Direct and to the point.

"Last Sunday, eh?" Mary MacLachlan stuck a pinky between her lips and considered the question. "Hm, let me see." She examined the ceiling as her other hand scribbled enigmatic calculations in the air. "Tuesday, right?" she confirmed with a quick downward glance, then more ceiling scanning and air calculations. Then finally, the answer. "No. No, she wasn't in last Sunday."

Warwick raised her own eyebrow and leaned forward onto the tabletop. "Are you certain?"

"Oh, aye. I'm right sure. I don't remember seeing her that night, an' I'd a been lookin' fer her." She turned a sheepish smile toward her manager. "I'm paid quite well," she assured, less than convincingly, "but I do depend on me tips. And seein' as how this Saturday is the first o' the month, well, me rent is due an' I been payin' close attention to me tips. No, if Jessie MacLeod had been here, I'd a known it. I'd a gotten that tip."

Warwick nodded, her expression inscrutable. She turned to Chisholm, whose was anything but, then back to Mary. "Thank you, Miss MacLachlan."

The waitress pushed the thanks away, practically curtsied to Quentin, then bounced back to her tables. Warwick and Chisholm gathered up their photograph, thanked Michael Quentin, and exited out onto the street.

"I knew it," Chisholm could barely control the exclamation.

"Hm," Warwick answered. "Let's see what they've got to say at the Frankenwald."

***

'*Frankenwald*' is a German word meaning, more or less, 'French forest.' It was also the name for one of the trendier nightclubs in Aberdeen, located in a newly gentrified neighborhood in the north end of town. The linguistic incongruity of a Scottish bar named after a German word for French terrain was given further life by the clubs intentionally asymmetrical facade and decor. Refurbished cement friezes shared the century-old entrance with bricks painted a shade of purple which could only be described as 'grape soda.' Inside, framed Degas prints shared wall space with neon light sculptures and mirrors advertising various brands of British and Irish beers. The serving bar appeared to be maple, with a seemingly never ending row of enormous wooden keg taps behind it. Flanking the bar was a billiards section on one side and a black linoleum dance floor complete with disco ball on the other. And way in the back was an eight foot tall elk, stuffed and mounted.

Somehow, though, the various decorations worked together to create a unified theme of incongruity. A dozen early patrons, each dressed differently from the next, continued the theme. The only thing that really wouldn't have fit in the eclectic tavern was a pair of on-duty lady police officers. Warwick walked in first; Chisholm closed the door behind them.

The bartender, it turned out, reflected his surroundings. He was taller than average, thick about the neck, chest and arms, and had long, greasy black hair pulled back into a pony tail, several days stubble on his fatty cheeks, and an eye patch from under which stretched the ends of a very nasty looking vertical scar. He was dressed in a white tuxedo, with tails. His plastic nametag said, 'Hello. My name is Günther.'

He was wiping down the counter with a rag of dubious cleanliness when the officers walked in. He looked up at them, then returned his gaze to the countertop without a word.

"Hello," Warwick commenced the introductions. "I'm Detective Sergeant Elizabeth Warwick of the Aberdeen Police. This is my Partner, Detective Sergeant Alison Chisholm. We'd like to ask you some questions." She held up her badge and I.D. to confirm her identity, and her seriousness.

Günther slowly raised his gaze from the countertop and leveled it at the officers. Then he looked down again at his rag. "I'm a wee bit busy just now." A Scottish brogue, not a German accent.

"It will only take a few minutes," Warwick assured. "we just have a few questions."

Günther didn't look up. "Ask your questions if you'd like. But I can't promise I'll answer."

Warwick glanced to Chisholm who shrugged in response. Warwick extracted Jessie MacLeod's photograph from her jacket pocket and placed it on the damp bar. "Do you know this woman?"

The bartender hesitated a moment then pushed the rag to one side and squinted at the likeness. "Should I do?"

"Her name's Jessie MacLeod," Warwick prompted. "I believe she's a regular customer here."

"Do you now," Günther replied with a grin. "Well, we've lots of regular customers, officer."

"Sergeant," Warwick corrected.

"We've lots of regular customers, Sergeant."

"And is she one of them?"

Günther frowned and pulled his rag back over. "I can't say."

"Well then, look more closely," Warwick instructed. "Can you tell me whether she was her last Sunday night?"

Günther did not in fact look more closely. Instead he resumed his wiping and repeated, "I can't say."

"Then think about it for a minute," Warwick ordered. She was losing her patience. "And tell me whether she was here last Tuesday night."

Günther stopped wiping and took a long deep breath. Then he stood up fully and exhaled through his nose for a rather long time. "I can't say," he reaffirmed.

"Listen, Günther. Maybe you don't understan—"

"Or maybe it's you what don't understand," the bartender growled back. "This is the hottest nightclub in Aberdeen right now. We've literally hundreds of regulars. And if the boss is lucky, that'll last about six more months. Then the regulars, they start going to the next hotspot, the boss closes up shop, and I'm looking for a new job. I see no reason to speed things up any by letting it be known that we help out coppers who come round asking questions about our regulars. So even if I did recognize the lass—which quite honestly, I don't—my answer is the same: I can't say."

Warwick considered this for several moments, then she peeled Jessie's photograph off the counter. "Thank you for your time, Günther. Come on, Chisholm."

Warwick turned on her heel and headed toward the door. Chisholm hurried alongside barely able to wait until they were outside to begin buzzing in her partner's ear.

38. The Suave and Debonair Mr. Grant

The knot in her neck was gone. The pain in her shoulders was gone as well. And her headache had receded, leaving just an empty tenderness behind her eyes. Her conversation with Prof. MacKenzie had relaxed Maggie thoroughly. She had expected, sought even, confrontation, but instead had found only soothing hospitality and sincere interest. The pleasantness might even have been magnified by its very unexpectedness and Maggie had left the academic's office feeling calm and refreshed.

She'd decided to take the long way home, enjoying her stroll beneath the summer sun, and for the first time that day, she forgot about the nightmares.

Maggie turned the corner of her apartment building and stopped. A thick smile unfurled across her face, starting self-consciously in one corner of her mouth but quickly blossoming across her entire countenance. Left tidily in the center of her welcome mat, atop the elegantly written 'Ceud Mìle Fàilte' were a dozen long-stemmed red roses, vased elegantly with a veritable bush of greens. She stepped over happily and extracted the card from within:

'Mo chridhe (I looked it up),

Tha mi duilich. Call me.

- Iain.'

"Oh yeah," Maggie mumbled to herself. "I was a jerk."

She unlocked her door and transported the flowers inside to display them proudly on her kitchen table. She sat down in one of the chairs there and stared at the card.

'Tha mi duilich.' Gaelic for 'I'm sorry.' He'd even spelled it right. But more importantly, they both knew he had nothing to apologize for; she was the one who should be apologizing—for forgetting about their Argyll rendezvous, and for then berating him over being concerned about her. So, in the end, the card meant he was man enough to swallow his pride for the sake of their relationship.

"Good play, Romeo," she whispered as she reexamined the card. Then she set it down and walked over to the phone.

"Good Afternoon. MacTary's Woolens." Iain answered.

"Tha mi duilich cuideachd," Maggie said.

"Er, how's that again?" Iain sputtered. "I don't think I heard you properly, miss."

"I said: I'm sorry too," Maggie translated. "Thanks for the flowers."

"Oh, it's you! Hello! So you liked the flowers, eh? Not too clingy, then?"

"Just clingy enough," Maggie smiled. There was a pleasant pause, then, "Dinner?" she suggested.

"Brilliant," Iain was quick to reply. "Where would you like to go?"

"Mm. You choose. Pick me up at six. I'll wear a dress."

"All right. Six, then. And I won't wear a dress."

"Good," Maggie laughed. She could feel her recent lack of sleep begin to catch up with her in the warmth and comfort of home. The back of her neck was heavy with fatigue. "I think I'll take a beauty nap before then."

"Och, you don't need to do that," Iain assured.

"Yeah, okay, that was too clingy," Maggie laughed.

"Aye, well, I couldn't just let it pass by either."

"Oh, you're right. You were screwed either way. That's why I like you so much. You know the score, but you stick around anyway." She laughed again. "I'll see you tonight, *mo chridhe*."

"Tonight, *mo chridhe*," Iain replied.

Then Maggie shuffled off to bed, the phrase lingering in her ears.

'*Mo chridhe*.' 'My heart.'

***

"Aye, right. Spellbook. Ballygoomy. Got it." Iain swallowed a mouthful of roasted potatoes then pointed his fork toward his dining companion. "But how did you end up in Wales?"

"Patience, grasshopper," Maggie raised a solemn palm to Iain's puzzled face. "And it's 'Ballincoomer,' not 'Ballygoomy.'"

"Aye, whatever." He waved the correction away with his fork. "So get on with it. How does my mysterious wee Maggie come to find herself in Aberwistwhich?"

"Aberystwyth," Maggie corrected again with a stamp of her foot and the slightest of pouts. Then she saw the twinkle in Iain's eye. "You knew that, didn't you? You're just teasing me."

"Well, I've heard of Aberystwyth, aye? But no, I can honestly say I've never heard of Ballygoomy." Then before she say anything, he amended, "Ballincoomer."

Maggie chuckled and took a sip from her wine glass. She could hardly begrudge him a little playful teasing. He'd been quite magnanimous and forgiving about her small faux pas of missing their rendezvous before going M.I.A. and incommunicado for two days, only to reappear and bite his head off.

He said he'd been worried half out of his mind. She'd been glad to hear it—in a sick, selfish, just-where-is-this-relationship-going? kind of way. She figured she owed him an explanation. At least.

But not every last detail. Complete candor wasn't necessary just yet. One word about black magic and he'd be out the door before she got the chance to utter the next one.

She stole a peek at his deep blue eyes.

But maybe not, she thought. He was being exceedingly understanding about her little Wales detour. *Maybe...? But no*, she decided. *No reason to broach that subject just yet. I'll burn that bridge when I come to it.*

"Okay." She set her utensils down and explained. About the Spellbook of Ballincoomer. About the ruins of the Ballincoomer Abbey. About the faded inscription on the ruins' stone walls. And about the internet café where she'd confirmed the presence of the Welsh Book of Souls at the library in Aberystwyth.

"From ancient ruins to an internet café?" Iain asked rhetorically. "Quite the juxtaposition."

Maggie opened her mouth to agree, but then closed it and stared across the table. "'Juxtaposition?'"

Iain sighed heavily. "It was in the same book as 'hence.'"

Maggie had to laugh. "I don't doubt it. Anyway..." And she finished her tale, including Gwen and Susan and the manuscript, but excluding the kidnapping and police interrogation. She did tell him about the nightmare, though; she needed some excuse for having been so mean to him.

When she'd concluded, Iain nodded thoughtfully. "Well, the whole thing sounds very interesting."

"Really?" Maggie squinted appraisingly at him.

"Oh, aye. Fascinating."

"Even the part about the orthographic differences between Old Gaelic and Old Welsh?"

"Och, especially that part." A boyish grin played at his mouth and eyes.

Maggie shook her head. "I don't know about you, Iain Grant."

Iain smiled broadly, his blue eyes sparkling. "Well then, stick around. There's a lot to learn."

***

A moonlit stroll up to her flat arm-in-arm with Iain—that would have been perfect. But it was late July at the 57th Parallel. Even at ten o'clock in the evening the sun was still shining brightly, albeit lower, in the summer sky. She'd just have to settle for the arm-in-arm part.

As the reached the door, Maggie squeezed his hand and looked up at him. "Would you like to come inside?"

"Aye, I would," Iain replied. "But I shouldn't. It's getting late and I need to be at the shop extra early tomorrow. Early delivery of tweeds direct from Harris."

Maggie's disappointment shone on her face, but she tried to understand.

Iain leaned down and kissed her pouting lips. "Another time?"

The pout curled into a smile. "Definitely."

39. Tea for Two

There was a message; the red light on Maggie's answering machine was flashing. But having just spent the last four hours with Iain, Maggie was fairly certain the message wasn't from him. And if it wasn't from him, then she didn't need to hear it just then. So she ignored the blinking red light and skipped off to bed, Iain's kisses still warm on her lips.

She didn't have a single nightmare.

In the morning, the day's first cup of coffee steaming in her hand, she pressed the answering machine's 'play' button:

"Hello, Maggie. This is Sarah MacKenzie. After you left this morning I realized I'd forgotten to invite you out to tea. I always take my new students out to tea. You know, a relaxed environment, get to know each other a bit better, discuss where you'd like to see your research go, things like that. I'm available tomorrow afternoon, or the next day, then—hmm, let's see—then not again until the middle of next week. So ring me up when you get in and we'll schedule something. Ta."

Maggie considered her coffee mug and the clock in turn. She felt a certain relaxation knowing where her next caffeinated beverage would come from. And at twenty after nine it wasn't too early to return Sarah's call.

Someone was in her office just then so she couldn't really talk, but a three o'clock tea at 'The Green Door Café' was agreed upon. Maggie made sure to get directions. Then she hung up the phone and strolled into the kitchen to make breakfast.

The cereal was gone before the coffee was gone. And the coffee was gone before the newspaper was finished. But eventually there was no denying that breakfast was over and Maggie reluctantly pushed herself up from the kitchen table and began the drudgery of cleaning up after herself. She washed the few dishes she'd used and dropped the newspaper into the recycling bin. Then she decided to change the water in the flower vase. She wanted Iain's roses to last as long as possible.

But as she pulled the bouquet from the vase, she inadvertently shoved her left thumb onto a particularly sharp and long thorn.

"Ow!" she shrieked. She followed up with a heart-felt, "Damn!"

The blood immediately began to ooze from the gash in her thumb-pad. Sucking the offending digit, she managed to complete the water change one-handed. She returned the roses to the kitchen table then extracted her thumb from her mouth and regarded the swelling droplet of blood rising from the center of her thumbprint. She let it grow and watched in morbid fascination as it reached critical mass, then broke free and slid down her thumb to splatter onto the table top.

'Infantsblood shall be spilt onto ancestral earth.'

Maggie reinserted her thumb into her mouth and squeezed her eyes shut. It had been a hell of a week.

The MacLeod kidnapping and the bloody words in the same Old Gaelic dialect as her Dark Book.

The Owen kidnapping and the bloody prophesy of the Welsh Book of Souls.

Not to mention Brìghde the Healer and the elusive Spellbook of Ballincoomer.

How did it all fit together? Or did it at all? Was she just wasting her time? She'd thought that perhaps she could help— maybe uncover something helpful to the police at least. But the police in Aberystwyth had been quite unfriendly; and she really didn't have anything to tell the Aberdeen police even if she were disposed to do so. And besides, didn't she have enough to keep herself busy?

Iain Grant and the promise of a late-summer romance?

Sarah MacKenzie and the impending responsibilities of her studies.

She really needed to figure out where her priorities lay. But she was relieved to remember that for today at least, fate had selected her studies. Professor Sarah MacKenzie, come on down!

Maggie grabbed a paper towel from the counter and wiped her blood off the kitchen table. Then she walked back toward the bathroom for a band-aid and a shower.

***

The 'Green Door Café' was well hidden. It was several blocks away from campus, just outside the invisible frontier which separated the student's Aberdeen from that of the city's permanent inhabitants. There was a small commercial district, dominated by eclectic boutiques with names like 'Retro Scotia' and 'Bibble's Baubles.' At the middle of the block, just past an upscale women's clothing boutique named 'Carrie Jean,' was a narrow opening to a small cul-de-sac alcove. Inside the alcove and tucked around behind 'Carrie Jean' Maggie stood the hidden entrance to 'The Green Door Café.'

The door was a dull white, not green. Good thing she'd gotten directions.

The interior continued the feeling of comfortable secretiveness. All told there couldn't have been more than a ten seats in the entire place. And this had been accomplished by shoving several small tables cheek-by-jowl between the narrow walls of the closet-like café. Still, rather than being cramped, the room felt cozy. This was likely the combination of the well-worn wood furnishings, the aged floral print wallpaper, the pleasant variety of framed watercolor prints, the baroque strings quietly filling the air from a pair of ceiling-bound speakers, and, most of all, the heavy-set gray-haired woman who looked up from the infinitesimal counter to give Maggie a warm smile that combined welcome with an unspoken understanding that, having found the place, she would undoubtedly come again. The woman let the smile fade, its residue still coating her lips, and returned her attention silently to the very thick book in her hands. Maggie reholstered her own 'hello' smile and stepped to the table in the back where sat, her back to the door, Prof. Sarah MacKenzie.

It was as she traversed the short distance to Sarah's table that Maggie finally realized who the professor reminded her of. The thick cascading brown curls, so prominent from behind, were exactly how Maggie remembered her own mother's hair, cuddling into it as a child. She didn't have a lot of memories of her mother, but she hadn't forgotten the smell and feel of the soft auburn locks across her face and nose. It was an exceedingly pleasant memory.

"Good afternoon, Sarah," Maggie offered in greeting as she reached the table.

"Afternoon, Maggie." Sarah MacKenzie didn't seem at all startled by the greeting in the quiet café, even though she too was engrossed in reading some thick tome. She turned her face up toward Maggie even as her eyes held the page just long enough to finish the last sentence. "And please, call me Sarah." She closed her book on a silver bookmark. "Any trouble finding the place?"

"No, none at all." Maggie took the seat opposite her mentor. "I'm glad you started the directions with, 'It can be a bit hard to find.' I paid pretty good attention after that. And the directions were dead on. Although I wasn't sure once I got here. The door," she nodded toward where she'd entered, "isn't green."

Sarah smiled warmly as she finally set her book down, silver bookmark slicing the volume in two roughly equal halves. "I think that's why I ended up falling in love with the place. It's a mistranslation from the Gaelic. This café has been here since 1740. It's changed owners over time, but it's always been here. When it was established, the owners were Gaels, and so they named it in Gaelic. After Culloden, when Gaelic was more or less illegal, they'd been forced to change the name. The owners claimed not to know exactly how to translate the name so some English bureaucrat who thought he spoke the language gave it a try. He missed the adjective though. The original name was '*An Doras Uaigneach.*'"

"'*Uaigneach,*'" Maggie repeated as she considered the word. "That means 'secret.' But the Englishman thought it meant 'green?'"

"Aye. The Gaelic word for green is '*uaine,*' apparently a bit too similar for the Englishman. So he decreed that they must call the place 'The Green Door Café' even though the front door was obviously not green. The Gaelic speaking owners thought it was hilarious," Sarah concluded, "so they accepted the English name, kept the Gaelic one in their hearts, and made damned sure no one ever painted the door green."

"Fantastic," Maggie enthused. "Don't you just love languages?"

"It's why I do what I do," Sarah smiled broadly. "Speaking of which, thank you again for meeting with me on such short notice. I always like to take my students out to tea right away. It's good to talk about academic interests and plans right at the beginning, before classes start up again and things get too hectic. And doing it over tea is so much more civilized than in that stifling little closet of an office they give me."

Maggie regarded the homey confines of the café. "This isn't much bigger," she joked, "but it's a lot more comfortable," she agreed. "Thank you for bringing me here."

"Not at all," Sarah waved away the thanks. Then it was finally time to talk shop. "So you want to study Welsh, do you?"

Maggie started to respond, but caught the 'No, not really' on its way out. And she suddenly regretted her earlier duplicity. She was so enjoying her visit with Sarah that she'd forgotten it was based on the misrepresentation that she wanted to learn Welsh.

Although, she supposed, she probably did 'want' to study Welsh—sort of. The way one 'wants' to eat broccoli: not because it's fun, but because it's good for you and afterwards you're glad you did it. So with Welsh. Maggie's true linguistic love was Gaelic, especially Scottish Gaelic, but also Irish Gaelic and their common ancestors Middle and Old Gaelic. Welsh on the other hand had never really interested her. Still, any good Ph.D. student in Celtic Studies should know at least a little bit of each of the four surviving Celtic languages and hence the course on Welsh she had suffered through so far; she was still getting around to that Breton class. In any event, she'd come to have tea with Sarah mainly because she liked the woman and needed an academic advisor anyway. She'd forgotten about the Welsh part. Time to eat her vegetables.

"Yes," she prevaricated, "very much so. I suppose I should admit my main interest is in Gaelic, but I feel I should—that is, I'd like to know Welsh too. At least a reading knowledge of it. And the older forms as well."

"Of course, of course," Sarah agreed, but before she could respond further, the thick old proprietress waddled over to their table.

"Are you ladies a' ready tae order, then?" she asked in a thick Highland brogue.

"Aye," Sarah replied after receiving an affirmative nod from Maggie. "I'd like a pot of Earl Grey and a raspberry scone."

"Very good. An' fer you, lass?"

"Er," Maggie paused. Sarah had just stolen her order. But no reason she couldn't follow suit. "I'd like the same actually. Earl Grey and a scone. Um, do you have blueberry?"

"Nae, love." The woman seemed genuinely ashamed. "Only raspberry and strawberry."

"Raspberry, then," Maggie acquiesced. "Thank you."

"Thank you, lass." And the woman trudged slowly back toward her counter.

"So, anyway," Sarah started up again, "your main interest is in Gaelic, then?"

"Well, yes."

"Good. Mine too."

Maggie was surprised by this. "Not Welsh?"

"No, Gaelic. Everyone has to have a primary interest," Sarah explained. "Mine's Gaelic—like yours. But I'm also very interested in Welsh, less so in Breton, and also a bit in Japanese."

"Japanese?" Maggie found that delightful.

"Well, Aye," Sarah replied proudly. "*Konichiwa, ogenki desu-ka?*" She suppressed a delighted laugh. "I think all languages are wonderful. You just have to find the ones that, well, that speak to you, if you'll pardon the expression."

"I will," Maggie graciously offered. "I suppose you're right.

Well, let's see if Welsh isn't ready to strike up a conversation with me."

"That's the spirit. So the interest in Gaelic, is that familial? You're of Scottish descent, aye?"

"Er, yes, on my mother's side." Maggie looked at her new mentor quizzically. "How did you know that?"

Sarah smiled again, that warm friendly smile. "Well, the 'Devereaux' seemed French to my ear, but the 'NicInnes' kind of gave it away."

"Oh, right," Maggie tried not to blush.

"I looked up your records when Robert—Professor Hamilton—called me. Margaret NicInnes Devereaux. That 'NicInnes' does catch one's eye."

"I suppose so," Maggie admitted.

"So 'Daughter of Innes,'" Sarah continued. "Is that on your mother's side?"

"Right," Maggie agreed quickly. "My mother and grandmother. They both had 'NicInnes' as their second middle name too. It's been given to every daughter of every daughter for thirteen generations, back to a woman named Brìghde Innes, who was a noble woman from around here. She was my great-great-great-and so on-grandmother."

"Brìghde Innes, eh?" Sarah considered the name. "Well, that's wonderful that you have that family connection. Family," she paused earnestly, "is very important."

The weight of this hanging thought was interrupted by the arrival of two small teapots and a pair of raspberry scones.

"Here you are, luvs," the proprietress announced as she set the goodies down on the table. Then she smiled pleasantly and strolled again toward the counter.

Maggie reached for her tea and scone, but while her right

hand made it to the pot of tea, her left was tackled halfway to the scone by Sarah's own soft hand.

"Oh!" Sarah turned Maggie's hand over to expose the wound from that morning's thorn. "What did you do?"

"Oh that?" Maggie too regarded her thumb, still turned upwards in Sarah's grasp. "I just stuck it on a thorn this morning. It's nothing serious."

Sarah examined the thumb critically, a slight frown creasing her brow. "Chamomile tea," she announced.

Maggie laughed nervously. "Uh, okay. I should drink chamomile tea for a stuck thumb?"

"No, no," Sarah finally released Maggie's hand. "Don't drink it; soak your thumb in it. Twice daily for fifteen minutes. Let it cool first, so it's just a bit above room temperature. Do that for three days. The oils in the tea will keep it from scarring."

Maggie stared down stupidly at her thumb. "Really?"

"Och, aye. It's an old Highland remedy," Sarah assured. "Works like a charm."

Maggie retracted her hand slowly, still considering her injury and Sarah's words. Her consideration was interrupted by more words.

"So, then," Sarah poured herself a cup from the teapot. "You're ready to branch out into Welsh. And exactly how much Welsh do you know already?"

This succeeded very well thank you in tearing Maggie's attention away from her injured thumb. For the second time since she'd arrived at the Green Door, she felt her comfort drain away like a receding tide. She'd already told Sarah—at their first meeting— what her Welsh proficiency was. But she'd lied, more or less, needing to overstate her abilities to make it believable that she'd understood, at least in part, the ancient manuscript of the Welsh

Book of Souls. Understood it without black magic, that is. And so now Maggie found herself faced with the dilemma of having to recall exactly what she'd said so as to remain, more or less, consistent. 'Oh, what a tangled web...'

"Er," she began weakly, "I've only taken a course or two in Modern Welsh. But I've studied enough other languages that with the aid of a dictionary, and a lot of patience, I was able to decipher a bit of what I found in Aberystwyth. But it really just showed me how much more I have to learn."

Oh, good finish, Devereaux, she applauded herself.

"The beginning of wisdom," Sarah winked over her teacup. "So what did you think of the manuscript, then? The Welsh Book of Souls, aye?"

"Er, yes." Maggie too sipped from her tea. She broke off a piece of scone but held off inserting it into her mouth. "As I said, I didn't fully understand it. But what I did understand seemed a bit, well, barbaric."

"Barbaric?" This characterization seemed to shock Sarah. "How so?"

Maggie chewed her bite of scone and swallowed. "Okay, maybe 'barbaric' isn't the right word. Maybe it was more, let me see, maybe 'bloody' would be better. Gruesome."

"Well, aye," Sarah conceded, "I suppose I could agree with that description. But those were different times, aye?"

"Of course," Maggie agreed. "It just struck me that there seemed to be a lot of blood letting required for most of their rites. But as you say, a function of the times, I suppose."

Sarah considered this with a silent nod as she too enjoyed a bite of raspberry scone.

"But still, there was one..." Maggie started.

"Aye? Which rite then?"

"No, never mind," Maggie stopped herself. She wasn't sure how to explain her ability to understand it. "I couldn't really read it all," she tried.

"Nonsense," Sarah encouraged. "Just tell me what you understood. Maybe I know it."

"Well, okay," Maggie acquiesced. "It involved—from what I could tell, that is—slitting the throats of two babies. I don't care what era it is, infanticide just seems barbaric to me."

"Aye. I know that one." Sarah took a thoughtful sip of tea. "But you know, what I found really interesting about that one," another sip, "is that it didn't actually require that the babies die."

Maggie set her scone down and blinked hard at the professor. To Maggie's recollection, the spell included the requirement that the babies throats be slit and their blood spilt into the ground. She wasn't sure how an infant would survive that. She said as much.

"Aye, I suppose so," Sarah conceded carefully. "But it really comes down to the wording of the spell, doesn't it? Do you recall the exact words used?"

Maggie had to shake her head. 'No,' she imagined herself saying, 'I cast a black magic translation spell that allowed me to recognize the meaning behind the words.' She settled for just the first word. "No."

"Well, the exact wording is something like, 'Two infants shall suffer their throats to be slit, and their blood shall be spilt into the earth.'"

Maggie looked askance at the professor. "Okay...?" She didn't see Sarah's point.

"It doesn't say the babies have to die," Sarah asserted.

"But how does an infant with a slit throat survive in Sixth Century Wales?" Maggie had to ask.

"Ah, well, quite simple," Sarah replied. "He doesn't. But nowadays—now, with modern medicine standing by to heal their wounds—I'd wager the rite could be performed without the babies having to die."

Maggie's brow creased deeply as she considered this. "Well, I suppose so, but—"

"The most important thing," Sarah interrupted, "would be to save the babies."

This phrase struck a chord inside Maggie that she didn't even know was there. "Save the babies...?"

"Aye." Sarah nodded, as she reached again for her scone. "Save the babies."

And suddenly Maggie knew exactly where her priorities lay.

40. Reasonable Minds May Differ

"Are you blind? It's as plain as the nose on your face!"

Warwick crossed her arms and leaned back in her desk chair. She understood that reasonable minds often differ and she was neither adverse nor unaccustomed to having her judgment scrutinized—it was part of the job. But there was no need for raised voices or insults. They were cops after all, not lawyers.

"There's no need to yell, Alison."

Chisholm, who had been pacing the floor like a caged tiger, stopped short and glared down sharply at the floor, pressing her fists against her hips. When, after a moment, she raised her face again, there was a self-conscious grin on it. "You're right, Elizabeth. I'm sorry. It's just— It's just that it's so obvious. She's guilty as hell. Jessie MacLeod is the kidnapper."

Warwick uncrossed her arms and rested her chin on a fist. "I'm not so certain..."

"Not so certain?" Chisholm echoed incredulously. Then she caught herself. "I'm sorry, but just think about it for a moment. You know as well as I do that eighty-odd percent of all kidnappings are committed by family members, and usually because they lost out on the custody arrangements."

"Statistics don't make a case," Warwick observed dryly.

"Of course not," Chisholm huffed. "But it's motive. Come on, Elizabeth, think back to the basics. Motive, means and opportunity. When you find all three of those in one individual, you've got your man—or woman, as the case may be. And Jessie MacLeod had motive, means and opportunity."

Warwick pursed her lips and offered up her opinion of this assertion, "Hm."

"All right, then," Chisholm finally sat down opposite Warwick and pointed to her fingers, "let's go through it."

Warwick leaned forward and folded her hands on her desk. "All right, let's."

"Motive." Chisholm ticked off the first finger. "MacLeod was divorcing her. He had physical custody of Douglas and even Jessie's lawyer admitted that no court was likely to take the heir apparent of the MacLeod chieftaincy away from the Chieftain himself. The only thing that might accomplish that would be some demonstration of his unfitness to have custody of Douglas. So she gains doubly by stealing her son back. First, she gets her son back. Second, she embarrasses MacLeod and gains the advantage in court. That's motive."

"I'll give you motive," Warwick conceded. "What about means?"

"Right. Means." The second finger was ticked off. "There was no forced entry, so we know whoever did it must have had a key to the townhouse. In her interview Jessie admitted she'd had a key before the divorce. Now, she claimed she returned it to him when he kicked her out, but she would have had ample time to make a duplicate. That's means."

"That's potential means," Warwick corrected. "But please, do go on."

"Opportunity." The third finger. "Now we know that she's got no alibi for that night. She wasn't at *Le Bistro Écosse* and she wasn't at *Frankenwald*. And not only is her alibi gone, but we know she lied to us. That's opportunity. And it's only reinforced by her deception."

Warwick nodded thoughtfully for several moments. Then she raised her own fingers and counted them off herself. "The motive is there, I have to admit that, but the means is hypothetical at best. We've no proof she kept a key. All we know is that there was no forced entry and so she would have needed a key to enter. But there are other ways it could have gone down. Similarly, the opportunity is pure speculation. All we know is that the waitress at the restaurant didn't succeed in getting Jessie seated in her section, and 'Günther' wouldn't tell us one way or another."

"Now wait a minute," Chisholm interrupted. "Günther told us she hadn't been in that night."

"No," Warwick raised a confident finger, "Günther said he didn't recognize her, and even if he did he wouldn't tell us. So she may well have been there, but Günther isn't saying."

Chisholm scowled across the desk at her compatriot.

"Now, throw in the fact," Warwick continued, "that Jessie is still very much around Aberdeen, and has yet to be spotted pushing a pram down Queen Street. If she kidnapped her own son, why stick around to be found out? Why not hot foot it to some Mediterranean beach to enjoy the company of her son in seclusion?"

"Maybe she's trying to throw suspicion off of her," Chisholm offered. "Maybe the child's with a relative, back on Skye."

"Or maybe she's innocent," Warwick countered. "Either way, it's a 'maybe' and you don't go arresting someone on a 'maybe.'"

Chisholm leaned back hard in her chair and let out a long, low sigh. She ran both hands through her long black curls and twisted them back into a loose, haphazard pony tail. "Wow," she half laughed the word.

Warwick waited for more but none was forthcoming. "Wow what?" she asked.

Chisholm exhaled again, then released the pony twist from her shoulder and leaned forward. "I just—" she began. "I just really thought you'd agree with me on this. I mean, sure, I'd expected you the challenge it, examine it critically, but agree with me in the end. I mean, it's all just so obvious. She's so obviously guilty. I thought for sure you'd see it too. Then we'd get Cameron on board, get the arrest warrant, and go pick her up. We find the duplicate key at her flat. And when we confront her with how her alibi didn't check out, she crumbles and confesses—or else feeds us some new alibi that she can't confirm. Either way, we've got the key and either a confession or another lie. Then we close the case with an arrest and hand it over to the prosecutors."

"The only problem being," Warwick observed, "I don't agree with you."

"Well, yes, that," Chisholm laughed nervously, "and the fact that I skipped a step in there."

Warwick raised an eyebrow. "Oh? Which one?"

Chisholm smiled sheepishly and began playing with her hair again. "The one where I convince you before going to Cameron."

Warwick's eyes flared. "You've already gone to Cameron?" She fairly shouted the question.

The answer came not from Chisholm, but from the knock on Warwick's doorframe. It was Cameron.

"Evening, you two." He stepped in, brandishing a several page report in his hand and a relieved smile on his face. "No doubt discussing the MacLeod case?"

"Quite right," Warwick confirmed through gritted teeth.

He waved the report gently toward the visiting detective. "Good work, Alison. Damn good work. And you really think she'll confess when we get her into custody?"

"I expect so." Chisholm turned to look up at Cameron but kept the corner of her eye trained on Warwick. "Or else she'll come up with another cock-and-bull story we can debunk—and one she won't have had time to prepare. One's as good as another really. If she lies, we'll destroy that alibi too, and we'll know she's a liar. If she confesses, then we've got her."

"Good, good, good." Cameron nodded, half to himself. It took another couple of moments before he noticed Warwick's sour demeanor. "What do you think, Elizabeth?"

"I think it's premature."

"Premature?" Cameron was taken aback. "No, no. It's not premature, I can tell you that. Overdue, if anything. I've spent half my day on the telephone with this superior or that. MacLeod's been calling every one of his friends and contacts—and that's quite a few, I can tell you—spouting off about how we're all a bunch of incompetent boobs. Not more than an hour ago the Superintendent gave me 'til the end of the week to find the MacLeod baby or he'll be handing the case over to the Yard." He clenched his jaw. "I hate the bloody Yard. Think they're so much better than us..."

Warwick and Chisholm sat silently, uncertain whether he'd finished.

"Sorry." Cameron caught himself again. "But why do you say it's premature, Elizabeth? I thought you and Chisholm had come to this conclusion together?"

"We were still discussing it," Warwick replied with a low glare at Chisholm.

"It's a very strong case against her," Chisholm felt compelled to assure. "Motive, means, opportunity. She's guilty all right."

"Hm." Cameron glanced down at the report again, a pensive scowl scarring his countenance. Without looking up he asked, "Motive's there all right. And the key to the townhouse?"

"I'm sure it's at her residence," Chisholm was ready with the reply. "I—I can guarantee we'll find it when we pick her up."

Cameron nodded to himself. "And her alibi?"

"We've verified it was a lie," Chisholm assured. "My guess is she'll feed us a new alibi, but she'll have no corroboration. None. Then we'll have her telling two different stories. That's almost better than a confession because it shows she's being deceptive. It shows consciousness of guilt. The jury will hate her."

Warwick crossed her arms and waited silently. She knew it was too late to affect his decision. He'd already made it; he was just double-checking his facts.

"She's guilty," Chisholm repeated. "And I'll get you the evidence to prove it."

Cameron chewed on his cheek as he continued to glare down at Chisholm's report. There was no way around it now, he had to make the call. "All right. Do it. Pick her up tonight, at her residence. I want to be able to search her flat. Find that key. And then get the confession." Then almost as an afterthought, he added, "And the child. Find out where the child is. I need the MacLeod boy in his father's arms by the end of business tomorrow."

"Will do," Chisholm replied eagerly as she jumped to her feet. "Will do. I'll grab a few of the boys. We'll case the flat, wait for her to get home. Then we'll nab her just as she's opening the door." She looked at her watch: five-thirty; they all knew Jessie MacLeod was likely on her way to some nightclub even now. "I'll have the key and her new alibi on your desk by morning."

She knew better than to look at Warwick, so instead headed

directly out the door, an observable spring in her step.

Cameron waited for a few moments, rubbing the white-fuzzed crown of his head as he pretended to read the report in his hand. Finally, he took in a deep breath and tore his gaze from the paper. When he looked at Warwick he looked tired.

"Sorry, Elizabeth. I've got to take a chance on this one." When she didn't reply, he went on, "Motive, means and opportunity. It's all there. The scientific method."

She smiled weakly and nodded, but didn't reply. Cameron nodded again and walked silently from the office, his continued perusal of Chisholm's report evidence of his misgivings at the course of action he'd just authorized.

Warwick watched him leave, then sat silently at her desk for a very long time. Ten, fifteen, maybe even thirty minutes passed, as she sat alone in her office and contemplated her remaining options. When finally she stood up, she walked straight to her map of Aberdeen. She extracted the upper right push-pin from the map and pulled the corner up ever so slightly before reinserting the thumb-tack about half a centimeter higher than its previous position. She stepped several steps back and admired the map. It finally looked straight.

She snatched the MacLeod file off her desk and stormed out the door.

41. MacLeod's Townhouse

"Dumb, Devereaux." Maggie made sure to whisper in the quiet of the cool, dark evening. "Stupid. And dangerous."

She'd had to wait for nightfall. A rather late proposition at the 57th Parallel the last week of July; it was well after eleven o'clock before she felt it had been dark enough long enough to venture out on her fool's errand.

In a way, though, the late sunset was a good thing. It had also given her enough time to confirm the complete lack of any reasonable alternative to her proposed course of action. It may be a dumb idea, but it was the only one she could come up with which would get her the information she needed in the time she needed it. Still, she couldn't help but wonder whether Breaking and Entering was a felony in Scotland.

Technically, she wouldn't actually be breaking anything, not if it worked out properly, but she was most definitely going to be entering. Perhaps simple Trespassing was just a misdemeanor. She absently wondered whether they deported for misdemeanors before shaking her head to clear it and stepping up to the cool stone wall of David MacLeod's townhouse.

She had not been idle as she waited for the sun to set. She had used the day's remaining light to case the townhouse. She got the address from the newspaper article she'd saved and then she made her way casually toward the crime scene, strolling past, casually, appearing to anyone, she hoped, like any other interested — but not too interested — Aberdonian. If there were cops around, then the whole thing was off. She might be planning on 'breaking' and/or 'entering,' but she sure as hell wasn't planning on 'getting arrested.'

The blue and white police tape still cordoned off the premises from the street. *'Crime Scene - Do Not Cross'* But there were no police officers hanging about; the place was deserted. Maggie supposed the city probably didn't want to pay even just one police officer to stand around guarding a crime scene which undoubtedly had been thoroughly investigated, probably multiple times, since the kidnapping. If there was any evidence the police were going to find, they'd found it. The only question that remained — and the hope that brought Maggie out into the dark night — was whether there wasn't some small piece of evidence which the police hadn't been able to find, but which Maggie might.

She looked around the small backyard garden of the townhouse. No one around. Good. She had strolled along the sidewalk in front of the rows of townhomes on Stuart Street. Just before the MacLeod house, she'd ducked into the back yard of the neighboring townhouse. It was late enough that she didn't expect to encounter anyone. And if she did, then she could plausibly deny any interest in their home; she'd just gotten mixed up, taken a wrong turn, silly American. But no one was about and she quickly hopped the short iron fence into the garden behind MacLeod's residence.

She had ignored the undoubtedly locked back door and stepped over to stand directly beneath the nursery window. The newspaper had also included a photo of that, if only to reinforce the obvious point that no one could possibly have entered the child's third floor nursery from the garden. But then, Maggie supposed, no one else could do this.

"<Tear asunder the bonds which chain me to the Earth. Deny Nature its order and raise my body to the hated sky.>"

It was a simple spell. The levitation spell. She had it pretty much mastered. She'd levitated books, pens, even pot pourri. Just never herself. But as she awaited that evening's twilight she supposed there was no reason that shouldn't work too. And she knew there was no time like the present to try.

Her ascent was shaky at first, but she concentrated and repeated the spell, whispering the Old Gaelic word for 'me' where she'd always said 'this object.' She'd expected to feel like she was being lifted, as if on an invisible forklift. But it wasn't like that at all. It was like she was falling—only in reverse. Like slipping away from something, being dragged away in a current. And she had to fight back a rather strong wave of panic as she imagined herself flying uncontrollably and irreversibly upward, toward the asphyxiating vacuum of outer space.

The window was fast approaching while her fingertips grasped frantically at the passing wall. As she reached the ledge outside the nursery window, she grabbed a hold of the window frame and thought as hard as she could to break off the levitation spell. She'd found that an unintentional break in her concentration could abort a spell, and similarly that a deliberate release of the spell in her mind would cease the effects of it. That's how she usually lowered the books, etc., that she levitated. She just hoped it would work this time too.

It did. She consciously shoved the spell away and let the certainty of gravity root her to the narrow stone ledge. She closed her eyes and let pass both the panic, and her motion sickness. When she opened her eyes again she realized, to her uncontrollable horror, that she was some twenty feet off the ground. She clutched to the stone frame of the window for all she was worth, an ironic fear of falling seizing her despite the mode of travel she'd used to arrive at her current location. Not wanting the think any more about it, she noted with relief that no one had bothered to lock the third-story window, threw open the sash and scampered inside Douglas MacLeod's nursery.

It was quiet as a tomb, and almost as dark. Unsettling thoughts considering the missing child who'd inhabited the small space, and the bloody fate that might await him at the end of a nearly forgotten Welsh prophecy. Maggie pushed the unpleasant thought aside, pulled a flashlight from her backpack and surveyed the chamber.

The word 'rannsachadh' came squarely to mind. The word was Gaelic and meant roughly 'to search,' but it had been borrowed from the Gaelic and brought into English as 'ransack.' There were no curtains, sheets, blankets or carpets to speak of in the small nursery. Nothing on the walls. What wood furniture as had been left by the police was scattered about the room as if tossed there by a giant at play. Scuff marks sliced at every angle across the fine hardwood floor, created a sickening crosshatch of despair in the stark glow of her flashlight. Only the crib appeared to be in its original position, standing silent vigil beneath the dried, brown, stained words from the newspaper photograph.

'I AM RETURNED TO FULFILL THE PROPHECY'

Whatever, Maggie thought and she hurried to the half-faded phrase which had stained the floor next to the crib. *This was where the real action is.*

'A THÁINMHNE NA DOHRGHATAS, SLÁINAICH AN LÁINABH A'SIO'

Or what was left of it; the thirsty floorboards had absorbed several of the more important letters. Not stopping to worry about it though, she knelt down next to the stains and swung her heavy backpack off her back. There was a divining spell in the Dark Book, and although she'd used the spell before to gather information about an event from physical samples left behind, it had been some time since she'd wielded it. She'd need to review it before proceeding.

The creak in the hallway decided otherwise.

Every house, even a townhouse, creaks sometimes, as walls and floors settle in rhythm with the continuous shifting of the earth beneath the structure; but those are the sounds of stress on vertical supports, the slight twist of a beam here or there. It was different, surprisingly different, Maggie noted, from the sound of someone shifting their weight on a squeaky floorboard just outside the nursery of a supposedly empty townhouse.

As quietly as she could, she set the backpack down on the floor, away from the Old Gaelic blood stain. Then she stood up and crossed over to the wall which held the door to the hall. She tiptoed lightly on the seam running between two lengths of boards, thus eliminating any squeaking she herself might cause. She'd trained the beam of the flashlight away from where anyone in the hallway might be able to see. She didn't turn it off completely — that would be a tip off that she'd heard something — but instead swung it to the opposite wall, its general glow still illuminating the room, but its exact location unclear.

Reaching the wall, Maggie paused for several short, shallow breaths. The smart thing, the sane thing, to do would have been to bolt right out the window and *'Bhaitit inh chaoimraighanh'* herself down to the ground. But wielding the magic always gave her an evil sort of rush and made her a little reckless, even itchy for confrontation. She knew all this, but still she couldn't quite stop herself. Bracing herself for what lay around the corner, and ready to cast a defensive levitation spell against the same, she dropped the flashlight and jumped around the corner.

"Ahhhhh!" she screamed.

"Hello, Maggie," replied Sergeant Elizabeth Warwick.

Maggie had been terror-stricken by the face she'd found waiting around the corner, eerily illuminated by the police officer's small penlight. Monsters and goblins and MacLeods she could handle. But there was no way Sgt. Warwick was going to buy any story Maggie could think to feed her. Maggie knew. She was going to jail. Still, she had to say something.

"Ho-Holy crap," she gasped. "You scared me to death." Not very professional, but it was honest.

Warwick grinned, the expression fully disconcerting in the weak glow of the penlight. "Now what's a nice girl like you doing disturbing a nasty crime scene like this?"

Yup. I'm going to jail.

"Er," Maggie started, but then stopped. She had nothing. Nothing credible anyway. She could hardly claim to have gotten lost on her way home from school. 'Oh, I always cut through the third floor of the MacLeod townhouse on my way home from my eleven o'clock lecture. I heard a rumor there was a kidnapping here a while back. That isn't true, is it?'

She sighed, the adrenaline-induced tingle in her fingertips beginning to subside, and wondered whether they served haggis in Scottish jails. Still nothing to be done now, and no story to be spun. "I— I thought I could help." That was true enough, she supposed.

Warwick's sardonic grin quavered for a moment then broadened into a genuine smile, one held also by her eyes. She reached over to the wall and flipped on the light switch, finally illuminating the hallway in overhead light. "That's good of you, Maggie," she said to the American's considerable surprise. "It's what I expected you to say. But," she paused and pursed her lips, "it may not be needed. An arrest is being made tonight."

Several dozen thoughts raced helter-skelter through Maggie's head, all vying for primacy in her now thoroughly confused mind.

"An arrest?" In her confusion, she'd forgotten to notice they weren't talking about what she was doing there. "Who?"

Warwick hesitated. She knew better. She really knew better. But then she shrugged. What the hell, she thought. It'll be front page news tomorrow anyway. "Jessie MacLeod. The baby's mother. And David MacLeod's soon to be ex-wife. She was about to lose the custody battle."

Warwick didn't find the explanation any more convincing from her own mouth than it had been from Chisholm's. She wondered if her doubt infected her tone. If it had, Maggie didn't seem to notice.

Instead Maggie considered the explanation for several seconds, the mish-mosh of competing ideas still spinning dizzily in her head. She grasped for a thought. "Is she Welsh?"

Now that, Warwick had not expected. She wasn't sure that she'd expected to find Maggie Devereaux at the crime scene, but she hadn't been surprised by it either. But the American's question came as entirely unforeseen. "Welsh?" she confirmed. "No, I don't think so." Then the inevitable follow up question: "Why?"

"Oh," Maggie began to reply, her senses beginning to return to her, helped no doubt by the newly stern expression worn by the police officer glowering at her. "Er ... no reason."

Oh, superb, Devereaux. Maggie mentally rolled her eyes at herself. There's no way she's going to believe that.

"Come now, Maggie." Warwick crossed her arms and intensified her stare. "There's no way I'm going to believe that. You asked that for a reason. You know something. Something that may help the investigation. What is it?"

"Nothing really," Maggie tried. "Just speculation, you know. And wrong speculation, I guess, if you're arresting the not Welsh ex-wife. Heh." This last syllable sprang from her nervousness; but she knew Warwick wasn't going to let her out of this one.

"First off," Warwick began, surprisingly calm, "I'm not arresting anyone." She let her gaze soften and proceeded, certain in her ability to extract the information from the American student. "In fact, I think they're wrong. I think Jessie's innocent. But I couldn't convince them. And I won't be able to without more information. If you know something, Maggie, tell me. Otherwise an innocent woman will go to prison."

Ouch. Maggie winced at the stinging injustice of it. That wasn't fair. Hitting below the belt.

"Not to mention," Warwick pressed her advantage, "ever finding the boy alive."

And she's down for the count. ...8...9...10! We have a winna!

"Okay." Maggie's shoulders dropped, half in relief. "I'll tell you what I know. For what it's worth," she was quick to add. Then she had a thought—a crazy thought—but one she decided to voice. "Will you tell me what you know in return?"

Stunned might be too strong a word, but Warwick was obviously surprised. After the shock faded from her eyes, it was replaced with a bemused smile. "No promises, Maggie. Tell me what you know. Then we'll see."

So Maggie did. Most of it anyway. Not the magic. But the kidnapping in Wales. And the prophecy.

"I think they might be connected," she concluded.

Warwick thought for a long moment, her arms crossed over her chest, one fist raised to support her chin. "Aberystwyth, you say? I could call down—"

"No!" Maggie interrupted. She also hadn't mentioned her interrogation by the police. "Er, that is— It's really not necessary. The police don't know anything. Er, probably, I mean. They probably don't know anything. Not that I would know."

"Maggie," Warwick began, her voice very like that of a schoolteacher, or a mother, or a mother who's a schoolteacher, "you're not a suspect, are you?"

"Suspect?" Maggie repeated incredulously. "No, of course not. Don't be silly." She shifted her weight and rubbed a nervous hand across the back of her neck. "More like a person of interest really. I told the police what I'd seen and they seemed to think—at first, that is—that I might be involved. But I'm not, of course, so, you know, there's no need to call them. Really."

Warwick frowned slightly but decided not to pursue it. "Hm," she commented. "Anything else?"

"No," Maggie answered with her own frown. "No, I really don't think so." She shrugged and glanced around the quiet townhouse. "I guess that's why I'm here. To find out more."

Warwick just stared at her, a perturbed look draped across her visage.

"You're not going to arrest me, are you?" Maggie finally asked. "For disturbing the scene. I hadn't even really gotten to that yet— Er, I mean, I wasn't going to disturb anything. Not really."

"Hm," Warwick repeated. "It's not a bad idea. But I'll tell you what." She stepped around Maggie and poked her head briefly into the nursery. "Everything looks fine in there. I'll go take a look downstairs. You must have come in through the ground floor, right?"

"Er, right." Maggie grinned nervously. "Of course."

"So I'll go downstairs and make sure everything's okay down there too. If so, you're free to go."

Maggie felt a wave of relief wash across her.

Warwick pointed down at a thick, paper-filled file on the ground next to where she had been standing. "That's my case file. Could you watch it for me? This may take a few minutes."

"Uh, sure," Maggie agreed.

Warwick started down the stairs.

"Aren't you going to make me promise not to touch your file?" Maggie asked after her.

Warwick turned around with a knowing grin. "Would it matter if I did?" Then she turned back and disappeared down the stairs.

Maggie waited for several seconds, her gaze shifting from the file to where Warwick had disappeared and back again. Finally she picked up the file and began to thumb through it as fast as she could manage.

Warwick's notes were on top. Her daily log of activities, chronicled by five minute intervals. Under this was a series of photographs—or more correctly stated, a series of documents with photographs paper-clipped to them. There were several bundles, each corresponding to a person. A person of interest, Maggie smiled to herself. The bundles consisted of handwritten interview notes to which was paper-clipped some sort of government issue photograph of the person, the person's name written on the white margin in blue ink. Driver's license photos, Maggie supposed, or passports— something the police could get easily. She perused each bundle carefully, interested in who Warwick considered to be persons of interest.

The first one was Jessie MacLeod. The ex-wife and mother of the missing child. The woman the police would be arresting that night. The one Warwick thought was innocent. Maggie skimmed the notes of the interview then turned to the next bundle.

Nellie MacQuarrie. MacLeod's nanny. And if Warwick's notes were to be believed, his lover. One of many no doubt.

Barry Nelson. MacLeod's business manager.

Impeccable dresser. Devoted to his wife.

Caroline MacDonald-Nelson. Nelson's wife. "Wow," Maggie whispered at the sight of Caroline's photograph. "She's gorgeous." A surgeon, too. Maggie tried not to think bad thoughts about her. She moved on to the next bundle.

Marsaili NicRath. A business rival of MacLeod's. He'd stolen control of her successful Gaelic news and culture website, but only because he wanted to shut it down. She'd hired a lawyer.

Glynis Campbell. NicRath's lawyer. And also Jessie MacLeod's. 'Conflict of interest?' Warwick had noted.

And there was one more photograph, paper-clipped to the inside back cover. Warwick was thorough, she had to give her that. But maybe a bit paranoid as well. It was a copy of an I.D. photo—from the Glasgow Police Department. 'Alison Chisholm, Sergeant Detective' read the type-written caption at the bottom. Now she had a face to go with Warwick's repeated references to a 'Chisholm' who was helping her with the investigation. Before Maggie could wonder why Warwick had gone to the trouble of obtaining her partner's photograph, she heard footsteps begin a squeaky ascent from downstairs. Maggie folded the file closed but neglected to set it back down on the floor.

"Finished," Warwick announced when she reached the top of the stairs.

"Yes, thank you," Maggie replied, handing Warwick the file folder. Then she realized what Warwick had meant. "Oh! You mean you—you're finished. Right. Good. Um... Am I free to go now?"

Warwick tried, mostly unsuccessfully, to suppress a smile. She tucked her file under her arm. "Yes, Maggie

Devereaux. You're free to go. I'll wait a few minutes after you. The front door's unlocked."

"Great. Thanks. I've just got a couple of things to fetch." Maggie ducked into the nursery and in a matter of seconds reemerged with her back pack and flashlight, now turned off. "I'll just be off now." And she hurried down the steps and out the front door, as Warwick sat down at the tops of the stairs and shook her head lightly, her faint smile belying the doubts in her heart. She hoped she'd done the right thing.

Maggie closed the door to the townhouse behind her and stood on the porch for several moments, her eyes closed and the cool night air drying the sweat at her temples. After several moments, she'd slowed her racing heart, then swung the backpack over her shoulders and started down the street.

So much for her career as a spy. She'd cased the place for hours, but still Warwick had managed to show up and scare the living daylights out of her. She wondered what else she'd overlooked.

"Dumb, Devereaux," hissed the shadow darkened figure across the street from MacLeod's townhouse, green eyes fixed on the receding form of the American student. "Stupid. And dangerous."

42. The Call of the *Bean-Sìth*

She was in the field again. The little red schoolhouse was right where she'd left it. Only now she was fully grown, a woman. Maggie straightened her shoulders. She stepped toward the structure.

"Don't."

Maggie turned around. There was no one there. She turned back. The schoolhouse was gone. In its place stood a small castle. A stone keep on an island in the middle of a small lake. There was no bridge.

She looked down. She was on a row boat. It was drifting across the dark loch toward the island. The sky above was gray and threatening. Without ceremony the boat slammed into the shore. She stepped off onto the rocky land.

She looked up. A great hill stood before her. The castle was out of sight. But Maggie knew it was atop the hill. She began to climb.

"Don't."

She ignored her mother's voice. She crawled on hands and knees up the steep, grassy embankment. At the top of the cliff she threw herself over the edge and looked up.

She was in a cemetery. In front of her stood a weathered gravestone. 'ELLEN NicINNES DEVEREAUX.' Maggie's mother. Maggie stood up and walked around the headstone. Her quest lay beyond.

The castle was a church now. A small stone kirk in the center of the cemetery. She walked toward it.

"Don't. Please." Her mother's voice again.

Maggie turned around. Now there were two gravestones. Ellen Devereaux's and another. 'CATHERINE NicINNES INGRAM.' Maggie's grandmother. This gravestone was silent. Maggie turned back.

She was inside the castle walls. The earthen floor was stained with blood. No one was about. The air was perfectly still. Then a cry pierced the air. It was the ghostly scream of a woman. It came from the nearest tower. Maggie ran toward the tower door. She dashed inside.

She found herself inside the church. Stained glass surrounded her. She heard another sound. She looked toward the balcony. The stained glass window there was shaking. It depicted a hideous dragon-like monster with seven heads. A hydra. The glass rattled violently. It shattered with an explosion of glass and light and color. In its place stood a real hydra, three-dimensional and terrifying. The monster flew on dragon's wings to the balcony ledge. It perched itself there, its fourteen reptilian eyes boring through Maggie.

Maggie stumbled backward. She reached for a weapon. There was none. The hydra unfolded its wings and dropped to the floor, feet from Maggie. Three of the heads let out a horrifying roar while the other four heads bobbed toward her.

Then she heard another cry. The ghost woman again. It came from behind her. She turned quickly. There was another gravestone.

'BRÌGHDE INNES GORDON.' It marked the entrance to a subterranean mausoleum. She ran to the stone and pulled. The hydra gave chase, its footsteps shaking the small kirk.

Maggie pulled the stone free. She dropped through the narrow opening into the dark room. It was a library. On the table nearest her was a book. The Dark Book. Her Dark Book. Next to it was another book. A small one. The ghostly cry was coming from within its pages.

She snatched up the small journal, then turned to look back up at the hole to the vestibule. The hydra roared again above her. Then one of its heads rushed down into the library, undulating on a long serpentine neck. Maggie swung the journal at the advancing head. The book transformed into a sword. The sword sliced the head clean off. The remaining heads screeched in agony above her. Maggie could hear and feel the beast flee from the church.

Maggie turned and looked down at the head rolling to a stop at her feet. She recognized its face. It was her own.

"Answer the call." It was her grandmother's voice.

Then she woke up.

Maggie sat up in bed. She was sweaty and out of breath, but not really scared. And she was sure of three things.

The castle was the Castle of Park.

The church was the small stone kirk on the castle's grounds.

And she needed a ride.

43. The Castle of Park

The Castle of Park was located only some fifty kilometers northwest of Aberdeen. More château than fortress, the four-story structure had once been a Highland tower house before being converted into one of the residences of the Gordon Clan Chieftain. Nowadays, while having remained in Gordon hands, the castle has been converted to a guest house. Maggie had overnighted there the previous fall, her interest piqued by a personal connection. Her great-times-ten grandmother, Brìghde Innes, had married a son of the Gordon chieftain and moved to Park. And it was on the estate's sixty acres that Brìghde had been buried. Maggie had found her ancestor's gravesite. In the cemetery next to the castle's kirk.

The kirk itself was a small stone structure, long since deconsecrated, its Gordon parishioners having dwindled in number and become more willing to travel to nearby Banff for mass. The one-story house of worship was boarded shut on Maggie's last visit and she had been unable to venture inside to see what treasures it might hold. That time she had traveled to Park with her aunt and uncle, Uncle Alex driving them halfway across the Highlands and back. This time Iain drove.

Iain steered his new convertible along Scotland's A96

highway. Maggie was taking in the passing scenery, her thick brown hair blowing behind her as the wind rushed past her face. She almost didn't hear Iain's voice.

"Thank you for inviting me along again on one of your little trips," he was saying. "Maybe one of these times you can drive," he teased.

"Hm," Maggie replied thoughtfully, "that would require me buying a car, I suppose. And I do so enjoy letting you drive me all around Scotland."

"I am quite good at it, aren't I?" he asked with exaggerated pride.

"Oh, quite," Maggie wholeheartedly agreed. "Really excellent, I must say. And I especially admire your ability to drop everything on a moment's notice to shuttle me around at my whim."

Iain laughed, but only halfway as he recalled his employer's reaction to another request for a day off. "Your uncle's getting used to it, I think. We've made an arrangement: for every day I miss with little or no notice, I have to cover the store alone on a Saturday. He and Lucy have been spending a lot more time together since you've arrived, I think."

"Well, that's good," Maggie replied over the rush of air. "And I'm glad he's making you available for my last second impulses."

"Oh, aye. He's a good man. And I think he felt bad I don't get to go with you to Park last fall."

"It was kinda your idea, wasn't it?"

"Perhaps," Iain replied cautiously. "But remember our concern that they might not let a Grant stay there, what with the historical animosity between the Grants and Gordons."

"Well, I don't suppose they have any cattle for you to steal," Maggie replied sardonically, "so we should be all right."

"I'm wounded." Iain clutched at his chest. "It's been

generations since the Grants stole any cattle from the Gordons." He laughed at the thought. "And anyway, cattle raids were all just a part of the romance of the Highlands, aye?" He reached out and took her hand.

She let him, but frowned down skeptically at their clasped hands. "Nice try, Romeo. Now pay attention to the road." She pointed at an upcoming sign. "We need to take this next turn off. Then follow the signs toward Banff. We should be there in about fifteen minutes or so."

Seventeen minutes later, Iain pulled his car up to the main entrance of the Clan Gordon's Castle of Park.

"You're in luck," Maggie whispered with exaggerated relief, "no wee school girls to bar your entry."

"Thank God for small mercies," Iain acknowledged as he pulled up the parking brake.

The castle consisted of three sections all painted a warm yellow-beige which stood out beautifully against the lush green of the grounds. The oldest section was a medieval looking tower, complete with a series of square cutaways in its parapet. The newer sections were a manor house equal in height to the tower and the four stories of hallways connecting the two. Maggie jumped out of the car even as Iain was undoing his seatbelt.

"I'll go check us in," she announced. "You get the bags."

Iain just chuckled and shook his head. He really did like her spunk, even if it meant being ordered around every now and again. "As you wish, milady." But she was already gone.

Then another thought struck him. Perhaps she was as excited as he was, and couldn't wait to get to the room—*their* room. After all, he remembered, it was their first overnight trip together. He jumped from the driver's seat and fairly yanked the bags from the boot.

As he walked into the lobby, Maggie stepped over to meet him.

"All right," she held up the room key, "we're all set. We're in the 'Black Watch Suite.'"

"Ooh, now that does sound impressive. A suite." Then his eye glinted and his voice found its salesman brogue. "Do you ken what the Black Watch is, milady?"

"A paramilitary force of loyalist Scots set up by the English crown after the Second Jacobite Rebellion to quell what Highlander foment might have survived the brutal repression that followed the rebels' defeat at the Battle of Culloden?"

"Er." He blinked at her. "Right."

"Come on," she tugged at his arm. "Let's settle into our room."

"Suite," he corrected.

Maggie smiled up at him, her eyes twinkling. "Why, thank you, Iain. Nice of you to say so."

And before he could reply, she pulled him up the staircase toward their waiting accommodations.

***

The room was very nice. Spacious, well decorated, comfortable, with a nice view of the grounds and its own bathroom. Iain didn't pay much attention to all that though. His mind was fixated on one little detail.

"There's two bedrooms," he observed. A suite.

"Er, right," Maggie replied uncomfortably. "It was, um, all they had left?"

Iain narrowed his eyes at her, uncertain. He was getting to know her pretty well.

She pressed on. "Yup, all they had left. But it's probably just as well. I've, well, I've been having nightmares lately—nothing too terrible, don't worry—but, you know, this way, I won't keep you awake."

He stepped over and grasped her arms. His eyes seemed especially blue as he looked down at her. "I don't think I'd mind being kept awake by you."

Maggie felt her face flush red. She suppressed a nervous giggle. "Er, right. Um, well, we'll just see how that turns out, eh?" She pulled away and began unpacking her bags, trying to ignore his stare on her back.

She couldn't tell him the truth. She was going to need an opportunity to sneak out that night after Iain had fallen asleep. Separate rooms would have been too obvious. And too cold. And just no fun at all. But separate bedrooms in the same suite would be good enough. She had considered perhaps trying to cast some sort of sleeping spell on him, but there was no such spell in her Dark Book; she would have been crafting, which was tantamount to playing with fire. One little syllable off and she might have ended up with the male equivalent to Sleeping Beauty or Snow White. And she doubted Iain would appreciate a big wet one from Prince William.

She also didn't want to inflict the nightmares on him. They had been the worst after she'd cast the translation spell on herself. Using the magic on herself was one thing. Using it on another, a friend, a boyfriend—she blushed again at the thought—well, that was quite another.

Having filled the small dresser with her clothes and toiletries she turned to Iain, who had not even unzipped his bag, let alone taken it into the other bedroom.

"Welp," she announced with her hands on her hips. "Shall we tour the grounds?"

Iain sighed, then tossed his bag toward the other bed

chamber. "Sure."

***

The clouds were beginning to roll in. Maggie and Iain walked across the castle grounds chatting and glancing skyward, wondering whether they would make it back before the rain started. They were almost to their destination, although Iain didn't know it. He thought they were wandering more or less aimlessly, letting themselves be drawn by the next interesting flower, garden, pathway. Maggie, on the other hand, was using the flowers, gardens and pathways to lead them to the kirk. They stepped through a row of bushes and found the stone church waiting at the end of their path.

"Oh look!" Maggie pointed in feigned surprise. "It's the little kirk we found last time I was here. Come on, I want to show you something."

She did in fact want to show him something. She also wanted to confirm the location of the kirk and whether it was still boarded up. It was indeed still boarded shut and Maggie made sure to study the doorway and windows as they walked past it into the small cemetery beyond.

"This," she said as they reached a weathered old grave marker of particular significance, "is Brìghde Innes' headstone."

"Oh aye?" Iain was genuinely impressed. "Your great-times-whatever-grandmother? Well, that's grand. Did you find it last time you were here?"

"Yeah, it was pretty exciting." She looked up at him, took his hand, then looked down again at the stone. "And, well, I wanted you to see it."

Iain smiled but didn't reply immediately. Instead, he leaned forward and squinted at the gravestone. "So what does it say?" It was in Latin.

"Er," Maggie too squinted at the worn etchings on the centuries old marble, "it says: 'Brìghde Innes Gordon. Born the fourteenth of April, 1600. Died the seventh of August, 1652. Wife of Alexander. Mother of Margaret. Healer of All.'"

"A healer," Iain repeated. "Just like it says on the portrait I got you."

Maggie smiled at the memory of that heartfelt gift. "Yeah, just like that." She was starting to feel bad for, if not deceiving him, at least not informing him fully either. "Come over here, there's another one."

This next gravestone held the dubious distinction of being the only one standing outside the cemetery's fence. The rail around the graveyard ran between the graves of James Wilkie and Margaret NicInnes Wilkie. Mrs. Wilkie was outside the cemetery.

"That," Maggie said, pointing to the banished grave marker, "is where Brìghde's daughter Margaret is buried."

"Outside the church grounds?" Iain asked with raised eyebrow.

"You noticed that did you?" An embarrassed grin accompanied Maggie's question.

"A bit hard to notice. And pray, what does her gravestone say?"

Maggie squinted again, but she knew what this one said. It was hard to forget. "Er, it says: 'Margaret NicInnes Wilkie. Wife and Mother. Born the 18th of January, 1620. Burned the 22nd day of December, 1644.'"

"Burned?!" Iain's startled voice carried across the silent graveyard. "She was a witch?"

Maggie was offended. "Of course she wasn't a witch!" she retorted automatically. "There's no such thing as witches." Then she remembered her Dark Book. "I mean, you know, not really. But they must have thought she was one."

"Well, that seems rather unfair," Iain offered, "to put it mildly." He paused. "Ever notice they never seemed used to burn men as witches?"

"Pretty suspicious," Maggie agreed. "I figure it means one of two things."

"What's that?"

"Either the men used it as an excuse to get rid of the uppity women they didn't like."

"Or?"

"Or," Maggie smiled up at him, "the men were too stupid to figure out the magic."

Iain laughed at this even as the first raindrops started to fall.

"Come on," Maggie tugged again at his arm. "Let's get back to the hotel before it really starts to rain."

And Iain gladly took her hand as they turned back toward the castle.

***

The suite also had a fireplace. Maggie hadn't expected to use it in July, but the rain had brought with it a cold front and the temperature had dropped noticeably by the time they'd finished dinner. The roaring fire was cozy. And unrelentingly romantic.

There was a couch in front of the fire and Iain and Maggie had cuddled up together in front of the dancing flames. A half an hour later Maggie knew they'd better stop or they wouldn't be using separate bedrooms that night. It was with the utmost reluctance that she resorted to 'the tap.'

At first Iain didn't realize what the tap on his shoulder meant, but then he regained his senses and gazed down at Maggie.

"What is it?" he whispered. "Is there something wrong?"

"Um." Oh, she really didn't want to say this, but the whole

point of the trip had been to sneak out that night. She'd wanted Iain along for companionship, and a ride. She hadn't anticipated simply wanting him. "I— I think we'd better stop."

Iain's eyes widened in incomprehension, then disappointment, then concern. "Why? Did I do something wrong?"

"No, no," Maggie quickly assured him. "No, it's not you. It's me."

"You?" He didn't understand.

"Um, yeah." Think, Devereaux. "Er, it's a female thing," she tried.

Confusion spread across Iain's countenance, but then he looked down the length of her body and thought he understood. "You mean...?"

Maggie grimaced. "Yeah. That time of the month," she lied. "Sorry."

Iain considered this for a moment, then rolled over and propped himself up next to her. "Oh, don't be sorry. You can't help that. I understand." His heaving chest told her that his mind understood, but his body was less certain.

"I'm really sorry, Iain." She touched his face even as she felt the squeeze on her own heart, for rejecting him—and for lying to him. "I—"

"Hush." He placed his hand over hers on his cheek. "I told you I understand, and I do. I'm here to be with you, not just to, well, not just to 'be with you.' you understand?"

"I do." And she felt horrible for it. Then she said what felt like the first honest statement to him in a long time. "Thank you, Iain."

He smiled, but didn't say anything. He contented himself to squeeze her hand and kiss it gently before pressing it back against his cheek.

***

It hadn't taken much convincing to ensure Iain took the inside bedroom. In addition to the fact that she had seized the dresser next to the bed in the main chamber, she had explained that she would be getting up repeatedly throughout the night to use the toilet—more alleged 'female stuff'—and would thus likely wake him up as she traipsed past his bed toward the bathroom every hour or so. It had been a full day, he had driven, and he was eager for some uninterrupted sleep.

One o'clock. She figured that was a safe time. By then he would not only have fallen asleep, but should be sleeping deeply enough that the sound of the door closing behind her wouldn't wake him. She threw back the covers, slid from the bed and quickly pulled on the clothes she'd brought: a black sweater, dark jeans and black shoes. Then she swung the Dark Book-filled backpack over her shoulders and slipped out the door and into the night.

***

The rain was letting up, but there was still a steady drizzle which spotted her glasses. Her flashlight illuminated her wet way and in a matter of some minutes she found herself back at the small stone kirk.

The windows had each been covered with a single large plank of wood, as if taken from the side of a crate. The front door—and near as she could tell, there was no back door—was blocked by several planks which had been nailed to the wooden door frame. She set her flashlight on the ground, its beam lighting up the raindrops falling next to the door, and grabbed onto the top board.

It barely moved on her first tug. But it did move a little. The nails had been pounded in some time ago and apparently never replaced. Years of the wooden planks swelling and shrinking with the seasons had loosened them from their moorings. She pulled again and the top board gave way, sending her reeling backward across the slippery stone path which led to the kirk's entrance. Emboldened, she repeated the feat with the four remaining boards and then, her hands stinging from the work, she pushed open the church's oak door, its rusty hinges groaning against their unexpected and unauthorized call to duty. She picked up her flashlight and stepped inside.

The flashlight's beam circled the interior of the church, illuminating in three foot circles the desolate interior of a Highland church put into disuse nearly a century before. The pews were gone—firewood, Maggie supposed, or some other use—leaving a cold stone floor stained from decades of dirt and weather seeping through the planks on the windows and doors. What stained glass as there had once been was long since shattered, the occasional small dark shard sticking out in front of the same wooden planks. Cobwebs filled the corners of the chapel and draped down from the beamed ceiling in sheets, a macabre veil pulled across the face of the ancient kirk. And the altar—the altar was abandoned, an empty stone stage at the far end of the empty stone church, the only sign of its once holy function being the discoloration in the stone floor where the offering table had once stood.

Maggie closed the door behind her and ventured inside, suddenly unsure of exactly what it was she was seeking. In her dream, Brìghde's grave marker had been in the floor of the church, but not only were there no such plaques imbedded into the stone blocks of the kirk's floor, but she knew full well that Brìghde's gravestone was outside in the kirkyard cemetery. So what was she looking for?

The only thing of interest were a few tarnished metal plaques scattered unevenly across the kirk's walls, between and beneath the empty window frames. She cautiously circled the perimeter of the church scrutinizing the plaques. The nearest honored the Gordons who had fought and died in the 1745 Jacobite rebellion against England. She stepped along the dirty, cobwebby wall to the next plaque. It commemorated the birth of a William Robert Gordon in 1731—and the death of his mother in childbirth. And so it went until Maggie reached the seventh of approximately ten such plaques. It was on the opposite wall from where she'd started and about halfway back toward the door. This tarnished plaque commemorated the marriage of one Alexander Malcolm James Gordon to one Brìghde Innes in A.D. 1619. Maggie knew this was it. But she didn't know what to do next. Remembering the dream, she looked down.

She was standing on one of the square stones which comprised the floor of the kirk. It was a bit over two feet square, as they all were, and rounded at the edges to create a rut between the stones. Unsure what else to try, she shifted her weight on the stone, first to one side then the other. The stone offered a wobble—slight to be sure, but there just the same.

She set the flashlight aside, pointing back at her and the floorstone by which she knelt down. She ran her fingers along the edge but there wasn't any room the get her fingers under the stone for leverage. She looked around for something akin to a crow bar, but saw nothing in the dim recesses of the empty chapel. Then she remembered the one tool she'd brought with her: the Dark Book resting heavily on her back. Without removing the backpack, she raised her hands over the floorstone and recited the levitation spell.

The stone scraped reluctantly from its moorings as Maggie demanded it raise itself into the air. Once it was several inches airborne, she gestured it heavily to the side and set it to rest with a hollow clunk on its stone neighbor.

Looking beneath where the floorstone had been, Maggie

found what she'd come for. The stone had served as the lid to a shallow stone capsule. Inside the capsule was a metal box. And inside the metal box was the small leather-bound journal from her dream. She opened it up and failed utterly to read it.

It was gibberish. Handwritten in black ink, the penmanship was exquisite, but the words made no sense whatsoever. She ran through her available armory of languages: English, Scottish Gaelic, Irish Gaelic, German, Latin, French. Nothing. She was considering attempting the translation spell again when she noticed something at the same time she remembered something.

She noticed that when a paragraph ended, the last line of the stanza would jut out from the right margin to stop halfway toward the left margin, rather than vice versa as one might expect. And she remembered that Leonardo da Vinci had written his journals backwards lest they fall into the wrong hands and he be accused of witchcraft. She looked down again at the journal.

It was in Scottish Gaelic. And its author had written it backwards.

The first line was: '*mag edaifh san nàf a maga saloè na liehb ug hboìrgs, sennI edghìrB gai ahtal-rahbael na oes-na e S.*' 'This is the journal of Brìghde Innes, kept that my knowledge might survive me.'

Maggie sat down on the cold, dirty floor and began to read.

44. Brìghde Innes' Diary

Monday, 22 December, A.D. 1645.

It was one year ago today that Margaret was burned as a witch. The time for mourning is now past. The time for action is now here. We must ensure nothing like this ever happens again. I shall send out coded missives calling together the coven. We shall meet in two moons here at Park. We must unite to eradicate the darkness which consumed my daughter lest someone else's daughter also be consumed in flame. We carry the torch of the Shining Folk, but we must shine without burning.

***

Thursday, 18 January, A.D. 1646.

Margaret would have been twenty-six today. I spoke with mother. She said the magic feels weaker somehow. I do not feel it myself. Still, I shall be sure to raise the topic with my sisters next month.

***

Tuesday, 26 February, A.D. 1646.

The meeting went well. We are united in purpose. We shall use our resources and our abilities to battle the dark magic and strengthen the light magic. The others reported that they felt no weakening of the light magic. All agreed to keep watch for any signs of such weakening.

***

Saturday, 29 May, A.D. 1646.

I visited with Rhonwyn ab-Morgan today. She was in Inverness with her husband on business. She convinced him to stop at Park on their way back south. She asked how I was doing since Margaret's death. I told her what I could. I also told her of mother's concerns. She said she thought she felt it too, but was uncertain. She spoke of a Welsh prophecy in which the magic eventually disappears. She stated her belief that the disappearance of the magic was connected to the phrase 'The Celtic Continent.' It was agreed that she would return in the summer with details. I shall reconvene the coven for then.

***

Monday, 4 June, A.D. 1646.

I spoke with Catherine today. She suggested calling for envoys from the other Celtic lands—'our sisters abroad' she called them—to see if they know anything of this prophecy. It was agreed, but we shall forego an envoy from Brittany just now given that the prophecy threatens to come to pass on 'The Celtic Continent.'

***

Friday, 1 August, A.D. 1646.

The coven was convened today. Ambassadors were also present from Wales, Cornwall, Ireland and Man. Rhonwyn brought word of the prophecy. If it is true, then the magic shall eventually abandon the Celts, and we shall be helpless against our enemies. It was resolved: our mission is now two-fold. We shall contain and destroy the dark magic even as we protect and preserve the light. As the prophecy is not meant to come to pass until centuries hence, a blood oath was taken. Each of us shall pass our charge, mother to daughter, as long as necessary. I shall pass mine to Margaret's daughter, Catrìona, when she is old enough to understand. The coven shall meet every seven years, or more often as is necessary to track our progress. I can only hope the day never comes where the dark arts of blood and death have survived while the light arts of soul and healing have perished.

***

Saturday, 1 August, A.D. 1647.

I had the most horrible dream last night. The light magic was gone. And a traitor, a Judas, had wrestled control of the coven, leading them toward the well of darkness, destroying all we will have worked for generation upon generation. It happened well beyond my lifetime or even Catrìona's. And so now I am tormented by two questions: Who will this Judas be? And will my own descendant be up to the challenge of stopping her?

Maggie closed the journal on her thumb.

"I don't know," she answered. "But yes."

45. A Hundred Thousand Warnings

The rain hadn't let up any by the time Maggie finally exited the abandoned kirk. She pulled the door to and replaced the boards, then scampered back to the hotel through the driving mist, Brìghde's journal tucked safely in her backpack.

Once back in the room, Maggie peeled off her damp clothing and laid it over the desk chair to dry, then crawled into the warm, welcoming bed. She managed to stay awake just long enough to feel sure that Iain had not been awakened by her return. Then she slipped off into dreams.

Iain had not been awakened by Maggie's return. He had, however, been awakened by his bladder shortly thereafter and emerged from his bedroom surreptitiously to tiptoe to the W.C. across the suite. He groped his way slowly toward the bathroom in the dark of the chamber, wanting to avoid waking Maggie by either the use of a light or the yell of an expletive after kicking a chair leg or some such. As he walked past the desk he set a probing hand onto Maggie's still damp clothes.

Thoroughly surprised he squinted through the dark toward her bed. She was there, safe, sound and visible under the covers, deep in peaceful slumber.

Hm, he thought. He wasn't sure what to make of it.

* * *

Iain squeezed Maggie's hand as they motored back inside the Aberdeen city limits beneath pink washed clouds. It was late—they had stayed at Park most of the day—but the mid-summer sun was just beginning to set. "Home again," he declared. "Thanks for a great get-away."

"Well, thank you for coming along," Maggie countered happily. "And thanks for the ride."

"Not at all. Iain Grant, Chauffeur Extraordinaire, at your service, milady." Then a smile curled his lips as he asked, "Have you any more mysterious trips planned anytime soon?"

"Mysterious?" Maggie repeated incredulously. "This wasn't a mysterious trip. It was just for fun. And to show you the Castle." That seemed true, for the most part.

"Hm," Iain replied, echoing his thoughts of his early morning trip to the loo. "Anyway, have you any such plans?"

"Well, actually," Maggie began, a bit sheepishly, "I was thinking of a trip to Brittany."

"Brittany?" Iain's voice held surprise, but approval. "Well, that sounds interesting. Why Brittany?"

"My studies," Maggie answered as she looked away at whatever the car happened to be passing just then. No need to tell him it wasn't her university studies.

"Hm. I figured as much. And when are you planning on going?"

Maggie looked down at her fingernails. "Tomorrow," she said quite matter-of-factly.

"Tomorrow?" Iain almost drove off the road. "You're going to Brittany tomorrow?"

She turned back to look at him. "Uh, yeah. It's kind of time sensitive."

Iain considered this for a moment. "During the summer break, your studies are time sensitive?"

"Uh, yeah." Time to change the focus of the exchange. "So you probably can't come along, huh?"

"Ha, not bloody likely." He paused for a moment to concentrate on a left turn then continued. "I'll be working every Saturday 'til Christmas if I up and leave for Brittany with no warning for, what, a week?"

"Probably just a few days."

"Probably just a few days," Iain parroted mockingly. But then he felt bad for it. "Well, maybe I can give you a ride to the airport. I, well, that is, I thought for some reason that we were staying over two nights at Park, so I've tomorrow off as well."

Maggie looked up at him, his eyes fixed on the road ahead. He really was a dear. "Thanks, Iain. It'd be great if you could take me to the airport."

"I'll pick you up too," he offered. Then remembering the debacle at Argyll. "Maybe you can just call me from the airport when you get back in town. Apparently, you never know when your plans might get altered. Those studies of yours can get pretty crazy, aye?"

Maggie had to laugh at that. "Aye, pretty crazy."

Iain shook his head. "Have I told you lately that you're mysterious?"

"Yes, I believe you have. Thank you."

"Not at all." The conversation had finally brought them to Maggie's apartment building. Iain pulled his car into the loading zone out front and pulled up the brake. He grasped her hand again. "Well, I have to tell you, Maggie, I kinda like all your secrets and mystery. It suits you somehow."

Maggie could feel herself begin to blush. "Um, thanks. I guess."

"And I think it's good to have secrets," he continued earnestly, "or it can be anyway. Just not lies."

She looked up sharply at him, the blush draining quickly away.

"Let's promise," he squeezed her hands. "Secrets are fine. But no lies. All right?"

"All right, Iain," she agreed immediately, moved by the trouble in his voice. "No lies."

He exhaled deeply. Then a broad smile flashed across his face. "Good. All right then. So here we are. Can I walk you up?"

Maggie smiled too, relieved their tense little moment had passed. "Please do."

They both stepped from the car and Iain fetched her bags from the boot. "So I guess I'll call you tomorrow morning to see whether you're still planning on going to Brittany, or if it's changed to Uruguay, or maybe Tokyo, and, assuming you are still headed somewhere, we can figure out what time I should pick you up.

Iain was watching Maggie's face, waiting for a reaction. But Maggie had stopped listening to him as her gaze fixated on her apartment door. Shortly after moving in she had gone out and bought herself a doormat with the words *'Ceud Mìle Fàilte,'* Gaelic for 'A Hundred Thousand Welcomes.' A bit trite perhaps, but very inviting. Far more so than the knife now shoved into her door.

Iain stopped his soliloquy and followed her gaze to the blade embedded at eye level into the wood of her door. They hurried over and discovered that the small dirk possessed a utilitarian as well as decorative function. Its blade tacked a small handwritten note securely to Maggie's door. On the note was written a single word, in a dark reddish ink that appeared suspiciously like blood. The word was '*Stad*.'

"It's a *sgian dhu*," Iain said of the small staghorn-handled knife. "A traditional Highland dagger. You wear one with your dress kilt, but they're just ceremonial anymore. Usually the blade isn't even sharpened." He pulled the knife from the door and slid a finger along the quite fully sharpened blade of the black handled knife, then stuck the stinging finger into his mouth and frowned. He handed the note to Maggie. "What does it say?"

"It says '*Stad*,'" Maggie replied, thoroughly disquieted by this turn of events. She looked at Iain with glassy eyes. "It means 'stop.'"

"In Gaelic?"

Maggie nodded her head. "Yes. And in Old Gaelic too," she noted with some alarm. "It's the same word."

Iain seemed struck dumb by this. He scowled down at the *sgian dhu* for answers, but received none. Finally he asked, "Does this have to do with your 'studies' too?"

Maggie didn't look up at him. "Yes."

"You're still going to Brittany?"

"Yes."

Iain thought for a moment. "I'm going with you."

"Yes."

Maggie thought for a moment herself, then crumpled the paper into a ball and looked up at her boyfriend. "Iain?"

"Aye?"

"Stay with me tonight."

He reached out and pulled her close to him. "Aye."

46. Rise and Shine

"Good morning, *mo chridhe.*"

Iain's voice jarred her awake. It had been a fitful night. She hadn't gotten enough sleep. Why was that? Her mind was still groggy.

She squinted up at the voice then squinted again at what she saw. She was trying to decide if she was still asleep. It was Iain. He was towering over her bed, holding a tray of what was obviously breakfast and dressed only, as near as she could tell, in one of her bathrobes. The pink satin one with the white quilted collar and the embroidered heart pocket. It was far too small for him and his muscular arms and legs protruded out from under the satin in way Maggie found disturbingly arousing. "What—?" she began, but then she remembered.

She looked him over with half-lidded eyes, then ordered, "Set that down and come over here."

Iain gladly obliged. Maggie reached up and, grabbing a hold of his face, kissed him hard and long. When she'd finished, she let go of him again and looked up at his satin manliness. "Thanks for last night," she purred.

Iain sat down on the bed next to her and placed an arm

across her sheet covered hip. "Thanks to you, milady."

She glanced over at the tray he'd set on her writing desk. "And you made me breakfast too."

"Aye. And I think it might even be edible."

"Well, then that was thoughtful of you." She looked up at him again. "Not a love 'em and leave 'em kind of guy, I see."

"Och, no," Iain grinned. "More like: love 'em, eat breakfast with 'em, and then leave 'em. At least leave 'em long enough to head into the shop and explain to your aunt and uncle how I'll be accompanying your studious self to Brittany for a few days."

Maggie pushed herself into a sitting position. "Well, good. That'll give me time too."

"For what?"

She flashed a mysterious smile at him, recalling their promise. "It's a secret."

"Uh-oh," he laughed. "Now I've done it."

"Maybe you need to do it again," she suggested, running a hand through his thick black hair and pulling his face to hers. "Come here."

"But breakfast will get cold," he protested through her kisses.

"Let it."

***

"Tell her Maggie Devereaux is here to see her."

"Is she expecting you?"

"No, but she'll see me."

"Hmph," the police officer replied dubiously, but turned from her receptionist's window to the telephone to ring Warwick's office.

Maggie crossed the small, uninteresting lobby and took a seat in one of the ugly plastic chairs. The nearest posting was on pink copy paper and reminded Aberdonians to buckle up. 'Click it or Ticket!' exclaimed the smarmy cartoon police officer.

After a few minutes there came a metallic clang from the large metal door on the opposite side of the lobby and Sgt. Elizabeth Warwick stepped into the lobby.

"Maggie," she greeted her visitor. "Good to see you. Come on back. I can spare you a few moments."

Maggie followed the police sergeant back to her spartan office. Maggie sat down and glanced up at the map of Aberdeen.

"Is that crooked?" she asked pointing to it.

Warwick suppressed a wince and decided to ignore the question. "What can I do for you today, Maggie?"

Maggie leaned forward and considered her options. The direct approach seemed best. "I was wondering if I could take another look at those bios you have in the MacLeod file."

Warwick couldn't suppress a grin. "Another look? You didn't look in my file the other night, did you?"

This took Maggie off guard. "Er, no. Well, yes. Maybe. I mean, well, you didn't tell me not to."

Warwick shook her head amicably at this display and slid the file from the corner of her desk to directly in front of her. She extracted the information packets in question. "You mean these?"

"Yes."

Warwick began reading off the names.

"Nellie MacQuarrie?"

"Yes." Warwick handed her the bundle.

"Barry Nelson?"

"Er," Maggie paused. "No." Warwick, intrigued, set it aside.

"Caroline Nelson?"

"Yes."

"Marsaili NicRath?"

"Yes."

"Glynis Campbell?"

"Yes."

Warwick paused at the last one. "Have you read the newspaper yet today?"

"Er, no," Maggie admitted. She didn't feel the need to explain why not.

Warwick looked down at the bio in her hand. "Jessie MacLeod was arrested the night before last, just as I told you she would be."

"You said you thought she was innocent," Maggie recalled.

"Yes. And it seems I was correct. She was released again the following day when her iron clad alibi came forward. She'd told us she was at a restaurant and dance club the night her son was kidnapped. That was a lie."

Maggie nodded along, not sure what the point was.

"In fact," Warwick continued, "she had spent the entire evening, and the entire night, in the company of one Barry Nelson—MacLeod's business manager, and husband to Dr. Caroline MacDonald-Nelson who made a habit of working night shifts at Aberdeen General Hospital's emergency room."

"Oh."

"And seeing as how Mr. Nelson, by coming forward, had simultaneously ruined his career and his marriage, it was determined that he was likely being truthful when he vouched for Jessie's whereabouts on the night in question."

"Wow," Maggie replied, unsure what else to say. "Have you talked to his wife yet?"

"No," Warwick replied simply.

"Why not?"

"Because she's gone missing," Warwick explained, a bit testily. "Just like everyone else in this bloody file. Caroline Nelson,

Nellie MacQuarrie, Marsaili NicRath, even Glynis Campbell. Every one of them has skipped town. We have no idea where they are."

They're in Brittany, Maggie couldn't help but think. Apparently this deduction made its way onto her face.

"But you know, don't you, Maggie?" Warwick leaned over her desk. "You know where they are."

"I— I'm not sure," Maggie replied, honestly enough. "I might."

"Where?" Warwick demanded. "Where are they?"

"Brittany?" Maggie offered tentatively. "Maybe. But I'm not positive."

Warwick sat back in her chair. "Brittany? Why Brittany?"

"Er, well," Maggie ran a nervous hand through her hair. "Like I said, I'm not exactly sure. It's just—"

She was saved by a knock on Warwick's doorframe.

It was Inspector Cameron.

"Sorry to interrupt, Sergeant." He offered an apologetic smile to Warwick then nodded politely to Maggie. "Good morning, miss."

He didn't seem to recognize her.

"But," Cameron continued, "have you seen Sgt. Chisholm yet this morning?"

Warwick frowned at the question, both in thought and in memory. "No. I thought she might be with you."

Cameron just nodded silently. Maggie could feel the tension in the room. She squirmed slightly in her chair as it shot over her head between the police officers.

"Hm," Cameron rubbed the back of his neck. Maggie thought he looked tired. "Well, if you see her, tell her I need to talk with her." He paused. "But then, you probably knew that, eh?"

Warwick replied with a curt nod and the inspector nodded too. "Maybe it was the MacLeod Banshee returned," he joked, half to himself, before heading back down the corridor.

Wrong prophecy, Sherlock, Maggie thought derisively, before remembering to return her attention to the sergeant.

Warwick leaned back in her chair and stared at her map, her mouth pursed into a troubled knot. "Maggie, I'm afraid I'm going to have to cut our meeting short. I think I need to go find our goodwill ambassador from Glasgow."

The word hit Maggie like a runaway truck. 'Ambassador.'

"Can we continue this later?" Warwick was asking as she stood up and gestured Maggie toward the door.

"Eh? Oh, sure." Maggie was only too glad to leave then. "Sure."

She followed the sergeant back into the lobby then stepped outside into the late morning sun.

She counted to five on one hand and to two on the other. Then she wondered how fast Iain could get them to the airport.

47. The Celtic Continent

"Good Lord, woman!" Iain's agitation was rising steadily as they waited in queue at EuroAir's ticket counter inside Aberdeen International Airport.. 'EuroAir:' proclaimed the banner behind the discount airline's ticket agent, 'We Get You There.' "Do you have any idea how expensive this is going to be? How are we going to pay for it?"

Maggie began to answer, then paused to consider her reply.

"Another secret?" Iain raised a suspicious eyebrow.

"No," Maggie replied shortly. "No secret. My grandmother left me an inheritance, a pretty large one, when she passed away last fall. I'll use some of that."

"Oh." Iain nodded thoughtfully. "You never told me that before."

"I haven't told a lot of people," Maggie replied. "It's not really the sort of thing you going around telling people."

"I suppose not," Iain had to agree.

"Next!" shouted the ticket agent. He was a slight man, only a few inches taller than Maggie, with narrow shoulders and thin arms. His thick black hair was wavy and just a little too long, curling into stray tufts at the temples and the base of his scrawny neck. When Maggie and Iain didn't immediately step to his counter, he repeated his command, his voice rising half an octave to a shrill screech. "Ne-ext!!"

Maggie, startled by his cry, hopped quickly to the counter. Iain followed more slowly.

"And what do you want?" asked the little man, making no attempt to hide his contempt for the 'customers' who insisted on interrupting his day. His blue plastic name tag read 'ROGER.'

"Er," Maggie began, a bit taken back by Roger's attitude, "we'd like two tickets to Brest."

"Brest?" Roger sneered.

"It's in France," Maggie explained. "Brittany."

"I know where it is," Roger huffed. He tapped something into his computer keyboard then studied the monitor. "You'll have to connect at London and Rennes," he seemed glad to announce. "That last one is France too," he added with another sneer.

"Thanks," Maggie grumbled.

Iain smiled but otherwise stood by silently, more than happy to let Maggie handle matters.

"When do you want to travel?" Roger asked with a bored sigh as he readied his fingers over his keyboard.

"Today," Maggie replied. "When's your next flight?"

"Today!" Roger gasped. "Good lord, woman! Do you have any idea how expensive that's going to be?"

Iain spun quickly away, coughing to stifle his laughter.

"Let me worry about that, Roger," Maggie shot back. "Just tell me when your next flight is and whether you have any seats left."

Roger frowned contemptuously at her order, but then sighed again very loudly and began checking the computer.

While he did so, Maggie considered the travel posters

framed on the wall behind the counter. There was the obligatory shot of the Eiffel tower and one for a music festival in Greece from last summer. As Roger stepped to the end of the counter where the tickets were printing out, Maggie was able to see the poster on the wall directly in front of her.

'*Jöjjön Magyarországba*,' it announced, above the convenient English translation: '*Come To Hungary*.' A bilingual poster for the approximately 6.8 billion people who don't speak Hungarian. The lithograph promoted an exhibition of artifacts showing that summer at Budapest's National Museum. Several such artifacts were displayed including a small bronze statue, a knife of some sort and what was either a plate or a talisman—all, according to the copy, collected from a newly discovered archeological site in the town of Visegrád, just north of Budapest. Maggie found the artifacts somehow familiar and as Roger returned to his station, tickets in hand, she leaned to one side and craned her neck to look around him, reading the bottom of the poster where stood the title of the exhibition.

'*A Keltik Vidék - Müvészet Europáböl Györg Románosz*'

'*The Celtic Continent - Artifacts From Pre-Roman Europe*'

"Here are your tickets," Roger slapped them down irritably on the counter. "The total is—"

"Wait!" Maggie shouted.

"What?" Roger shrieked in surprise.

"What?" Iain asked, at first concerned something was amiss. But then he saw the look in her eye.

"Never mind," Maggie instructed, pointing at Roger's chest but still staring at the Hungarian poster. "Never mind Rennes. We need two tickets to Budapest."

***

"Next!" Roger shouted without looking up from his

computer.

"When's your next flight to Brittany?" Sgt. Elizabeth Warwick asked as she stepped up to the counter.

Roger glared up and raised a derisive eyebrow. "What is that—some sort of joke?"

Warwick hid her confusion. "It's no joke, I assure you." She extracted her badge and I.D. and showed them to the ticket agent.

Roger straightened up, nodded and tapped at his computer keyboard. "There's a flight to Rennes at 12:04," he explained. Then his sneer returned and he slapped at two torn up boarding passes still sitting on his counter. "Unless of course you want to wait for me to print out your ticket, then change your mind and go to Budapest instead."

The confusion couldn't be hidden this time. "How's that?"

So Roger explained about the snotty little American woman with all the cash and her tall lummox of a Scottish boyfriend and their sudden and irritating decision to forego the tickets to Brittany he had so diligently printed out and instead take the 8:57 to Budapest, by way of London and Berlin.

"So if you want to do that, tell me now before I print out your damned ticket. The next flight to Budapest leaves at 11:18."

Warwick looked at her watch. Ten-thirty.

"So what'll be?" Roger demanded, "Brittany or Budapest?"

48. Blood Rite

Visegrád was founded in 872 by the earliest Hungarians, Magyar invaders from the Central Asian steppes. The city stood atop a great hill overlooking the Danube Bend, the point where the waters of Europe's longest river turn ninety degrees to flow due south, on their way to cleave Buda and Pest before progressing toward their final destination in the Black Sea. The Magyars hadn't been the first to recognize the area's strategic significance and they wouldn't be the last. After them came Huns, then Turks, then Austrians. Before them came the Celts.

The Huns and the Magyars eventually merged to become Hungarians, converting to Christianity and building churches and castles to rival any of Central Europe. In the 15th and 16th Centuries the invading Muslim Turks conquered all of southeastern Europe up to Vienna, an area which included Visegrád. The churches were converted to mosques, and the castles were reduced to ruins.

But the Huns and Magyars had built their cities upon the ruins of those whom they had vanquished. The Celtic holy sites, often chosen for their symbolic importance atop the highest hills, were swept aside to make way for Hungarian fortresses and castles.

Centuries later, when the Turks and the Austrians and

finally the Russians were expelled from Hungary, and the Hungarians set about the business of rebuilding their country, one obvious priority was to rebuild the historic castles and monuments which dotted their countryside. The ruins of Visegrád's castle, perched atop the highest hill in the city and presiding over the most breathtaking view of the Danube below, were among the first to be selected for renovation and soon efforts were underway to rebuild what could be rebuilt and preserve what could not. Experts from throughout Europe descended on the small town of 1,800 and began the painstaking archeological work required to properly preserve and restore on of Europe's oldest castles. It was during this renovation, while excavating the earthen bowels of the castle's deepest recesses, that workers unearthed, quite literally, a startling find: several dozen bronze sculptures and tools buried in the ground beneath the castle. It was immediately assumed and quickly confirmed that the artifacts were from the earliest inhabitants of the Danube Valley: the Celts. Experts put the age of the artifacts at somewhere around 3500 B.C., making them the oldest known relics of the pre-historic Celtic culture which had once dominated Europe. The artifacts were carefully extracted and sent to the National Museum in Budapest, the inevitable exhibition being advertised from one end of Europe to the other, while the renovation and excavation work continued in Visegrád, the upper floors of the castle ruins open to the public, but the lowest floors strictly off limits.

Maggie needed to get to those lowest floors.

But first she had to get rid of Iain.

They'd arrived in Budapest around four-thirty. Then a forty-five minute bus ride up to Visegrád. Iain had been mostly patient and compliant but he'd insisted on finding a hotel before taking in the scenery. And he couldn't skip dinner. So an early dinner and then the twenty-five minute walk up the hill to the castle ruins. She'd tried to persuade him to let her visit the ruins alone, but he would have none of it. Whenever she pushed too hard all he had to do was mention the *sgian dhu* in her door and she would remember why he'd come along in the first place. He actually had the dirk his pocket still and would extract it demonstratively, saying something to the effect of, "I think I'd rather I came along."

But it was now or never. They had reached the top of the hill and were stepping through the ruined outer walls of the fortress. Maggie was convinced that the MacLeod boy and the unnamed Welsh girl had been spirited to the small town on the Danube bend, to be murdered in the ancient Celtic ruins beneath the castle. But she was at a loss as to how she could explain it to Iain without sounding completely insane. So either she had to convince him of the facts and to come with her—a conversation likely to include discussion of the Dark Book and its magic—or she had to save that conversation for later and send him away somehow. She opted for the later. Secrets were okay, she reminded herself, just no lies.

"Iain?" She batted her eyelids and licked her lips pitifully. "Do you think you could run back down to the city and buy me a bottle of water?"

It wasn't completely a lie, she told herself. She was a little thirsty after all.

Iain stopped dead in his tracks. "Back down to the city?" He looked down the hill in exaggerated horror and fatigue. "We just got up here. It took us almost half an hour. It'll take me an hour to go get you water."

Maggie sat down on a short ruined wall. "I'll wait here. Thanks."

Iain goggled at her. "But—" he started. "I mean— Are you sure you need water?"

Maggie coughed lightly and offered an exaggerated swallow. "Oh yeah, definitely. I usually bring water, but I didn't bring my backpack."

Iain winced in guilt at this observation. Maggie had left her backpack back at the hotel room. When she'd picked it up—with its water bottle, flashlight, and Dark Book—Iain had asked, 'Why are you bringing that?' Unsure how to explain without mentioning the magic, she'd agreed to leave it behind. She hoped it hadn't been a mistake.

"I'd come with you," Maggie went on, trying to sound weak and parched, "but I'm afraid I'll get dehydrated." She looked up at the setting sun. "It's still pretty hot out."

It was at that and Iain wiped the sweat off his brow. "Aye. So you can see why I'm no thrilled at walking down and than back up that hill again."

"I know, Iain. And thank you. There a lot of boyfriends who wouldn't do that for their girlfriend."

Maggie usually avoided calling him her 'boyfriend.' She was embarrassed by the term, feeling rather schoolgirlish, and they let the nature of their relationship go unspoken. But just as with the quiet man whose rarely raised voice commands that much more respect when it is raised, so too did this uncommon use of the terms 'boyfriend' and 'girlfriend' possess irresistible power.

"Er," Iain stammered. "That is—" He rubbed the back of his neck and looked again down the hill. "Well, I suppose it won't take as long to go downhill..."

"Thank you, Iain. Thank you so much."

Iain frowned. He wasn't entirely unaware of being manipulated, but he wasn't sure what there was to be done about it. "All right, I should be back soon enough. Try not to look at the entire castle before I'm back. I'd like to see a bit of it too."

He turned toward the hill, then turned back. He extracted the *sgian dhu* from his pocket and pressed it into her palm. "Here. Take this." He looked her in the eyes, worry shading his own. "Just in case."

Maggie nodded, then slipped the dagger into the pocket of her shorts. "Thanks again, Iain. Hurry back."

Just don't hurry too much, she thought, and stood to watch him disappear around a bend in the steep downhill path. Then she turned and dashed inside what remained of the castle.

It took a moment for her eyes to adjust to the darkness. The only light came from a series of light bulbs screwed into white plastic sockets bolted to the stone ceiling and joined by black electrical wire. Several displays crowded the entry, explaining the history of the site, the exhibits on display, and the general lay out of the open areas of the castle. To view these areas one needed simply to follow the series of signs which led away and to the right back toward those parts of the castle already restored. To the left was a large, white, plastic sheet, twenty feet wide and hanging from the ten-foot tall ceiling to the stone floor, effectively blocking view of whatever lay beyond. A dozen waist high metal posts stood sentry before the plastic sheet, their velvet ropes drooping menacingly between them. Each rope bore a laser-printed paper sign: '*Behajtani Tilos - No Entry*'.

Maggie looked around the stone foyer. No one was around. Likely a function of the time of day. The sun was setting. The sign in the center of the lobby explained even further. The castle would be closing to visitors in ten minutes. She'd have to come back with Iain tomorrow.

She ducked under the nearest velvet rope and sneaked around the plastic sheet.

Behind the plastic lay two things: a towering stone wall only a few feet from the plastic, and an arched doorway in said wall, holding a staircase leading downward. To the lower levels, no doubt, those still undergoing renovation and excavation. Maggie considered her timing. Any legitimate workers had likely gone home a few hours ago. The lower levels would be abandoned. Or at least they should be. She stepped to the top of the dimly lit stone staircase and paused.

From her pants pocket she extracted the rubbing from Ballincoomer. An intricate Celtic knotwork circle surrounded by three parts of a prophecy: 'The ban-shee shall return to claim her legacy'; 'Infantsblood shall be spilt onto ancestral earth'; and 'The magic of the Celts shall be reignited.'

Considering the smeared pencil image, a thought struck her. *Just where does a circle begin?* And with this though in mind, she shoved the rubbing back into her pocket and began her descent.

Again bare light bulbs had been bolted to the ceiling; few and far between, they cast a most inadequate light. The steps themselves were cracked and worn, some stones wobbling beneath her feet, others sloping off into impossible rounded lumps.

Seventeen steps down she found herself at the mouth of a long, dim hallway. The ceiling was low and the breadth of the passageway was little more than Maggie's own shoulders. The word 'catacomb' came to mind. Dirty stone walls brushed past her as she followed the widely spaced light bulbs toward the end of the long passageway. When she'd traversed its twenty-yard length, the hallway bent to the left, revealing another worn staircase leading downward into darkness. Maggie followed it down.

The next passageway was very much like the first. Again a narrow low-ceilinged corridor, again the dirty stone walls, again the widely-spaced bare light bulbs. The only difference came about halfway down the corridor—when the lights shut off. Closing time.

She was in complete and utter blackness. She waited a moment for her heart to slow and her eyes to adjust. Neither did. There was simply no light for her eyes to adjust to; she was as good as blind. And given this, her heart chose not to slow, but rather to race faster, as panic-driven adrenaline flooded her veins.

Pull yourself together, Devereaux, she told herself. You're not that far down. And the corridor back upstairs doesn't have any pitfalls—none that you noticed anyway. It'll be easy enough to grope your way back upstairs.

She turned around in the darkness and took the first tentative step back toward the lobby.

Maybe her eyes were adjusting after all. She could see the faintest outline of a shadow ahead of her. It was her own shadow, cast out in front of her, black against the almost black of the passageway walls.

She stopped. And looked over her shoulder.

There was the faintest of lights coming from the end of the corridor. It barely illuminated the arched end of the passageway, but in the otherwise complete darkness, the light was distinctly visible. Just as distinct as the faint voices she could hear coming from the same location.

Turning around again in the near darkness, she stepped carefully toward the end of the corridor, the light, and the voices.

The passageway ended in another staircase down to another narrow corridor. The difference this time was that the passageway was only about half the length of those above and ended in an arched doorway that led out onto a stone balcony. Maggie crouched down behind the short stone balcony wall and peered over the edge to the activity below.

She was at least thirty feet up. A steep stone staircase to her left hugged the wall and doubled back on itself to lead down to the excavation site below. Scaffolding adorned two of the three stone castle walls which burrowed into the earth and created, together with a natural rock face, a large sunken chamber the size of a typical auditorium. This impression was reinforced by the circular rings of a recently unearthed stone foundation which created the outline of an amphitheater in the dusty floor. And it was inside this ghost of an amphitheater, on the stage as it were, where they had assembled.

There were ten of them. Just as she'd expected. Six from the coven standing in a circle with the children in the middle, and four standing off to one side dutifully attentive to the proceedings. The four 'ambassadors.'

From Ireland, Kitty McCusker.

From Wales, Gwen Palmer.

From the Isle of Man, Susan MacGowell.

And from Cornwall—Maggie shook her head; she should have known—from Cornwall, Officer Kernough. '*Kernow*' was the Cornish word for 'Cornwall.'

They'd been watching her, trailing her, making sure the seventh member of the coven—Brìghde Innes' descendant—didn't get too close.

The coven. The female-line descendants of the coven Brìghde Innes had established almost four-hundred years earlier to stop the dark magic and preserve the light. There had been seven then, but only six now—because Maggie's Grandma hadn't told her everything. Maggie was Brìghde's female-line descendant; she would have completed the coven, but they'd thought better of approaching her—at least directly—until her feelings on their plans were known. And once known, Maggie was not welcome. Hence the *sgian dhu* in her door.

They had conspired to kidnap both the MacLeod boy and the Owen girl. The Owen kidnapping would be forgotten soon enough, especially with Kernough's help, but the MacLeod kidnapping, that would take some finesse. He was too important for the police to move slowly on it, or the media to not to report on it. So they'd had to set up a fall guy—or woman in this case. Jessie MacLeod. And once she was safely behind bars, they'd high-tailed it out of town and back to the 'earth of their earliest ancestors' to perform their bloody ceremony.

Marsaili NicRath. MacLeod's rival. She'd likely chosen the precise noble to victimize.

Glynis Campbell. NicRath's lawyer. And Jessie's too; she was more than able to feed the young girl dubious legal advice.

Caroline Nelson. Wife to MacLeod's C.O.O. She'd undoubtedly manipulated her husband into the affair, with her long hours and indifferent attitude, banking on the fact that he'd never come forward to corroborate Jessie's alibi if doing so meant throwing away both his career and marriage.

Nellie MacQuarrie. MacLeod's nanny. No wonder the newspaper said there were no signs of forced entry. She'd let the others in—or carried the child down to their waiting hands.

And Detective Sergeant Alison Chisholm of the Glasgow Police Department. To make sure Jessie MacLeod was arrested. Warwick had been right to be paranoid—of course.

That left the sixth member of the coven. The leader. The one who had subtly approached Maggie without her even knowing it. The one who had translated the ancient prophecy. Who had maneuvered young Nellie MacQuarrie into MacLeod's bed. Who had drawn on Glynis Campbell's legal expertise to frame Jessie MacLeod. And who now planned to exploit Caroline Nelson's medical knowledge to save the lives of the babies whose throats she was about to slit. Prof. Sarah MacKenzie held up a razor-sharp silver blade and spoke.

"As the prophecy has foretold, so has it come to pass." Her voice echoed off the empty cavern's vault-like walls. "The last of the magic has abandoned the Celts, leaving us powerless and all but stateless, subjugated by the invaders who stole our homeland. But today all that ends. Today the prophecy shall be fulfilled. The blood of these children shall mix with the oldest Celtic earth and the ancient Celtic magic shall be reignited—into our hands. The might of the Celts shall be restored to us."

Wow, Maggie pushed a loose strand of hair away from her face, she's nuts.

"We call upon the spirit of our founder. Our founder whose progeny deserted fair Celtica and left our coven weakened in number—but stronger in resolve. We call on your spirit, Brìghde Innes, the *Bean-Sìth*, to bless our endeavor with glorious success."

'What?!!' Maggie wanted to shout out, but she held her tongue. Brìghde Innes? How dare she? Brìghde wasn't a *Bean-Sìth*, she was a *Bean-Slànaighear*. A Healer. She would never have condoned this sort of blood-letting. How dare she call on my ancestor? But it gave Maggie an idea. A crazy idea, she knew, but then again she considered her situation.

MacKenzie stepped into the circle and knelt before the two swaddled babes. She lowered the blade to the first child's throat. Maggie couldn't see whether it was the MacLeod boy or the Owen girl, but it didn't really matter. She was out of time. She'd never descend the stairs in time and a shout would only push the blade to quicker work, MacKenzie intent on finishing her task before Maggie could stop her—and she hardly expected the good doctor to be able to save two infants with their throats slit ear to ear. This was her only chance. She yanked the *sgian dhu* from her pocket.

'Blood drawn by an enemy's blade / Ancestor summoned in bloody circle made.' An abbreviated version of a spell from her

Dark Book. Her only chance. She gritted her teeth, closed her eyes—and sliced the blade across the palm of her left hand.

Oww!! Holy Hell! Owww!! Tears welled in her eyes even as the blood began to flow from the palm of her left hand. She caught her breath and transferred the knife to the bleeding hand, then repeated the act against her right palm.

Oowwww!! The pain forced the blade from her hand; the resultant 'cling' echoed throughout the chamber. MacKenzie looked up from where she was about to draw her own blade across Douglas MacLeod's soft neck.

"What was that?" she demanded of the others.

Maggie leaned forward onto her bleeding hands, then smeared her hands across the dirty stone blocks to outline a bloody circle, several feet in diameter.

"<Blood of my blood, answer my call. Follow the dark forces to our shared lifeblood and come you to me now.>" She was in too much pain to whisper, but she didn't yell either. The words slipped past in mid-volume desperation.

The effect was immediate. A shaft of light—an evil red light—shot forth from the full width of the circle and pinned itself against the ceiling above. Then a scream, the most horrible scream Maggie had ever heard, pierced the chamber. The cry of a mother torn from her child, a wife torn from her husband, a spirit torn from her afterworld. Maggie curled onto a ball on her side and covered her ears with bleeding palms, a vain effort to block out the cry which permeated everything in the room.

"Who dares?!?" cried the blood red apparition of Brìghde Innes' ghost, soaring from its bloody portal into the air above the coven. "Who dares call me?! Who dares call Brìghde Innes?!"

Maggie elected not to raise her hand just then.

She did however manage to lean forward onto the balcony

ledge and look down at the cove. They were fleeing. They ran toward the darkened doorways at the far end of the excavation site. Maggie didn't know where they led, but the women below knew at least that they led away. All except Sarah MacKenzie, who remained kneeling before the children, now red-faced and screeching in their own right.

"Who dares summon me to this plane? Who dares disturb my slumber?! And with the magic of demons, no less!" Her beautiful but ghostly face contorted in agony. "Who dares torment me thus?! Who burns my soul with the rancid touch of evil magic? Release me at once, I demand, lest once tainted, I burn for eternity in the lake of fire!"

Oops! Maggie spun around and swung a foot across the bloody circle, breaking its ring in two places. The motion brought her squarely onto her bum, her back against the balcony railing. But the circle was broken, and with it the spell, releasing her ancestor from her torment. She hadn't expected that side-effect.

The apparition sighed in divine relief, like the sound of a thousand violins, then faded to a shapeless pink vapor. Then the vapor dissipated and the soul of Brìghde Innes was gone.

Maggie sat leaning against the balcony ledge for a long moment, her ears ringing, her head spinning, her heart racing, and her hands bleeding. She wasn't even sure where she was for a moment. But the voice brought it all back to her.

"Show yourself, Maggie!" MacKenzie shouted. "I know you're here somewhere!"

Maggie hesitated, but then shrugged. Why not? She turned around and slowly stood up, rising like a ghost over the banister. She didn't say anything. She didn't have to; MacKenzie saw her.

"There you are!" MacKenzie shouted shaking her knife up toward Maggie's perch. "I knew you wouldn't understand. Your grandmother never told you the truth. You don't understand what's at stake. The babes wouldn't have died, Maggie, they wouldn't have died. But now..." She trailed off and looked down at the two bundles squirming and crying at her feet.

"Don't do it, Sarah." Maggie exhorted. "Don't. It won't work. The magic is gone. Accept that."

"The magic is gone?" MacKenzie cried out. "Gone, you say? How the bloody hell can you stand up there and tell me it's gone when you just summoned a ghost right before my very eyes. Gone, you say!"

This was no time for a lecture on dark versus light magic. She had to save the babies. She stepped over to the stairs and began to descend.

"Stay right where you are!" MacKenzie screamed, waving the blade wildly in front of her.

"C'mon, Sarah. You don't want to do this." But Maggie stopped at the top stair just to be safe.

MacKenzie threw her gaze down at the children then back up at Maggie. "Don't take another step!" she warned.

Maggie went ahead and took one anyway. Slowly so as not to startle MacKenzie too much. Maybe she would realize what she was doing and drop the knife and just run away. No such luck.

"You take one more step, Maggie Devereaux," MacKenzie bent down toward the swaddled infants, "and I'll slice the little buggers where they lie."

Now that's an illogical threat, Maggie thought. She gave voice to her skepticism. "Isn't that what you're going to do anyway?"

Sarah MacKenzie regarded the helpless children before them. "Aye, Maggie," she replied with an evil grin. "It is." And she sliced the blade across Douglas MacLeod's throat.

Douglas' gurgled yelp was entirely drowned out by

Maggie's panicked, "NO!" But before she could make it down the steps, MacKenzie repeated the atrocity against the Owen girl. Blood spurted forth from their innocent throats and into the dry, thirsty earth beneath them. MacKenzie stood up over their bleeding forms and raised her face toward the heavens, throwing her arms wide. Awaiting the rushing torrent of white magic spewing forth from the earth into her greedy hands, no doubt.

But of course nothing happened.

The prophecy was now fulfilled. But MacKenzie had it in the wrong order.

Maggie half sprinted, half jumped down the stairs. It was taking too damned long. When she finally reached the bottom, she raced toward the children, screaming the whole way, "No! No! Nooo!!"

MacKenzie dropped her face and shone panicked eyes toward Maggie. She was clearly surprised by the ineffectiveness of her blood rite. Maggie was fast approaching. She stepped two uncertain steps backward, then threw down the knife and ran for one of the darkened exits, flailing at first but then settling into a full sprint.

Maggie couldn't have cared less about MacKenzie's flight at that point. She'd reached the children.

"Don't die, babies." She pressed a hand against each one's throats—only to feel the faint pulse of blood with each beat of their tiny hearts. At least they were still alive.

Bean-Slànaighear. Healer. Healing spell. But there is no healing spell. There is no healing spell.

She couldn't even try one. She'd never found the Spellbook of Ballincoomer. Damn Kitty McCusker. And Damn Sarah MacKenzie.

Then she remembered the newspaper photograph.

"*A tháinmhne na dohrgatas, slánaich an mhac a'sio!*" she cried. "*Slánaich a' chaile a'sio!*"

'Forces of Darkness, heal this boy! Heal this girl!'

Nothing.

"*A tháinmhne na dohrgatas, slánaich an mhac a'sio! Slánaich a' chaile a'sio!*"

Still nothing.

Oh, God! What am I going to do?!

Then she saw MacKenzie's blade lying just a few feet away. She sprang forward, snatched it up and in one motion sliced the back of her hands this time, spilling the blood running through the raised veins there. She circled the freshly drawn blood across the earthen floor of the cavern. "Grandma!" she cried.

The red light returned, shooting again to the vaulted ceiling some fifty feet above. Then the light shaft faded to reveal the glowing red apparition of her grandmother.

Maggie didn't wait for a greeting. "What's the healing spell?"

Her grandmother's expression was as pained as Brìghde's; the same dark magic tore at her spirit. She shook her head sadly and explained, "There is no healing spell. Not any more."

Maggie's eyes were running over with tears. "Then what do I do?!" she demanded, blood running down her forearms from her clenched fists.

Her grandmother's spirit fought against its agony. "What you must," she counseled. "The magic need not be dark."

Maggie looked wildly at the dying children then again at her grandmother. "Thank you," she said, then kicked away a portion of the bloody circle to release her grandmother's soul.

Maggie snatched up the knife again. Time to craft.

"<Burn!>"

This had the desired effect. The blade immediately began to

glow red—the same evil red that had enveloped the ghosts of her ancestors. She turned toward the stricken infants.

"God forgive me," she whispered, then seared the knife against Douglas MacLeod's bloody neck. He let out a gurgled scream and his small body shook violently within its blanket. The smell of burnt flesh stung Maggie's nostrils.

She released the knife, liquified skin sticking to it, and repeated the barbaric cure on the Owen girl. She too was wracked with half-mute screams and violent jerking. Then both children were still.

Shock, Maggie hoped. Dead, she feared.

"Stand aside!"

Maggie turned and saw a large man running toward her. He was stocky, with thick black hair, and was dressed all in black. He knelt down and clutched Douglas MacLeod to his breast.

"I didn't—" Maggie began.

"I know," Taggert replied. "I know, lass."

He lifted up Holly Owen as well.

"Did I kill them?" Maggie asked from her seat on the ground, eyes streaming tears and hands oozing blood front and back.

"Nae, lass." He placed an ear to each child's chest in turn. "Indeed, you may have saved them."

Then he turned and jogged lightly toward the doorway from which he'd entered. "Good work, lass," he called out again over his shoulder, then he disappeared into the blackened tunnel.

Maggie collapsed onto the earth, not really sitting, not really lying. Her hands hurt, her lungs hurt, her eyes hurt, her heart hurt. "God," she wheezed, "what just happened?"

"You tell me."

She bolted up into a full sitting position. Then sprang to her feet. "Iain!"

"Tell me," he repeated. He was standing at the bottom of the staircase she had used to descend into the excavation pit. He was holding a bottle of water in one hand. "What just happened here?"

She considered her bleeding hands, dirty clothes, teary eyes. This would be a test of her powers of persuasion.

"Well, you see—" she began.

"Don't," Iain interrupted. "Just don't. You promised me: no lies." He looked down at the bottle of water in his hand. In disgust, he threw it to the ground. "I told you I'd give you your bloody secrets, woman, but damn it, no lies!"

Maggie was unsure what to say. He was really angry. She'd never seen him this angry. She'd never really seen him angry at all.

"I saw what you did, Maggie." The words hissed past his lips.

The knife, she immediately thought. *He saw me put the knife to the babies throats. He thinks I hurt them. Okay, that's easy enough. He just doesn't understand.* "The knife, you mean? I can explain—"

"Not the knife!" he bellowed. His voice echoing off the walls. "Damn the knife! I saw what you did their with your, your, your damned witch's circle."

Oh hell. The black cat was out of the bag.

"Iain," she started gingerly, but he would have none of it.

"What the bloody hell was that? you can summon spirits? you can make a knife glow like the bloody sun? you can heal wee babes whose throats are slit side to side? What the bloody hell are you?"

"I'm— I'm Maggie."

Iain shook his head wildly. "No. No, you're not Maggie. You're not the Maggie I know. Or not the one I thought I knew at any rate. What do you do, then—just say 'Ach Lach MacTarnagach!' and turn people to stone?"

"It's—It's not like that," Maggie protested.

"Oh aye? And what's it like?" He was beside himself. "What is it bloody like?!"

Maggie's eyes filled again with tears. "I—I can't explain."

Iain glared at her, unspeaking, unmoving. Finally, he spat on the ground. "Then don't." And he turned around and began climbing the stairs.

"Iain!" she called out after him. "*Mo chridhe!*"

He stopped.

"I need you to understand," she begged.

Iain Grant stared down at the ground for the longest time. "I don't know if I can, Maggie. I don't know if I can."

And he disappeared up the stairs.

Maggie ran to the bottom of the stairs and looked up at where her heart had just vanished into the darkened passageways of the castle. She frantically wiped the tears out from under her glasses, smearing blood across her cheekbones like an ancient warrior.

"Iain!" she cried. "Iain! IAIN!!!"

But there was no reply.

Epilogue

"*Köszönöm.*" The man exited the taxi, stepped to the front window and handed the driver a bank note. "*Tessék a viteldíj. A többi a magáé.*"

The taxi driver nodded in thanks, wondered at the man's perfect grammar but strange accent, and pulled slowly away. The man ignored for a moment the destination he'd reached and stood instead gazing down at the Danube below. Tall and fit, with an air of authority about him, he wore a suit of the finest summer wool, a brilliant silk tie, and Italian leather shoes. The light breeze flirted with his strawberry blond hair, but it retained its shape, combed straight back from his face. Finally, without a shrug, he turned and walked toward the ruins of Visegrád Castle.

He passed through the front entry, surveyed the lobby, tucked a large bill into the '*Donations*' box, then waited for the few other early morning patrons to depart the foyer for the museum within, before stepping over the barrier rope, ducking behind the plastic sheet hanging from the ceiling, and disappearing through the stone doorway into the dim passageways below.

He emerged at the other end on a stone balcony overlooking the excavation site. There was no one working yet that early on a

Saturday morning. He scanned the dirt and stains on the balcony floor, kicking gently at some brown debris, but declining to bend down or touch anything. His hands still in his pockets, he turned and descended the stone steps to his left.

At the bottom of the stairs he stepped out onto the earthen floor of the cavernous chamber. Stepping slowly at first he scanned the perimeter and then made his way resolutely to the center of the ruined foundations, in the middle of the recently excavated concentric stone rings.

Here he crouched down, careful not to touch his suit pants to the ground, and inspected the stained earth. He extracted a hand from a pocket and ran a finger through the dirt. Then he picked up a handful of the loose earth, rubbing it between his fingers and holding it up for closer inspection. Once satisfied, he tipped his palm and let the soil pour down again past his face, with its inscrutable black eyes, neatly trimmed goatee, and long mottled scar running the length of his left cheek.

He stood up again and brushed the dirt off his hands. He tugged his suit coat back into position and straightened his tie. Then, looking again at the stained earth, he spoke.

"I know you were here, Maggie," said Devan Sinclair. "But where are you now?"

END

THE MAGGIE DEVEREAUX PARANORMAL MYSTERIES
Scottish Rite

Blood Rite

Last Rite

THE DAVID BRUNELLE LEGAL THRILLERS
Presumption of Innocence

Tribal Court

By Reason of Insanity

A Prosecutor for the Defense

Substantial Risk

Corpus Delicti

Accomplice Liability

A Lack of Motive

Missing Witness

Diminished Capacity

Devil's Plea Bargain

Homicide in Berlin

Premeditated Intent

Alibi Defense

THE TALON WINTER LEGAL THRILLERS
Winter's Law

Winter's Chance

Winter's Reason

Winter's Justice

Winter's Duty

Winter's Passion

ALSO BY STEPHEN PENNER
The Godling Club

Mars Station Alpha

ABOUT THE AUTHOR

Stephen Penner is an author, artist, and attorney from Seattle.

In addition to writing the Maggie Devereaux Paranormal Mysteries, he is also the author of the David Brunelle Legal Thriller Series, featuring Seattle homicide prosecutor David Brunelle; the Talon Winter Legal Thrillers, starring Tacoma criminal defense attorney Talon Winter; and several stand-alone works.

For more information, please visit *www.stephenpenner.com*.

www.ingramcontent.com/pod-product-compliance
Lightning Source LLC
Chambersburg PA
CBHW070733180626
46818CB00007B/2829